THIRD AND TEN

A NOVEL

CAMELLIA BOOK ONE

MARIE VEILLON

HOMEGROWN PUBLISHING LLC

First Edition October 2023

Second (Revised) Edition September 2024

ISBN 979-8-9889657-6-3 (ebook)

ISBN 979-8-9889657-5-6 (paperback)

ISBN 979-8-9889657-7-0 (hardcover)

Cover design by @cindyras_draws

marievwrites.com

 Formatted with Vellum

AUTHOR'S NOTE

This novel could be categorized as a "minty rom-com" or a closed-door romance with the door cracked open. It incorporates Christian themes, especially Catholic views on prayer, marriage and family, and chastity.

It includes heavy innuendo and discussions of sex, chastity, fertility awareness, and natural family planning, as well as some semi-steamy and fade-to-black love scenes, implied nudity, crude humor, and mild language; however, any explicit spice happens off-page. If it were a movie, it would probably be rated PG-13.

Additionally, please be aware of the following content and depictions, which may be controversial or triggering for some readers: pregnancy and childbirth; women's health, especially postpartum; body-consciousness; alcoholism; family loss and death; cancer; adoption, legal guardianship and child custody; and parental abandonment. It is my intent to treat these topics with the sensitivity they deserve, and I promise to deliver a HEA in the end.

On a lighter note, the writing style of this book purposefully reflects some of the grammatical and syntactical quirks more common to those who speak and think in a Cajun accent. In other words, it sounds weird on purpose.

3RD AND 10

— **See also,** *3ʳᵈ **Down and 10 Yards to Go***; The offense's last chance to gain the ten yards required for a new set of downs before having to decide whether to give the football to the opposing team, try for a field goal, or risk going for it on fourth down; The situation often referred to as "third and long," as the offense has a long way to go under increased pressure and in a short amount of time.

for Josh,
my very own romance novel MMC,
who loves me so much better
than I deserve most days.

THIRD AND TEN

PROLOGUE
(SEVENTEEN YEARS AGO)

JD

"Whoa ... what are you doing?" I ask, backing away from the lips of the eighth-grade girl my brother's been crushing on for the past few months. A slow song continues playing in the background.

She looks equally stunned and embarrassed. "I thought we were going to ..." She mumbles and adjusts her lips over her braces. I can't even begin to understand why I'm supposed to be eager to stick my tongue in someone else's mouth, especially one full of metal and lime-green rubber bands.

I drop my hands from her sides, taking another step back. "I only wanted to talk to you about my older brother," I say awkwardly.

"I can't believe—wait, *what*?"

"You're Summer, right? Aren't you in the same grade as Blake?"

She cringes. "Yeah, and I know Blake Bourgeois. Everyone does. But did you just say he's your *older* brother?"

I nod carefully.

"Um, what grade are you—"

"Sixth."

She runs her tongue over her braces again, and the way she

scrunches her nose makes it look like she's trying not to barf. "So ... what are you doing at an eighth-grade party?"

"My parents told me I had to follow Blake here."

And he wasn't happy about it, either. I thought I'd make it up to him by trying to be his wingman, but this is quickly turning into another one of those times when I do something stupid to impress my brother and end up pissing him off instead.

"And you assumed it was okay to ask me out? Like, you really thought I'd *date* you?"

By now, I know "date" really means "make out" in this context. I may be young, but I'm not stupid. I'm also big for my age and play up a couple years in most rec sports, so Summer isn't the first person to assume I'm older. Which means I overhear entirely too much for my age.

And even though I *like* girls, I don't really get it. Whatever happened lately to Blake and his friends that makes it impossible for them to think about anything but girls or parts of girls must not have hit me yet. I'm honestly afraid of getting older after listening to the gross stuff my 13U baseball teammates have been saying all season.

I sigh, reminding myself that I have a job to do. "You seem really nice, but to be honest, I'm just here for my brother."

Her expression softens. "You mean, Blake sent you to talk to me?" Now she's back to batting her eyelashes and poking her chest out.

I peel my eyes away from Summer to search for Blake, but he's nowhere to be found. "He didn't exactly send me," I admit after a while, and her face falls again.

The song ends, and nearly all of the couples begin separating, with the exception of the pair beside us. In fact, they're still too busy swapping spit to notice the way everyone's gawking at them. I recognize the guy—Landry Reed, an older kid from my football league— just as I notice his hand creeping up his date's chest. She pushes him away immediately, frowning in disgust.

Then, something weird happens to me when the girl plants her hands on her hips. I swallow hard as my eyes run over her. For the first time, I think I understand why my brother and his friends can't stop talking about boobs, and why dudes like Landry are willing to embarrass themselves in public to get a hand on one. Because *this* girl is different. She's ... softer. She doesn't need to stick out her chest to attract attention, and I doubt she likes the way people are staring at her now. A strange feeling settles in the pit of my stomach, just from watching her.

"JD? Hel-*lo*?" Summer calls, bringing me back.

"Huh?" I blink a few times. But I'm too busy listening to the other couple's argument to pay any more attention to Summer.

"Gah, Tenley, I thought it's what you wanted," Landry growls, and I'm suddenly fighting the urge to turn and punch him in his big dumb mouth.

Tenley frowns harder. "Well, it wasn't," she retorts angrily, and her blue eyes meet mine for a second.

Wow.

She's pretty. *Really* pretty.

But she seems sad, and I don't like that.

And I'm impressed because she was brave enough to call Landry out in front of everyone.

I almost blurt out my thoughts aloud while she's still looking at me. Then I think about saying something nice to her, maybe even making her laugh at Landry's expense, but stupid Summer interrupts again.

What could Blake want with Summer when there are girls like Tenley in his class?

"I asked you where your brother went," Summer repeats, and Tenley finally looks away, to my dismay.

"I, uh, well ... I don't know."

"Then help me find him," Summer whines, grabbing me by the hand and pulling me along.

And this is what I get for trying to suck up to Blake. No doubt I'm getting my ass kicked later.

She drags me around as we continue searching, and I notice a minute later that Landry and Tenley are looking for someone, too.

Eventually, Blake emerges from the pool house—along with

Landry's sister, Loren—only to walk into some kind of standoff with Landry. I have no clue what's going on, but I *would* like the chance to knock Landry out for making his girlfriend feel so bad earlier.

I make my way over, purposefully bumping his shoulder and waiting for Blake to jump in. But he's too busy watching helplessly as Tenley leads Loren away. I turn to shoot Landry another warning glare. How many people does this jerk need to hurt in a single night before one of us fights back?

Then I remember we're practically the same size, despite a three- or four-year age difference. I'm just about to call him out when Blake finally decides to step in.

"Come on, man, we're leaving," he commands. I stare at Blake for a second, trying to convey how badly I need to wipe the smirk off Landry's face, but the look I get in return says, *stay out of it.*

I settle for throwing my shoulder into Landry's again as I trail my brother, disappointed that he seems more interested in chasing Loren than sticking around to give Landry what he deserves. I use the opportunity to catch one more glimpse of Tenley as her blonde pony-tail bounces behind her, and the next thing I know, Blake turns back to lay Landry Reed out with a single sucker punch.

———

TENLEY

"Lo ... I'm so sorry," I say, my cheeks reddening. "And not just about whatever that was back there with Blake Bourgeois."

But my best friend only nods and continues crying softly. She can't even face me. And I deserve it because I'm the jerk who ditched her for her older brother. Although she's known about my crush on Landry for years and how badly I've been wanting him to give me my first kiss, I *did* technically abandon her for the one person she hates the most.

Because I'm the worst.

And after the devastating news I got this morning, you'd think I'd be more willing to lean on my most trusted friend.

"I mean it. I shouldn't have gone off with Landry. If it makes you feel any better, he ruined the moment by trying to steal second in front of everyone," I explain.

She sighs, crossing her arms and kicking a loose rock on the edge of the driveway as we wait for my older sister to pick us up. "It doesn't make me feel better, Ten. It just makes me want to kick him in the junk for trying to take advantage of you," she mutters, her smirk betraying her.

"I wouldn't stop you," I return, and she finally looks up and grins.

"Can we pretend you aren't talking about my brother for a minute so you can tell me what it's like?"

I roll my eyes but humor her. "Weird. Sort of gross. Kind of fun at first, but then things got sloppier and more uncomfortable as it went."

"Of course it was gross! You wasted your first kiss on Landry, you ding-dong."

I elbow her softly, trying to hide my smile. "Don't worry. You're still my favorite Reed."

"It was that bad, huh?" she asks, chuckling.

"Eh, I'm not sure I'm built for kissing," I return. "But I couldn't enjoy it, anyway, not when I felt like I'd betrayed you. I really am sorry."

"I know," Loren says, her tone soothing as she yanks my arm down and squeezes it. It's as close as I'll let her get to hugging me. I'm not even sure why I thought I'd enjoy dancing with a boy or even kissing one when I've always been a huge fan of personal space.

We're interrupted by a horn as my sister's car pulls up, and we climb into the back seat, kicking a couple of liquor bottles around the floorboards as we get settled.

"Where to, ladies?" Tessa asks condescendingly from the passenger seat. Some guy I've never seen before is driving, and I cast an uneasy glance at Loren. She mirrors my concern.

"Home, please," I reply.

"Aw, did the party get too out of hand for my sweet little angels?" she teases again.

"Sure. Let's go with that."

"Someone's a little sassy," our driver remarks in an amused tone.

"Ryan's right. Sounds like you could use a drink," Tessa adds, lifting the bottle she's holding and shoving it under my nose.

"We're fine, thanks," I grind out.

"How about you, Lo-Lo? Or are you too green for a sip of the hard stuff?"

Loren scowls. "Who you calling *green*, Tess?"

Tessa's hand flies to her chest in mock surprise. "Then I guess you aren't as innocent as you pretend to be, either? What, did the two of you play a sexy game of Spin the Bottle?" She turns back to me. "I imagine you've gotten a few propositions by now with that rack of yours, Tenley Jean. Kiss any boys tonight?"

I look away in annoyance, but Loren tilts her chin up daringly and responds. "What if we did?"

I'm not sure whether she's standing up to Tessa or admitting to messing around with Blake in the pool house, but I wouldn't put either of those past her. My sister and her boy toy laugh loudly, only further upsetting Loren. Then Tessa thrusts the bottle at her again. "You two badasses should be able to handle a small swig, then."

"Get it out of her face, Tessa," I order. It's not the first time she's shown her true colors in front of Loren and me, but I imagine Tessa's extra-lousy behavior tonight has something to do with the bomb my parents dropped on us earlier.

Loren's gaze holds firm as my sister stares her down.

"Oh, wait, I forgot. Your mom drinks enough for all of us, right?" Tessa starts, snickering to herself as we drive up to the house. Loren ignores her, and we bolt from the car as soon as it stops.

"I'm sorry," I repeat as we walk inside, and Lo squeezes my arm again.

"Hey, girls," my mom greets us from the living room. She sounds happy to see us, but I know she's just putting on a brave face right now.

"Back so soon? I thought you two had a sleepover," my dad says, his voice slurred. He looks tired, most likely because of the new medications. My mom explained to Tessa and me that the treatments will probably make him feel sicker before they actually help him get better.

"It was a boy-girl party," Mom corrects him. "Their first, remember?"

"Oh, that's right," he replies, forcing a smirk. "So, how was it? Any special slow dances or …" He clutches his throat and tries to disguise his coughing, and my mom hands him a glass of water. "Did you have a good time?" he rasps after a few sips, but I can tell he's in pain.

"Yes, sir," Loren answers, then glances at me. She knows something's up.

"We did," I add with a sigh.

I hate the way this feels. I've always shared everything with Loren, but now I'm apologizing for my sister and keeping my parents' secrets.

"Yeah, so, good night," I call out before turning and ushering Loren to my bedroom.

"Hey, is your dad okay?" she asks as soon as we're alone. "He seems … off."

I look away, preparing myself to deliver another lie. "He's fine."

"Hmm. It sounded like he was drunk or something," she reflects as she sits on the edge of my bed.

"Well, he's not," I say and turn my back to her.

"I don't know, Ten. I'm pretty sure I can tell by now. I do have plenty of practice, after all."

My eyes sting, and I swallow hard. "He's not drunk," I repeat, more harshly this time. "And having a mom who can't stay sober for more than a day at a time doesn't give you the right to assume the worst about everyone else's parents." I bite my lip as soon as I say it, unable to face her.

"Wow. Tell me how you really feel, then," she replies after a while, her voice breaking.

"I'm sorry, but you're not the only one with family stuff, you know." I turn and keep my eyes trained on the floor.

"Actually, I *don't* know. Because you never said anything," she whispers.

"It's hard to get a word in when we're always talking about your problems." I cringe because it's mean, and I feel terrible already. But it seems like the only way to get her to drop the subject.

I cross my arms over my chest and glance up at her. Her eyes are wide and glistening, as if she can't believe what she's hearing, and she looks so sad that my chest aches.

"I didn't realize I was such a burden to you," she says through a quiet sob, wiping the moisture from her cheeks. "But don't worry. I'll stay out of your way from now on."

She inhales deeply and collects her overnight bag before she turns to march out. I open my mouth to say something, but it's too late. She's already slammed the door behind her.

And I don't allow myself to chase after my best friend, because deep down, I know she's better off without me.

CHAPTER 1
TENLEY

MAIS LA.

I grimace at the speaker of the drive-thru when I hear, "Sorry, ma'am, we don't do salads anymore."

"Oh, well, what about a grilled chicken wrap?"

"We have a crispy chicken burger," the voice crackles. Because grilled anything would be way too much of an ask.

I sigh, figuring I might as well do it big if this is turning into a cheat meal. "Just give me a cheeseburger with fries. And a Coke."

There aren't many fast-food options back home, probably since Cajuns believe good food isn't cooked until the chef finishes drinking. So I've opted to grab something before I leave civilization, knowing this is the first of many conveniences I will miss after living in an actual city for the past decade.

As soon as I'm back on the road, I hit a huge pothole and spill half of my soda. I grumble to myself and scarf down the disgusting bag of junk as I drive the last fifteen miles or so to my hometown, the main highway cutting through an endless progression of rice fields and law office billboards until I reach the city limits.

Welcome to Camellia, Louisiana
Home of the Mighty Yellowjackets
and Former LSU Tiger JD Bourgeois, III

The sign I pass on my way in looks a bit more faded than I remember, including the strip the town added later honoring the hometown kid who'd played college football. I glance at the familiar storefronts lining Main Street as I pull up to the lone traffic light, noting a few changes. Besides the set of loud truck pipes a couple of blocks away, the only sound is the click of the light switching back to green. It's another stark contrast to the hustle and bustle I've grown used to.

I finally arrive at the modest Acadian-style home on the outskirts of town and slowly pull into my parents' driveway to park beside an older-model pickup truck. My heart constricts as I glance over at the well-loved F-150 with a faded fleur-de-lis sticker on the back glass, knowing its owner likely hasn't been in the driver's seat in a while. I force myself to bury the stinging remorse as I grab a couple of bags from the trunk of my new Audi, which I only bought to ease the transition.

My nephew swings the door open and greets me with a smile as soon as I reach the front-porch steps. "Aunt Ten," Ethan acknowledges me with a light kiss on the cheek and slides a duffle bag from my shoulder, lightening my load in an instant. He looks at least an inch taller since I saw him last month, and his dark-green eyes are even more striking than I remember. But I figure overnight growth spurts are the norm for a fifteen-year-old boy.

"Any more bags in the car?"

"Just a few, but we can get the rest later." I'm planning to keep most of my luggage packed for now, optimistically hoping to secure my own place as soon as I can. Although I've resigned myself to a new job and an extended stay back home, I'd like to maintain some of my independence until I return to my real life back in Waco, Texas.

My mother's wearied appearance on the front porch draws me back. Raising a teenager and nursing a terminally ill adult have been taking their toll. "Hi, Mama," I say and accept another cheek kiss. I'm not usually this affectionate, but the rest of my family is. It's also fairly common down here. Mom squeezes me tightly before leading me inside with a hand on my back.

"Is Daddy awake?" I ask after dropping my bags unceremoniously in my old bedroom and returning to the kitchen. Another cultural norm in Louisiana—most of the living happens in the kitchen, because food is life.

She sighs heavily. "He's been finding it harder to rest at night. I'm sure he'll fuss me for letting him sleep through the day, but I can't bring myself to wake him when he finally gets some relief." She glances at the clock on the stove. "It is time for his medicine, though."

"Let me get that," I say quickly.

She smiles softly and hands me the spiral notebook serving as my dad's chart. It's been a while since my mom last worked in a clinical setting, but her notes still reflect her decades of nursing experience. According to this schedule, my dad's care has become a full-time job. I swallow hard, ashamed for selfishly thinking I would come home to help and expecting to live apart from them. The gravity of his condition weighs on my heart again.

Ethan returns and briefs me on more of their routine while my mom busies herself around the kitchen, and I finally make my way into the living room to wake my dad. He's resting in his recliner. A twin-sized hospital bed is stationed nearby, which I know he hates. This isn't the first time we've been through this—he survived a bout with throat cancer when I was a teenager. We hadn't gotten to celebrate his recovery, though. By the time he'd made it into remission, my older sister passed away unexpectedly, just after giving birth to Ethan.

Now the cancer has returned to my father's lungs with a vengeance, and the oncologists all agree that it's the beginning of the end, spurring my impromptu decision to uproot my life and return temporarily to my hometown in South Central Louisiana.

"Hey there, Tenley-girl," my dad drawls in a sleepy voice after I begin adjusting some of the devices responsible for keeping him alive.

"Hey, Daddy," I return and kiss his cheek. "*Comment ça va?*"

"Ah, *ça va, ma jolie fille*," he answers in French. "I hope your drive wasn't too bad?"

"Not at all." We're both fibbing. Things are obviously not going well for him, and the roads between Texas and Louisiana are notoriously rough.

"Have you talked to Ethan? He's probably going to need a ride to football practice this afternoon."

I hand him a few pills and a glass of water. "They're practicing on Labor Day?"

"Coach ain't one to cut them any slack, but that's why they're going to be good this year."

"Hmm. I'm actually about to head over to meet with Dr. Simms and the clinic staff. I'm sure I can drop Ethan off at the field and pick him up on the way home."

I frown as he struggles to get the medicine down before speaking again. "Aren't you going to stick around and offer your services as an athletic trainer to the team?" he suggests with a broken laugh.

"I'm afraid I've let my water-girl certification lapse."

"Oh, I'm sure those boys would still be happy to have your help," he says, smirking. "You know, some of your old friends have moved home, too. You probably went to school with half of Ethan's teachers and coaches."

I don't have the heart to tell my dad I haven't kept in touch with any of my childhood friends over the years or even bothered to attend a reunion. My career has kept me so busy that I've barely had time to visit my family. Not that I could boast about any close friendships from high school, anyway. At least, not once my home life became so complicated.

Unlike my sister, I'd made it a point to lie low back then. Besides helping at home during my dad's first round of cancer and eventually after Ethan was born, I did my time in extracurriculars, earned good grades, and worked as an athletic trainer for the football team. But that was all. I was determined not to become one of those girls who peaked in high school.

Then I went off to nursing school, which took so much time and energy, and college Tenley turned into a more mature, determined version of high-school Tenley, who kept her head down and took everything seriously. And adult-workaholic Tenley is certainly no better.

Nearly every version of me since middle school has been bad at relationships and friendships, because being so driven makes me incapable of forming a deep connection with anyone in case they might need me—or I might need them. It's a lot easier this way. Besides, I don't mind being alone.

"I'll keep an eye out for some of my classmates while I'm around," I answer after a minute, feigning interest for my dad's sake.

"I bet you'll find some familiar faces at Ethan's football games, for sure."

I nod. "Anything else I can get for you?" I offer, changing the subject.

"I may be dying, but I'm not completely helpless yet," he replies. "*Je ne suis pas gâté.*"

"That *is* what I'm here for, you know, to spoil you. Although I also got tired of only catching Dallas games on Sundays." I purposefully ignore his morbid sense of humor.

He chuckles, which triggers a short coughing fit. "And at least I'll go out knowing I raised you well."

CHAPTER 2
JD

"Nice job out there today, Tate," I say, dropping one hand onto the helmet of my junior quarterback and using the other to shake his face mask playfully. "I'm feeling the new footwork."

"Thanks," he returns. "Coach Blake's been working with me. Now, I just gotta get that slant right."

"It'll come, man." I walk on, slapping a few of the others on the back and doling out positive feedback with an occasional side of constructive criticism. "Big E," I call out to number twenty-three. The young running back turns before he reaches the doors of the locker room.

"Yes, sir?" he asks, his eyes wide.

My nickname for him seems a bit ironic since I'm looking down at him, but I'm used to towering over everyone, at least since I retired from playing professional football and started coaching high schoolers. "Your blocking's improved. I liked you in that matchup with Trevor today." I hold out my fist as a proud smile spreads across his face, and he bumps his knuckles against mine.

"Yeah, he was pretty mad about that," he says with a light laugh. "You must have missed the next play when he laid me out."

I shake my head and laugh with him. "Oh, I saw it. And then you held your own again on the next one. You kept battling."

"I did juke him on that kickoff return, too."

The back of my hand makes a low *clack* against his shoulder pads. "There you go. I may have to let you start on special teams this year."

His smile transforms into an ear-to-ear grin. "Sweet."

"Need a lift today?" I lean in and ask a little lower. It's not an offer I usually extend to the whole team, but Ethan's home situation is different. I try to help him out as often as I can without giving him special treatment, and he's grateful each time I do. In fact, he's probably one of my favorite students—friendly, obedient, kind, and hard-working—an anomaly among teenagers these days. Maybe being raised by his grandparents has given him a different perspective.

"Thanks, but I'm good. My Aunt Tenley's coming to pick me up."

"Oh, right. I guess that means she's back?"

"Just got in today. But I may need a ride home on the days she has to work late, so you're not completely off the hook yet," he says with a hopeful glint in his eyes.

I reassure him of my standing offer and follow him into the locker room, addressing a few more of the players before talking to each of my assistant coaches.

"See you tomorrow, bruh?" Blake asks as we walk outside together.

"Yep." He opens his mouth to speak again, but I lift a finger to cut him off. "And before you ask again—*no*. I'm still not interested in your blind date this weekend."

"Why the hell not? Trust me, she'd show you a good time." My brother smirks wolfishly.

"Mostly because we don't share the same taste in women ... or the definition of a good time, for that matter."

He rolls his eyes. "Come on, JD. The last few girls I set you up with were all hot."

"Maybe until I tried engaging them in conversation." I sigh, reminding myself to play nice. "Look, man, I appreciate the offer. But I'm ready for a real relationship, and I'm tired of getting my hopes up for nothing. All this casual dating has started to seem pointless ... and boring."

"That's only because you don't allow any of your dates to 'entertain' you. There's nothing wrong with having a little fun until you find *the one*, you know," he adds that last part mockingly. "When's the last time you got—"

I interrupt him with a loud groan, sensing his need to say something else inappropriate. "Get out of here, Blake."

"Whatever you say, boss," he concedes, tossing the football he's been holding at my head. He's taken to calling me that since he started volunteering as one of my assistant coaches, mostly to remind everyone that he isn't so keen on being ordered around by his younger brother. But Blake is the type of perfectionist whose pride forces him to do his job well and settle for conveying his resentment through a few passive-aggressive remarks.

"But I think you just answered my question," he adds, proving my point.

He walks off, leaving me to pick up the stray equipment near the bench. I'm squatting down to grab my clipboard when I notice a pair of black-and-gold-sneakered feet which look decidedly more feminine than I'm used to seeing near the sidelines. My eyes lift to scan the stranger standing across the fence.

Damn.

My stomach flips. She's gorgeous.

She's on the taller side, wearing fitted black scrubs and a white lab coat over what appears to be the most amazing hourglass figure I've ever seen on a real-life woman. I watch as her dark-blue eyes search the area around the locker room. There's something vaguely familiar about her face, and I continue gazing at her, inventorying a slightly upturned nose and shoulder-length, wavy blond hair. I like that she isn't overly made up. I mean to look away after a while, but she puts her hands on her hips, inadvertently opening her coat to reveal a tiny waist in contrast to the nicest set of big, beautiful—

Um, capital letters?

Her name and a couple of her credentials are embroidered over the pocket, which I admittedly only notice because I'm gaping at her chest.

Tenley Robin, DNP, CNM

She must be relatively smart if she's got multiple acronyms listed on that fancy lab coat. I haven't even heard her speak yet, and I'm already intrigued.

"Um, hi? I'm here for Ethan," she says with an awkward wave in front of my face, bringing me back from my thoughts. I don't realize how hard I'm staring until she gives me an uncomfortable look.

"Oh, uh, sorry. Just kind of ... blanked out for a second there," I reply, attempting to cover up the fact that she caught me checking her out, even though I left my mouth open and everything. I scramble to form a coherent response until Ethan's name triggers a few details from recent memory. "I'm Coach JD. You must be E's Aunt Tenley. I've heard a lot about you."

I toss the football into a pile and transfer the clipboard to my left side so I can extend my right hand over the fence. She takes it reluctantly, and I don't think I've been this nervous or excited about touching a girl since middle school. But she tugs her hand back and discreetly wipes it on her thigh as if she's trying to rid herself of my cooties.

And now I'm staring again. How does she manage to make scrubs look so hot, anyway? Aren't they supposed to be frumpy and shapeless?

Crap.

I forgot I'd been patting the sweaty backs of about forty teenage boys just prior to offering my hand to this lady. I turn my head and cringe, scolding myself and attempting to get it together before facing her again.

"Nice to meet you," she replies with a tight-lipped, polite smile. It's the kind you give when you accidentally make eye contact with someone on the elevator or when someone holds the door open for you but ends up inconveniencing you because you have to rush over to relieve them of their duty.

Come on, JD. Make small talk like an actual human.

"He's a great kid, you know. I'm not really supposed to pick favorites, but if I could ..."

Her smile stretches a little wider, looking more genuine this time. "Yeah, I guess he's not so bad."

I nod, sensing the unpleasant stench of football equipment lingering in the air and praying she doesn't associate the smell with me. I clear my throat awkwardly. "So, uh, how's Mr. Jude doing today?"

She looks away quickly, pulling the corner of her bottom lip in between her teeth, and her eyes begin to water. "He's ... you know, he's hanging in there." She sticks her hands in her pockets and digs a toe into the grass, obviously trying not to cry.

"That's ... good."

Great. He's freaking dying, you idiot. Why would you even go and ask such a stupid—

"Well, it was great to finally meet you in person." I cut off my inner monologue with my best attempt to end the conversation politely and salvage what's left of my pride, but this whole interaction is going to hell in a handbasket. "Ethan should be out soon. Just let me know if you guys need anything."

I turn abruptly, planning to tuck tail and jog back to the locker room as fast as possible, but instead I trip as I nearly bowl over Ethan.

"Whoa, sorry," he apologizes, putting his hands on both sides of my arms to right me, despite my obvious size advantage. I clear my throat again, feeling a bit emasculated, and glance over my shoulder to see if Tenley has noticed the exchange. It looks like she's trying not to smile.

"You're good, E. I'll see you tomorrow," I say quickly, shaking off his grasp and stooping to pick up the clipboard I dropped.

"Wait, Coach, I wanted to introduce you to my Aunt Ten," the little jerk says, smirking down at me. "Unless you two already got the chance to talk?"

I stand and notice his shoulders shaking lightly as he stifles a laugh, and the crowd gathered outside the locker room tells me Ethan wasn't the only witness to my failed attempts at being smooth. I can hear a few of the guys catcalling and snickering over in the distance.

I hit them with my best teacher glare, and they silence themselves before shuffling back into the locker room. Ethan also has the good sense to drop his head and scamper away as soon as he sees my jaw clenching. "But, yeah, I'll see you tomorrow, Coach," he calls, most likely afraid of the number of extra laps he'll be running later if he keeps this up.

I don't look back as I stomp over to the locker room, the remaining players scattering like roaches the second I walk in.

"Any of y'all got something to say to me?" I demand. Most of them keep their eyes trained on their own feet.

"Come on, Coach," one of the seniors says, shuffling over and reaching out to pat my shoulder. "A guy like you shouldn't be striking out that easily. You almost made that nice lady cry. What happened to the sauce, man?"

I press my lips together, trying to keep my laughter contained. Who am I kidding? He's right. But the truth is that it's been a while since I've bothered to put much effort into my love life, despite wanting to be in a relationship so badly. Finding a single woman my age with values that are comparable to mine is hard enough; uncovering one of those in a town this small seems impossible. I've gotten offers since my return to Camellia a handful of years ago, but most of them have been intended for some ex-ballplayer and not for the real me—not that I was really intrigued by any of them, anyway. Regardless, whether it's due to the infrequent practice or my lack of interest, I've apparently lost my touch now that I've finally found someone I want to impress.

And I'm not exactly sure why, but I'm *definitely* interested in impressing Tenley Robin.

Okay, yeah, she's obviously stacked. But she's also willing to put her family's needs above her own, judging from the way she uprooted her life to be here now, and I like that she wasn't afraid to walk out onto a football field to pick up her nephew. Maybe it's those values in conjunction with everything Ethan's been saying about her that makes me think I could like her already, but there's something about her drawing me in, even after that single disaster of a conversation. Either way, I'm not giving up that easily. I'll just have to work on making a better impression, or at least manage an interaction that doesn't end in either laughter or tears.

"What the hell do you and your country-ass mullet know about *sauce*, anyway, Landreneau?" I finally say, cracking a smile and play-fully shoving him out of my way.

The rest of the locker room breaks out into new fits of laughter. I take a few steps forward, then pivot back around to give them all the death stare again, silencing them within seconds. "For the record, I wasn't shooting my shot or anything like that with Ethan's aunt. I was just being polite. It's part of my job to reassure your parents that I'm a decent guy."

"Yeah, but she's ..." A kid named Damien gestures crudely with both of his hands, but Ka'von, my star wide receiver, shushes him, and Damien wisely trails off once I turn my glare on to him.

"Let me find out that any of you said a single word about Ms. Tenley again, good or bad, and you'll be flipping tractor tires until your arms feel like they're going to fall off," I declare, stepping forward to poke him in the chest. Damien shoves his hands behind his back.

"Got it?" I search each of their faces.

"Yes, sir," most of them grumble in unison.

"Good. Now, clean this place up before you shower. Y'all's stink is salting my game."

CHAPTER 3
TENLEY

"So," Ethan starts as I pull away from the football field.

"So?" I question hesitantly. An awkward silence fills the cab for a minute before he bursts into laughter. "Okay, what's so funny?" I totally don't get teenagers. But, then again, I've never really acted like one myself.

"Nothing." But the fact that he's wiping his eyes leads me to believe it's *something*.

"What could I have possibly done that's so embarrassing?" I ask defensively. "I barely even said anything."

"You really don't know what happened back there, do you?"

I shrug.

"Coach JD *obviously* thought you were a snack," he says, cracking up again at the end.

"Wait, what does that even mean? And why does it sound so inappropriate?" I eye him, and he raises his brow innocently.

"It's not like that. I just meant he seemed ... very interested in you."

"Oh, I guess I thought he was just being polite."

I'm not actually *that* unobservant. I could sense when the guy was checking me out and noticed his awkward demeanor throughout our exchange. But I certainly don't know JD Bourgeois well enough to surmise whether he'd conducted himself any certain way toward me just now. Sure, we went to school together, but he was a grade or two behind me, and I can't remember interacting with him much outside of football. Watching someone play ball on TV doesn't exactly equate to knowing him, either.

"Seriously? He went from sigma to mid as soon as he saw you," Ethan declares, gaping at me like I have three heads.

"Are you even speaking English right now?"

He sighs impatiently. "Look, I've never seen Coach JD act that lame in front of anyone before. Normally, all he has to do is show up and smile, and everyone drools over him and gives him whatever he wants. Old ladies, principals, football dads ... they practically worship him around here. I mean, he's super corny, but people love it."

My eyebrow shoots up. "Just because he played a little college football and looks like a Hemsworth, everyone seriously treats him like a god?"

He narrows his eyes at me. "Wait, you think he's hot, too, don't you?"

I recoil. "Whatever, I wasn't even looking hard enough to notice." I glance back at Ethan's expression. He isn't buying it. "I mean, he's generically good-looking, I guess. But not really my type, especially if he's the player you say he is."

"First of all, you're the one who just called him a Hemsworth. I'm pretty sure those guys are everyone's type, Aunt Ten." I roll my eyes at him, but he has a point. "Secondly, I don't think Coach JD is a player. He could probably get with any of the women around here, but he's not like that. He's just really likable."

"What do you mean?" I blurt out the question. But only because I want to know what kind of influence he might have on my nephew.

Ethan turns to face me from the passenger seat to elaborate. "He's actually a pretty good guy. He doesn't act like he's better than anyone because of what he's accomplished, and he goes out of his way to be an awesome coach. He never minds giving me a ride back from practice. Some days we stop for food on the way home, especially since

Pop's been sick again. He says he figures Mawmaw doesn't have much time to cook. And he even came over to help me mow the lawn last weekend."

"Wow. That's all ... very nice of him," I reply, regretting not coming home sooner again.

"He's always doing that kind of stuff, and not just for me. Besides, I spend enough time around him to know if he were dating a bunch of women at once, and I'm positive he doesn't have a girlfriend."

I glare at him from the side, sensing an ulterior motive. "Are you ... you're not telling me this because you're trying to set me up with your coach, are you?"

"Oh, no, ma'am, I swear." He holds up his hands innocently. "I just thought you should know he isn't a creep or anything."

I nod silently.

"So," he begins again, "just to be clear, would you say the vibe is more Chris or Liam? He's totally giving Liam, right?" He barely gets the rest of it out before breaking into a fit of giggles.

I reach out to shove him playfully in the shoulder. "You're too *canaille* for your own good."

Ethan's not wrong, though. JD does resemble the youngest Hemsworth brother, with his large stature, light-brown hair and beard, and prominent nose, none of which I mind in the least. Perhaps he's a little scruffier than the actor, but from the initial looks of it, he more than makes up for it in both height and muscle volume.

Okay, so I fibbed when I said JD wasn't my type or that I hadn't bothered to check him out. Tall, sturdy former football player with huge arms and a heart of gold just sounds like a dangerously dreamy combo I need to stay the heck away from right now.

"Fine. I won't bring it up again," Ethan says reluctantly, pulling me back from my thoughts. I feel my cheeks flush a little, as if he's read my mind and knows I've been giving his coach the once-over. "But for the record, I'm pretty sure he was being weird because he was nervous around you. Like, in the good way. I bet he asks about you later."

I bite my lip. I haven't even considered dating anyone in Camellia.

Truth be told, JD sounds like a genuinely decent guy. Except for being a couple of years younger than me, he also fits the profile of my previous romantic interests—not that there have been many of those in a while. I think back to the last time I dated—Chad, another football player—and realize that it's been years since my last real relationship. I've also never been good at dating or relationships in the first place.

Regardless, even if I had the time or the mental capacity for men right about now, I'm not sure how long I'll be here. And I'm not willing to risk making Ethan feel uncomfortable by getting involved with his coach. He obviously admires JD, and I'm glad he seems to have found a good role model.

"Aunt Ten?" he calls. I've drifted again. "What should I say if he asks for your number or something? Do you even have Snapchat?"

I shake my head lightly. "I don't think that's a good idea. Your coach seems nice and all, but our lives are complicated enough as it is, don't you think?" I smile tentatively at him, though he looks disappointed. "Dating just isn't on my priority list right now," I add quickly.

"Whatever you say," he replies with a shrug. "But maybe it wouldn't be so bad if you found someone who would make you want to stay home this time."

Ah, there's his motivation.

I reach over and squeeze his shoulder affectionately as I'm overcome with guilt. "I'm sorry I've been away so long, Ethan. But you are more than enough to make me want to stick around for a while. I promise I'll be here as long as you need me, okay?"

He nods and smiles back at me, looking somewhat relieved. "Okay."

"Besides, I'm just starting to catch on to your Gen-Z language. You can't get rid of me now."

CHAPTER 4
JD

"Hey, E, still need a ride home today?"

"Yeah, Coach, if you don't mind. Aunt Ten had a delivery this afternoon, and there's no telling how long that'll take."

I can't help it when my ears perk up at his mention of Tenley. I've admittedly been making it a point to hang around by the gate at the end of practice most days just to get a quick look at her again.

Okay, so it's more like a long, hard stare while she walks around the car after giving up the driver's seat for Ethan, but I'm sure I've been playing it off well.

"So she's stuck at the hospital again?" I ask as we fall into a routine, and I hand him a bag of football equipment to carry to my truck.

"Yeah. She said she'll be taking over a lot of the deliveries for Dr. Simms now."

"Oh. I didn't realize our population was big enough to keep Dr. Simms that busy in the first place."

"Apparently women come from all over to have their babies in Camellia because our hospital's so nice, especially if you want to go all natural or whatever. She tried explaining more of it the other night, but it sounds sort of gross," he continues, tossing his backpack into the back seat. "But she did say something about letting babies come on their own time and that when she gets called out to help a mom in labor, it could be hours or even days before she gets to finish her job."

We both climb into the front and buckle our seat belts. "I see. So, she's kind of like an OB-GYN but ... crunchier?"

"Sure, I guess."

I nod, pretending I'm not fishing for more information as I crank the truck and pull out of my parking spot near the home gate. Ethan's been going on about Tenley for the past couple of months, so I doubt he's noticed my prompting in all of our conversations lately. "I guess her, uh, boyfriend probably doesn't appreciate her having to work those crazy hours, though." I make the mistake of venturing a quick glance at his face. He's already trying his hardest not to crack up.

I furrow my brow. "I'm just making small talk."

"Yes, sir," he says, barely holding back his laughter. "Weather sure is nice, too. And how 'bout that Saints game last weekend?"

I roll my eyes. "Are you going to tell me whether she's single?"

He snorts, amused by my desperation. "Don't you think I would have mentioned it by now if I thought I'd be getting a new uncle?"

"Right." I nod quickly, as if it isn't too late to act like I haven't been working up the courage to ask him about Tenley's relationship status all week or that I'm not relieved by his answer. To be fair, my social media stalking hasn't been very successful since all her accounts are private. How else am I supposed to get my intel?

"I hate to be the one to tell you this, Coach, but you're not fooling anyone. You look at Aunt Ten the same way I look at Caidence Fontenot."

Busted.

I cringe. "Have I really been that obvious?"

He huffs at me. "Worse. Everyone's been calling you 'Coach Thirsty' behind your back."

I curse under my breath. Blake warned me about my new nickname, but I've been hoping he was just messing with me. "I'm sorry. I don't think I'm usually this lame around women."

"I figured," he says. "And just so you know, I wouldn't have minded if you wanted to ask her out. I even tried to talk you up a little bit, be your wingman and all. But I don't think she's interested. Sorry, man."

I feel the instant pangs of disappointment, even though I'm flattered by Ethan's blessing. He really is a great kid, and sometimes I enjoy spending time with him more than I do with guys my own age. Though, I'm not sure if that says more about me or him.

"Oh ... well, thanks for trying. I appreciate it."

"Yeah, no worries."

We drive in silence for a minute before I change the subject. "Speaking of Caidence, how are things going?"

He puffs out his cheeks and exhales loudly. "She knows I exist, but barely."

"Hang in there, bro. I have a feeling you'll make an impression when the time is right. You've been looking good at practice. I bet she'll be watching from the sidelines."

"Maybe," is all he says, looking down at his lap.

I reach over to shove his shoulder playfully. "And hey, now that school's started again, I can always assign a group project. I can be a good wingman, too." He laughs at me, and his expression lightens.

"You know," he begins again, his smile growing. "Technically, Aunt Tenley didn't say she wasn't interested *in you* ... only that she wasn't interested in dating anyone at all right now."

I keep my eyes on the road, trying not to grin like a silly teenager at the slightest bit of hope. "So, you're saying there's a chance?"

He laughs heartily at the *Dumb and Dumber* reference, even though the movie is much older than he is. The others usually glare at me as if I'm an alien once my inner nerd rears its ugly head, but Ethan is one of the only kids who indulges me by laughing at my jokes and recognizing my movie references.

"By the way, if this conversation ever comes up again, I haven't said anything. I don't think she'd appreciate it if she suspected I was setting her up."

"What conversation?" I feign ignorance, and he chuckles again. "For the record, I'd only ever repeat something you told me in confidence if I thought you were in danger. So I expect you to extend the same courtesy by not telling your aunt and everyone else that I'm really just a huge dork," I add with a smile.

"The guys on the team would never take you seriously again if they knew you were this lame."

"Nah, I'm still bigger than all of you."

"Fair enough."

I laugh again as we near his house. "What about dinner?" I ask, knowing how hard it must be for Mrs. Therese to keep a teenage boy well-fed while tending to her sick husband. Ethan once let it slip that she hasn't been able to get to the grocery store as often as she used to, so I make sure to check on their eating habits by working it into our conversations.

"Aunt Ten's been keeping the fridge stocked. And she cooks about as good as Mawmaw does, except she always makes us eat a salad or something healthy on the side."

"All right, then," I say as I pull into the driveway. "Maybe I'll have to crash dinner at the Robin house again."

"For sure," he confirms. "I'll figure out a way to get you an invite." He retrieves his bag from the back seat before reaching out for a fist bump. "Thanks again, Coach. I appreciate you always having my back."

"No worries, Big E. I got you."

"See you tomorrow?"

"See you tomorrow. Oh, and don't forget to start looking over your bio notes for our test later this week," I yell after him as he walks up the front-porch steps. He nods and waves without turning around on his way inside.

Before I can back out, I sense movement behind me. I watch Tenley drive up in my rearview mirror before she parks and gets out of her fancy car, lugging her purse and dragging her feet. I figure I should wait for her to make it to the house before leaving, mostly to be polite and only somewhat so I can check her out.

I offer a short wave, and she barely glances at me when she passes. But she surprises me by calling out over her shoulder as she trudges up the steps. "Hey, Coach."

"Uh, hi, Ms. Tenley."

Can't I even manage a non-awkward hello?

She turns to face me. "Thanks for bringing Ethan home. I was worrying I wouldn't make it out of the hospital in time when he texted to say you'd already offered to give him a ride."

I smile. Technically, Ethan asked me for a lift first, probably because he knew we'd get here around the same time as Tenley.

My mini wingman.

"Yeah, of course. It's nothing. I don't live much farther down the road, and I always enjoy hanging out with E," I lean out of the open window to reply.

Attaboy. Nice and easy. Don't say anything stupid this time.

"Sure, you do," she says, narrowing her eyes at me. "I'll bet you're just itching to spend some quality time with the kids you deal with all day at school, in addition to the three extra hours at practice."

I swallow, pulling my arm back into the cab with me. Maybe this isn't the day for a nice conversation, after all. "Well, you know, I don't mind helping out when I can."

She cringes. "I'm sorry, that came out wrong. I didn't mean to be a jerk. I'm just so tired that everything probably sounds sarcastic," she explains with a weary sigh. "What I should have said is that I appreciate your help because I can imagine you're ready to get home by now. I'm sure teachers and coaches don't get paid overtime."

"No worries, you're fine." But her apology instantly goes to my head, as if it makes a difference that she cares enough to be nice to me. I'm sure she's just grateful for the help in general, but my ego takes it as an open invitation to flirt again.

"And hey, I may not get paid a whole lot, but there are a few other job perks. You know, summer vacations and holidays off, free school lunches, an unpaid moving crew at my disposal ... invitations to dinner and home-cooked meals courtesy of my favorite student's grandma and maybe even his very cute aunt ..." I continue, smirking playfully.

She crosses her arms and eyes me from the front-porch steps, totally ignoring my compliment. "Is that so? Wouldn't some of that be considered unethical? At least, the part about the student's family bribing you with food?"

"Louisiana law says it's not a bribe unless the cost of the meal exceeds twenty-five dollars. I always make sure to eat exactly twenty-four dollars' worth of your mom's famous gumbo when she offers for me to stay."

"Uh-huh," she replies, holding back a smile this time.

I know Ethan just said she's not interested, but her responses are encouraging, and I can't pass up the chance to make my intentions clear now that we're sort of alone. I turn my ball cap around, then lean a little farther out of the window to stick out my left arm and rest my palm on the top of the frame so that my muscles are on display. I absolutely need to play up my advantages here.

"Never even been tempted to eat more."

"Right." Her smile grows wider, and despite her obvious exhaustion, she's at least interested in the conversation. "And if my mama's gumbo couldn't tempt you, nothing else will."

Though her arms are crossed, she keeps her body turned toward me and takes a step down, creeping closer. And hot damn if her eyes don't flicker to my arm. I flex involuntarily, but she looks away quickly once she realizes I've caught her checking me out.

No, no, it's okay, look all you want. Hell, I'd get out of the truck right now and take this whole dang shirt off if you want to see more—

I clear my throat, trying to bring myself back. "Oh, I don't know, Ethan's been talking up your culinary talents lately. From what I've heard, your pork stew and corn bread might be good enough to push me over the line of ethical appropriateness—if I were lucky enough to score an invite, that is."

She throws her head back and laughs, and I can't help but think about how badly I'd like to put my lips on the parts of her neck she's exposing. I take a deep breath and exhale softly, trying to hide the evidence of my attraction. She'd undoubtedly freak out if she could read my mind, and rightfully so. I've never been the type to undress a woman with my eyes, but Tenley Robin is doing something really strange to me.

"Coach Bourgeois, you are shameless, aren't you?" She glares at me with an annoyed expression, but I can tell she's still enjoying our back-and-forth.

"Just JD. No need to be so formal when you're about to ask me over for dinner later this week."

She rests her hands on her hips again. I love the way it shows off her figure. "Well, *Just JD*, as much as we all appreciate everything you do for Ethan, I'm afraid corn bread and stew aren't on the menu this week. But I'll be sure to send you a bowl of leftovers the next time I make it."

I press my lips together, forcing a smile. She's letting me down gently, and I can't blame her. We barely know one another, and she's made it clear that dating isn't a priority for her. But none of that means I have to stop trying to change her mind. Impatient as I may be, it's also obvious I need to set my sights on building a friendship first.

"I'll take what I can get, I suppose," I reply after a beat, bringing my arm back into the cab and getting ready to make an exit with the sliver of pride I have left. "Just be sure to write your name and number on the container, so I can return it later. Wouldn't want anyone to think it was a gift and bring the total past the legal limit, you know."

She nods again and fidgets with that bottom lip between her teeth, making my stomach dip. The longer I'm around her, the worse off I become.

"Yeah, I'll do that," she says after a while, eyeing me skeptically. "Have a good night, Coach JD."

"You too, Ms. Tenley," I return, raising my window. "See you around."

I heave out another sigh as I shift my truck into reverse. But not a second later, I'm forced to slam on the brakes. I mutter a few bad words after I lurch to a stop mere inches away from bumping into Mr. Jude's old truck. My heart is still thumping when I steal a quick glance in the mirror and find Tenley watching with a hand over her mouth, stifling her amusement. I shake my head and curse my stupidity a few more times before I finally reach the road.

Will I ever be safe from making a complete and total fool of myself in front of her?

Not likely.

But at least I was able to gather more information from our exchange. I review a list of findings as I turn down my road and remind myself that as long as Tenley is coming around to see Ethan play football, I'm thereby granted the opportunity to see and interact with her. And since football season is just getting started, there should be plenty of opportunities.

Then again, maybe she really isn't interested in dating and only wants to be friends. Or maybe she isn't interested in *me* at all, beyond being politely appreciative of my caring for Ethan.

I walk into my house and throw my keys onto the kitchen island before stopping to grab a beer from the fridge. Then I take a sip and run a hand over my face as I lean back against the counter. I'm afraid I'm going to need better advice than an inexperienced teenage boy can offer if I want to entice Tenley to give me the time of day. Reluctantly, I slip my phone from my back pocket and start a new text thread.

JD

I need help.

BLAKE THE SNAKE

LOL. What's wrong, Coach Thirsty? Miss Aunt Tenley still isn't falling for your golden-boy charm and your big muscles?

I groan. I knew seeking my brother's help would be painful, but he's the only person I trust with this. He could have at least pretended not to know what I was going to ask or even spared me the "Coach Thirsty" reference, though.

JD

Ha ha. Laugh it up while you can. But don't think I won't remember this when you eventually find the woman who doesn't immediately fall for your "charm."

And yes, I am willing to admit that I'm in over my head.

BLAKE THE SNAKE

First of all, the day when I need your help to get a woman will *never* come.

But what's the big deal about Tenley Robin, anyway? Don't get me wrong, she's hot, but you usually care more about personality, and you hardly even know her. She seems a little stuck up, especially for you.

JD

Idk, man. She's different, more mature. Maybe I only like the version of her I've heard so much about from Ethan, but I honestly can't stop thinking about her, and that doesn't happen often for me.

Besides, haven't you been trying to get me to go on more dates?

BLAKE THE SNAKE

Fine. I'll bite. How did you strike out this time?

I give Blake a play-by-play of my conversation with Tenley and Ethan's failed attempts to convince her to give me a shot, hoping he has some sort of magic formula that'll change Tenley's mind. Because if there's anything my brother's good at, it's getting women to notice him.

BLAKE THE SNAKE

She's probably just got too much going on. You know how most women have the power to block out sex and focus on important stuff.

Then again, maybe she's not into the age difference. Or maybe she thinks she's too good for you.

JD

Was she like that in high school? I remember her being one of the hotter athletic trainers, but that's all.

BLAKE THE SNAKE

She was quiet and mostly kept to herself. Her sister Tessa attracted a lot more attention.

JD

Yeah. Let's make sure Ethan never really hears about that.

BLAKE THE SNAKE

Right.

Look, maybe you're just making yourself too available. I bet she'd pay more attention if she thought she couldn't have you.

JD

You think I should play hard to get?

BLAKE THE SNAKE

Let's start by dialing down the desperation, at least.

JD

Wow, thanks. Great advice, bro.

BLAKE THE SNAKE

Hear me out … Friend-zone her first, flirt with another woman around her, and once she thinks you're not interested, find a reason to take off your shirt in front of her. It'll work. Trust me.

JD

I don't like any of that.

Except maybe the shirtless part.

BLAKE THE SNAKE

I'm pretty sure I know what you're going to say,
but have you thought of making her a friends-
with-benefits offer? You never know. She might
be into that kind of arrangement.

I consider Blake's suggestion for a second, but that's as long as it takes for me to solidify that I want more than a casual hook-up with Tenley—or with any woman, for that matter. Whatever it is I'm feeling for her goes beyond physical attraction or lust. And, even though I don't know her as well as I'd like, my instincts tell me there's a reason I can't seem to get her off my mind. But try explaining that to my brother.

JD

No.

BLAKE THE SNAKE

I figured.

JD

We weren't created to separate sex and love,
man. You'll never be happy as long as you keep
your life disordered.

BLAKE THE SNAKE

Thanks for the unsolicited sermon, Padre. 🙄

I'm just saying, if you can't have both, settle
for one?

JD

I'd rather not settle.

BLAKE THE SNAKE

Suit yourself, bro. At least give the whole stalker
approach a rest, though.

JD

Yeah, thanks. I'll start there.

CHAPTER 5
TENLEY

"No offense, but I want my doctor," says yet another expectant mother.

I press my lips together and force a smile. "I'm sorry, Mrs. Thibodeaux. Dr. Simms had to go to the hospital. But I am well qualified, I promise. I'm a nurse practitioner and a certified midwife, and I've attended hundreds of deliveries at birthing centers and in hospitals."

"Birthing centers?" She regards me thoughtfully as she rubs her belly. "As in, natural and unmedicated births?"

"Yes. But I understand if you'd feel more comfortable waiting for Dr. Simms, especially since he's been taking care of you all this time. I just wanted to introduce myself and offer my help." It's disheartening, but I can respect my patient's wishes, especially when she's so close to delivery and grasping at any semblance of familiarity.

"So, what you're saying is that if I insist on waiting for Doc Simms to get back, I'll be here all afternoon?" she ventures.

"That's probably the case," I reply, turning my palms up and hoping to seem slightly less threatening.

"All right," she finally acquiesces.

I give her a more genuine smile this time, doing my best to put her at ease by asking questions and making small talk. Once she divulges that this is her fourth baby and she's had some complications in the past, I have a greater appreciation for her hesitance to accept a new caregiver. But by the end of the exam, I feel like she's at least given me a smidgen of her trust, especially once I make a point of going through her birthing plan with her. We're on friendlier terms now, anyway.

"How many kids do you have, Nurse Tenley?" she asks as I walk her back to the lobby.

"Oh, none for me. I enjoy working with you mamas and your littles so much that I haven't even found the time to look for Mr. Right," I deliver my well-rehearsed joke. "And I suppose he's a pretty important ingredient."

She chuckles and pats my shoulder reassuringly. "That's how it was for me. I'm a chemical engineer and a recovering workaholic. I never thought I'd even want kids, and then—out of nowhere—my husband appeared, and he somehow managed the impossible task of sweeping me off my feet. Now here I am, forty-four and on baby number four."

I smirk. "Eh, my feet are planted pretty firmly," I counter. "I think I'll just settle for spoiling my nephew and getting my newborn fix at work."

"Be careful, before that statement falls on your nose one day," she replies with a wink.

I laugh and bid her good luck, and I'm pleasantly surprised when her next appointment block appears on my column of the schedule. It hasn't been easy winning patients over, but I'm finally making some headway.

I finish up my charting around noon, just as a few of the staff pop into my office and invite me to lunch. Although I would usually make an excuse not to go out, I'm flattered by the gesture and join them at a Mexican restaurant not far from our clinic. And, aside from the exercise in willpower it takes to limit myself to one round of bottomless chips and margaritas, I genuinely enjoy myself.

After a surprisingly amusing lunch, I drive home and find my mom in the kitchen. "Hey, Mama," I greet her.

"Oh, hey, baby," she replies, adding an air kiss near my cheek. "You're home early today."

"Yeah. Dr. Simms is pretty good about making sure we don't have to come back after lunch on Fridays. How is everyone today?"

She turns her mouth to the side. "We've been better. It was a rough morning."

I sigh heavily. "Anything I can do?"

She shakes her head softly and turns back to the dishes she's just dropped into the sink. I join her and pick up the rinsing, and we continue the chore in silence for a few minutes before she speaks again. "Are you going to Ethan's game tonight?"

"That's what I planned, but I don't mind staying behind if you'd like to go. You might enjoy the fresh air."

She takes her time drying off her hands before she speaks again. "Tenley, I ..." Her voice breaks off, and her eyes grow watery.

"Hey, whatever it is, all you need to do is ask. I can go watch Ethan play or stay home with Dad. I'm here to help, remember? I don't want you to keep trying to do it all alone."

"That's just it. I know it seems like I'm being antisocial, but I just don't know how much time I have left with your daddy. And I love Ethan more than life itself. But I'm not exactly a spring chicken anymore, and I'm afraid that raising a grandchild while nursing your father through multiple rounds of cancer has taken its toll on me, too. I'm ... tired."

I stare at her for a second, noting how she's started to reflect her age. Her formerly light-brown hair is gray and thin, and her face is gaunt, with newly etched lines appearing around her eyes and mouth. I think of my sister for a second, since they've always shared a strong resemblance, and wonder if Tessa might have aged similarly if we hadn't lost her to a rare postpartum complication at the age of nineteen.

"Of course you are," I agree. "You've been Superwoman for years. Let me help."

"I'm afraid you don't understand what I'll be asking of you."

I shake my head. "What do you mean?"

"Tenley, I've been running on fumes for the past few years. But once this is all over, I'm going to need some time to rest. And I can't do that while I'm raising a teenager."

I suck in the corner of my bottom lip as I finally grasp her meaning. I'm an idiot. All this time, she's been waiting for me to offer to take over as Ethan's guardian, but I've been too self-involved to notice. Guilt swirls around in my chest again. Of course, I love my nephew. I just don't love the idea of having to face some of my biggest fears by assuming the role of foster mother.

What are my options, though? The rest of my family has been making sacrifices so that I could go off to pursue my dreams and live carefree. It's my turn to help, and a few years of supervising a self-sufficient, smart, respectful teenage boy shouldn't be all that hard. It's not like I'll be changing diapers or staying up with a crying baby, after all. Tending to Ethan is the very least I can do.

I step closer to my mother and wrap my arms around her. She returns the hug after a second, most likely surprised I've initiated the exchange. "I'm sorry I didn't get it on my own, but of course I'll do whatever you need for Ethan. And I apologize for waiting so long to come back and pull my weight." I let go of her so I can be sure she's heard my offer. "But I mean it. If you want me to stay around for a few years and help, I will. If you want me to find another place for Ethan and me to live, just say the word."

She lets go of the tears she's been holding in and they stream down her cheeks as she pulls me back in to hug me tightly. "Thank you, baby. I wish I didn't have to ask you for something this heavy. I never wanted you to inherit so many of my responsibilities, but Ethan needs at least one parent who can give him the love and attention he deserves. And I want you to have this experience, too."

I'm tempted to ask what she means by that last part, but I figure it's better left alone for now, especially since I have more important questions to ask. "But what about his biological dad?" I venture. "I mean, did you ever ..."

She frowns. "No, not exactly. Tessa gave me a name when she first told me she was pregnant. She claimed he didn't want to be involved.

I wrote to him when Ethan was a few years old, but he never responded. Then I reached out again a couple months ago, once we found out your dad's cancer was back. He still hasn't answered."

I nod thoughtfully. "Could that become a problem for us later?"

"I spoke to a lawyer about it, as well as about transferring guardianship to your name, just in case. He said it should be an easy transition since no one else was named on the birth certificate. And I hope the two of you will stay here for a while longer, at least for your dad's sake. There's no point in moving Ethan out of the only home he's ever known at a time like this, anyway, don't you think? Or making you spend all your money on a place to live when we have the room," she rambles on.

I humor her, though, because I can imagine her relief after finally getting this burden off her chest. "Of course, we'll stay a while. It's not like we wouldn't be back for dinner every night anyway, right?" I chuckle lightly, and she sniffles through a smile.

"I don't know, I think your cooking might be better than mine."

"I doubt that will ever happen." I grin at her.

"Well, I guess it's a good thing we settled this today," she says, turning back to the dishes as if we weren't just having a life-altering conversation.

"I'm afraid to ask why," I reply, my tone dry.

"It's parent night, so Ethan needs a field escort for the ceremony before the game."

I cringe. "This was your plan all along, wasn't it?"

She laughs heartily. "*Mais*, of course it was. I've already filled out the paperwork so that they'll be calling out your name to represent your sweet, handsome nephew. Ethan was already planning to ask you if you'd walk with him."

I throw my head back with a huff, trying not to smile at her. "I see where your grandson has learned to be so *canaille*."

She says nothing but purses her lips as she continues wiping the countertops, and I move to pour myself a glass of tea from the fridge.

"Fine," I concede after a minute. "Do I have to wear something special?"

"I had a shirt made for you. It's hanging in your closet. Be there at six. Oh, you'll probably want to bring my cowbell for the game. And Tenley?" She turns to face me.

"Yes, ma'am?"

"Try not to spend too much time staring at Ethan's coach and pay attention to the game. I know JD Bourgeois and his brother are both easy on the eyes, but you've got to at least pretend to watch the boys play ball for a bit."

I choke on a sip of iced tea. "Okay, first of all, you shouldn't believe anything Ethan tells you!"

She raises an eyebrow at me expectantly. "So, you and JD haven't been flirting and making sweet eyes at one another for the past couple of weeks?"

"I don't know what you're talking about. But for the record, I have no intention of dating *anyone* in Camellia," I declare as I walk off to change. I laugh to myself when she grumbles a sarcastic response I'm sure I wasn't supposed to overhear.

The truth is that while I've been too blind to recognize my mom's attempts to bring up Ethan's guardianship, I *have* inadvertently noticed JD's lingering gaze each time I pick up Ethan from practice. I simply refuse to flatter myself by thinking he's interested in me, since he must have his pick of all the available women around here. I figure his attention is more likely out of concern for Ethan's well-being and that he's only watching to ensure I'm taking good care of one of his favorite students. Either way, I don't think it's wise to read too much into JD's flirting or his "sweet eyes."

Back in my bedroom, I find the shirt my mom commissioned on my behalf. I click my tongue in disgust once I realize it's at least two sizes too small. Surely, she's done it on purpose, hoping to advertise my assets for me. I trade my scrub top for the T-shirt, anyway. The collar dips entirely too low, which means the girls are getting some screen time tonight, like it or not. I tug on the fabric, attempting to stretch out the shirt, then try readjusting my boobs, all without success. Eventually, I give up on any chance of modesty or propriety and can only hope I don't embarrass Ethan in front of his friends with his football number stretched out so awkwardly across my chest. I groan in frustration and stomp out of my room.

"Seriously, Mom?" I ask back in the kitchen, gesturing to the disaster of a neckline. "You're about as subtle as a billboard or a fake dating-app profile."

"I don't know what you mean, *cher*. I think that shirt is quite flattering," she replies, pressing her lips together and trying not to laugh.

"I'm calling Mrs. Sandy and getting her to make me another shirt in an actual adult size next week."

She shrugs. "Suit yourself. In the meantime, I think Coach might have a hard time concentrating on the game while you're wearing that. You'd better sit up high in the bleachers, so *he's* not tempted to stare at *you* all night."

CHAPTER 6
JD

I STAND ON THE SIDELINES, SUPPOSEDLY CONCENTRATING on my playbook. But I can't stop my eyes from wandering, and the game hasn't even started yet.

Earlier, I watched Ethan escort Tenley down the field for parent night. It's the first time she's worn something other than scrubs around me, and if I thought I liked her curves before, it's only because I hadn't seen her in jeans and a fitted V-neck tee until tonight. I'm even more sprung on her than I care to admit at this point.

And now I'm pretending to study a route that none of my players even understand while I observe Tenley's interactions with an old classmate. They're talking near the entrance to the bleachers while Shaliene, my homecoming date from junior year and another former athletic trainer, hands over her fresh-from-the-oven baby. Tenley expertly tucks the blue swaddle into her arms, and the baby immediately nestles up to her very plush chest, looking cozy and comfortable within seconds. I continue to stare as she gazes down at the baby fondly, her lips moving as if she's murmuring something to him.

I never thought I could be so envious of an infant. I realize after a minute that I've closed my playbook and defaulted to standing here and gaping at her again. But I can't stop myself. I'm midway through compiling a list of Tenley's qualifications for making and nourishing babies when, suddenly, my angelic view is blocked by something much more offensive.

"Yeah. That's a big fat *NO*, Coach Thirsty," Blake says sternly with both of his hands on my shoulders. He physically turns my body to face the field, despite my protests.

"What? There was a baby. Am I not allowed to look at the baby?"

"We all know that's not what you were staring at, big boy. In fact, you were probably scaring all the other mothers and children in the stadium with that look on your face," he grumbles, his eyes darting around nervously.

"What look?" I ask incredulously.

"You have a problem, bro. I'm starting to worry about you," he says quietly, his tone more serious.

I open my mouth to defend myself, but I'm not even sure how to explain that watching your crush hold a baby and fantasizing about making one of your own isn't creepy but actually nice and wholesome. Well, it had started out wholesome, anyway.

"I know. You're right. I just ... I can't stop thinking about her, but I also can't get close to her."

"You need to get her out of your system," he suggests. "Man up and ask her out, once and for all. And if she says no, go out with someone else until you forget about her."

That isn't how I'm wired, and Blake knows it. And somehow, nothing about the way I'm wired even matters with Tenley around, anyway.

"Or, you know, keep stalker-staring at her from afar and pestering Ethan for little tidbits of information, making yourself look sketchy and desperate, losing your edge, and damaging your reputation with the other women in town ..."

"I don't care about my reputation ... and I don't want any of the other women in town," I reply, pouting childishly.

"I know, buddy," he concedes after a second, patting me on the back. "Let's just go play some football. We'll worry about Miss Aunt Tenley later, huh?"

I roll my eyes, secretly pleased with my big brother's willingness to help me. It isn't often that Blake shows his softer side, but he's always taken good care of me, especially since we lost both of our parents a few years ago.

"Yeah, all right," I concede, clearing the emotion from my throat. "Just throw something at me if I get stuck staring again, would you?"

He chuckles and swipes the playbook from my hands. "I'll send one of the trainers over with a bottle of water. Come on, we still need to figure out that route before game time." We walk back toward the offense, and I sneak a quick glance over my shoulder, just to have something to hang onto for later.

I do my best to focus on the game after that. We're playing one of the toughest teams on our schedule tonight, so there isn't much room for error. Music blares over the press-box speakers as I walk down the line and greet each player and coach with a handshake, a fist bump, or a tap on the helmet. It's one of our pregame rituals, after our locker-room prayer. It's important to me that they all know their coach is behind them, that I'm confident in their abilities, and that I trust them to do their jobs. Plus, being a hype man is literally the best part of what I do.

"You good, two-three?" I ask as I approach Ethan.

"I'm ready, Coach," he says, his expression serious.

"You're on returns tonight. Get out there."

He shoots me a wide grin, an unspoken token of gratitude. Ethan's been grinding to earn his place on the team as a running back, and though he's still an underclassman, allowing him an opportunity on special teams during kickoff returns signifies his promotion to RB3 on the team. I can also see him moving up before the end of the season, if his work ethic sticks.

The crowd gets louder behind me, and I slap Ethan on the back as he takes off with the rest of the special teams crew. Then I continue along the sideline, making sure I thank the athletic trainers for their hard work ahead of time.

I readjust my headset and take my place around midfield, just as the ball sails up and over into Ethan's arms. He secures it well, cradling it within the crook of his elbow, and wastes no time in charging the mass of defenders.

Looks like it'll be number twenty-three, sophomore Ethan Robin, on the return for the Yellowjackets.

Then I cringe once I realize he's about to get a rough introduction to a couple of their bigger guys. I tense up, anticipating the hit, but he successfully jukes the first player, shuffling his feet and darting around him before repeating the move another time and breaking free from the crowd.

And he's at the fifty ... the forty ... Robin makes another one miss, and he's down to the twenty-five now ...

I run down the sideline, following Ethan as his legs eat up the distance to the end zone with only a couple of defenders left on his heels. One of them makes a last-resort dive with only a yard to go, their pads cracking when they collide, and Ethan gets lost at the bottom of a dog pile.

Robin is finally taken down at the goal line with a big hit by Gradney after a good seventy-yard run!

The refs blow the whistle as they attempt to pull everyone away, and I take a celebratory leap once they signal for the touchdown, even though the excitement is short-lived.

TOUCHDOOOWWN, YELLOWJACKETS! But it looks like Robin is a little slow to get up. Let's hope he's all right, folks.

My heart drops to my toes when I notice Ethan stays down after the rest of the crowd thins. He's clutching his left ankle with his knee pulled up to his chest and his helmet on the ground beside him. I usually leave the athletic trainers to tend to injured players, but I instinctively jog over this time.

"You good, Big E?" I ask as one of his teammates offers him a hand. Ethan pulls himself up, but he hisses and nearly loses his balance when he attempts to shift his weight onto his left foot. A couple of guys rush over to duck under each of his arms, supporting him as he hobbles to the sidelines.

"I'm okay, Coach. It's just my ankle," he replies, though his face betrays his calm response. The rest of the guys who have been taking a knee stand again, and the crowd applauds as Ethan gets to the bench. The trainers immediately begin unlacing his cleats, and I know I need to let them do their job so that I can do mine. Yet I can't see past making sure he's all right, especially since I'm already feeling guilty about letting Ethan push himself too far in an effort to prove his worth on the field tonight.

"I've got it, JD." I hear Blake's voice in my headset, and I turn to watch him signal the next play call to our quarterback. He glances over and gives me a confident nod. It's an assurance that he'll cover for me, as I seem to have forgotten that I'm supposed to be acting like a head coach right now and not an overly concerned parent.

I squat in front of Ethan, who is still grimacing in pain while the trainer removes his sock. To my relief, I don't see any signs of an obvious break, but there's already a noticeable bruise and some swelling on the inside of his foot.

"It's probably just a sprain," Ethan volunteers, but I can tell he's just trying to keep me from worrying.

"You're done for the night," I say brusquely. There's no way I'm letting him back on the field until he gets cleared by a doctor.

"I'm sure I just need some tape." But I glare at him until he drops his protest.

"Hey, superstar, what happened?" I gulp when I hear a softer voice.

Ethan forces a smile for Tenley when she comes around. "I'm fine. Just twisted my ankle," he lies again.

"What a way to celebrate your first big-boy touchdown," she says mirthfully. She kneels beside me, her arm brushing against mine when she takes his foot in her hands to examine his ankle. I notice she doesn't seem bothered by the current conditions, which include Ethan's sweaty foot and the damp patch of grass beneath us. Then I remember that not only has she done this before, maybe even for me, but that she's also earned a few nursing degrees since then.

"Does it hurt in a certain spot or when I turn it one way or the other?"

"Mostly on the inside, when I try to put any weight on it," he admits.

She nods and releases his foot, dusting her hands off on her thighs. "I guess we ought to get it x-rayed, just to be safe." I'm a little bit in awe of her calm demeanor. This is my job, and I'm not even that collected.

"Hey, boss, just a heads up, but you look like you could use some water," I hear Blake calling distantly over the radio. I adjust my headset and avert my eyes once I catch on to his warning.

"Will you, uh, take him to the hospital now?" I ask.

"Might as well," Tenley answers, standing from her position on the ground. It takes all I have not to glance up at her. "Just let me bring my car closer. Can someone help him over to the home gate?"

"We'll get him to you," I assure her.

"I'll meet you there," she tells Ethan before she walks off. I shift my focus back to him, trying to avoid watching her go.

"Let's get these pads off, then." I direct the others to help him remove the layers of gear. "Are you sure you're all right?" I lean in to ask.

"I'm good, Coach, I swear. I probably just need some ice," he replies with a strained smile.

"Come on, I'll walk you to the car." I support him as he rises to stand, and one of the trainers brings over a pair of crutches we keep on hand for these situations. He seems to get the hang of using them after a few steps, but I continue walking alongside him anyway. Most of his teammates turn and offer some encouragement, and Tenley is already waiting in her car by the time we make it to the gate.

Ethan lowers himself into the passenger seat, taking the crutches before I hand him a bag of ice. "Text me as soon as you find out what's going on," I command.

"I will. Thanks, Coach."

We trade fist bumps, though there's still a tightness in my chest that probably won't resolve itself until I know he's okay. "Put that on now." I point to the ice pack. "Maybe some ibuprofen?" I suggest, finally looking over at Tenley.

She smiles warmly. "I'll take good care of him, Coach. I promise," she says with a tinge of humor in her voice.

"Right. Okay. Good luck." I back out and close the door as Ethan waves shortly, and they drive away. Then I blow out a ragged breath as I jog toward the sidelines.

"Welcome back," Blake says without turning to look at me. "Care to join us, boss?"

I roll my eyes and check the scoreboard. Apparently, Blake called for a gutsy yet successful two-point conversion attempt. "I don't know. Looks like you've done a damned good job in my absence," I remark, genuinely impressed.

He smirks at me, leaning back on his heels and crossing his arms. "We've been managing without you, Coach Thirsty."

I huff, and he snickers to himself. "How is he?" he asks, covering up the microphone on the headset.

I lift a shoulder and let it drop. "Hopefully it's just a sprain. I asked them to let me know what they find out at the ER."

He reaches over to pat my arm lightly. "I'm sure he'll be fine," he reassures me, just before our quarterback launches a ball my way.

"For E," Tate says, grinning, and I mirror his expression, unexpectedly brimming with pride.

The last few seconds of the game clock tick away before Ethan texts to say that it's only a mild sprain after all. I exhale as relief floods through me. Then I selfishly reflect on the fact that he'll probably be missing practice for a while, which means that I won't get to see Tenley. I scold myself and try to take my brother's advice by setting her out of mind before I congratulate my team on their win, wishing it were easier to quit thinking about Tenley Robin.

CHAPTER 7
TENLEY

Bourgeois, Fontenot, & Guillory, Attorneys at Law

I narrow my eyes at the sign in front of the law office where my mom sent me. I should have remembered that there aren't many lawyers in Camellia, and Ethan's assistant football coach is one of them. I'm sure my mom has hired one of the other, more experienced attorneys, though I imagine Mr. Donald Guillory has been around long enough to have written the laws himself.

I walk into the repurposed Craftsman-style home. It's probably one of the oldest buildings in town. "Good afternoon. You must be Ms. Robin," the well-dressed receptionist greets me. She looks familiar enough that I think she might have been a few years behind me in school.

"Tenley," I correct her with a forced smile. "My mom said she set up an appointment for me?"

"She did. Mr. Bourgeois will be ready for you in a second. Just let me tell him you're here."

I sigh. Of course I'm meeting with frat boy Blake instead of old man Donald or harmless, middle-aged Mark. It's beginning to seem like I can't go anywhere without running into a Bourgeois or someone willing to bring them up in conversation.

The receptionist reappears and leads me down the hall to one of the offices. I peer around the room as she introduces us, already feeling uncomfortable with all the signed jerseys plastered on the wall, especially since most of them are sporting a "BOURGEOIS III" patch on the back. There are also a few encased footballs and baseballs on the back bookshelf.

I redirect my attention when Blake stands and leans over his desk to initiate a polite handshake. He's almost as tall as his younger brother, though a good bit slimmer and more clean cut. Blake's what I would call classically handsome, with his light hair, sharp features, and blue eyes. Luckily, I've known him since kindergarten and have built up an immunity to his infamous charm, if not a distaste.

"Find something interesting?" he asks, hiking his thumb back.

"Oh, uh, yeah. That's an impressive collection." I try my best to recover, hoping he doesn't think I'm checking him out or fangirling over JD's old jerseys. "JJ Watt?" I inquire, gesturing toward one of the autographed footballs as I settle into a fancy leather chair across from him.

He cocks an eyebrow, seemingly impressed. "Yeah, a gift from my brother. Of course, most of this was."

I nod, trying to remain impassive at his casual mention of JD. "That's a pretty cool perk, I guess."

"Definitely. But we all know he makes friends wherever he goes, right?" I can sense he's measuring my reaction carefully as he sits behind his desk.

I try to force a light laugh without sounding overzealous. "I can imagine."

Dammit. Now he probably thinks I've been imagining things about JD.

Blake only smiles warmly and clears his throat, signaling that it's time to get down to business. "So, your mom called me the other day and said you'd be coming in to file for guardianship of Ethan?"

"Right, yes. That's the plan."

"How's his ankle, by the way?" he inquires, and I'm surprised at the genuine concern in his expression.

"Better. The doctor will probably clear him to return to football this week, though I think making the front page of the newspaper and getting a hand-delivered game ball from his coach may have helped with his recovery."

Ugh. Now *I'm* bringing up JD again.

"I'll bet." He laughs quietly before he goes back to shuffling the papers on his desk, and I'm grateful he doesn't dwell on my comment. "Do you have any questions about the process?"

"Could you maybe walk me through the basics?" I ask with a hopeful smile.

"Of course," he begins. "Since Ethan's legal birth certificate didn't name his father, your mom and dad were granted legal custody at your sister's passing, and we'll basically be transferring those rights solely to you. There are other options, like emancipation—which would make Ethan legally responsible for himself—and adoption, but Mrs. Therese said y'all would prefer to leave Tessa's name on Ethan's birth certificate."

I nod, taking in all the information. "I think we're going with guardianship. So where do we start?"

"We typically file for temporary custody first, and then proceed to finalizing guardianship—or full custodianship, in Louisiana—at a second court date, given no one else throws their name in the ring. The proceedings will take at least a few months, barring any complications."

"But with my parents agreeing to everything from the beginning, it should go pretty smoothly?"

"Yes, assuming no one steps up, claiming to be Ethan's biological father. And as far as I know, your mom made repeated attempts to contact a candidate but never received a response."

"Mm-hmm," I agree quietly. I've never met the guy my mom suspects is Ethan's father, since my sister kept his identity a secret from everyone else, but I know he isn't worth a damn if he refused to even acknowledge the possibility of Ethan being his son. It's his loss, as far as I am concerned.

"You'll also need to prove you're a suitable guardian with an adequate home," Blake continues. "Your mom said you'd be filing solely? No, uh, spouse or significant other that might come into play?"

"Nope, just me," I answer.

Yeah, this isn't awkward at all.

"The next step is to establish yourself in the community since you're filing for custody here. Unless you plan to move Ethan with you to … Waco, was it? If so, you'd have to file in Texas." He looks down as if he's reading the information from his notes, but I get the feeling he's just feigning professionalism and knows exactly where I've been living.

"We're not going anywhere, at least until Ethan graduates from high school. I also signed a one-year contract at Dr. Simms's practice with the option to renew next year, and I was just granted hospital privileges in town."

"And Ethan is on board with this? I'm only asking because it does help, given his age."

"He is," I answer shortly.

Ethan and I got the chance to talk about our situation over the weekend while he was laid up with a sprained ankle. He seemed optimistic about the transfer of guardianship, though he did ask for additional reassurance of my plan to stay with him in Camellia for the indefinite future.

Blake jots down some notes after peering at a calendar. "I think we'll be able to get you in for the initial hearing within a month. I'll have Jada give you a call as soon as we get on the court docket. We'll need Ethan there, and it probably wouldn't hurt if you could bring your mom or someone else close to the family who could serve as a reference. Maybe even someone well-known in the community, like Dr. Simms?"

"I'll try."

"Some additional routine advice I give to all my clients in your situation: It's best to lie low and be careful what you share on social media for now. You wouldn't want any unbecoming photos to surface, much less to get pulled over for a DUI or arrested in a bar fight." He clears his throat awkwardly. "Not that I think you'd have a problem with any of that, of course. It's just my job to advise you against it."

"Got it."

He finishes his notes, punctuating the last bit with a dramatic flourish of his pen. "Do you have any other questions for me?"

I ask him about a medical consent form, since it came up during last Friday's visit to the ER, and I thank him when he promises to draw up the paperwork.

He stands, offering his hand again. "I'm happy to help. Ethan's a great kid, and I'll do everything I can to make sure this works out for you guys."

"I appreciate that, Coach Blake," I say as I shake his hand. "How exactly did you end up with that title, anyway, since you're not a teacher?" I curse myself as soon as I blurt out the question, realizing where I've accidentally led the conversation again.

He crosses his arms and smirks. "I suppose you might recall I played football in high school, too." He's fishing, since he knows I'd remember supplying his water when he'd been the starting quarterback. "Although I wasn't as talented as my brother, I helped him train over the years. And I'd just finished law school around the same time he got the head coaching position, so he asked me to come on as an offensive assistant. I guess he still needed me around, you know, to keep him out of trouble."

I laugh politely. "Right," I say as I look away, only for my eyes to land on the small plaque adorning one of the framed LSU jerseys.

Joseph Drake "JD" Bourgeois, III

Maybe I could start a drinking game while I'm home. Except if I were to take a shot every time someone mentioned JD, I'd be walking around drunk all day.

I blink a few times and turn my attention back to Blake when he speaks. "It's funny how some of us who couldn't wait to get out of Camellia have found our way back, isn't it?"

"Yeah," I reply carefully. "I guess it is." I can't help but feel like he's scrutinizing everything I say, though I'm unsure why. Maybe he just exudes these skeptical lawyer vibes all the time now.

He nods and walks out from behind his desk, gesturing for me to go ahead. "It's not so bad, you know," he says over my shoulder, guiding me with a hand on my back as we reach the door to his office.

"What?" To my dismay, his proximity throws me off-kilter for a second. But I'm not attracted to him or intimidated by him; I just don't care for his invasion of my personal space. I glare at him, and he drops his hand and allows me to cross the threshold alone.

"Living in Camellia, I mean. It's nice. We all sort of have each other's backs. I don't know about you, but I missed that when I left." He attempts to save face with his explanation, shooting me a wide but artificial-looking grin, complete with some of the most perfectly white teeth I've ever seen. In this moment, I can't help but note how different Blake looks from his brother, with his smile contained to the bottom half of his face while JD's seems to spread so that even his eyes crinkle on the sides.

But I'm not supposed to be thinking of JD right now—or noticing things about him at all.

I force my lips to form my own polite almost-smile in response. "Yeah, I could see that. Everyone's been so nice since I've been back, and we've had a lot of help with Ethan and my dad. Hopefully I can return the favor by ushering in the next generation while I'm here."

Blake's eyebrows shoot up questioningly, and I realize how awkward that sounds. "You know, by delivering a lot of babies," I add, trying to save us both the embarrassment. But he only blinks a few times, still confused. "I'm a midwife, Blake. That's why I work with Dr. Simms."

"Oh, right, yes." He finally catches on, to everyone's relief. "I heard 'nurse practitioner' and figured family medicine ... but yeah. That makes sense," he adds, stumbling over his words. It's slightly entertaining to watch him squirm, until it dawns on me that he might think I was volunteering myself to *make* all those babies with someone, maybe even with his brother, and now *I'm* thinking about that and—

"Nope, certified nurse-midwife," I reiterate with a light chuckle, forcing all thoughts of JD from my brain again. "Bring me all the babies, but like, everyone else's, not my own."

Oh, no. This whole ship is going down now.

"Same, but you know, with teenagers—for football." He cringes when he realizes that he's only making it worse.

It's time to get out of here before I say anything else dumb or am forced to think about a Bourgeois brother again. I've certainly had enough for one day. "Yeah, well, thanks for everything," I begin, scrambling back to the waiting room.

"Of course, glad to help. Just make sure you give your contact info to Jada here, and she'll reach out to you as soon as we get that court date set up. Or give me a call if you have any questions before then."

He gestures toward the receptionist before adding, "Jada, will you please hand Ms. Robin a card with my personal number, just in case?" Then he delivers an awkward wave and a "see you later, Tenley" before disappearing into his office again.

"I didn't realize you and Blake were old friends," Jada remarks with a bubbly smile, handing me a blank form on a clipboard.

"Classmates," I say as I fill out the form. "I'm originally from Camellia."

"You must go way back," she replies, exchanging the clipboard for a business card. "He doesn't usually give his cell number to clients."

I lift my shoulder. "He also coaches my nephew's football team."

"Then you must know his brother, too. Aren't those Bourgeoises just the best?" she asks with a hint of mischief in her eyes.

I nod, realizing I'll never find a safe space again so long as I live in Camellia. "Aren't they, though?"

CHAPTER 8
JD

ALTHOUGH THE CIRCUMSTANCES ARE UNFORTUNATE, WE get a Friday night off when the coastal team we're scheduled to play is hit with a tropical storm. Thankfully, the damage isn't devastating, but an overwhelming sense of guilt inspires me to forego our regular Saturday-morning team meeting and organize a small supply drive instead.

"Thank y'all for coming out to help," I call out to the football team and spirit groups. "We'll be accepting donations for the next couple of hours. Let's get a crew stationed out front to unload everything as people drive up, and the rest of you can work on sorting what they bring in. A volunteer will drive everything down to the people in Cameron later this afternoon, so we'll need a little help to load up the trailer, too."

The noise level in the gym immediately rises as the kids begin shuffling around and pairing off to attend to some of their duties. I pull out my phone to post another reminder on social media, hoping to get at least a few members of the community to show up.

"Hey, Coach," a familiar voice greets me.

"You're late, E," I reply automatically without looking up. "Still trying to milk that sprained ankle?"

"Sorry, it's my fault." I glance up to find Tenley standing in front of me. "I accidentally slept in after a late night at the hospital," she explains, looking remorseful.

My pulse immediately quickens. "Oh, well, it's all good, then."

"Figured you wouldn't mind," Ethan retorts with a smug look.

I narrow my eyes at him slightly, and he thanks Tenley for the ride before scampering off to find a job. She holds out a bag in front of me, but it takes me a second to wake up and accept her offering since I'm too busy trying not to react to seeing her in fitted leggings.

"I grabbed a few things. But if you notice anything missing after you get all the donations in, I can bring more when I come back for Ethan."

"So, uh, you're not busy today?"

"Not particularly."

"We could use your help," I lie.

She glances around, probably noticing how bored most of the kids look. "Could you really?"

I shrug innocently. "I was hoping to get your opinion about what household items and toiletries might be needed the most?" I phrase it as a question, hoping to bait her into staying. "Unless you're still tired, that is."

She hesitates, eyeing me skeptically. "I guess I could stick around for a bit. But I am on call."

"I'll take you for as long as you're free."

Ugh. Why does everything I say in front of her have to sound so lame? Hasn't Blake been telling me to make myself look less desperate and more unavailable?

"Okay, then," she answers, still studying me as if she can't believe I'm really this weird. "Where do you want me first?"

Oh, no. Please. Don't.

I inhale deeply, trying to collect myself before I blurt out the first thing that comes to mind. Because, you know, "in my lap" might sound a little sketchy.

"Uh, well ..." I scan our surroundings nervously as I try to think of something, *anything* to keep her here. "Why don't I show you around while we wait for the donations to start coming in? And then you could tell me if we're missing any categories?"

She lifts a shoulder. "Sure."

I smile and gesture toward the first few sections we've taped off and labeled, waiting for her to lead the way. She strolls along the perimeter of the gym, quietly announcing each category as if she's committing the names to memory. I follow her like the obedient puppy I am, shooting Ethan a dirty look when he walks by with a box of canned goods and puckers his lips to mime a few kisses at me.

Of course, that's also the moment Tenley finally turns around to address me. Her eyes dart back and forth between Ethan and me before she speaks. "I noticed you don't have a section for baby stuff?"

"Oh, no. I guess that's one we forgot."

"They could probably use diapers, wipes, and formula. There's usually a shortage during hurricanes."

"Right. Well, thanks. See, I'm glad I asked for your help," I say, relieved when Ethan walks away. I call on a couple of girls from the dance line and ask them to designate a space for the items she just suggested.

"You're also missing a section for feminine-hygiene products," she adds once she has my attention again.

"Uh, yeah. That stuff's probably important, too," I answer awkwardly.

She smirks and goes over to the girls, explaining what to do. "I figured I'd handle that one for you," she remarks when she returns with amusement in her eyes.

I mouth a "thank you," and she chuckles lightly, the sound of her laughter making my stomach flutter. We walk back to the front of the gym together as the students flit around us.

"Maybe I should hang around a little longer in case you need me to pick up the baby and feminine products later," she volunteers, to my surprise. It hasn't taken her long to get invested.

"That would be great." I flash her a wide grin, and she smiles back shyly before she looks away, making my heart quicken at the possibility of having the slightest effect on her. Then she reaches up and begins twirling her ponytail around her finger, and I get myself stuck staring again.

"So, what would you like me to do until then? Just stick me wherever you need me."

Gah. Just. NO.

I clear my throat. "There may be more volunteers than I originally thought. But you could help me supervise for a while, until something comes up."

"Okay."

I lead her over to a table and chairs, gesturing for her to sit before settling down next to her. "Tenley, I feel like I owe you an apology. I might have come off a little too ... friendly before," I begin, her expression shifting immediately. "It's just, Ethan talks about you so often that I can't help but feel like I already know you."

Her face relaxes again. "Yeah. Same, I guess. I hadn't realized how much time you guys spend together. We're really grateful for everything you do for him, by the way."

"I enjoy hanging out with E. And since I don't have anyone waiting for me at home, it's kind of nice when I get to fall in with the rest of your family."

Dude. That is so not less desperate.

I cringe as soon as the words leave my mouth, and she looks down and presses her lips together, as if she's a bit embarrassed for me. "What I meant to say is that helping Ethan has been rewarding for me, too. I lost both of my parents a few years back, and ..."

"You and Ethan have a lot in common?" she finishes, her voice tinged with sadness.

You're only making things worse, you idiot.

"I'm sorry. That was insensitive of me."

"Not at all," she reassures me quickly, even touching my forearm for a moment. "It's really kind of you to sacrifice your time to make sure Ethan doesn't miss out on anything. And I'm sorry about your parents." She glances up at me, her expression softer. I only nod this time, terrified of what I might say if I open my mouth again, especially now that she's initiated a millisecond of physical contact.

Fortunately, we're interrupted by one of the kids who has accepted a cash donation and is asking what to do with the money, and Tenley offers to hold onto it.

I'm eager to ask her more questions as soon as we're alone again. "So, E tells me that you're a midwife and that you get to deliver babies?"

"Among other duties," she says with a short laugh. "But getting to attend a birth is usually the highlight, even though I often get called out of bed in the middle of the night for it, as was the case last night."

I blink a few times, trying not to let my mind wander into Tenley-in-bed territory. "I take it you're a fan of babies?"

She sighs dreamily, and I almost do the same. "For sure. I was still at home when Ethan was born, and I loved helping with him. Then I became a labor and delivery nurse, which was great—except for when I disagreed with the pushy male doctors," she explains, turning in her chair to face me. Her eyes brighten as she continues. "I basically became a midwife and went on to get my doctorate so I could pretend to be in charge while I let the mamas do it their way."

"I like that," I say, trying to turn on a little charm. "But technically, that makes you *Doctor* Tenley, right?"

"More commonly, Nurse Tenley."

"That's kind of amazing, you know."

"I can't imagine doing anything else," she says with a shrug, attempting to downplay my compliment.

"I don't know how you manage it, though. Just thinking about holding all those newborns is enough to give me baby fever," I joke. But it falls flat, and her expression tells me I'd better change the subject quickly if I want to keep her talking. "But, uh, besides that, how has moving back to Camellia been going for you? I mean, apart from your dad being sick, of course."

She mulls it over before answering. "It's actually been a blessing in disguise, in a way. I hadn't realized how much I missed my family. Work is a little slower than it was in Waco, but that's not such a bad thing now that I have more responsibilities at home. I'm not sure if he mentioned it, but I'm going to be taking over as Ethan's legal guardian now, so ..." She trails off when another student approaches with an envelope of cash and adds it to her stack.

"Yeah, he told me about the guardianship stuff. Congratulations," I offer.

"Thanks. I hope I don't screw up too badly."

I furrow my brow, sensing the uncertainty in her tone. "You don't sound excited."

"No, no." She shakes her head quickly. "It's not that. I love Ethan. I'm just not so confident in my underdeveloped parenting abilities."

I lean in as if I'm imparting an important secret. "Teenagers are impossible. Don't take it personally if you hit a few bumps in the road. Just be glad you're starting out with a pretty good kid and that you still like him, for now."

Her smile widens again as she opens her mouth to speak, but we both flinch at the next interruption.

"*Mais, gardez donc.* Aren't you two working hard?" my brother drawls from across the table. I straighten up and shoot him a dangerous glare. Blake may not think much of Tenley or my crush on her, but he certainly knows how badly I've been dying to engage her in a real conversation.

"We've been collecting the cash donations," I fire back. Tenley bites her lip and looks down at the envelope of money, and I want to jump over the table and knock the stuffing out of him for making her squirm.

"That's nice." He raises his brow as if he's trying to give me a signal, or maybe he's warning me about coming on too strong again. "It'll be a good example to bring up later at the custody hearing, Tenley. Might I suggest a social media post?"

"Wait, you're her lawyer?" I ask incredulously.

He clears his throat loudly, a smug look crossing his face. "Now, Coach, you know I can't answer that."

I turn to Tenley, who nods reluctantly. "He is."

"How the hell did that happen?"

"The Robins needed an attorney, and I happened to be available when Tenley's mom called." Blake stifles a smile and explains with widened eyes, another cue for me to calm down. "Well, that, and Mrs. T requested me," he adds in a cocky tone.

"She did, did she?"

"Because he already knew Ethan and our situation," Tenley interjects.

I clench my jaw and nod, unsure whether I should feel relieved because my brother is a damned good lawyer and Tenley and Ethan are in great hands, or if I want to give in to the urge to protect them from Blake the Snake.

"Exactly. So, how about that picture?" He holds up his phone and calls out for Ethan while I cast a tentative side glance at Tenley. She looks about as uncomfortable as expected, given the circumstances.

Ethan comes over with one of the signs outlining our cause, and Tenley stands to pose beside him. "Get in there, JD," Blake encourages me. "It'll help to have a trusted local authority figure," he says with a satisfied smirk.

I sigh but stand and follow orders, my eyes darting over to Tenley again. "Is this okay?" I ask quietly as I sidle up next to her and place a hand on her shoulder. I inhale slowly and deliberately, trying to seem less obvious while savoring the opportunity to get this close to her. She smells amazing, of course, wearing some light, clean perfume that must have been made just for her. It's the perfect blend of citrus and floral and has just become my new favorite scent.

"Uh, yeah, you're fine," she whispers before Blake instructs us to smile.

He snaps a few shots, and we separate as soon as he lowers his phone. "I'll just text those to you later," Blake tells Tenley, and I have to check myself before I growl at him.

Well, I may have accidentally let a small caveman grunt escape. Blake looks more than amused.

"What are you going to do with that cash?" he asks.

"Tenley suggested we use it to buy a few items that most people don't think to donate," I explain, trying to calm myself.

"Very economical. What time are they coming to collect all the supplies?"

"Around one."

"Then y'all should probably go ahead and get to shopping," Blake replies, coming around to sit behind the table with us.

Tenley glances over at me. "That's not a bad idea. I could run out and grab what we need while you finish up here," she offers. But I'm still thinking too hard about throat punching my brother to answer her right away.

"Well, JD, aren't you going to offer to help the lady? You can't just leave her to do all the heavy lifting on her own, not when you could be putting all those muscles to use." Blake gestures at my arm as he leans back in a chair, making himself comfortable. "Don't worry. I'll stay behind and look after everything."

"I'm sure I'll be fine." She shakes her head as she rises from her seat.

I jolt to my feet, almost knocking over my folding chair in the process. "No, Blake's right. I wouldn't want you to have to load everything up yourself. I'll take you in my truck."

She shrugs, fidgeting with her ponytail again. "Okay, then."

I feel Blake's foot nudging me in the butt as soon as she turns to look for her purse, and I swat him away and glare at him again. He mouths a "you owe me," to which I return a "fine."

"Ready?" she asks.

"Yep," I answer too quickly.

I lead her toward the door, stopping when we pass Ethan. "Hey, we're, uh, making a quick run to the store for more supplies," I tell him, motioning to Tenley beside me.

"Oh, should I ... come with you ... to help?" he asks, looking back and forth between us.

I shake my head, desperately trying to send him a telepathic signal. "Nah, we're good, right?"

"Sure," Tenley answers politely. She sounds less than enthusiastic, but I'm so desperate to spend time with her that I push ahead.

"We'll be right back," I say, winking at Ethan. He smirks, and a few of the other football players give me the nod or mutter Coach Thirsty comments as we walk past. I plow straight into the locked side of the double doors before successfully opening the other side, making Tenley snort, but none of it dampens my mood as we walk toward the parking lot together.

CHAPTER 9
JD

I'VE NEVER BEEN MORE NERVOUS AS I HURRY OVER TO OPEN the passenger door for Tenley, and she thanks me quietly before climbing inside my pickup. I reach for the ball cap sitting on my dash and put it on backward before settling in the driver's seat, praying it will activate some semblance of swagger.

Then I crank the truck, and Tenley's eyes widen when the Jonas Brothers song I'd been listening to blares over the sound system.

"Sorry," I mumble as I lower the volume. But as soon as I hear her giggling, I'm ready to throw my pride out the window just to amuse her. "Don't tell anyone you caught me in my Jonas era."

Technically, it's her fault I was bingeing their *Happiness Begins* album in the first place. I've been trying to channel my crush into wholesome outlets, and there's only so much time I can spend working out and revising my playbook before my mind wanders back to her.

"You mean, Ethan doesn't know about your secret playlists by now?" she asks, smirking. "I know you're younger than me, but if you like this stuff, I imagine there are more boy bands lurking in your rotation."

"Yeah, he doesn't seem to mind singing along to *NSYNC when he needs a ride badly enough. And, for the record, you can't be more than a year or two older than I am," I clarify, glancing over as I pull out of the parking lot. Her lips are moving as she quietly mouths the words. I can't help it as my smile spreads even wider, but she stops once she notices I'm watching her, biting her lip as her cheeks turn a few shades darker.

"Weren't you a football trainer in high school?" I ask, changing the subject.

"I was."

"I thought you looked familiar when I first saw you picking up Ethan, then I remembered you from my brother's class."

"You were pretty busy back then. I'm sure you were too thirsty to notice who was supplying your water on the sidelines," she says nonchalantly.

My brain short-circuits for a second, and I barely handle simultaneously freaking out about her using the word "thirsty" and subduing the urge to make a corny *Waterboy* reference.

"Maybe, but I definitely remember *you*."

Okay, that was kind of smooth.

She doesn't respond, but I think I catch her blushing again. We're both quiet as I pull up to the only traffic light in town, and she picks up the rosary I keep in a cup holder as a reminder to say a decade or two on my way to work in the mornings.

"What's been your favorite part about coming home?" I begin, startling her. She drops the beads as if she's guilty of uncovering something personal. "Besides your family, what else did you miss while you were out in Texas?"

"Oh, that's easy. The food."

"Really?" I ask as the light changes.

"Absolutely. Authentic Mexican food is great, and there aren't as many healthy choices out here, but I wholeheartedly missed stopping for boudin on a Saturday morning or being able to find good sausage and tasso for a gumbo when the weather changes."

"And you like to cook, right?"

"I do. Unfortunately, that means I've also been eating entirely too much since I've been back," she says with a smile.

"You're making up for lost time. I'm sure a few good meals won't hurt," I return, and she rolls her eyes playfully.

"What about you? You spent some time away for football, right?"

I inhale deeply, pretending to think over my answer while I'm willing my heart rate to slow down. "I'd have to say, after the people and the food, I didn't realize how much I liked hearing my last name pronounced correctly until it was gone."

She laughs. "Yes, I forgot about that. It's so refreshing to be a *Roh-BANH* again and not a *RAH-ben*. I can't imagine how your name gets butchered."

"I know the announcers had a hell of a time with it when I was still playing ball."

"I bet," she agrees. "Oh, yeah, and catching the right football games, of course. It's nice to be back in range of the home team."

My phone chimes before I can address her football reference, and my truck's audio system announces that I have two new messages from Blake the Snake.

"Do you want me to read them?" asks the robotic voice.

"NO!" I yell, making Tenley jump. "Sorry," I mutter. "I just don't trust my brother to be appropriate most of the time."

She smiles warmly. "Siblings are like that."

I remind myself not to complain about my brother since he's literally all I have left, especially in front of Tenley. "I hope he's been okay, you know, as your lawyer. Blake can be ... well, *Blake*."

I check my phone as we reach the next stop sign. He's texted the photo from earlier, along with instructions to forward it to Tenley so I'll have an excuse to get her number. I suppress a grin at his antics.

"Don't worry, he's been a gentleman," she replies, another smile playing at her lips. "But I already knew what to expect, so I haven't exactly given him the chance to be anything else."

I can't help but chuckle out loud that time. "Good. He just sent that picture to me. Do you want to text it to yourself?"

"Sure, thanks." She takes my phone and punches in her number, and I'm entirely too excited to hear a *ding* coming from her purse a second later. "To be honest, I doubt I'll do anything with the photo.

It seems a little cheap to brag about doing volunteer work just to make myself look good before the hearing," she explains.

"Yeah, that makes sense."

"Don't get me wrong, I appreciate Blake's advice, but I'm not really big on social media in general, and I'd prefer not to start making out-of-context posts now."

So she's not stuck up after all; she's just more reserved and less pretentious than most. Her modesty is only another reason to like her, one more thing that sets Tenley apart.

"What if I posted it with a bunch of other pictures from today? I could just tag you so it'll show up on your profile, but it won't look so staged."

She considers my proposition. "That could work. Thank you."

"No worries. Just make sure we're friends." I nudge my phone to signal my permission for her to make a friend request from my account, and she takes it.

Nice.

I'm still celebrating on the inside when I drive up to the store, and Tenley hops out before I can make it around to open the door for her. It's not like we're on a date or anything, after all.

"All right, lead the way, Nurse Tenley," I say, acquiring a shopping cart as we walk inside.

She glares at me with a suppressed smile as she motions toward an aisle with a diaper display at the end. I follow obediently as she skims the shelves, grabbing several different canisters of baby formula and dropping them into the buggy. Then, she begins gesturing to boxes of diapers and wipes, while I add each selection to our haul. Our efficiency is so impressive that I indulge myself in thinking about how natural it feels to shop for baby supplies together—even if the other shoppers are staring at us like we're crazy for gathering enough formula to feed an entire nursery with no baby in sight.

"That should do it," Tenley announces after she ends up on the receiving end of another dirty look. I tip my head politely at the woman eying us up as she passes, and her expression softens. There are more than enough diapers to go around, lady.

"We can spend the rest on feminine-hygiene products ... if that's okay with you," Tenley adds, ignoring the interaction.

"I trust your professional judgment."

She smiles, seemingly pleased by my comment, and walks on. She obviously likes helping, and I'm beginning to suspect she's enjoying my company, too. I trail closely behind her as she rounds another aisle, twirling her ponytail as her eyes scan the rows. Then she stops abruptly and bends over to examine a box on the bottom shelf. My heart thrums loudly as I take in an eyeful of her backside in those athletic leggings.

Oh, my damn.

I grip the handle on the shopping cart until my knuckles turn white, desperately trying to resist thinking about whether she feels as soft as she looks.

What in the hell is wrong with me? When did I become the kind of guy who stares at women and imagines ... well, the things I'm imagining right now?

She pops upright and tosses something into the buggy, and I clear my throat and turn my gaze away. But she does a double take, stepping back and crossing her arms over her chest.

"Why, Coach, are you blushing?"

My eyes widen in panic. "What?"

"Are you really that embarrassed by the tampon aisle?" she asks, trying not to laugh.

I shrug and smile coyly, relieved that she still seems oblivious to the way I'm always looking at her. "Maybe just a little *honte*. I'm not exactly used to accompanying a pretty lady through this department, so I'm afraid my role is best limited to pushing the cart and enthusiastically agreeing with your selections."

She only shakes her head in amusement and turns back to the shelves. Then she adds a few more packages before deciding we have enough.

"Of course," she grumbles to herself when her phone sounds.

"Everything okay?" I ask as I push our cart over to the checkout line.

"Yeah, I just got a message from the hospital. It's probably nothing serious, but I need to go in to check on a patient."

I should be disappointed, but I'm too busy gloating over the fact that she doesn't sound eager to leave. "That's too bad. Now I'll have to unload all these tampons by myself with the whole team watching," I say, nudging her gently. She smirks at me, and my stomach flutters.

"Wow, that's a lot of baby stuff," blurts the cashier as we approach, bringing me back from my trance. I recognize her as one of my former biology students.

"It's for the tropical-storm victims," Tenley explains.

"Oh, that's nice," Maddie remarks, studying us a second longer. Then she picks up a phone and makes a call to the owner over their intercom system, and he walks over a minute later to help with our cause by offering us a discount.

"It's nothing," he says as Maddie moves over for him to punch in a special code on the register. "You're the one I should be thanking, Coach. We're all so grateful for everything you do around Camellia."

Tenley raises an eyebrow before paying with the cash we collected earlier, and I pile everything back into the shopping cart.

"How about a photo? I'll be making a big post later to recognize all of our donors," I offer when our benefactor comes around to shake my hand.

Another employee volunteers to take our picture, and I pull Tenley in to join us before she can protest. I cup my hand around her shoulder, holding her a little more firmly this time, and she surprises me by leaning in as we pose. My smile definitely isn't forced.

We finish our transaction and head out to the parking lot, falling into an easy rhythm as we load my truck. "Sorry, I know that photo op took an extra minute of your time," I apologize before I crank the engine. "But I didn't want to turn down the help."

"No worries. It's not an emergency, but I do need to go in to work soon."

We pull away in silence except for the radio, until she clicks her tongue. "You know, Ethan warned me you'd be like this."

"He did?"

"Yeah. He said people usually just fawn over you and give you whatever you want."

"Oh," I say, unsure of how to react. "I guess it might seem that way sometimes."

"He also raves about your generosity. But I suspect that's why everyone in Camellia is so willing to dote on you all the time. They're just grateful."

I glance over at her, attempting to read her expression. She looks thoughtful. "Ethan only sees what I want him to see, most of the time," I offer. "I do my best to be a decent role model for the guys, so I'm not surprised to hear he believes all that about JD, the socially responsible football coach." Then I lean over and whisper, "But most of the time, I'm just JD, the dorky teacher who watches too much TV and gets nervous around beautiful, intelligent women."

She laughs as I turn into the school parking lot. "For the record, he idolizes both versions," she remarks, making the corners of my mouth turn up, even if she's still refusing to acknowledge my compliments.

I kill the engine and turn to face her. "Then I hope you don't mind if your nephew turns out to be a closet nerd."

She smiles back at me. "That would actually be sort of ideal." Then she motions to her phone again. "I should get to the hospital."

"Right."

By the time I go around to the passenger side, she's already stepped out and is offering the envelope of leftover cash. "Thanks again for today," I say as I take the money. "I, uh, enjoyed hanging out."

"Thanks for letting me help," she returns shyly. "Will you tell Ethan that I'm headed to work?"

"Yeah, sure. I can bring him home on my way back, if you want."

"That would be great. Bye, JD." She gives me a half-wave before walking to her car, and I watch as she drives off.

"Wow, how did that go?" Blake's voice brings me back when he manages to surprise me for the second time today.

I heave out a sigh. "I'm not sure. I probably need to lie awake all night and review the game film first."

"That good, huh?" He chuckles and moves over to open the tailgate. "I practically set you up on a date. Don't tell me you blew it."

"I don't even think I blew it this time. She's just out of my league, I guess."

"You've got to be kidding me," he grumbles, his tone shifting.

"She's not stuck up, all right?" I climb into the back of the truck and slide the boxes forward. "It might take her a while to open up, but she's actually cool as hell. Everything I suspected I'd like about her seems to be true. She's smart, thoughtful, and mature. She cares about the same stuff I do. We make each other laugh, and I think we both enjoyed going on a glorified tampon run together, so there's that." I hop down from the truck bed. "It just feels like she's immune to my flirting."

"Hmm. Did you ask her out yet?"

"No," I admit. "I was working up to it, but she got called to the hospital."

"And you're sure she wasn't looking for an excuse to get away? You didn't say anything else dumb or fart in front of her, did you?" Blake asks, narrowing his eyes.

"I managed to hold it in, on both counts," I retort. "She actually seemed disappointed about having to leave."

"*Mais*, then what's the problem?"

We each grab a stack of boxes and head to the gym. "I don't know," I groan. "Maybe she does like me, just not enough to overlook her no-dating policy. Maybe she thinks I'm nice, but I'm not her type, or maybe she doesn't find me attractive at all."

"That's an easy fix. Just make yourself sexy, kid," he says plainly.

I roll my eyes. "If I knew what she was into, I'd certainly have tried it by now."

Blake stops me as we reach the doors. "Wanna know what I think?" I lift a shoulder in a shrug, and he continues. "You need to be more aggressive. If you're going to keep going for *desperate*, then it's past time to pull out the big guns, literally. Tenley's noticed you've got the body of a Watt brother, trust me. But she needs to see more of it."

"Oh, okay. Let me just find a reason to take my shirt off in front of her and make sure she fully understands, then," I mumble sarcastically. I've always seen my size and build as an advantage with women, but maybe Tenley isn't into bulky, retired football players. I glance at my brother again. She probably wouldn't refuse me if I were more like Blake—a clean-shaven professional who wears a fancy suit to work instead of faded khakis and a monogrammed polo.

Although, I *have* caught her checking out my arms a couple times …

"All right. Plan B. If you really want to move this along without throwing yourself at her, then you have to make her jealous," Blake proposes with a wide grin.

"I'm not sure I like the way that sounds—or the look in your eyes right now, if I'm being honest," I reply warily.

"You're overthinking this, man. Convince her she's not your only option. If she gets jealous, you'll know she's interested. And if she doesn't care, at least you'll have learned she's not worth the headspace anymore."

I sigh. "I'll consider it."

"You do that. Because I happen to know what Tenley likes, and I'm absolutely certain that you're exactly her type," he says, a cocky look on his face now.

"And how in the hell would you know that?" I growl.

Blake chuckles. "Touchy, are we? It's probably the lack of—"

I shove him into the locked side of the gym doors and dart inside before he can retaliate, like the annoying little brother that I am.

By the time we wrap up the supply drive and I bring Ethan home, I've already resigned myself to spending another Saturday night alone on my couch with a pizza and a college football game.

Pathetic, I know.

To be honest, I could be on a date right now if I were willing to let Blake set me up. The problem is that I don't want to settle for a casual hookup, and the only woman I'm interested in dating doesn't seem all that interested in dating me.

Besides that, I've never really enjoyed going out all that much, which also means I've outgrown most of my old friends. I'm ready to spend my weekends with someone I really care about, someone who needs me to keep her warm on the couch while we stay in and binge Netflix. Someone who wants to start a family together.

If only that someone wanted me back, I think as I balance the pizza box against my hip and unlock the front door.

Is it really too much to ask to have Tenley Robin waiting for me on the sofa with a big fuzzy blanket and a football game on the TV when I walk inside? I wouldn't mind one bit if she were wearing those tight leggings and holding a cold beer in her hand, while we're at it.

I exhale loudly as I flick on the lights and step into my empty house. I should adopt a dog. It'd be nice to be greeted by someone who's happy to see me when I get home each night. But I guess it'd be irresponsible since I work so late during football season. Maybe a cat, then?

Like I said, pathetic.

I bring my pizza into the living room and search for something to watch. I settle on a matchmaking reality series, the one where they basically set people up on blind dates at the altar. I could apply for the show myself, but I'd run the risk of getting paired with someone who didn't share my values, or even someone who's just plain nuts. On second thought, I probably take marriage too seriously for that.

Those other *Bachelor*-style dating shows aren't my cup of tea, either. I've never been a fan of juggling multiple romantic interests at once, and I don't think I'd care for the lifestyle that accompanies reality-TV success.

I'd even found myself considering whether I was being called to religious life a while back, entertaining the possibility that my growing disinterest in dating was intended to steer me toward the priesthood. But after speaking to Father Conrad, I concluded that I still have a deep desire for marriage and family life, much to my relief. Father said that I would feel a pull, that I could trust the Holy Spirit to lead me to the right vocation in the same way I was drawn to teaching and coaching. By then, I'd already started to suspect there was something special about the connection I shared with Ethan. Then Tenley showed up at the football field a few weeks later, and there was an undeniable tug. Now, every time I think about Tenley, each time I see her and Ethan together, I feel that pull again. And it's only been growing stronger by the day.

A wave of relief washes over me as I recognize this longing for what it is—divine intervention. And if the Holy Spirit is actually putting these desires in my heart now, then I can't ignore that, right? I may be making a fool of myself by everyone else's standards, but I know I can't give up on Tenley yet.

I smile to myself at the irony as I take out my phone. Having to accept my brother's help in this situation seems exactly like the kind of joke God would find entertaining.

JD

Fine. I'll try it your way.

BLAKE THE SNAKE

Figured you'd come around.

We'll start with Plan A. Your girl singled out that signed JJ Watt football in my office all on her own the other day. Like I said, you're definitely her type. You just need to show her what she's missing.

CHAPTER 10
TENLEY

I wake on Sunday morning to a steady buzzing and the smell of fresh-cut grass. I peek through the curtains to find Ethan trimming around the edge of the house over the sounds of a lawn mower running in the distance.

I've slept in again after spending most of the night at the hospital, not making it to bed until the early-morning hours. Although it's been busy and tiring, I'm starting to adapt to life here. Truth be told, the adjustment hasn't been as difficult as I feared, and I'm starting to enjoy all the rushing around with Ethan and becoming more comfortable at work.

My mom greets me as I pad into the kitchen, pointing to a fresh pot of coffee. I eye her curiously before I pour myself a cup and join her at her post in front of the window.

"What's so interesting out there?" I ask, taking my first sip.

She says nothing but gestures toward her view of the backyard with her right brow cocked. I move closer and peer out the window, nearly choking on my coffee once I finally see what has her so entranced.

It must be the sweaty, toned, and shirtless football coach passing by on the riding lawn mower.

"Good Lord," I accidentally blurt out between coughs, making my mom chuckle beside me.

"Yes, bless Him," she adds, pulling me closer. "And all His creation."

I inhale deeply before attempting another sip. "So, uh, why is JD Bourgeois riding around half-naked on Daddy's lawn mower, anyway?"

"Who the heck cares?"

"Fair enough," I allow, neither of us able to peel our eyes away. We stand together and watch intently as he glides back and forth, cutting neat rows across the yard, oblivious to his captive audience. It's just like before, when JD recruited me to help with their supply drive. He seemed blissfully ignorant as nearly every woman we passed in the supermarket checked him out, some of them even sizing me up and conveying their distaste. I imagine my mom and I look just as ridiculous now, our heads turning side to side as he passes, both of us mesmerized by his rugged build.

I allow myself a thorough perusal while I hide behind my coffee cup. JD's workout regimen obviously prioritizes bulk over definition, and I am here for it. It's too late to pretend I haven't stolen a quick glimpse at his arms before today, but the uninhibited view only proves that I am indeed a fan of his giant biceps. My gaze roams over his torso, appreciating his broad shoulders and chest. I carefully regard his powerful form as it tapers down to a waist devoid of the sharply defined abs that societal standards deem attractive. Surely there are some women who prefer this look, solid and muscular for the sake of being strong and not simply for show, as if he spends more time working than working out.

Fine. It's me. I'm some women.

"You know, this isn't the first time he's come over to help Ethan cut the grass," my mom begins, reminding me that I'm not alone. "But it *is* the first time he's done it without a shirt. Just sayin'."

I nudge her gently and give her a side-eyed glare. "It's still hot out."

"It sure is."

"Ma!"

She shrugs. "Unlike you, I have no problem admitting that JD is a fine piece of—"

"MA!"

"Work. I was going to say work. And that he's apparently very sweet on you."

I roll my eyes, knowing that if I don't somewhat concede, she'll only make it worse. "I'm not blind. But we've been through this before. I also have a lot going on, and dating is the last thing on my mind."

She waves her hand flippantly, as if my very legitimate reasons for putting my social life on the back burner aren't valid. "Or maybe you're just afraid to pile on another reason to stick around?"

I furrow my brow. "No." But it's a lie, and we both know it.

"Do you really think yourself too grand for little old Camellia?"

"Of course not," I huff. "If anything, it's the opposite," I add quietly.

"So, you think he's too good for you?"

I bite my lip and stare down at my mug. "JD shouldn't have to settle for something complicated or for someone who can't give him the time and attention he deserves."

"Hmm. Well, I happen to think you're selling yourself short and that you'd be surprised at how easy it could be with the right guy. I'd also venture to say that JD deserves the chance to decide for himself what he wants."

I'm not usually one to let my mom have the last word, but I'm out of defensive plays. We continue to sip our coffee in silence, neither of us willing to continue the conversation or to walk away from the view.

"Guess we could fix them something cold to drink. We owe them that, at least," my mom says, eventually. She steps away to find a pitcher, leaving me pondering her words while the caffeine works its way through my system.

Just as I bring the cup to my lips for the last sip, Ethan jumps up in front of the window and taps loudly on the glass, scaring the living daylights out of me. I flinch and shout a few profanities, splashing the rest of my coffee down the front of my shirt in the process. He doubles over with laughter on the other side, evidently surmising exactly why I've been standing there for so long.

I take a step forward, dropping the empty mug into the sink and using my palm to make a loud thud on the window. "I'm going to pay you back for that later, kid!" I scream loud enough for him to hear me, my face flushing.

"I was only checking on you," he calls back. "You look like you might have been daydreaming ... or having a stroke," he says with feigned concern for my well-being and a knowing smile.

"Someone has to make sure you're doing a good job," I return.

"Oh, is that why you were supervising so carefully?"

My mom chuckles from across the kitchen. I narrow my eyes in my best attempt at intimidation, but he only laughs to himself as he walks off to restart his trimmer.

As soon as Ethan clears my line of sight, JD rides by again, bobbing his head and continuing on as though he's missed the entire exchange. He *is* wearing sunglasses and earbuds, so maybe noise-cancelation has saved me from humiliation, at least this once.

Yeah, right.

He stops the mower abruptly, right in front of the window, then stretches his long, muscular arms, lifting them over his head and giving me an even better look at his triceps. I gulp, wondering how I've gotten myself into this situation, forced to attend a gun show against my will. He twists his neck and spins his cap around. Then he reaches down to restart the mower, but not before turning to face the window and aiming a smirk my way. The engine roars back to life as JD continues down the row, leaving me there with my jaw hanging open.

"You know, you'll have to acknowledge him eventually," I hear my mom say as she brushes up against me.

I swallow hard. "We're friends. I thank him all the time."

She scrunches her nose. "I think he may be looking for a less *friendly* form of gratitude, baby."

"Mo-om," I groan.

"Enjoy it while you can," she starts, ignoring my protests. "In a few years you'll be griping at him to mow the lawn and shaving his back for him so he doesn't scare the neighbors when he takes his shirt off."

I sigh. "You do realize I'm not going to randomly marry and live happily ever after with Ethan's football coach just because of a few nice gestures, right?"

"You could start by inviting him to stay for dinner, though," she murmurs, taking a pitcher of sweet tea out to the front porch. I roll my eyes as I follow with a few glasses of ice.

She sets the tea down on a small side table, just as the mower quiets down. I look away once I see JD walking over, pulling a shirt down over his head and replacing his cap.

Thank God.

He and Ethan trudge up the steps, and my mom greets each of them with a cold drink and a cheek kiss, thanking them for their labors. I cross my arms in front of me, regretting my decision to stay in this old sports bra instead of changing into a more proper under-wire death trap and replacing my coffee-stained pajama top. And the fact that JD's T-shirt is missing its sleeves only compounds my discomfort, since I can't help but watch his arms flexing and glistening as he raises a glass to drink.

My mom nudges me until I blurt out an awkward "thank you," then I sit on the porch swing, becoming increasingly self-aware of my messy morning bun.

"No worries," JD answers between gulps. "I was actually hoping to borrow Ethan to help me back at home since we're finished here." He settles across from me in the nearest chair, sliding his sunglasses up over his cap and casually glancing down at my bare legs as my mom refills his drink. His massive hands make the glass he's holding look comically small.

"We've figured out we can get everything done before the hottest part of the day when we double-team both yards," Ethan adds, using the collar of his shirt to wipe the sweat from his upper lip. "And we already went to church this morning. Coach likes going to early Mass."

But why do they always have to double-team *me* like this? The two of them are so much cuter together—not that I think JD is cute.

I finally admit defeat and allow my gaze to return to his arms. They're pink and slightly sunburned toward the top, as are his neck and the bits of his shoulders I can see over his collar. I tell myself he only took off his shirt earlier because he was trying to even out his tan and not because he's a total exhibitionist. Although I suspect he wanted me to at least survey the view, especially since he's torn open the armholes wide enough to reveal the extra back muscles that reside on top of his normal human muscles. He tilts his head and exposes his throat as he swallows the last of his second glass. Then a single bead of sweat drips down beneath his collar, and I gulp along with him.

The hell with cute. JD Bourgeois is freaking *hot*.

But only in a totally objective, non-datable way ... right?

I blink, forcing myself to look away and tightening my arms over my chest. My mom glares at me knowingly, her lips pursed in a cue for me to wipe the drool off my chin.

"Aunt Ten? Is it cool if I go to Coach JD's?" Ethan asks expectantly.

"Uh, well, don't we have to go to Mass?" I realize too late that Ethan already addressed that detail while I was busy gawking. He stifles a laugh, having caught me checking out JD for the second time today. "Right, sorry. You went this morning. So, yeah, that's fine."

Ethan's still smiling to himself when he announces he's going to grab his things, and my mom snatches the empty pitcher and follows him inside before I can scamper away first.

"Nice PJs," JD remarks once we're alone. I glance down at my dingy New Orleans T-shirt and matching shorts, then bring my knees up to wrap my arms around my shins.

"Believe it or not, they were a gift from my dad," I reply, and he nods appreciatively, a smile playing at his lips.

"That tracks. He's definitely one of the most loyal fans I've ever met. I can't imagine he gave you much choice in the matter, either."

"It's a good thing I've always liked football, I suppose. And you?" I'm not sure why I engage him in conversation, except maybe to defuse some of the awkwardness.

"You mean, do *I* like football?" he asks, grinning. I roll my eyes playfully, and he continues. "Saints fan, born and raised, though I was partial to the Texans for that little while they kept me on the payroll."

"Fair enough." I bite my lip, having forgotten that I'm talking to a former pro. I'm not sure how, since he certainly looks like he could still hold his own on the football field. I keep my eyes down, feeling more and more self-conscious in JD's presence by the second.

"Tenley," he begins after a while. "I, uh ... I was thinking ... I mean, hoping ..."

I glance up to find him staring at me with my stained pajamas and my messy bed head, and I suddenly feel like I can't bear to let him see me like this any longer. Luckily, the front door creaks as Ethan steps out onto the porch again.

"Ready, Coach?"

JD looks away, his lips moving as if he's scolding himself. "Yeah, let's go, bud," he finally says to Ethan.

"Later, Aunt Ten," Ethan bids me as he passes by.

JD stands reluctantly and places his empty glass on the table. He glances my way one more time and gives me a halfhearted smile before he and Ethan get into his truck and drive off. I exhale slowly, considering what he might have wanted to say before I go inside.

"Nice PJs," my dad calls as I join him in the living room.

I narrow my eyes at him. "I guess you have good taste."

"Maybe it's just the way you're wearing them," he counters.

"Ha ha," I return sarcastically as I plop down onto the couch.

I unlock my phone out of habit while my dad switches the channel to a football highlights show. The analysts discuss their predictions for next week's LSU matchup just as the former Tiger tight end appears on my timeline, making me roll my eyes again.

It really is unfair how JD manages to be everywhere all the time.

I study the picture he'd tagged me in earlier. The two of us are posing beside the grocery-store owner, and the way I'm leaning into JD with his arm wrapped around me implies a certain level of comfort or even intimacy between us.

My eyes dart around the room nervously before I take the plunge and click on his profile. I scroll down, careful not to accidentally like any of his older photos. Most of his posts seem impersonal and generic, save for a few photos with Blake. I close one platform and open the next, snorting quietly when I see a TikTok he made with some of his students. He's a terrible dancer, which makes me smile a little too easily. I continue scrolling backward on his Instagram until I pass a few gym selfies, which I've never been a fan of until now, and eventually happen upon some posts from his football career.

I audibly gulp and blink down at the screen. Then I force myself to look away, hoping my heart rate is escalating because I'm paranoid and not because I've been staring too hard at JD in a fitted uniform with those giant hands of his wrapped around a football. I close the app quickly, resigning myself back to the TV.

But I. Am. Weak.

By the next commercial break, I retreat to my room to Google him, and the results are *not* disappointing. I swipe over a few different photos of him on the field or in a locker room until I unintentionally click on a sideline interview. His voice is deep and breathy when it comes through the speakers, and his chest heaves beneath the pads as he wipes his sweaty brow with the back of his arm. He grins proudly at each of his LSU teammates when they interrupt to congratulate him on the touchdown he'd apparently just scored, making me realize how young he must have been when this was originally recorded. I pause the video and throw my phone down onto the bed, disgusted with myself. Then I groan and vow never to do *that* again.

I could probably convince myself that there's no harm in allowing some detached appreciation of JD's physique, except I know he'll pop up entirely too often in person, and things are already awkward enough. I'm not here to admire anyone, much less to go looking for the temptation to act upon any kind of attraction.

Not that there is any attraction on my end—only appreciation.

Still, I pick up my phone, close all the windows, and clear my browsing history, just in case temptation strikes again.

CHAPTER 11
JD

"Hey, JD," one of my colleagues greets me as I walk into the teachers' lounge.

"Hey, Loren," I return with a sigh, grabbing my lunch out of the fridge. "How goes it today?"

Loren's a fellow Camellia native, having graduated a couple of years ahead of me, along with Blake. Her dad is probably the most respected football coach in our school's history, but she was definitely more of a scholar than an athlete. And, despite having so little in common throughout high school in addition to our comical size difference, Loren and I formed a bond as soon as I began teaching and realized we were the lone optimists of the teachers' lounge.

It's not that I don't love my job and the rest of my coworkers, but the increasingly difficult working conditions have taken their toll on most educators, leaving us all disillusioned at best and perpetually tired and grumpy at worst.

Plus, Loren always keeps the good snacks in her classroom.

She purses her lips. "Eh, same old. Counting the days until Thanksgiving." I nod knowingly, because all teachers live and die by the countdown until the next break.

"How's Damien been doing in your class?" I inquire about one of my football players as I sit beside her at the lunch table.

She blows out a breath. "He actually managed to stay awake for a full hour today."

"I guess we can call that 'growth,' " I say with a chuckle and offer the bag of chips I've just opened.

"The bar has been set low, my friend." Her smile contradicts her sarcasm as she plucks a chip from my bag.

"Funny how that phrase applies to nearly every conversation I've had today," I grumble, sounding more like one of those fussy, old veteran teachers.

She furrows her brow and fixes her gaze on me. "Something bothering you, Golden Boy? You don't seem like your usual sunny self."

"Well," I begin, ignoring the nickname. Loren may be petite, but she more than makes up for it in wit. She continues staring at me expectantly as she sneaks another chip and crunches away. "There's this ... situation. It's not exactly school related."

"Oh, a *dating* situation?" she asks, settling in. "Do tell."

I cringe. We *are* friends, but not the kind that dish about their love lives. Until now, our conversations have been mostly limited to work and our favorite TV shows. But I think I can trust Loren, and I certainly need all the help I can get.

"It's technically not a dating situation either, although I'd really like it to be," I say after a while.

"But she's not interested?"

"She's been giving me mixed signals. I think she might be more averse to dating in general than to me, but I don't know how to move past that."

Loren straightens up in her chair, suddenly looking uncomfortable. "Um. This isn't, like, one of those times when you're being hypothetical but you're really talking about the person sitting right next to you, is it?"

"No, no," I reassure her quickly, holding my hands up in a panic. "I mean, no offense, you're great and all, but—"

"But I'm no Tenley Robin, right?" She smirks and takes another chip, leaving me with my jaw hanging.

"Wait, how did you know I was talking about Tenley?"

She shrugs. "I overheard Ethan saying she was back in town. Also, a few of his teammates were messing with him the other day, something about calling for his 'Uncle Coach Thirsty.'"

I groan. "Was Ethan upset?"

"He seemed okay with it," she replies thoughtfully. "I mean, he didn't mind joining in your roast."

"Of course he didn't." I roll my eyes. "So, how do you know Tenley?"

"We were best friends all the way through middle school, you dork." This time she confiscates the entire chip bag. "We've grown apart since then, though. I haven't spoken to her in years, but I was hoping to run into her soon and remedy that."

"You were?" It's sad that I'm getting this excited for any connection to Tenley, though I should have remembered she and Loren were in the same class.

"Sure. Suppose she'll be at the pep rally later?"

"Probably." As if I hadn't already grilled Ethan for that information earlier today.

"Perfect. I may be able to help with your situation. Are you thinking what I'm thinking?" she asks eagerly. I can almost see the wheels turning in her head. "And before you say anything, the answer isn't 'Tenley's boobs.' Although, we should all be thinking about that according to Damien's description of her."

I accidentally growl, making her laugh as she gets up and scoots her chair in. Her head barely reaches my shoulder, even though she's standing.

"Calm down, Coach Thirsty. For the record, those kids are all rooting for you ... even if it's mostly because they think you'd take it easier on them if you had a girlfriend," she says, walking backward and bobbing her eyebrows suggestively.

Then Blake surprises us both by flinging the door open and barreling into the room, just in time for Loren to plow into him. She stumbles as though she's backed into a brick wall, and he leans down to grab her shoulders and help her regain her balance.

"Ugh. Watch where you're going," she protests, shrugging out of his hands and moving to stand beside him.

"It's not like I'd have seen you unless I'd been staring at my feet, Reed," he replies with a smirk.

"Yeah, well, you don't belong in the teachers' lounge, remember?" Loren fires back. Blake's smug expression transforms into a resentful sneer.

"I'm here for my brother. He's in dire need of my dating expertise," he grumbles, and I snort. "What could the two of you possibly have to discuss, anyway?"

Loren narrows her eyes. "I was just offering my own assistance, as it were."

Blake blinks, looking surprised, then turns away. I can't help but laugh at the way they're standing parallel to one another, arms crossed and scowling. The two of them have been rivals for as long as I can remember, with Loren winning the academic upper hand by eking out Blake for the title of valedictorian over a decade ago, and my perfectionist brother never forgiving her for being smarter than him.

"You probably shouldn't be wasting your time with an amateur," he adds after a second, addressing me as if Loren wasn't currently stationed a few inches away from him. She scoffs before he continues. "There's a lot riding on this, and we could all stand to benefit from you finally getting laid."

"I'm not trying to sleep with her. I'm trying to ... relationship her," I declare. They're both holding back a laugh now, Loren's lips twitching and Blake's nostrils flaring. "Okay, let's say I'm trying to accomplish both. Regardless, I'm failing miserably."

"Then it's time for Plan B—" Blake says.

"We should try making her jealous—" Loren offers at the same time.

They glare at one another, issuing a silent challenge until Loren finally speaks again. "I'll see you at the pep rally, JD. Let me know if you want to take me up on my offer."

Blake huffs, and Loren rolls her eyes. "You're going to use *her* to make Tenley jealous? You'd be better off planning one of those cheesy promposals, with a handmade sign and all. How about, 'You're a perfect TEN, and I'm just trying to score'?" Blake holds his hands out as if he's picturing the poster in his mind, still facing Loren but obviously directing his suggestion at me.

Loren's shoulders drop, and she turns away and her eyelashes flutter. I'm sure she'll fire off another sharp comeback any second, but she stays silent.

"Do you always have to be such an ass?" I bark at Blake once I realize she's trying not to cry.

He clears his throat, seeming remorseful now. "Sorry, boss."

"He wouldn't know how to be anything else," Loren finally replies with an indignant sniff. Then she scampers away, leaving Blake with his hands in his pockets and a broody look on his face.

"What are you actually doing here, anyway?" I ask after he shakes off their encounter.

"I had to bring over a form to renew my coaching authorization. I figured I'd hang around for the pep rally, but I guess the good people of Camellia don't need my help to pay homage to the great JD Bourgeois and all his majesty."

I stand and toss my trash, refusing to take the bait. "Cool. Well, I'll see you in the gym, after I grab my scepter and my crown." I learned long ago that my brother's love language is "sarcastic douche."

He snorts and follows me down the hall to the sanctuary of my classroom. "And I also came to see if you needed any help with the Tenley situation," he adds as I unlock the door. "But I guess you've already gotten a better offer."

"Maybe I have."

He cocks an eyebrow. "You and Loren actually have a plan?"

"Yep," I lie.

His curiosity is killing him. "Aren't you going to tell me about it?"

"No, I don't think I will," I say in my best Captain America impression as I sit behind my desk and begin sorting papers.

He grunts and saunters over to the board, examining some of the signatures, artwork, and social media handles that high schoolers tend to leave behind. For some unknown reason, teenagers seem to think we teachers want their constant feedback, and their critique methods range from proclaiming a simple, "That's why no one can stand you!" when I uphold a project deadline to scribbling an enthusiastic, "Brittany G + Britney F love you, Coach JD!" on my dry erase board.

"Well, I sure as hell hope Brittany G and Britney F aren't involved, or you might find yourself needing more of my advice than you think," he remarks.

I roll my eyes. "No worries, man. It's all legal."

Blake wanders off and picks up a plastic model of a human heart, fiddling with it absentmindedly. "Just tell me you don't seriously think talking to Loren Reed is enough to make Tenley jealous."

I shrug, enjoying how much this is getting under his skin. "Why not? Loren's cute. She's also smart and really funny—she's a catch."

"I've always found her to be an intolerable smartass, but if you think Loren's so great, then why don't you just ask *her* out instead?"

It's a valid question, but I'd rather use this opportunity to mess with him than give him a completely valid answer.

"She's cool, but I don't think there's any chemistry. It's more of a brother-sister vibe with us."

He nods and sets the heart back down on a shelf.

"Which is good, because it'll make things less awkward later if we have to resort to PDA to get Tenley's attention," I add, because I can set the bait, too.

He turns abruptly and narrows his eyes at me. "Wait, you're not actually going to kiss Loren ... in front of everyone?"

I grin. "It's not like I'd be leading her on. Lo understands. In fact, she's the one who came up with the idea." He glowers at me as I'm unable to stifle my laughter. "Although, I don't think a school-based make out session was part of her plan."

"Right. I just ... I wouldn't want you to compromise your standards or do something out of character for Tenley's sake," he mutters.

"Sure," I return, laughing louder now. The bell rings, and Blake stomps over to the board and erases the student blurbs, just to make his resentment clear.

"Relax," I tell him. "I promise not to let Loren Reed corrupt me, okay?" He grunts again, and I punch him in the shoulder as we walk out to the gym.

The pep rally goes over the same as the last hundred or so I've attended, with the exception of Tenley's presence rattling me, of course. I wave at her from the gym floor when she takes her place in the bleachers, and she shoots me a polite smile before hiding behind a group of other parents. I puff out my cheeks and force out a breath as I stare longingly in her direction.

"I'm sorry, Coach," Ethan says when he approaches. "I've been trying to throw your name around in front of her. She's just ... too busy to notice, I guess."

A couple of other guys pat me on the arm as they pass on their way to the student section. "Don't give up, Coach JD," Tate adds encouragingly. I must be making my Coach Thirsty face again to warrant their pity.

"Thanks for trying, E," I say, suppressing my wounded pride. "I haven't forgotten about my half of the deal, though. Group project next week?"

"Yeah?" He glances over to the side where Caidence stands with the rest of the cheer squad. She smirks at him and fluffs her ponytail, and I swear the kid's got actual hearts in his eyes.

I tap him in the chest. "Yep. And your class has been too noisy lately, so it looks like I'll be assigning partners myself."

"Wait, just the two of us? I don't know," he panics. "What if I get too nervous?"

"Then I'll help you," I reassure him.

"You will?"

"Yeah, just make up some excuse to call me about the project, and I'll play along."

He nods excitedly and offers me a fist bump. "Dude. You're, like, a way better wingman than me."

"Yeah, I'd hope so, since I've probably kissed a few more girls by now," I say with exaggerated condescension.

He gives me a playful shove and darts out of my reach. "I'm going to ignore that one, Coach Thirsty!" he yells, taking the bleacher stairs two at a time while I glare daggers at him.

Blake joins me again as the rally begins, and I worry he'll give me more flack when I get called to the floor to make a speech. But he looks surprisingly proud when I glance over to catch his expression.

Then Loren sidles over to me toward the end, making it a point to ignore Blake when he tries to resume their usual banter. "Introduce me when she passes, then follow my lead," she instructs, attempting to lean up and get closer to my ear. I nod, and we station ourselves near the exit so I can catch Tenley on her way out.

I clear my throat when she approaches, and Loren places her hand on my forearm, turning to face me as if we've been having an intimate conversation. "Oh, hey, Tenley," I call as she walks by. "How's it going?"

She stops reluctantly, almost as if she's been hoping to avoid me. "Hey, Coach. Everything's fine, thanks." Then her focus shifts to Loren, and I swear her composure falters for a second before she forces another polite smile.

Loren takes her cue. "Oh, my gosh, *Tenley*? Is that you?"

Tenley's eyes widen in recognition. "Loren? Wow ... it's so good to see you."

Loren opens her arms, and I'm surprised when Tenley readily embraces her. "I thought I'd heard you were back in town," Loren says over Tenley's shoulder. Then she turns to scold me playfully. "It almost sounds like the two of you've been hanging out without me."

I shrug, glancing coyly at Tenley. "We run into each other pretty often, you know, because of Ethan."

"Ugh, I'm totally jealous. We should definitely catch up, Ten," Loren proposes, settling in at my side. I swallow hard, unsure of what I should do next. Then I feel one of Loren's petite hands curling around my elbow, so I lift my arm slightly, making sure it's in Tenley's line of sight.

"I'd love that," Tenley replies with a more earnest smile. She looks back and forth between us. "You look amazing, by the way," she blurts out. Then she cringes as if she hadn't meant to say it out loud.

Maybe she doesn't want us to know she's sizing Loren up? Maybe she's actually bothered by the attractive woman on my arm?

And now I've got to take a couple of breaths to slow my heart rate.

"Thanks. You're making those scrubs look pretty darn hot, yourself," Loren returns. I clamp my mouth shut before I'm tempted to say anything stupid while Loren wags her eyebrows at Tenley and gets her to laugh.

"Well, I'm sure you both need to get back to work," Tenley says after a while, trying to extricate herself. I feel Loren nudging my side, but I'm frozen.

"Maybe we'll run into you at the game? I'm on concession-stand duty tonight," Loren offers.

"Sure. I'll be on Aunt Tenley duty."

Loren throws a hearty elbow into my ribs this time, making me hiss. I try to disguise it with a cough. "Yeah, she's, uh, got a special shirt and everything," I say when I finally manage to find my voice.

Come on, man.

Tenley bites her lip, looking amused. "My mom had it made for me."

I nod and shoot her a flirty smile. "Remind me to thank Mrs. T later. I mean, we need all the support we can get."

"Right," Tenley agrees hesitantly, and I think she might even be blushing.

Loren pinches the inside of my forearm, and I take it as a signal to continue. "So, I'll see you tonight? I'll be the one on the sidelines wearing the coach's headset."

"And I'll be the one in the bleachers wearing Ethan's number." She rolls her eyes demurely.

"I'm sure I'll be able to pick you out of the crowd."

Tenley's cheeks flush even darker. "Good luck tonight, Coach. See you around, Loren."

I exhale in relief as I watch her walk off.

"Holy shit, JD," Loren exclaims.

"What?"

"First of all, spend enough time in the gym?" she asks, squeezing my arms and contorting her face. "What do you plan to do with these things, anyway? Crush cars? Move furniture? Lift heavy machinery?"

I snort as Blake returns, his eyes zeroing in on Loren as she grips my arms. I flex my muscles, making her giggle, and she drops her hands before she continues. "Secondly, you should have warned me that you'd turn into a pathetic simp as soon as Tenley came around. How am I supposed to work with that?"

I shrug apologetically. "I can't exactly help it."

"See, I told you this would never work," Blake mumbles under his breath.

"No, no, there's something there, I can tell," Loren says thoughtfully, ignoring Blake's tone this time. "We've planted the seed. I think we just need to give it a little water."

CHAPTER 12
TENLEY

"What took you so long tonight, anyway?" I ask Ethan as we make it to the nearly vacant parking lot.

He shrugs with forced nonchalance, but I notice his eyes darting over to a group of cheerleaders tossing their pom-poms and bags into the trunk of a car. He stops in his tracks when one of them turns and smiles brightly in our direction, a set of well-defined dimples accenting her beautiful, tawny-brown complexion.

"Ah, I see." I watch him grin back at her until she lowers herself into the back seat. "What's her name?"

"Caidence," he says on an exhale and starts walking again.

"She's cute. Are you guys ... dating? I'm afraid to ask what you call relationships these days."

He frowns. "Tonight was the first time she really talked to me. But we're going to be partners for our next bio project."

"Oh. So she waited around to talk to you about the assignment?" I ask, lacing my arm with his.

"She doesn't know about it yet." Then one side of his mouth curls up into a smirk. "Coach JD's not assigning partners until next week."

I bite my lip, suppressing a smile at the lengths JD is apparently willing to go to make Ethan happy.

"Hmm. Then maybe it was the touchdown you scored in the third quarter or that onside kick you recovered to end the game," I offer, and the back of his neck flushes. "Or maybe she just thinks you look like a snack."

He presses his lips together, trying not to laugh as he rounds my car. "You get points for trying, Aunt Ten." But then he groans and points out a deflated tire on the passenger side.

"*Mais la*," I grumble, kicking the saggy heap of rubber. "It's definitely flat."

"Good thing Pop showed me how to change a tire," Ethan declares proudly. "I've got this."

He makes his way to the trunk, trading his football bag out for the spare and gathering the tools as if he knows exactly what he's doing. I watch him appreciatively for a second before I bring the rest of the gear over to where he's crouching beside the flat tire, and I'm impressed when he manages to jack the car up successfully. However, we hit a major roadblock when it's time to remove the old tire.

"The lug nuts are just too tight," Ethan admits. "They must have used an impact wrench to get them on."

"You were doing a great job so far."

"I think it was the leftover adrenaline from that game, but it's starting to wear off. I'll need to call in bigger muscles," he explains.

I glance around the deserted lot. Of course, JD's truck is one of the few vehicles left. "Do we really have to ask *him*, though? It feels like we bother him all the time."

I'm not exactly thrilled about the prospect of facing JD after our latest awkward interaction. To my dismay, I mentally stumbled over seeing him with another woman this afternoon. And it didn't help that the woman clutching at his arm was my former best friend, Loren Reed.

It's not like I suspect Loren has grown up to be any less amazing than the quirky and bubbly girl who used to sleep over at my house every weekend and subject me to *Lord of the Rings* marathons so we could drool over Orlando Bloom together. She seems just as charming and good-natured as ever. She's also pretty—really pretty. Loren's always been a natural beauty, and now she looks like a modern-day Audrey Hepburn.

But it's glaringly obvious that if JD is into Loren, he couldn't possibly have been intentional about flirting with me all this time.

So, then, why did he do it again, right in front of Loren?

I wish I could say I didn't care. As much as I shouldn't bother worrying about why JD Bourgeois has been staring at me like I'm the last woman on Earth while he's obviously seeing someone else, the truth is that I can't help but feel something stirring in the pit of my stomach every time he looks my way. Because even though I don't *want* to like him, he's still walking around in the body of a tight end and doing all these good deeds, like setting Ethan up with his crush. And dammit if "nice guy who loves kids, tall and muscular with gorgeous eyes" isn't my freaking type.

There's probably a reason why most of my exes and celebrity crushes were all football players. I mean, Orlando Bloom is dreamy, but I'd prefer a Watt brother any day of the week—specifically a TJ.

"Aunt Ten? We don't exactly have anyone else to call," Ethan reminds me, bringing me back to the present. "And you know he doesn't mind helping."

I hang my lip and whine once more before giving in to the inevitable. "Fine, let's go get the muscles."

He smirks at me before setting down the torque wrench and leading me back to the football field. JD and his brother are walking out of the locker room when we approach, and it only takes a second for Ethan to convince them to help.

"Oh, I almost forgot," JD says as we pass the concession stand. "I promised Loren I'd walk her to her car. I don't care for anyone going out to the parking lot alone in the dark, especially this late."

Of course. No way the human golden retriever would let that happen.

"If you want to go ahead, I could wait around ..." Blake begins, trailing off as soon as JD cocks an eyebrow. "But I guess you might need my help. Why don't you just go inside and see if Loren's ready?"

"She's ready!" Loren calls, rounding the corner of the building a second later as if Blake conjured her up. She greets each one of us and listens as JD explains our predicament, and we all make the awkward trek to the lot together.

JD clears his throat as we near my car. "I'll, uh, be right back," he announces, then gestures for Loren to lead the way. She turns and winks at me before they walk off together, and I realize I'm wearing a less-than-friendly expression. I busy myself with opening my car door and pretending to sift through my purse, determined not to stare.

"What's going on with them?" I hear Ethan ask Blake. When I turn, the two of them are standing together, arms crossed, watching the scene play out in front of us.

"Hmm," Blake grumbles. "Not sure. Must be new." Then he slips his phone out of his pocket and makes some excuse to go over to his truck.

My curiosity finally gets the best of me, and I join Ethan to observe quietly as the couple stops in front of an older-model sedan. Loren faces JD and places a hand on his forearm while she speaks, and he laughs as he steps closer. Then, once she opens the door and sits inside, he leans over to continue their conversation, stretching his arms as he grips the door in his left hand and the frame with his right.

I turn my attention away quickly when there's an even stronger pang in my gut than before. That uneasy feeling must be the result of watching another couple interacting, I tell myself.

I certainly hope it is, anyway. Because I am absolutely *not* jealous.

I'm not, right?

My face flushes as JD stoops and reaches in to touch Loren again, maybe to tuck a strand of hair behind her ear.

I'm admittedly disturbed. But I'm not jealous. I'm just irked because the guy who's been hitting on me was already seeing someone, particularly someone who is the opposite of me in nearly every way, making it clear that he was never really attracted to me.

Or maybe I'm embarrassed because I've been reading too much into his flirting. Which would also mean I'm angry, because he was sleazy enough to enlist help from Ethan and maybe even my parents to get me to like him.

It's a good thing I *don't* like JD, then. Thank goodness I haven't fallen for his charm or his "trying to be a good role model for the kids" act and that I've been able to resist thinking about his physical appearance in *that* way.

Well, most of the time.

Some of the time?

Although, it's hard not to notice his massive shoulders flexing beneath his polo shirt right now. It would be practically impossible to ignore the bulging muscles in his back, straining against the fabric as he rests his right forearm across the frame of Loren's car. The way the hem of his sleeve can't seem to contain his ample biceps certainly isn't *not* sexy.

Shit.

His head turns quickly in my direction, and his eyes meet mine as he catches me staring. I want to look away, but I can't, and he knows it. He flashes me a cocky smile before he pushes himself back to a standing position, his massive hand splaying over the door as he shuts it.

Then Loren rolls down the window and reaches out to him. He grasps her hand for a second, and it looks like his thumb is rubbing the inside of her wrist. And I know I'm in trouble, because I swear my skin begins tingling in that same spot.

Oh, no. This is not happening.

I am not *that* attracted to JD Bourgeois ... I can't be.

I shake my head lightly to clear the intrusive thoughts when I hear Ethan calling my name.

"Hmm?"

He's looking at me with a knowing smirk. "I asked if you were okay ... because you growled."

"I didn't ... growl."

He stifles a laugh. "Yeah, you did. It kind of seems like you're jealous."

"Pfft, of course I'm not jealous," I squeal incredulously. "I'm just annoyed. It's late, and I'm tired. And I wish I didn't have to wait all night for the muscles to finish saying good night to his girlfriend before we can get this dang tire changed and go home."

"Come on, Aunt Ten. They're just talking. You don't have to get so worked up about it," he continues, clearly amused. "Although, I'm sure Coach would be more than happy to make it up to you."

"Oh, stop it. You know I'm not interested in JD, not in that way," I lie.

"Sure sounds like you are."

"That's impossible because I'm not into guys who flirt with every woman they see or who would stoop to using a kid to set them up."

Ethan's tone changes, his upper lip curling in disgust. "We both know he's not like that."

I groan, because deep down, I know he's right, despite the way tonight has gone. "Okay, look, I do think JD is a decent guy, and I am totally grateful for all the stuff he does for you. But I'm not desperate enough to date your coach just because he's nice to us."

Ethan coughs awkwardly, and his eyes flicker around me. I guess he isn't used to getting scolded, especially by me.

"I mean it, Ethan. Stop trying to set us up. It's not gonna happen," I declare a little too forcefully. I may be projecting my feelings, just a little.

"Yes, ma'am," he answers this time, pressing his lips together and glancing over my shoulder. I instinctively turn to follow his gaze, and my stomach drops.

Because, of course, JD would be standing right behind me. And one glimpse at his face tells me he's heard every word of my unnecessary rant, though I don't know whether I've just provoked or demoralized him.

JD looks away and shakes his head, as if he can't believe I'm this shitty.

But I definitely am.

"Yes, ma'am," he echoes Ethan. I flinch and open my mouth to speak, but I suppose there isn't much room for an apology with my foot lodged so far back in there.

"Um, I'm sorry. That probably sounded way worse out of context," I begin rambling.

He holds up his hand to stop me. "No need to explain. Your private conversation is none of my business, even if it was apparently about some other loser who also goes by JD."

I keep my eyes trained on the ground as he walks past me and claps a hand over Ethan's shoulder, then he makes his way around the car without another word. I turn and shield my face with my hand, beyond mortified.

"What the heck, Ethan? Why didn't you tell me he was *right there*?" I whisper through my teeth.

He shrugs innocently. "I didn't know you were going to go off about the guy. Now this whole situation is going to be even *more* cringe."

I follow Ethan to the other side of the car, just as Blake returns. We all supervise as JD squats to pick up a wrench and twists it over one of the lug nuts, loosening it with barely a strain. He moves on to the next one, stifling a small grunt as he forces the wrench to turn over.

Oof.

I audibly gulp as I watch his arms flexing. I cross my own arms over my chest, willing myself to look away and act as bored as possible. But I inadvertently make eye contact with Blake instead, and he's grinning at me as if his only reason for coming back was to watch me ogle his brother.

It isn't my fault that JD's arms look like sexy tree trunks tonight, okay? And did he really have to come to my rescue again, especially after what I just said about him?

I think I might be growling again.

"You okay, Tenley? You seem ... thirsty," Blake says, his eyes narrowed.

"I'm fine," I snap.

JD glares at Blake until he looks slightly remorseful. Ethan doesn't mind laughing at my expense, though.

"All right, E. Want to take over now?" JD asks.

"Thanks, Coach," Ethan says and gives me a stern look, as if he's the parent reminding me to use my manners.

I sigh. "Yes, thank you."

JD keeps his eyes down as if he can't even bear the sight of me anymore. "No worries. Just have Ethan text me once you've made it home safely." Then he walks to his truck, seemingly without giving me a second thought.

CHAPTER 13
TENLEY

"Would you like to invite some of your friends over for dinner?" I ask Ethan on the morning of his sixteenth birthday. "I'm making your favorite."

My parents woke him earlier this morning to give him his gift. We all got a little emotional when my dad handed Ethan the keys to his old pickup truck, and my mom promised to bring him to get his license as soon as I'm able to leave work to sit with my dad this afternoon.

"I could ask Caidence ..."

"That would be nice." I smile.

"... And you could call Coach JD."

I narrow my eyes. "Why would I do that?"

"Because you still feel guilty about what you said last Friday."

I turn to the sink, hoping he misses the way I wince at his accusation. "Even if that were true, I can't just invite him to dinner out of the blue without giving him the wrong idea," I explain, washing a coffee mug.

"Don't worry. I think he gets it now," he mutters.

"Oh. You've talked about ... that incident?"

Ethan crosses his arms and leans back against the counter. "Do you even care?"

"I don't have to be romantically involved with someone to care whether I hurt his feelings," I say defensively.

"He hasn't brought it up. But that's probably because you *did* hurt his feelings."

I know I did. The only time I've seen JD since our run-in after the football game was at church the following Sunday morning, and he barely even acknowledged me when he'd stopped to talk to Ethan on his way out. Truthfully, I've only been going to Mass because it's a requirement for me to serve as Ethan's confirmation sponsor, but the fact that JD apparently attends regularly and receives Holy Communion has triggered my guilty conscience ... as well as some other surprising sentiments I'm not willing to admit.

I groan as I shut off the water and dry my hands with a dish towel. "In my defense, he *did* kind of parade around in front of me with Loren after he's been ..."

Dammit. I forgot I'm supposed to be in denial about JD's interest in me.

"He's been what?" Ethan asks with a satisfied grin.

I roll my eyes and toss the towel onto the counter. "You know what."

"Well, maybe he just got tired of waiting for you to go out with him," he retorts.

"Well, technically, he's never asked me out," I fire back, mirroring Ethan's posture and crossing my arms. "Not that I want him to," I add quickly.

"That's not what your face was saying while you watched him change that tire the other night," he mumbles under his breath.

"What are you even?" My voice goes suspiciously high. "Ugh. You're ridiculous!"

"*I'm* ridiculous? Aunt Ten, you're the one getting all worked up over a guy who 'technically' hasn't even asked you out."

I open my mouth to respond, but I've got nothing, so I settle for pouting.

My mom walks into the kitchen again, glancing between the two of us and noticing the tension. "What on earth are you two arguing about this early in the morning?"

"Nothing—"

"Coach JD—"

We both answer at the same time. She shakes her head and turns her gaze to me, as if she's asking my side of the story first.

I heave out a sigh before I begin. "After the game last Friday, we had to get JD's help to change that flat tire, and Ethan provoked me until I laid down the law about not going out with his football coach just because he's done us a few favors. Naturally, JD overheard what I said, and even though I've already apologized because the delivery was admittedly a little harsh, Ethan wants me to invite him over for dinner. However, I think it would be inappropriate, and I don't want to risk leading him on."

"Ethan?"

He huffs. "Maybe I went too far the other night. But she's totally missing the point."

"You mean, she doesn't want to admit she was only bothered by what you said because she's scared shitless, seeing as though she has a weakness for your football coach's big muscles and his even bigger heart?"

Ethan snorts. "Exactly."

My cheeks immediately start to burn, and I barely manage to blurt out some unintelligible objection.

"That's almost the same noise she made when she was forced to watch JD get cozy with Ms. Reed," Ethan says as he and my mom laugh. At this point, I'm just hopeful my dad's still napping in the other room because he'd undoubtedly be siding with Team Date-the-Retired-Football-Player.

"He's trying to make her jealous, too?" Mom nods appreciatively. "I didn't think JD had it in him, but I guess I shouldn't have underestimated him after the sexy lawn-service stunt."

I furrow my brow and turn to Ethan. "What's she talking about?"

"Uh, would you look at the time? Gotta get to school ..." He grabs his backpack off the table and darts toward the door.

"You're not going anywhere without me yet," I grumble, ignoring the way my stomach immediately dips at the notion of JD colluding with my friends and family to get my attention. My mom continues chuckling to herself while I angry-pack my things and stomp out of the kitchen after Ethan.

He slumps in his seat as we pull out of the driveway a minute later. "You still owe me an explanation," I demand.

"Don't I get a free pass on my birthday?"

"Nope."

"Fine," he says with a sigh. "But you can't convince me you don't really know why he's been going around shirtless and getting other women to grope his arms in front of you."

My breath catches in my throat at the same time a range of emotions hits me—fear being the foremost. But I'm silent as I continue driving, afraid to incriminate myself or imply my mom was right.

"Look, he just wanted a shot with you, and I wouldn't have helped him if I didn't trust his intentions," Ethan continues, his tone softening. "You don't have to go out with him or anything, but can you at least try being nicer, for me? I hate it when things are weird between all of us." Some of my anger subsides, but only because he's piling on more guilt.

Still, I can't take JD seriously if he's only been plotting and scheming this whole time. I don't appreciate being manipulated, and I don't like how he equated jealousy to attraction.

It's a good thing it didn't work, anyway.

Although, I'd be lying if I said a small part of me isn't relieved to hear JD doesn't seem interested in Loren, after all.

Maybe petite brunettes aren't his thing?

Wait, no—I don't care what JD likes. I'm upset, because he was probably leading Loren on and using her to trick me into feeling something for him.

Hmm. I wonder if he prefers curvy blondes ...

I shake my head to rid myself of the rogue thoughts. "At least tell me you didn't let the air out of my tire," I finally manage aloud.

"Of course not. The flat was just dumb luck." He smirks. "All I did was stall you for a while. And to be honest, I'm pretty sure Coach Blake's been coming up with most of these ideas, anyway. JD loses all his rizz around you."

I glare at him, a reminder that I'm clueless when it comes to teenager terminology. Ethan rolls his eyes. "He has no game. You make him nervous."

"Oh."

I disregard the way my stomach dips again and attempt to focus on the important stuff. It does seem more likely that Blake would come up with some of these schemes before JD would. And to be honest, Ethan's attachment to JD and his commitment to shipping us, though misguided, are sort of endearing.

"No more," I say after a while. "Promise me you'll stop with all the conspiring?"

He sighs. "I'm sorry. I'll quit trying to push the two of you together."

"Thank you," I reply, a bit surprised by his confession.

"And you'll apologize again and invite him over for dinner tonight?" he asks hopefully. I groan, realizing he's already set the next trap, and I'm walking right into it.

I agree anyway.

We drive up to the school, and I reach over to squeeze his shoulder. "I hope you have a great birthday, and good luck at the DMV later. I'll see you and your fancy new Louisiana driver's license tonight."

"Thanks," he returns with a smile, his green eyes shining. Then he uses his phone's front-facing camera to ruffle his hair before stepping out of the car, making me laugh to myself.

I feel a little lighter by the time I get to work a few minutes later, until I remember I still have to uphold my end of our deal by talking to JD. But when I pull out my phone, there's already a welcomed distraction in the form of a text from a random number.

UNKNOWN

Hey Tenley, it's Loren Reed. I got your number
from Ethan. I was hoping we could get together.

I stare down at the message, surprised and even flattered that Loren bothered reaching out to me. The thing is, I have no idea how to respond.

Loren and I had been close when we were younger, but it was mostly my fault we grew apart. I'd purposefully distanced myself once my home life got complicated, thinking I was saving her from worrying about me while she was already struggling to deal with her own problems. And even though I'd apologized for the way I'd acted toward her once my family's issues became public knowledge, our relationship had never been the same. I eventually made new friends in college and then through work, but I always kept myself guarded. I never allowed anyone in, not the way I had with Loren.

I'm still wary of her involvement with the JD situation, but she *is* offering an olive branch by initiating a conversation after all this time. I suppose the least I could do is return the courtesy. A casual meetup probably wouldn't hurt, especially since she's one of Ethan's teachers and building a good rapport within the community could help me both at work and with Ethan's custody arrangement.

I may also be feeling a bit remorseful after the unkind thoughts I had when I saw her hands on JD's arms the other day.

I settle for responding with a polite "glad to hear from you," and we make plans to get coffee together. Then we continue texting back and forth between my patients and her classes for the next couple of hours, leaving me genuinely excited about rekindling our friendship.

Talking to her like this feels ... nice.

LOREN

So, this might be a bit presumptuous of me, but
you should know that JD and I are just friends.

I scrunch up my nose as I stare down at her last message, unsure of what to say again. Even though I don't know for certain that JD and Loren were only pretending to be an item in front of me, it seems obvious after everything Ethan disclosed earlier. So I figure playing dumb is the safest move, at least for now.

TENLEY

Oh, well … that's too bad. I thought you guys made a cute couple.

LOREN

He's the best, really—but not my type.

TENLEY

I don't know him all that well, but he seems like a really nice person.

LOREN

He totally is. And he speaks very highly of you.

I blink down at the screen. Has JD really been talking about me to his friends? And does this mean Loren might be reporting everything I say back to him?

I guess it's a good thing I've been treading lightly, otherwise I might have accidentally fessed up to something as embarrassing as Googling JD and staring at pictures of him in a football uniform while I'm ovulating.

Not that I actually do that … anymore.

TENLEY

He's been very kind to my family so far, and we're especially grateful for his help with Ethan.

LOREN

Sounds like typical JD. I'd say he's just being himself, since he's considerate and helpful toward all his friends, except I noticed he couldn't keep his eyes off you at the pep rally the other day. 😊

I swallow hard as I read Loren's last text.

Have I really been that oblivious of JD's interest in me? My face heats up unexpectedly as I run through our interactions over the past few weeks, especially once I recognize all the times Ethan or even Blake may have had a hand in things. And the longer I think about it, the more I suspect this is indeed another setup.

But wait, isn't JD supposed to be mad at me? Why's he sending Loren in for more recon if he doesn't even want to talk to me right now?

Ugh.

I was terrible at this stuff as a teenager, and it seems like I've only gotten worse as an adult. I take my time with my next patient and walk myself through a few different scenarios before deciding to stick to the truth—or to what I think should be the truth, anyway.

TENLEY

Okay, he may have flirted with me before, and I do think he's a great guy. But I'm not really looking to get involved with anyone right now.

LOREN

Right. Gotcha. I just thought I'd put it out there, you know, since we're going to be besties again and all.

TENLEY

Look at you, already pulling wingwoman duty. 

Unfortunately, work's getting busy. Talk later?

LOREN

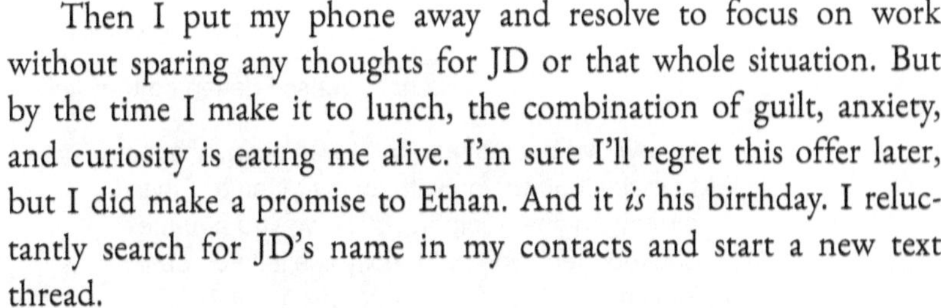

Then I put my phone away and resolve to focus on work without sparing any thoughts for JD or that whole situation. But by the time I make it to lunch, the combination of guilt, anxiety, and curiosity is eating me alive. I'm sure I'll regret this offer later, but I did make a promise to Ethan. And it *is* his birthday. I reluctantly search for JD's name in my contacts and start a new text thread.

I linger over the button for a second before tapping send. He deserves an explanation after the offensive comments he overheard. After all, he really has been nothing but kind to my entire family, and I shouldn't be in danger of leading him on by showing him some common courtesy. Hopefully JD will accept my apology and allow this whole dinner-invitation thing to go over smoothly, and we can all share a completely platonic meal as mature adults. I chew my lip as three dots appear, signaling his incoming reply.

My jaw falls open while I sit in shock. Then those little dots pop up again.

He *would* try to defuse the situation with humor ... and maybe even a little more of that flirting that I've been pretending to hate.

JD

confused face selfie

Are you sure you have the right number? This is JD, btw.

TENLEY

JD

So, what has Ethan requested for dinner?

TENLEY

His favorite: pork stew with corn bread

JD

Wow. Last week you said you'd never be desperate enough to go out with me, and now you're trying to seduce me? Women …

"Talking to someone interesting?"

I flinch when one of the medical assistants walks into the break room and catches me twirling my ponytail around my finger while I grin down at the phone.

"Uh, no, just … nobody special," I reply, slipping my phone back into my lab coat pocket. I like Mackenzie, but she's also the biggest gossip in the office.

She grabs her lunch from the fridge and sits next to me as my pocket buzzes. "That doesn't look like a texting-nobody-special smile. That looks like a booty-call smirk or a flirting-with-my-crush simper."

"I don't do crushes … or booty calls."

Mackenzie shakes her head, staring me down as she chews on her sandwich, and I bite my lip nervously. "Well, aren't you going to check that?" she dares me.

"Fine," I concede with a sigh. I pull up the message, and she scoots closer as if I've invited her to read it with me.

JD

I'm sorry … that was supposed to be a joke.

> I should have just asked what to bring to dinner.

> And look, I understand what you meant the other night. I apologize for coming on so strong before, and I promise I'll do my best to stop making things weird.

Well, shit. Even though this conversation began as my apology to JD, I still managed to screw it up and make him feel bad about flirting with me ... again. It's another reminder that I shouldn't be having flirty text conversations in the first place.

"Wait, this guy's sending you selfies? What's he sorry for? And what does he mean by 'coming on so strong'? Good Lord, is that JD Bourgeois?" Mackenzie squeals as she reads over my shoulder.

"There's nothing going on, I swear," I blurt out. I click the side button and put my phone to sleep, despite her protests.

She leans back in her chair, aiming a judgmental glare my way. "Hmm. Jesus knows when you're tellin' a lie, sis. And so do I."

My face heats up, and I let out an awkward cough. Then I excuse myself before ducking into the filing room to text JD back.

TENLEY

> You're fine. See you this evening? Don't worry about bringing anything.

JD

> I'll be there.

CHAPTER 14
JD

Of course, Tenley would wait until I've officially given up on her to invite me to dinner.

I have spent the past week avoiding her and attempting to wipe her out of my thoughts, only allowing myself to replay the memory of her telling Ethan "it's not gonna happen" until it starts to sink in. Because I've been wrong all this time, mistaking that tug she elicits in my chest for something stronger.

Who was I kidding, anyway? God wouldn't have led me to fall for someone who isn't interested in me at all, right?

Regardless of where these feelings originated or how much they've grown, I've come to terms with the fact that Tenley and I aren't going to be together. Pining after her has been so damned frustrating, and I'm tired of trying to figure out what she wants from me. I've finally convinced myself that it's time to move on, once and for all, and her name pops up on my phone in the middle of class.

Then all that "leave Tenley alone" stuff is instantly forgotten, and my heart is hammering at the mere idea of seeing her again. Maybe I'm stupid for thinking I could talk myself out of wanting her, but I can't keep setting myself up for disappointment like this. I'll just have to settle for being Tenley's friend ... her pathetic and loyal friend who will always be available to change a flat tire since he'll be spending his life alone.

Luckily, I'm able to respond to her since my students are taking a test. And even though I probably come off entirely too eager once again, at least I get a more sincere apology from her. I also vow not to hit on her anymore, and I'm determined to uphold my promise for both our sakes.

No one complains when I end practice a little early that afternoon, and Ethan rushes by me on his way out, barely stopping long enough to flash a wide grin and a set of keys, proving he'll no longer be needing my help to get home. I have to check my emotions once I realize I've lost my excuse for hanging out with him so often, but I paste on a smile as I congratulate him and assure him that I'll be there for dinner. Then, I grab a shower at home and stop at the gas station for a gift card before heading to the Robins'.

I take a fortifying breath as I knock on the door, reminding myself that I'm only here for Ethan and not because I'm a hopeless fool. His grandmother opens it a second later.

"Glad you could make it, Coach." She leans in to press her cheek against mine for an air kiss.

"Thanks, Mrs. T," I reply, genuinely glad to be welcomed into their home. I walk around to the living room, greeting Mr. Jude next. He seems to be in good spirits, and we talk football for a few minutes until Mrs. T comes back to administer a dose of medicine.

I excuse myself and follow the scent of roux into the kitchen. My breath hitches at the sight of Tenley in front of the stove. It isn't fair that she should be a great cook on top of everything else. I still hold traditional values in pretty high regard, but I'm not one of those guys who thinks a woman's place is limited to the home. By the same token, I like to eat, and I can't help but admire Tenley's domestic capabilities as much as her professional competence. I clear my throat to alert her to my presence, ignoring the urge to walk up behind her and wrap my arms around her waist.

"Hey. Need any help?"

She cranes her neck around to look at me. "Oh, hey, JD," she returns, a smile spreading across her face as if she's happy to see me. It's like a punch to the gut, triggering that "not gonna happen" track that's been playing on loop in my brain. "I'm just finishing up, but thanks. Make yourself at home," she adds before setting the spoon down.

I nod and lean back against the counter, trying not to stare too hard as she bends to pull a cast iron skillet of corn bread from the oven. It's equally difficult not to fantasize about this all being real one day—Tenley waiting to greet me with a kiss when I get back from practice, or vice versa when she works late for a delivery, then trading stories about our day while we make dinner together and wait for Ethan to join us. Maybe we'd even have one of those cute couples' rituals, like patting one another on the butt every time we cross paths in the kitchen—

"Thirsty?" she asks, knocking me back to reality.

"What?" I respond, straightening up as panic sets in.

"Do you want anything to drink?" she tries again, regarding me suspiciously.

"Oh, uh, yeah. Water would be great." I exhale and will away the heat rushing to my cheeks.

She retrieves a bottle from the fridge and hands it over as her mom enters the kitchen. "Thanks," I mumble before I unscrew the cap and take a few gulps.

"So, where's the birthday boy?" I venture once I get my heart rate down a little.

"I think he's still in the shower," Tenley answers.

Mrs. T passes through a door on the back side of the kitchen and returns a second later with a basket full of laundry. "I forgot to put these away earlier," she says. "He might actually be waiting on a clean towel, so I'd better go check on him."

She rushes past me, not noticing when a couple of items fall off the top of the stack. I automatically stoop to pick up the clothes from the floor, just as Tenley comes closer for the same reason. Without thinking, I pluck a bundle of black fabric and hold it out for her. Her eyes widen and she lets out a soft gasp, so I glance down to see why she's panicking about whatever's dangling from my fingertips.

Holy mother of over-the-shoulder boulder-holders...

I am holding Tenley's very sexy, very lacy bra. In fact, I'm suspending it midair. Its generous cups are hanging open, providing my cursed imagination with an all-too-clear representation of the actual size of her assumed voluptuous chest. And, boy, have I underestimated that figure. I gape at the bra for a second longer with my jaw slack, fighting the urge to pull a Gollum and keep it for myself. But she reaches out to snatch it from my hand before I can say "my precious."

"Um, sorry, I didn't realize ..." I begin awkwardly, trailing off once my gaze meets hers. She looks absolutely mortified. Her face is completely flushed, and there's a gleam from the tears that have already started pooling in her eyes. She pulls her bottom lip in between her teeth and mumbles something unintelligible, making me regret inadvertently stopping to examine the bra before handing it back to her. I may have given up on convincing Tenley to go out with me, but I still care about her. And the last thing I want is to make her feel bad.

I can't understand why she's so upset, though. Not only are we both adults, but she's a medical professional who practically examines women's body parts for a living. And while I'm certain Tenley's too modest to enjoy accidentally flashing her undergarments in front of anyone, it's not like she's actually wearing them right now. Or that I'd seen her embarrassing granny panties—only her beautiful, lace-encrusted, bust-enhancing lingerie.

I mean, she had to have bought a black bra with the intention of feeling and looking sexy, right? Why else do women wear underwear that looks like *that*? And why should it bother her if I see it, anyway, when she clearly has no romantic interest in me?

I furrow my brow as I continue studying her reaction. She finally turns away, tucking the bra under her arm before scurrying out of the room. I blow out a breath and rub my hand over my face, frustrated and wondering if I'm ever going to manage a simple interaction with

Tenley. It seems like all I ever do is upset or irritate her, even when I try my best to rein in my attraction and act friendly.

"Oh, baby, I'm sorry. Did I drop some of your things?" I hear Mrs. T asking Tenley on her way back to the kitchen. She winks at me before returning to the laundry room with the empty basket.

I press my lips together in a smile when I realize she set her daughter up. Or maybe she set *me* up because she needed a good laugh. Either way, my mind's still reeling.

I mean, who knew they actually made bras with three rows of hooks in the back? Does it help compensate for the added weight in the front? Is it one of those things, like, the harder you have to work to get it undone, the bigger the prize? There are so many questions floating around inside my head now.

Tenley interrupts my inappropriate thoughts once again when she walks back into the kitchen, stopping abruptly. "Are you seriously laughing at me?" she asks as she regards me incredulously.

Truthfully, I *am* doing my best to stifle an immature giggle, but not for the same reasons she's imagining. "No, no—of course not," I reply innocently.

"You know, God makes women of all shapes and sizes. I guess you haven't had much experience noticing the ones who wear cup sizes past the letter D, though, based on your reaction just now. But I see these women every day, and I hear their stories and how they are made to feel terrible about themselves because they don't fit someone else's mold," she scolds me with her hands on her hips.

Man, I love it when she stands like this, her fists digging into her sides and pulling her shirt in tighter so I can study her curves. Apparently, she's assumed that the size of her bra offends me when, ironically, she'd probably kick me out of her house if she knew exactly how much seeing her underwear has turned me into an infatuated adolescent boy again.

"Well, Nurse Tenley," I begin, smirking at her and feeding off her annoyance. I know I promised not to flirt with her anymore, but I owe it to her to correct her misconceptions, don't I?

I take a few steps forward and lean down to whisper beside her ear. "I only reacted that way because I *definitely* noticed the cup size of that bra, and now I'm probably ruined for all other women. And, for the record, I *definitely* would have wanted to make its owner feel really good about herself, because I happen to think her shape and size are perfect."

I linger for a second before I pull away, sensing her nervousness. Her breathing slows down and she shivers once, despite what looks like her best effort to seem unruffled by my proximity and my comments about her body. However, I remind myself that I'm not here to bother her. Regardless of whether she likes me, she's not willing to act on it. And I promised myself I would walk out of here with my pride intact at the end of the night.

"But I didn't want to make you—I mean, the anonymous bra owner—feel uncomfortable," I add, taking a few steps back and leaning against the nearest countertop. "So I thought it best to keep my compliments to myself."

She narrows her eyes, obviously upset, though I'm not sure whether she's angry because I called her a hypocrite or because she didn't intend to react to me at all. I cross my arms, flashing her a cocky smile and maybe even a slight flex—you know, just for good measure.

Yep. There it is. One tiny, infinitesimal glance down to check out the guns.

I knew it.

But dammit if I can keep my own composure with her staring me down like that. Every time she shows the smallest bit of interest, my body reacts before my brain can catch up, and I transform into a goofy, awkward teenager again.

Before I pick up on what's happening, I see the corners of her mouth turn up into a satisfied smile. Then she bites her lip and gestures hesitantly to the counter. "JD, you ... um ... I think you might have bumped into Ethan's cake."

I cringe, finally realizing that I have, in fact, leaned back onto the tall, multilayered chocolate cake resting behind me. I'm growling in frustration when I feel a light touch on my arm. It's Tenley, gently urging me forward. I reach back to find that, sure enough, there's a blob of brown icing smeared across the bottom half of my shirt. Based on her expression, I've successfully managed to make it look like I shat myself.

"I ruined his birthday cake, didn't I?" I groan.

She shakes her head quickly, barely concealing a smile. "Nah, I'm sure I can smooth this out. You might be wearing some of it for the rest of the night, though."

"What's wrong?" her mom asks, walking over to us once she returns to the kitchen.

"I'm just a bull in a china shop," I grumble. "Too big and clumsy for every room."

"*Mais, cher*, that's nothing," Mrs. T replies, laughing lightly. "Tenley can help you wash up. I'll grab one of Jude's old T-shirts for you."

"Come on, Coach," Tenley says, looking entirely too amused as she leads me down the hall to an empty bathroom. She gathers a washcloth and soap while I stand there like a helpless toddler, then leaves the supplies on the counter before she slips away, chuckling quietly. And I'm not sure whether to feel disappointed or relieved when she doesn't offer to wipe my backside.

I glare at the pathetic man-child in the mirror and scold myself for being so lame before I attempt to clean myself up. I quickly give up on reaching around and decide to ditch my shirt, slowly and deliberately peeling it up over my head to avoid spreading the chocolate. The door creaks softly, and I look up to find Tenley standing in the open doorway again.

Her eyes widen for a second before she averts them. "I'm sorry, I should have knocked first. Uh, here. Hopefully this fits." She holds out a faded Saints tee. I can't help but smirk at her as I let my shirt slide down my forearms, leaving me completely topless. Then I take the T-shirt she's offering and push my hands through the sleeves, pausing there.

"Would you mind checking to see if I left anything behind?" I ask, turning so she has no choice but to inspect my bare back.

I twist around to watch her from over my shoulder, flexing for her again. "Ah, no, everything looks … fine," she squeaks.

"Cool, thanks." I turn back to face her as I pull the fresh shirt down over my head. It's a little tight, so it takes a few tugs to get it past my chest.

"No problem," she whispers, then bites her lip as her eyes dart over my torso.

I open my mouth to say something flirty again, but Ethan interrupts me when he clears his throat from behind Tenley.

"I'm not even going to ask what excuse you used to get shirtless this time," he declares, watching our exchange from the hallway with a grimace.

I grab the chocolatey shirt and follow Tenley when she darts out. "It's probably for the best," I answer, patting Ethan on the shoulder.

But she surprises me by stopping to take the balled-up fabric from me. "Let me throw that in the laundry for you. I can send it back with Ethan later."

"Thank you," I'm forced to say again, though the idea of having one of my shirts smell a little like Tenley isn't so bad.

Yep, still pathetic.

We all go into the kitchen, and Tenley makes a quick stop in the laundry room before everyone sits around the large dining table. I find myself sandwiched between Ethan and Tenley. At least I won't have to fight the urge to stare at her across the table.

"Where's Caidence?" I ask Ethan.

"She's working at the cafe tonight. But she wants me to stop by later to show her my truck," he says with a cocky smile. I nudge him playfully, making him laugh. "So, uh, you guys made up?" he leans over to ask quietly.

I lift one shoulder in a shrug. "I guess. She apologized. I accepted. Either way, I'd never turn down a free meal."

"You know I can hear you, right?" Tenley leans over and whispers conspiratorially. Ethan laughs again.

"Oh, I'm sorry. You probably don't appreciate the way I was

talking to Ethan about you behind your back, right?" I retort, narrowing my eyes.

She scrunches her nose. "Who's ready to eat?"

I smirk as I stand and gesture for her to serve herself first, waiting for her to return to the table so I can push in her chair for her. Her eyes flicker over to me with a warning, but I can't help the way I was raised.

Mrs. T adds some homegrown cucumbers and tomatoes to my already overcrowded plate once I sit. Then she leads everyone in a blessing and invites us to dig in. I shovel a forkful of rice and stew into my mouth and let out a loud, involuntary groan.

I turn to Tenley with stars in my eyes. "This is ... *so* good."

"Thanks," she replies shyly, trying to disguise her smile with a bite of food. I can tell she takes pride in her cooking from the way she reacts to my compliment.

Unless, maybe ... it's a reaction to *me*?

I *did* sort of moan.

"*Oui, c'est bon*," says Mr. Jude with a smirk.

"It's bussin', Aunt Ten. Thanks for cooking," Ethan adds.

I try the corn bread next, growling appreciatively this time. Then I set the slice down and lean back to suck the butter off my fingertips, watching for her response.

She stops chewing and brings her glass to her mouth, taking a deep gulp.

"Wow, Tenley. Ethan wasn't kidding." I reach my arm around to rest on her chair back. "I've never been so tempted to break the rules. But I could certainly eat twenty-six-dollars' worth of this, as long as you promise not to report me to the ethics board."

She forces a fake laugh and takes another sip, and I notice her ears turning red.

Interesting ...

No, wait—*not* interesting. I'm making her uncomfortable again, which I promised not to do.

Her parents exchange knowing glances across from us, and I

realize I may have gone too far. I remove my arm and turn back to my plate, attempting to tone down the desperation.

"Slow down, there, Coach. You're gonna make yourself thirsty," Ethan says with a warning glare, and I give him an apologetic look in response. I keep my mouth busy after that, finishing off two servings of food in between laughing at Mrs. T's funny stories about Ethan as a toddler.

And it's the best meal I've had in as long as I can remember.

CHAPTER 15
TENLEY

WE CUT ETHAN'S BIRTHDAY CAKE AFTER DINNER. MY MOM adds a scoop of ice cream over each slice to camouflage the spot that ended up on JD's back, and we all go out to the front porch to enjoy dessert.

We laugh again about the cake mishap, and JD smears chocolate icing on Ethan's nose in an attempt to shut him up after he keeps making jokes about "Coach serving cake," whatever that means.

It isn't long before Dad gets tired, and Mom brings him inside just before the sun begins to set. Ethan waits patiently for permission to take the truck out for a spin. As soon as I say he can go to Caidence's, he abandons us with a quick "thank you, bye."

And that's how JD and I end up alone on a porch swing.

"That kid's got it bad," he says after we watch Ethan drive away.

I chuckle lightly. "He does. But Caidence seems like a nice girl."

"Yeah," he agrees. "He could do much worse. She gets pretty good grades, works at her family's business, and is super respectful. Although, I'm not sure how much he thinks about all that so long as she's wearing a skirt on the sidelines every Friday night."

I glance over. It's getting darker out, but his smile is still visible, as well as the outline of his chest and shoulders in that tight T-shirt. His arm stretches lazily over the back of the swing, and he pushes us back and forth with the slightest movement of his foot. Then his eyes meet mine for a second, causing a definite twinge in my chest, and I force myself to look away.

He's too easy to read tonight. There's something different in his expression that says he isn't just a harmless flirt after all and that his feelings for me run deeper than friendship or simply physical attraction. I can sense him staring at me longingly, as if the dark has made him bold. But I know that if I turn to face him right now, it will be too hard to keep pretending I don't know any better. And if I acknowledge his feelings, I'll have to concede to mine, too.

I'm not ready for that.

"For what?" JD asks.

Crap. How much of that did I say aloud?

"I'm not ready for Ethan to be driving ... and dating, I guess." I try awkwardly to recover, hoping all my thoughts haven't slipped out so easily.

"I thought the same thing earlier when I realized he won't be riding shotgun with me anymore," he says, his tone wistful. "But that's the deal with teenagers. As soon as you think you've got it figured out, they go and attempt something else adult-like, and you've got to start all over again, right?"

I pull my feet up and cross my legs as he continues swinging us. "I'm not sure I'm equipped to handle first dates and custody court dates in the same month, though."

He's silent for a minute before he answers. "For what it's worth, I think you're doing an amazing job. You've made sure he has everything he needs and that he feels safe and loved."

I have to swallow the lump in my throat before I answer. "Thanks."

"And if there's anything else he might need, I'm here ... for both of you. Don't be afraid to ask."

But what scares me is the way he's implying he wants to be helpful in *other* ways, since we both know Ethan won't be needing a ride home from practice any time soon.

"You already do too much."

"Hey," he says, his voice deepening and drawing my gaze back to him. "It's okay. You don't have to do it all on your own."

I turn away again, the tears pooling in my eyes. Why does he insist on being so nice to me, despite my inability to treat him with the same courtesy? What could he possibly see in me that makes him so desperate for my attention? And why is this conversation making me so emotional?

"Tenley." He says my name softly, and his fingertips leave a trail of warmth over the back of my hand as he tries to comfort me. "I'm sorry, I didn't mean to upset you."

I sniffle quietly, trying to hide the evidence. He groans and pulls his hand away, probably because he's annoyed with me. But when I turn, he's running his fingers through his short hair, tugging at it in frustration. "Why do I always say the wrong thing around you?"

"It's not you. It's hard for me to admit I might need anyone," I confess, to my own surprise.

"Well, I promise I'm not just trying to suck up to you or to make you feel like you owe me anything. I enjoy spending time with Ethan ... and with you ... your whole family."

I sigh heavily, willing the waterworks away for now. "I really do appreciate all your help, JD, and I'm sorry again for what I said the other night. It's not like I think you've been doing things for Ethan just because you're trying to ... get with me." I cringe as I stumble over the last part.

"Oh. So, you *don't* think I'm trying to 'get with you'?" he asks. His eyes are narrowed, but a smirk plays on his lips now. I shake my head, feeling my cheeks heat up. And now I'm the one who's grateful we're still sitting in the dark.

That is, until my mom has the courtesy to turn on one of the porch lights, casting a warm glow our way. "Wait, are you ... blushing?" he asks incredulously. "Is it because you had to give me a compliment?"

"No," I lie, shoving him in the chest. But I realize I've made a huge mistake as my hands collide with a sexy brick wall. I shouldn't be touching any remotely sexy parts of JD—or any other man, for that matter.

"Your cheeks are getting darker by the second," he leans in and whispers. "Is it because you're worried I'm trying to get with you now?"

"Leave me alone," I grumble, still flustered with him so close. But I'm better off letting him think I'm embarrassed by what he said and not losing my composure over the physical contact I just made with his muscles. You know, the ones I can see flexing and straining beneath that threadbare T-shirt each time he moves.

Whose idea was it to stay out here with him, again?

"I'm sorry. I'm not supposed to be making things weird, and if your face is any indication, we've definitely crossed over into weird territory," he says, his tone light.

"And this isn't weird for you?" I return. And now it sounds like I'm flirting back.

His brow rises. "Which part? Making a fool of myself while picking up your bra? Having to squeeze into your dad's old T-shirt because I basically sat on Ethan's cake? Ending the night with a romantic swing on the porch, just the two of us?" He pauses for a second before adding the last question. "Or finally hearing you acknowledge my huge crush on you?"

I turn away and bite my lip, taking a second to collect myself before facing him again. "You really are shameless, aren't you?"

He shrugs, his gaze locked onto mine. "Maybe I just really like you."

My eyes dart down. "You're making it weird again."

"I'm sorry," he repeats with a sigh. "I can't help it. And I know you're probably not that into me, Tenley, but the truth is ... I can't stop thinking about you."

My heart thumps so loudly that I can barely hear him. He waits until my eyes meet his again before he continues, making it nearly impossible to keep my expression neutral.

"I'll try my best to keep my feelings for you to myself, if that's what you really want. But I'm hoping there's at least a small part of you that feels something for me, too."

I watch his chest as it rises and falls, and then the muscles in his throat contract as he swallows, as if his confession has taken a lot out of him.

"You can't ... you barely even know me," I say in a small voice. "There's nothing special about me, anyway."

He smiles in disbelief. "I know how much you love your family. I know you enjoy helping people and that doing the right thing is important to you, even when no one is watching. I know you don't like attention, even though you deserve it, and that you're not too proud to apologize when you've hurt someone. You're real and genuine, while everyone else only seems to care about looking good on social media." He shrugs shyly. "I told you, I've spent plenty of time thinking about what makes you special."

"I hope you at least managed to take a break from thinking about me while you were with Loren the other night, though."

Wait, *that's* how I answer him? He's basically pouring his heart out, and my reply is to bait him into talking about his attempt to make me jealous? Seriously, *what* is wrong with me?

He huffs and shakes his head before he responds. "You can stop pretending you don't know why I offered to walk Loren to her car. And for the record, there never was or will be anything going on between Lo and me."

I open my mouth to reply, but nothing comes out. He's right; I already know too much. Yet, I'm still relieved to hear him say it out loud, to admit that he's more interested in me than Loren.

He looks down at his feet for a second before swinging us back and standing up on the return. "I should probably get going. It's late."

"JD, wait." I know I have to say something now if I want to avoid hurting his feelings again. "I'm not good at this kind of stuff, okay? I'm sorry for assuming you were just flirting all this time and for not taking you more seriously. I guess I figured you joke around with other women the way you do with me," I blurt out.

He shrugs, his hands sinking into his pockets. "I haven't found any other women worth flirting with since you came home."

Oof.

My heart feels heavy, as if it's struggling to keep beating. There's a tiny voice in the back of my mind that is screaming at the top of her lungs because JD is a good man, and I'm crazy for pushing him away. But I don't have the emotional capacity to even consider how I might really feel about him with everything else on my plate, much less to handle a relationship. And it doesn't take a genius to see that JD Bourgeois is a relationship kind of guy.

I take a deep breath. "You're sweet, JD, and very charming. I like spending time with you, but my life is already so, *so* complicated. I'm always on call, and my family needs me right now. Ethan's hearing is coming up soon, and I can't think about anything else until all that is settled. You should want to be with someone who can give you the attention you deserve."

"Tenley, I'd never try to pressure you into anything. But I'm also entitled to make up my own mind about who and what I want. I'm well aware of what I'm getting myself into, of how I could fit into your life," he says, his voice deep and stern. "So, how about you tell me what you actually want instead of reciting a list of your objections?"

I frown as anger and embarrassment bubble up to the surface. I can't believe he has the nerve to call me out like this ... until I stop and realize he's right. I've been selfishly making decisions on JD's behalf and operating under the assumption that dating him would require so much effort on my part, when all he seems to want is to make my life easier.

Hell, he's been killing himself just to get me to notice him. That's got to count for something, too, right?

"Tenley?" He moves closer again, and the way his nearness awakens butterflies in my stomach like I've never felt before only proves I've been lying to myself. Refusing to acknowledge that I'm drawn to him doesn't make it any less true.

I squeeze my eyes shut, straining as if there's a rubber band around my heart that could be easily stretched. I think about the way my insides melted earlier when he said I'd ruined him for all other women, then again when *he* nearly ruined *me* by asking me to stare at his bare back and making me listen to his reaction to my cooking.

But as soon as I try to extend the rubber band far enough to include anything close to dating, relationship, or commitment, I panic, and the band snaps back into place.

And it stings. What I want and what I can manage are still two different things.

"And if all I want is a friend, at least for now?" I offer quietly.

"For now?" he asks.

I shrug, and he nods thoughtfully, his large frame casting a dark shadow over half of the porch. Then I notice a mischievous twinkle in his eyes. "Yeah, of course. I mean, the friend zone's a little more disappointing after handling your underwear earlier, but I'll take what I can get … for now."

My jaw drops, and I swing forward to mime a kick to his shin. He dodges it playfully. "I thought you just said you weren't going to tease me anymore!"

"Eh, I think I deserved that one," he says, grinning.

"Fine," I concede. "Consider it your consolation prize."

"Really?" he asks, his hand immediately flying up to his chin in mock thought. "You're giving me a friend-zone perk?"

"Boob jokes are the least I can do, I suppose."

"In that case, I have a very important question for you."

"The girls and I were afraid you might," I reply dryly, trying not to sound even remotely flirty.

"I just need to know, Tenley … are all of your bras that sexy?"

That is decidedly *not* what I expect him to ask, especially not in that deep, gravelly voice.

Can you wear that bra as a hat? Do you still have to wear a life jacket, or do those things help you stay afloat? How do you even run without giving yourself black eyes?

Those are par for the course. But I can't self-deprecate myself out of this one. His eyes darken while he awaits my response.

I clear my throat, willing away the heat pooling inside. "You're not very good at boundaries, are you?"

He lets out a low whistle. "I'll take that as a yes, then. Which, for the record, should be enough to hold me over … *for now.*" He bends slightly, addressing my chest next. "Ladies, enjoy the rest of your night."

Instinctively, I bring my hand up to hide the way he makes me smile and blush at the same time, and he straightens up, acknowledging my simpering with a satisfied smirk of his own.

"Good night, *friend*. Thanks again for dinner," JD says with a wink. Then he turns and jogs down the steps with entirely too much optimism for a guy who's just been friend-zoned, and I watch him walk away entirely too closely for someone who isn't totally into him.

CHAPTER 16
TENLEY

Homecoming week is not for the faint of heart.

There's the decorating, themed dress-up days, pep rallies, parades, senior court presentations, toilet papering, high-school reunions, bonfires ... and then the football game and a semiformal dance. My head is spinning with all the activities and responsibilities as the parent of a varsity football player. I can't imagine how I'll survive once Ethan becomes a senior and has to serve on the homecoming court. Hell, I'm still doubting whether we'll both make it out alive this year.

After recruiting my mom and me to help put together his grand proposal, Ethan tried backing out of his plan to surprise Caidence at cheerleading practice and ask her to be his date to the dance. He got so nervous that he needed a pep talk from both my dad and JD before he could work up the courage to go through with it. And he's been driving me nuts ever since she said yes, keeping me busy with every-thing from getting his dress clothes ready to picking out Caidence's corsage at the florist.

I haven't even had time to feel sentimental or reflect on my own homecoming memories, although they were mostly limited to the football games since I was more reserved than the average teenager. Having an older sister who was known as *that* former Homecoming

Queen—the one who hid her unplanned pregnancy until she couldn't anymore—prompted me to keep a low profile. And now, as a parent, I just hope Ethan can fall somewhere in between. I want him to enjoy high school more than I did, but I feel the need to protect him from his mom's fate at the same time.

"I'm not letting him take the truck," I repeat to my mom. We're sitting on the couch, watching my dad rest. "I'd rather just taxi them around myself."

"Ethan's a good boy. He'll be responsible," she argues. "I'm sure he'd like to drive his date now that he can."

"I bet he would. But I'm also sure there'll be some alcohol going around, and I'd rather not let him risk getting on the road if there's a chance that he or anyone else in town might drink and drive."

She shrugs. "I guess you're right. Either way, it's your decision to make now."

I roll my eyes but know she means well. "I thought this would be easier since he already sleeps through the night and wipes his own ass, but parenting teenagers might be harder than tending to newborns."

"You and I both can agree on that one, my girl," she mutters, and I feel guilty for triggering thoughts of my sister. Not that we never talked about Tessa after her death, but I know my parents felt some culpability for allowing her to make the choices she had as a teenager. Tessa had been really good at hiding her promiscuity and partying from them and disguising herself as the perfect, bubbly, popular class favorite, though. And I'm grateful they ultimately managed to come to terms with their loss by not placing too much of the blame on themselves and turning to one another and their faith. Having Ethan to raise probably helped, as well.

"Look, if I'm going to do this, I'm going to do it my way, and I really need you to respect my decisions," I begin with a renewed appreciation of my mom's strength. "But I still need your help and value your advice, so thank you."

My mom's expression softens, and she leans over to kiss my cheek. "Well, I think you're doing a great job, so far."

"Thanks," I murmur, trying not to get choked up before heading out to the football field. "I learned from the best."

"Since you think so, mind if I offer one more bit of unsolicited advice?"

I eye her suspiciously. She has that gleam in her eyes, the one she gets each time she butts into my love life. "I suppose I have to hear you out now, don't I?"

"I know you've vowed not to date or get romantically involved since you've moved home, but—"

Yep, there it is.

I shake my head quickly. "Mama, I'm not wearing that tight shirt you had made for me again. And I'm not going to throw myself at JD."

"Who said anything about JD?" she retorts with a sassy hand on her hip.

My face flushes a little. I'd be lying if I said he hasn't been on my mind since our talk on the porch swing the week before, but it's not like I can admit that without having to make some other meaningful declarations.

"I was only going to suggest that you reconsider your no-dating policy in general, because I'd like Ethan to continue having a father figure in his life. I'm not saying you should shack up with the first guy who asks, but I do think seeing you happy and settled would be good for him. It's important for a young man to have a decent role model, particularly one who will teach him how to be a good husband and father."

"But he's had that for the first sixteen years of his life, hasn't he?"

"Yes, I'd like to think he has. But he's still a kid, and he's going to need that kind of guidance now more than ever."

I look away, exhaling loudly. "Okay. I'll think about it." If she only knew that even considering the idea of dating someone with the intention of settling down feels like opening a big, scary can of worms.

"That's all I'm asking," she says, as if getting me to reevaluate my entire life plan is no big deal. "And for the record, I was absolutely talking about JD," she adds with a smirk. "He'd fit the bill, don't you think?"

I clear my throat and will my face not to get any redder. "I suppose he will make a fine husband one day, for the right person."

"Very fine," she repeats.

"Mom."

"Tenley."

I press my lips together, trying not to give anything away. "What is it with you people and your obsession with JD Bourgeois?"

"Oh, I don't know. He's gorgeous and generous and adores both you and Ethan ..."

I groan. "He's great, okay? But—"

"But what? Your only objection is that he lives in Camellia? *Mais*, so do you," she fires back, using her hands for emphasis. "Why are you so intent on leaving again?"

I shrug thoughtfully. "Because things are harder out here. My life was much simpler back in Texas."

She huffs. "That's a load of crap."

"Maybe I just don't want to get stuck like you did, okay?" I blurt out, cringing as soon as the words leave my mouth. "It seems like all you've ever done is make sacrifices for us, and you never really got to live your own life."

She shakes her head, her expression softening. "Then you misunderstood. Taking care of y'all has been a blessing, not a burden. Serving others is the only way to fulfill our greatest purpose. It's why we were created. What good are any of our gifts and talents if we can't use them to love and serve one another, whether we do it at home or at work?"

I blink, trying to digest what she's saying. My mom has always been a faithful woman and has done her best to instill those qualities in her family, but she's never been one to rattle off Scripture verses. She's probably been doing a better job of living her faith all this time, leading by example, and I haven't paid enough attention to notice her piety before now.

"I'm sorry. That wasn't a very nice thing for me to say. I didn't really mean it, anyway," I offer after a while. She nods in acceptance of my apology, so I continue. "I honestly don't mind the service part. I guess after seeing everything you've been through, I just figured having a family would be more complicated than focusing on a career."

"Of course it is, but it's also more rewarding. And although the two are not mutually exclusive, one is more important and more precious than the other. Do you think your dad cares much about having a fancy job title or missing out on a guys' night right about now? And the chance to spend this time with him, and the time I got to raise your sister while she was still here, I wouldn't trade any of that."

I sigh. "I get it. And I appreciate everything you've done for us. I just can't picture myself getting married or having kids," I admit, crossing my arms to ease the dull ache in my chest.

Her eyes water as she stares at my dad resting peacefully in his recliner. "Well, baby, it breaks my heart to hear you say that." She stands abruptly and walks into the kitchen, leaving me both relieved and disappointed about not having to delve any deeper into my confession.

I sigh and rub the back of my neck, flinching when I hear my dad cough. "Hey, there, Tenley-girl," he says, his voice rough with sleep.

"Hey, Daddy. How was your nap?" I ask as I move to check his oxygen levels.

"Oh, I wasn't sleeping, I was just resting my eyes," he fibs with a mischievous smile.

I laugh and readjust his blanket over him. "Can I get you anything before I head out to Ethan's game?"

"I'm fine, and I'm sure your mama's going to take good care of me while you're out."

He's right. She will. Because she was made for it, unlike me.

"Homecoming game tonight, is it?" he asks after an awkward silence.

"Yes, sir."

"How was our boy feeling this afternoon?"

"A little nervous, but I think he's ready," I answer. "He's been getting more playing time."

He fidgets in his chair, trying to get comfortable again. "He told me Coach has been working with him on a few new plays this week."

Ugh.

Can I just stop blushing or feeling a flutter in my stomach every time someone brings JD up in conversation? He's literally unavoidable at this point.

"Yep."

"Make sure you tell both Ethan and JD good luck for me."

"Sure."

"Tenley," he begins, his voice weary. "I want you to know that I agree with your mom."

I take a step back from helping adjust the pillows behind him. "You do?"

"I think you owe it to yourself to give JD a shot. What's the harm, you know?"

I huff. "I've you told you all already, with everything else I've got going on, there's no time left for dating or relationships."

He reaches out to grab my hand. "Make time."

"That's easy to say, but hard to fix."

"Then you'd better fix it while you still can," he replies in a more serious tone, patting our joined hands. "Besides, I've always liked that kid."

"JD?" I ask, trying not to laugh at the thought of him as a "kid."

"Yeah, he's a hard worker. He hasn't minded helping with Ethan. And he's done a hell of a job with the lawn, don't you think?"

"Hmm?" I squeak, immediately ready to die of embarrassment once the realization hits me. Has my dad been watching our interactions all this time? I expected him to cite JD's football records as a credential before mentioning his topless grass-cutting services.

He's still smiling when he continues. "You know, your mom and I aren't just trying to set you up with a nice guy in the hopes he'll get you to stick around. JD may be young, but he understands some things that you haven't learned yet, that I had to learn the hard way. Careers and freedom are nice while they last, but they're only temporary and unfulfilling on their own."

"Oh," is all I can say.

"Promise me you'll think about it, at least?"

"Okay, Dad." I lean down and press my cheek against his. "I've got to go. Love you."

"I love you, too."

I debate whether I want to talk to my mom again, but I know I'll feel guilty if I walk out before settling things. "I'm leaving for the game," I announce in the kitchen. "Dad's awake."

She nods without turning around, and I think I hear her sniffling. "Mom?"

"Yeah, okay. Give Ethan a good-luck kiss for me," she finally replies as she faces me, her eyes still red-rimmed.

"What's wrong?" I take a few steps toward her, but she rushes past me.

"I just ... I'm sorry," she replies, forcing a smile. "I overstepped again."

"It's okay. I know you just want to help."

She nods. "You'd better get going if you want decent parking and a good seat in the bleachers. I'm sure it'll be packed out there. I'll see you when you get back."

I grab my purse from the kitchen before I go, still reeling from everything my parents have said in the past half-hour. I guess I can appreciate where they're coming from. They've had a great marriage and simply want the same for me, and they're probably both feeling sentimental with my dad living out his last days. I just don't understand why they think I can't be happy with the life I have or that I'll suddenly shift my priorities after one date with JD.

Besides, JD deserves better, I tell myself as I get to the football field. He's worthy of a relationship based on something more meaningful than physical attraction or convenience. While I can't offer him that, I am certain there are plenty of other women willing to try.

And, speaking of the devil...

I haven't seen JD much over the past week or so, though we have been trading some friendly and borderline suggestive texts in between the busyness of homecoming. But something flitters around inside my stomach when I find him standing in the center of a crowd on the sidelines. A few of his old friends must be in town for the festivities, and it looks like he's regaling them with a story, laughing and waving his hands animatedly while holding his audience captive. His coaching headset hangs loose around his neck, but he's missing his trademark ball cap tonight, and I notice his hair looking a little longer than I'm used to seeing it.

It's cute. *He's* cute.

I sigh, willing myself to look away. But then his eyes meet mine for a second, and he literally does a double take to shoot me a wide smile. I involuntarily simper back at him, self-consciously tugging on the waistband of my shirt. His gaze travels down my body and up again, his smile fading into something more heated and forcing my heart to beat faster before he shifts his attention back to the group. After his confession the other day, I assume he isn't disgusted by what he sees. I *hope* he isn't, anyway—a realization that honestly scares me a little.

I blow out a frustrated breath and take off toward the concession stand, determined to keep my eyes from drifting back to him. But I come to an abrupt halt when someone grasps my arm.

"Hey," JD says, having left behind his fan club. "Everything all right?"

Besides needing my stomach to stop with the fluttering, already?

"Sure, I'm fine," I lie, trying to soften my expression.

He shrugs. "You looked a little upset when you walked by."

"Oh, I just ... I have a lot on my mind." I force a small smile.

"Was your dad feeling okay today?"

I study him for a second before I answer. "He's good. Actually, he wanted me to wish you luck if I saw you before the game, so ..."

"And what about your, um, Aunt Tenley shirt? You know, the other one ... with the v-neck?" he asks, gesturing over his chest. "How's she doing?"

I roll my eyes and cross my arms, equally surprised by his cheekiness and amused by the apparent success of my mom's little stunt. "She's fine. Living out her retirement in the back of my closet. Thanks for asking."

"Would you let her know I miss seeing her around?"

"I really set myself up with that whole boob-jokes clause, didn't I?"

"I'd tell you I've been trying to come up with new material, but then you might assume I've also been thinking about your amazing assets all day, and I wouldn't want to make you feel weird about our new dynamic or anything."

"Or you could just swear you haven't been doing that, and I'd believe you, thereby salvaging our friendship."

Ope. Am I flirting back?

"But honesty is important between friends, isn't it?" he returns, smirking. "And I did promise to make those mental images of you in that black bra last me a while." He leans closer, whispering the last part and making me squirm.

I drop my arms and roll my shoulders back before stuffing my hands into my back pockets. "You mean, the one I'm wearing now?" I ask innocently, and I watch as his eyes glaze over and his jaw goes slack. "Though, I have to admit, just between us, the lace is a little scratchy," I add, tugging on one of the straps and letting it snap for good measure.

Whoa. Did I really just say and do all that?

He stares distantly as he reaches to rub the back of his neck, seemingly at a lost for words, then he shakes his head in defeat.

"What's wrong, Coach, didn't think I'd ever be able to hold my own?" Although if he keeps his arm up in that position any longer, I'm going to get tongue-tied myself.

He looks away and thankfully drops his arm as a smile spreads across his face again. "I guess now that you've officially friend-zoned me, you can finally let loose and be yourself?"

I shrug. "Maybe."

"Do you always flirt this hard with your friends, Ms. Tenley?"

"Not usually," I answer plainly. "But it feels like you're abusing your privileges. Someone needs to put you in your place before you utter the phrase 'bosom buddies.' "

"Hey, that clause was supposed to include unlimited boob puns. I want my money back."

"Too bad I don't keep a wallet," I say, patting my collarbone to imply I've stashed my money in my bra.

He licks his lips, his expression getting more serious. "You know, it's not nice to play—"

But he's interrupted by some guy I barely remember from school yelling, "JD, get over here, man! You'll never guess who I found!"

I glance over and notice that a couple of women have joined their group. I don't recognize either of them, but they're both very pretty, despite being severely overdressed for a high school football game. I turn back to JD, nodding my head in their direction.

"Looks like you're needed elsewhere, Coach."

"Yeah. I guess I've got to get to work at some point, too. I am on the clock."

For some reason, I feel the urge to reach out and touch him, even just to poke or pat him on the arm. I bring my right hand up to twirl my ponytail around my finger instead. "Good luck, then."

"Thanks. Have a good night, Tenley."

I bite my lip and nod, watching intently as he turns and walks away.

Wait, what?

Did I just purposefully flirt *hard* with JD?

I'm totally guilty, and I don't think I've ever enjoyed flirting this much. Also, how is it fair that his butt looks so good in those khakis?

I finally go on to retrieve a cold water from the concession stand, trying not to glance back in JD's direction. But I can't help that I want to see the way he interacts with the others, even just to have a rubric by which I can rate our exchanges.

It seems like he's trying to keep the conversation short, slowly backing away as he speaks. One of the women grabs his arm and leans in to talk to him, making me feel something unpleasant in the pit of my stomach. But he forces a polite smile as he reaches into his pocket for his phone, inadvertently sloughing off her hand. Then he makes an announcement to the whole crowd and looks my way before pulling up his headset and jogging over to the sidelines.

And I grin to myself, because I like that he can't help but steal a glance at me, even when he has all eyes on him.

CHAPTER 17
JD

I GLANCE AT MY REFLECTION IN THE MIRROR, REALIZING I've been grinning like an idiot all day even though I'm dreading the rest of the evening.

I made the stupid mistake of letting Blake and some of our old teammates talk me into going out later tonight, despite being utterly exhausted. Homecoming makes for one of the longest weeks of the school year. Not to mention, I'm already worrying about my students going to the dance later, particularly Ethan and the rest of the football team. I know firsthand that the temptation to make any number of poor decisions will be overwhelming, but I hope they'll all use whatever bit of common sense they have at that age.

So why am I smiling again?

The simple answer is that Tenley flirted with me, and I mean flirted *hard*. The long answer: she'd encouraged me to picture her in her underwear, even going so far as to describe it for me and to pose so that I could create a mental image, and I've been very obedient to her wishes since then, like the good friend that I am.

I'm honestly lucky we played one of the weakest teams in our district last night, because I'd been so distracted by the sudden shift in her attitude toward me that I'd made a few bad play calls. Then, as if the sexy pregame interaction wasn't enough, she'd had the nerve to sit near the bottom of the stands and ruin my concentration for the rest of the evening. I could feel her staring at me the whole time, especially when the team celebrated our win by dumping a cooler over my head, leaving my shirt soaking and clinging to my chest.

Something has definitely changed over the last few days, and although she claimed just last week that she only wanted friendship from me, she's been sending me signals ever since that we're past the "for now" stage.

Needless to say, it's been killing me not to find an excuse to see her today. All I want is to watch her reaction when I tell her I'm still thinking about her and that damned black bra. Instead, I'm being forced to pretend I'd prefer going out drinking with a bunch of dudes over hanging out with Tenley and Ethan and having a beer on my own couch.

I finish primping just as my phone chimes, and I inhale sharply when I see Tenley's name on my screen instead of one of the guys from our group text. My heart quickens as I open the message. It's a picture of Ethan and Caidence dressed up for the dance. I relax and smile at the photo, laughing at Ethan's nervous expression.

JD

They look great. I hope they have a good time.

Tell E to behave himself or else. 

TENLEY

They said thanks!

Will you be at the dance?

JD

No, teachers don't chaperone anymore—too much liability and all. Plus, it's terribly uncomfortable watching your students try to twerk in formal dresses.

TENLEY

laugh react

> JD
>
> Are you going?

> TENLEY
>
> I was, but now I'm on call. And I don't want Ethan to drive himself, so I'm sort of looking for a backup DD, just in case …

> JD
>
> I'll be hanging out in town with some old friends tonight, but I don't mind if you want to keep me on standby.

> TENLEY
>
> Cool, thanks. Hope you have a great time with your friends. You deserve a night out, Coach.

> JD
>
> I could say the same for you. But I guess you have to lie low when you're on call?

> TENLEY
>
> Mostly, yeah.

> JD
>
> Well, just text me if you need me. Anytime.

> TENLEY
>
> *heart react*

Ugh. We've been hovering so close to the edge of the friend zone and making progress with every conversation, even if it's still painfully slow. Is it so wrong to hope she reads into my messages and assumes I mean for everything to sound more sexy and less friendly?

Because I definitely do.

I try to shake my thoughts of Tenley as I head out. But by the time I meet up with the guys, half of them are already annoyingly drunk and hitting on one of the girls behind the bar, who also happens to be a former student of mine. Well, I suppose she's technically a grown woman now that she's old enough to work in a place like this, but it's hard for me to think of the kids I taught as adults sometimes.

"Hey, try to enjoy yourself, huh?" Blake nudges me after I very unsubtly tell one of my ex-teammates to lay off the barely legal bartender and remind him how lucky he is to have a wife and baby waiting for him at home.

I shrug. "I'm sorry, teaching high school kind of ruins the local party scene, man." I take a small sip of the beer I've been nursing for the past half-hour.

"Are you sure that's why you look so miserable?"

"I guess I just don't have as much in common with them anymore," I reply.

"Hmm. For the head coach of an undefeated football team at homecoming and a guy who has the attention of most of the women in this bar, you seem ironically unhappy tonight," he points out, his concern etched on his face.

I look down, picking at the label of the bottle, purposefully ignoring his bait. "I worry about them, you know? I remember some of the stupid stunts we pulled back then, and I just don't want to see any of those kids getting into trouble tonight."

"I'm sure Ethan will be fine." Blake reads me all too well. "He's got a good head on his shoulders."

"Yeah. You want anything?" I hook my thumb over toward the bar.

He eyes my full bottle suspiciously. "I'll walk with you." I guess I'm in for yet another big brother heart-to-heart, except sometimes I'm not so sure that Blake's heart is involved.

"JD, I need a favor," he says once we're away from the crowd. "On behalf of a friend."

"Yeah?"

"Ethan's custody hearing is next week. Do you think you could be there as a character witness for Tenley? I don't think her mom can make it."

I shrug, trying to downplay my excitement. "I could probably swing it, as long as I can find a sub."

"Good. I'd feel better if she had at least one person there to vouch for her, just in case the judge wants to verify she's fit ... you know, that she'd make a good mother."

I ignore the way he's bouncing his eyebrows suggestively. "Does it necessarily need to be me? I mean, you could say as much about her as I could, right?"

"Not exactly, since I'm her lawyer. Besides, you're the perfect choice since you're well-known around here and the best equipped to blindly gush about Tenley Robin and her maternal qualities." He smirks.

I elbow him, attempting to hide my smile. "Fine. Do I need to show up in a suit and tie or what? Can I wear my regular clothes?"

"I definitely recommend the suit," he says. "For Tenley, though, not the judge. I'll text you the details later."

"All right." I'd like to play it cool, but I settle for seeming slightly less than giddy about the getting the chance to help my favorite people and having Blake's encouragement to go after Tenley again.

We each grab a fresh drink from the bar and rejoin the group, and I feel a little less uptight after that. About an hour later, though, I get a text from Ethan's phone.

BIG E

> Hey Coach, this is Caidence. I'm worried about Ethan. I think he's been drinking. And when I asked how he'd be getting home, he said he was planning on calling you. Do you think you could come to the dance and help me with him?

JD

> No worries. I'll be there in a few.

I gesture over to Blake, explaining to him that Ethan needs me. He shakes his head as he laughs but tells me to let him know once we're all home safely. Then I give the rest of the group some excuse about chaperoning duties before I go.

I drive over to the rec center where the dance is being held, grateful that I only had a few sips of my beer. Then I rush into the building and immediately begin searching for Ethan through the rows of wide-eyed, sweaty teens, half-dressed in formal wear, all of them parting the way before me as if I'm a leper. To their credit, teachers don't belong here. We aren't exactly humans with real interests and emotions, after all.

I finally spot Caidence sitting cross-legged on the floor beside the frumpy pile of dress clothes containing Ethan. "Hey," I say as I approach them. "Thanks for texting me. What's going on?"

She shrugs shyly. "I think he had a couple of drinks, maybe even a few too many?"

"Where'd he get it?" I ask, crouching to assess Ethan's state. He's floppy, almost unresponsive, and my stomach turns. "And have you called Tenley?"

"I don't know where he got the alcohol. When I asked him who to call, he unlocked the phone and opened your contact, but I texted Ms. Tenley, too."

I sigh, continuing to try to wake Ethan to no avail. "Has he been vomiting? Did he fall and hit his head or anything?"

"I don't think so. He hasn't been like this for very long, though. Coach, is he gonna be okay?"

"I think he'll be fine, eventually. But I should probably take him home. You did the right thing, Caidence. And I hope he hasn't ruined your night by acting like a total dumbass," I say, looking up at her.

She nods quickly. "Yes, sir. Thank you."

"I'll have him call you tomorrow with an apology," I promise, attempting to pull him up from the ground. But he's dead weight. "Shit, kid. You've been working out," I mumble more to myself than to him as I squat again, this time maneuvering Ethan so I can sling him over my shoulder like he's a sack—a very heavy sack.

All right, knees, don't fail me now.

I know I'm asking for trouble since one of my knees has, in fact, failed me before, but there's no saving face now. I inhale deeply, grunting loudly like the old man I've become as I barely manage to stand with Ethan's upper body hanging limply over my back.

Then I turn and see Tenley walking through the door, her hand flying to her chest in a panic. I make my way over to her while the students back out of our way again. Come on," I say when I get to her. "I'll meet you at your house. He's out cold."

"He called you first?" she asks, sounding wounded as she trails behind me.

"He got Caidence to text me from his phone."

"Do you think he's got alcohol poisoning?"

"I honestly don't know. I couldn't get an answer as to how much he drank." I continue walking to my truck, relieved to hear Ethan groaning when his head bounces off my back.

"Could you just put him in my car?"

"I'll have to follow you home to get him out later, anyway. And it's easier to unload him if he's sitting higher."

"Oh. Okay."

I open the passenger door to my truck before flopping Ethan's listless body into the seat.

"Ugh," he moans. "I think I'm gonna be sick."

"The hell you are," I growl, walking over to grab a water cooler from the bed of my truck, removing the lid and tossing it back, then planting the jug in Ethan's lap. "If you get puke anywhere else but in that bucket, you're dead."

He wraps his arms around the cooler as if it's a life raft, resting his cheek on the rim. I slam the door shut and walk around to the driver's side, and Tenley follows me again.

"Meet you at your place?" I offer.

She nods, her eyes filled with concern. "JD, thank you again."

"No problem."

She walks off reluctantly, and by the time I climb into my truck, Ethan has started filling his makeshift barf bucket.

I roll the windows down, letting in the cool night air. "You all right, bruh?"

"Maybe."

"You've got some splainin' to do, Lucy."

He groans again, his head rolling back onto the headrest. "I'm sorry."

"I'm sure you are, now. What and how much did you drink?"

"Just a few swigs. One of the guys ... he had some bottles in his car."

"Why?"

He doesn't answer, and his chest rises and falls as he drifts off. "E?" I reach over and shake his shoulder to wake him.

"Hmm?"

"Why did you drink so much, Ethan?"

He lets out a deep breath. "I was just so nervous, you know, because of Caidence. And then I started thinking about Pop, and my mom ... and my biological dad. He's been calling me."

"So, you just wanted to take the edge off, then?" I huff. "And instead, you ruined Caidence's night and made yourself sick." I know I'm being a little harsh, so I bite my tongue and resign to save my lecture on the dangers of using alcohol to cope with one's problems for later.

Then I rewind that conversation.

"Ethan, did you just say your biological dad's been calling you?" As far as I know, that isn't supposed to be happening. Or, at least, it hasn't happened before.

"Yeah," he breathes. "Mawmaw wrote him a letter a while back, and he recognized me in the newspaper from earlier in the season, when I scored my first touchdown. We've just been talking and stuff."

Well, maybe it's okay since Mrs. T wrote him the letter? This goes beyond a coach's jurisdiction, doesn't it? Yet I can see how it's affecting him from the decisions he's made tonight.

I sigh and venture on because I already care too much about Ethan to let this go. "And are you okay with that, him reaching out to you?"

"He's all right so far ... it's just weird."

"Does your aunt know?" I ask as we pull up in front of their house, but he's already started heaving again, so I have no choice but to drop the subject.

I get out and walk around the truck, holding my hand up to warn

Tenley as she nears. "Give him another minute," I tell her, and she nods.

"I'm sorry we ruined your night out," she begins quietly.

"Don't be sorry. I'd rather be here with you guys, anyway."

She crosses her arms and looks down, probably embarrassed by my honesty. "I don't know. I can't imagine your other friends letting their kid throw up in your Gatorade cooler."

"You've got a point," I admit with a slight smile. Then I turn and bump my elbow against the window a couple of times to get Ethan's attention. "Ay, you done in there or what?"

"No," Ethan moans, followed by more coughing.

"He's going to be fine, by the way. He's half-coherent now, but he should feel better once he finishes clearing out his system," I explain.

"Did he tell you what happened?"

As much as I'd do just about anything to get on Tenley's good side, I'm not willing to throw Ethan under the bus or put my nose where it doesn't belong. I am concerned, though. "He thought he'd look cooler if he drank a little, and it caught up to him."

She nods. "I figured as much. I just hope this doesn't come up in court next week."

"I seriously doubt anyone would fault you for the kid getting drunk at homecoming. He's sixteen. It's not like you bought the alcohol for him. And at least you cared enough to have someone on standby in case this happened, right?" I try to reassure her, but she only nods again. "I'll help him inside once he's done in there," I offer. "But I'm leaving that bucket so he can clean it out and return it in the morning."

"I assume you'll need it back pretty early, too?" she asks, her expression amused now.

"Oh, yeah. I'd like to watch him walk it out to the road for the garbage pickup after he does all that work to clean it," I say, chuckling.

"I'll make sure he replaces it later. And I imagine you'll have a nice *Afterschool Special* talk prepared?"

"Absolutely, except my version usually begins with a *'mais* bruh' and ends with early-morning Mass. If that's all right with you, of course."

"You have my permission to knock some sense into him any way you see fit," she says, smiling. "I trust you."

Before I can properly react to that, Ethan taps on the window to signal he's done. I stare at Tenley a second longer before I turn and open the door, burying my face in the collar of my shirt and going for the bucket first.

"I'll get that, JD," Tenley says behind me, so I back up and let her take care of it. She has a few choice words for her nephew as she shuffles over to the side of the house to set the cooler down.

"Come on, wingman. Up you go." I lean into the passenger seat so Ethan can fold over my shoulder again, and he doesn't protest as I carry him into the house. I wave at Mr. Jude in the living room before stopping to greet Mrs. T with a cheek kiss as usual. She hands me a bottle of water for her grandson, looking more amused than worried, and I continue on to Ethan's room and drop him onto his bed.

"Coach," he begins as I search the room for a trash can.

"Yeah?"

"I'm sorry again. Thank you for coming to get me and for not telling Aunt Ten everything."

"Drink some of that water. And don't thank me yet. I'm still planning to make you regret your decision in the morning."

"I already do," he mumbles after taking a few sips from the water bottle. "Coach?"

"Yeah, E?"

"Sorry I barfed in your cooler." Then he lies back and immediately begins snoring.

I laugh to myself and turn to walk out, but my breath hitches when I find Tenley leaning against the doorframe. She clears her throat and looks away quickly. "I'll pretend I didn't hear that if you want me to."

"For his sake, anyway."

She nods again, then she gestures toward the front of the house. "Walk you out?"

CHAPTER 18
JD

I bid Tenley's parents good night before following her out to the front porch.

"It looks like I've found myself in your debt, once again," she begins, and I think she might be stalling. "What will it be this time? Another dinner at our house?"

She's offering to feed me? Unprompted?

Our eyes meet for a second, and I'm tempted to finally ask her out on a real date, though I don't want to push my luck just yet. "I thought I told you to quit keeping count. I don't want you to feel like you owe me anything," I say instead.

"So, you're really going to turn me down?" she asks, smiling playfully. "I thought you liked my cooking."

"Your cooking is delicious, but your company is even better, if I'm being honest," I return.

"Mm-hmm." She looks away, but it's too late to hide how much she actually enjoyed my cheesy line. "Is there anything I can say that you won't twist around and use against me?"

"Tenley, of all the things I'd like to hold against you, words have never crossed my mind."

She throws her head back and laughs. "There you go again." Then her expression falls, and she narrows her eyes as she stares at something over my shoulder. I turn and spot the security camera mounted on the porch overhang.

She crosses her arms and shifts her weight to one side. "I would invite you to stay a little longer, but I'm sure your friends are waiting for you."

"I meant what I said earlier."

"Either way, I'll have to offer you a rain check. I have a feeling we're being ... monitored," she says, pulling a face at the camera.

"Really? Are we that interesting?" I ask, gesturing back and forth between us.

"Apparently." She looks embarrassed again.

I take a step closer, hoping to salvage whatever we had going a second ago. "Well, if Ethan's passed out and Blake's nowhere around, then that must mean your parents have been getting some ideas about shipping us, too?"

Her face flushes. "Your brother?"

I shrug. "Blake's like a Sour Patch Kid. He gets sweeter with time."

"I guess I could see that."

Tenley slips her hands into her back pockets and glances uncomfortably at the camera. She's dodging the question I asked about her parents, though I already know the answer.

"How about you walk me to my truck, and then I'll get out of your way?" It's risky, but I'm betting she'll loosen up without the audience.

She nods, and I lead her out, dragging my feet. "So, can I really name my price this time?" I begin again, opening the door and leaning back against the driver's seat.

"I don't know. I feel like you may have taken advantage of my last offer." Her eyes run over me as if she's checking me out.

I lick my lips, thinking I should wear jeans around her more often. "You didn't sound so helpless when you were teasing me last night."

"Maybe you regret the boob-jokes clause, too, then?" She smirks and steps closer.

I let out an exaggerated exhale to disguise my nerves. "Oh, yeah. Definitely. I, uh … I didn't realize a bra could be so … distracting."

"It is rather itchy."

I huff and try to play it cool. "And I'm the one who turns everything around on *you*?"

"I'm just trying to hang in there, Coach."

I pause for a second, slowing things down. It's all very, very promising, but I'm afraid to read too much into her reactions. "Does that mean I'm not making you feel uncomfortable anymore?" I venture.

"I think I'm just better equipped to handle you now."

My bad shoulder feels tight after all that heavy lifting, so I reach up without thinking and latch my hands onto the edge of the doorjamb. Then I notice the way her eyes are glued to my arms as I'm stretching.

"And I think I like the way that sounds, Ms. Tenley," I reply, my voice a little deeper this time.

She rolls her eyes and turns away. "Are you always like this?"

"Only with you," I say, dropping my arms. She groans, making me laugh again. "I'm sorry, I'll quit."

She glances back at the house. "You'd better name that price before my mom starts peeking at us through the blinds."

"Hmm, that's a lot of pressure. I may need to think it over first."

"Nope." She shakes her head. "The offer expires when you leave."

"It's like that, is it? Can I ask for something to be redeemed in the future, at least?"

"Sure."

"Anything I want?" I grin.

"Within reason," she corrects me.

"A favor *or* an object?"

"I'm not giving you my bra," she declares, her eyes narrowed. "Bras this size aren't cheap, and there's a twenty-five-dollar gift limit for public servants, remember?"

I click my tongue. "Damn, okay … think, JD …"

"Is there really nothing you want from me?" she asks, her voice still tinged with humor.

"Oh, it's quite the opposite," I return, laughing incredulously. "I'm just trying not to waste my one shot."

"And I figured you'd have something prepared, since I'm supposedly all you ever think about." She rolls her eyes playfully, but I don't miss the way she keeps daring me to ask her out. As much as I'd like to follow her lead, I'm also worried about losing this momentum. I need to do something to hook her now.

"You're right, I've definitely thought this through before. But I'd been expecting three wishes, and I'm afraid of getting buyer's remorse again."

She bites her lip to hide her smile. "I'm not a genie, you know. I'm only giving you a few more seconds to make up your mind."

My instincts are yelling at me now, urging me to make a move. I grab one of her hands and use it to pull her in gently, and the contact sends a wave of heat throughout my body.

"I think you know exactly what I want." I let my eyes travel down to her mouth, just to make my intentions clear. "But since we're just friends, we'd have to be careful to keep it ... you know, friendly."

"I see." Her voice cracks, and I gravitate closer again.

"Tenley, I'll stop if you want me to," I mumble. "Just say the word."

She shrugs one of her shoulders slightly. "A deal's a deal, I guess."

Hot damn, is that a yes?

My pulse throbs in my ears, and I attempt to regulate my breathing as I reach out with my free hand and grasp her hip, drawing her toward me once more. She stares up at me, letting me lead her, and I remind myself that I can't just pull her in and shove my tongue down her throat. I need to get this just right, to carefully toe the line between scaring her away and making it count.

I lean in, inch by inch, until my nose is even with hers, and her eyelids flutter closed. Then I bring my right hand up to lift her chin slightly, holding her there as I close the space between our lips as painstakingly slowly as possible, despite the electricity drawing me in.

She inhales sharply at the contact, shifting her weight into me and pressing her deliciously full bottom lip against mine. But I stay still, ignoring the heat burning me up from the inside out and allowing her a moment to acclimate. I'm desperate to make this perfect for her, and I need her fully present so she can remember every detail later.

After a few seconds, I pull away and barely brush my lips over hers, and she follows me as if I've activated a magnet inside each of us. I slide my hand up to cradle her cheek, holding her steady while I deepen the kiss again, urging her mouth open until she yields. Then I tilt my head and gradually slip my tongue inside. She takes it in willingly, mingling it with her own.

And it's all so, *so* good.

Tenley clasps her hands around the back of my neck as she lets out an adorably gratified sigh, and I nearly relinquish the last of my control at the sound. But as soon as I think it's safe to bring things up to normal speed, her phone rings, making her flinch and breaking the seal between us. I hold her face still, though, resting my forehead against hers while we stand there for a second longer, both of us breathing hard.

"You should probably check that," I murmur, her lips mere centimeters away from mine, tempting me again. But I know Tenley well enough to understand that she needs the space to process and that I'm much better off leaving her wanting more. I lick my lips one more time and inhale deeply as I let her go, leaving her standing in the same position, her eyes heavy-lidded and her own lips still parted.

"Sorry," she whispers, as if it's the best she can manage.

She's making it nearly impossible to resist the urge to pull her back in while she's so mouthwateringly flustered, and I'm struggling to convince myself that stopping now is an investment for later. But she looks thoroughly dazed, maybe even a little intoxicated, and knowing that I'm the one who's done this to her is unbelievably hot.

All I can do now is hope I've read her correctly and delivered the kind of first kiss that will inspire plenty of repeat performances. I like my chances when I see her blink a few times as if she's still trying to regain consciousness before pulling her phone out.

"It's the hospital. I've got to go in," she explains apologetically.

I nod. "Duty calls."

"Yeah." She slips her phone into her back pocket and brings her thumb up to her mouth demurely.

Too late to look shy now, babe. I already know you taste like cinnamon and that your bottom lip fits perfectly against mine.

"So, um, got any more favors you need done around here?" I ask, intending to sound fun and flirty again, but my voice comes out too deep for her to miss my meaning.

The corners of her mouth turn up, and she drops her thumb. "I thought friends don't keep tabs."

"I guess you're right. We *are* friends, after all."

"Mm-hmm."

"Good night, Tenley," I say, reaching out to brush a finger over her arm, just to see if I can make her squirm. It works—another good sign. "Don't forget to have that little twerp of yours report to my house early in the morning with a clean cooler. And make sure he's dressed for church."

"Will do, Coach. Good night."

I watch her hips sway as she ambles into the house without stopping to look back, then I climb into my truck and drive home. I review every second on the way, and I'm still smiling to myself when I strut inside and pull out my phone.

JD

Got E back home safely.

BLAKE THE SNAKE

I'm glad he's all right. Thanks for the update, man.

You coming back to meet us?

JD

Nah, I'm already home.

BLAKE THE SNAKE

Come on, bro. You just need someone to take your mind off she-who-shall-not-be-named.

JD

I don't think that's possible. Plus, I'm not going to leave Tenley's place and go straight to hooking up with someone else.

BLAKE THE SNAKE

Why the hell not? Let's find you a nice girl to make out with for once.

JD

Already done. 😌

BLAKE THE SNAKE

You ... WUT?

JD

I kissed Tenley.

Read that again.

BLAKE THE SNAKE

I'm speechless.

JD

So was she by the time I was done.

BLAKE THE SNAKE

Was it everything you dreamed of and more? 😏

JD

Shut up.

But yes.

It was one of my better moments.

Until she got called to work. 😕

BLAKE THE SNAKE

Look at you, man, finally crawling your way out of the friend zone.

gif of battered soldier

JD

gif of a smiling turtle

CHAPTER 19
TENLEY

My skin feels unpleasantly sticky, and I try to disguise the way I have to adjust my shirt as Ethan and I scoot down one of the rows in the parish courthouse. I'm already stress-sweating, which is always fun for a big-busted girl like me.

I don't foresee any reason why the judge won't grant my petition for temporary custody, but tell that to my anxiety-riddled brain. I glance over at Ethan, forcing a tentative smile for him. He smiles back warmly, and I can see the gratitude in his eyes. I can't help myself as I reach out and hook my arm through his. Maybe I hadn't planned for this or even expected it, but becoming his guardian definitely feels right. I continue staring at my nephew and reflecting satisfactorily on my emotional growth until I notice his head turning in recognition.

"Hey, you came!" Ethan whispers excitedly as we're joined by some tall, hot stranger in a suit.

I lean back quickly. What the heck is *he* doing here? And why does he look so different today?

"Of course I came," JD replies in a hushed tone, but his voice is too deep, and the bailiff passing by with the judge's last customer gives him a warning scowl.

I turn to the left to find a familiar pair of hazel eyes already staring back at me. "JD? You're here. And you ... shaved?" I ask incredulously, only to get the same glare from the bailiff.

He winks and shoots me a dimpled smile, and I shiver. I whip my head around, hoping to disguise my widened eyes and attempting to get my thoughts in check, but it's impossible as long as I can feel JD staring at me with an ear-to-ear grin.

This isn't the scruffy dork stuck in a football player's body that I've grown accustomed to seeing regularly over the past few months. *This* is a grown man. And he looks annoyingly and distractingly good.

Someone announces the judge's arrival, and I carefully allow myself another peek as we all stand. JD's no longer facing me, but I can tell from his smug expression that he knows I'm checking him out.

And sadly, I can't help myself.

I bite my bottom lip and inventory the changes he's made since I last saw him. A dangerously adorable pair of dimples is visible now that his jawline is completely smooth. His light brown hair is longer than usual, which I only notice because it looks so nice parted to the side. He's wearing a navy suit that must have been tailored to fit him, and, *holy cow*, does it fit him. I let my eyes run over the fabric as it hugs his well-defined shoulders, swallowing hard when I realize it's probably an old game day suit from back when he played football.

Ethan nudges me with a gentle elbow to the ribs and a knowing smirk on his face, letting me know my ogling has become too obvious, and I catch a slight quirk in JD's smile before redirecting my attention to Blake's ongoing exchange with the judge. But my thoughts immediately drift back to JD's lips, and Blake shoots me a warning glare when the judge has to call my name twice to elicit a response.

It's like they all know exactly what's on my mind, and I'm still powerless to control it. What the heck is wrong with me? Why am I standing here undressing JD Bourgeois with my eyes instead of acting like the rational and responsible adult I came here to prove that I am?

Sure, I've never been able to convince myself that JD isn't attractive and sweet and basically great. I can no longer deny developing my own crush and maybe even legitimate feelings for him. And I admittedly haven't been able to stop thinking about the kiss we shared the other night. But I've never had tunnel vision when a man entered the room before, and I don't know how to deal with this kind of distraction.

I take in a deep breath and exhale slowly, telling myself that this is simply an inconvenient combination of physical attraction, increased stress, and a poorly timed hormonal shift. None of the reasons for my sudden interest in JD matter, anyway, since our situation remains the same. I'm still convinced that dating him wouldn't be in anyone's best interest, especially not Ethan's. Besides, I've been able to keep my cool around JD for the most part. Today shouldn't be any different.

Although, that was before I'd witnessed him rising from the ground with Ethan draped over his shoulder, like my own personal superhero. Before we began sending one another increasingly flirtier texts all day, before my stomach started cutting flips every time he looked at me, and before he'd kissed me like *that*.

How had he managed so much restraint the other night, anyway? He'd lured me into thinking he was going to keep things casual and "friendly" before ambushing me with that ridiculously hot kiss. Then he just continued living as if it hadn't happened, without so much as a reference to it in any of the texts we've exchanged over the past thirty-six hours, including the "good luck" message I received from him this morning. Meanwhile, I've been stuck in my own head, consumed with reliving my very detailed memory of that night and asking myself all kinds of other dangerous questions, like how to keep pretending we're only friends after this, what might have happened if we hadn't been interrupted, whether JD always kisses that way—so composed, yet so intense—and why I'd even let him kiss me in the first place. Just thinking about his quiet confidence as he'd pulled me in and pressed his lips to mine has my temperature rising all over again.

I blow out another breath, still trying to figure out what's changed between us. Maybe I've finally let JD wear me down to the point that I've given up on resisting him, or maybe it's my family's influence.

Maybe I just plain wanted him to kiss me. Because I like him. I like JD Bourgeois a lot ... probably more than I should.

One more glimpse in his direction, and I'm absolutely sure that's the case. I'm also very certain I want him to kiss me again, without any interruptions.

"I'd like to meet in my chambers for a minute," I vaguely hear the judge announcing through my suit-wearing-JD–induced brain fog before I'm ushered into a side room.

I watch JD shamelessly as he follows Ethan and Blake, and he stops to hold the door open for me. Then I hold my breath as I pass, hoping to avoid having to answer to my ovaries, who are demanding to know whether he smells as good as he looks.

He still manages to ruin my concentration when the tip of his finger deliberately skims the inside of my wrist, eliciting a gasp from me and leaving a trail of warmth up my arm. Just the slightest brush of his calloused skin over mine has me losing my balance and stumbling through the doorway. I hear him snort quietly in amusement as I scurry away quickly, frantically trying to put some distance between us after discovering that he does, in fact, smell even better than he looks right now.

Gah, what's happening to me? Unexpected physical touch has always irritated me in the past. Yet here I am, melting into a pathetic puddle over a fingertip graze, and he hasn't even spoken a word to me so far today.

The judge's voice brings me back again, and I squeeze my eyes shut, attempting to refocus. It was only a light touch on the wrist, after all—barely any contact. He probably didn't even mean for it to be that sexy. This is perhaps one of the most important moments of my life, of Ethan's life, and I can't let this sudden lack of self-control jeopardize our future.

Blake explains our situation while the judge listens impassively. "No father was listed on Ethan's birth certificate, your honor, nor has one been identified for certain. His biological aunt, Ms. Tenley Robin, is the only adult relative who is both financially and physically capable of providing for Ethan since her father's unfortunate illness, and she's more than willing to assume legal guardianship in order to allow Ethan's grandmother, Mrs. Therese Robin, to care for her husband."

I smile hopefully as the judge turns his attention to me. "I see," he says, pausing for a second before he continues and addresses the extra accessory in the room. "Well, if this isn't the boy's father, then—"

"I'm here to vouch for Ms. Robin in the place of her parents, your honor," JD finishes for him, his voice giving me the chills again.

The judge eyes him suspiciously for a second before he recognizes him. "Hmm. You're JD Bourgeois. Aren't you two brothers?"

"Yes, sir, but I'm also Ethan's football coach and science teacher," he adds quickly. "I've gotten to see Ms. Tenley take on the role of Ethan's guardian since she's come back to Camellia to care for him. And she's done an outstanding job, in my humble opinion."

"And in what capacity have you witnessed this?" the judge asks, his tone still skeptical.

"I can tell you she's been getting him to school every morning, teaching him how to drive on the way back from practice in the afternoons, and even making him home-cooked meals and helping him with his school projects at night. She's made sure Ethan has everything he needs, including discipline and stability, and she's been in the stands for every one of his football games. She even came down to the field to tend to him when he was injured. I wish I could say all my students had as much support at home, but the truth is that Ethan is a lucky kid."

I gape at JD in disbelief. He's talking me up entirely too much.

Although, technically, I *have* been doing all of those things. I survey the room and see Ethan nodding and grinning proudly in agreement, as well as Blake smiling encouragingly at JD as he continues.

"Most of all, your honor, I think Ten—uh, Ms. Robin—wears her heart on her sleeve."

I drop my eyes, my face flushing. Then I hear JD clear his throat, and I glance up to find him staring back at me. My stomach swirls, and a wave of heat climbs up my entire body until even the tips of my ears must be red.

"Anyone can see how much she loves her nephew and that she'd do anything for him, just from the way she looks at him. I can't imagine Ethan could find a better guardian or a more selfless and devoted parent," he finishes, his eyes still locked onto mine, the intensity in his gaze overwhelming me.

Selfless? Devoted? Is he still talking about me?

The look on JD's face says that he wholeheartedly believes in my parenting abilities, even if I don't, and that he's been observing and evaluating my maternal qualities very, very closely all this time. I gulp, desperately hoping the judge has heard enough, because I can't listen to any more of JD's compliments without wanting to pull him down by that tie and—

Whoa. Down, girl.

"Well," the judge begins, abruptly ending my inner monologue. "It's hard to argue with a resume like that," he says with a smirk. "But, ah, what about your living arrangements?"

Blake coughs awkwardly, obviously picking up on something I haven't. "Oh, your honor, JD is just a family friend. Tenley and Ethan are planning to remain in the same home as Mrs. Therese and Mr. Jude for now. They all felt it would help with the transition."

My face heats up again in embarrassment, but at least Blake has the sense to reroute that conversation before we all have time to dwell on its implications. I don't dare to check JD's reaction.

"And you plan to stay here permanently?" the judge turns and asks me directly.

"Yes, your honor, at least until Ethan graduates from high school. I'm under contract at Dr. Simms's practice here in Camellia and was recently granted hospital privileges as an attending midwife. I couldn't leave very easily now, even if I wanted to—but I don't," I say, tripping over my defense.

The judge nods thoughtfully, pausing for a moment before he continues. "Seeing as though you are one of Ethan's closest relatives and the only one present today, I see no reason not to grant your petition for temporary custody, Ms. Robin. I'd like to talk to Ethan alone for a minute to ascertain his wishes, then we'll take a short recess and meet back in the courtroom to make all this official."

It seems odd that the judge emphasizes the word "temporary," and although Blake explained that cases like ours usually happen in stages, it feels a little less official than I expected. But he reassures us that everything is fine, and I excuse myself for a quick trip to the ladies' room and a reprieve from JD's presence.

I stare at my reflection in the mirror for a second. Why has my heart decided to wait until this very moment to wake up and overrule my brain? Apparently, all he has to do is say I'd make a decent parent, and I'm putty in his hands.

Even so, I can no longer ignore that a very significant part of me *really* wants to explore these feelings with JD. And although I assume he won't mind if I make a move, I also think he'll expect a date to follow shortly, and maybe even a real relationship.

My face relaxes as I realize I'm not as terrified at that prospect anymore, and I'm still eager to convey my gratitude for all those nice things he just said about me in the same way I rewarded his last favor.

Then I groan and shake my head, trying to bring my thoughts back to the more important stuff I have going on, like the custody hearing. I can't get used to this new lack of focus. I apply a fresh coat of lipstick, run my fingers through my hair, and blow out a breath to hype myself up.

The guys are waiting to escort me back into the courtroom when I emerge. This time I end up sitting beside JD, and his hand ventures over to cover mine. He strokes my pinkie with his thumb, triggering a response throughout my whole body and awakening parts of me I haven't regarded in a long time. Unfortunately, this also includes a disproportionate number of previously unused sweat glands.

Everyone stands as the judge reenters, and I take a second to free my hand and peel my blouse away from my dampened skin, desperately trying to get some fresh air to the girls. We remain standing as the judge reiterates the conversation we had in his chambers. But then he adds a bit that even has Blake fidgeting and looking nervous.

"Since young Mr. Robin is sixteen, the court will honor his request and grant temporary custody to Ms. Tenley Robin, effective immediately. We will revisit the situation in another month or two, after the family attempts to contact the young man's alleged father one more time, as the goal is always the reunification of children with their biological parents whenever possible. Case dismissed."

He taps the gavel, and I feel Blake's hand on my elbow, ushering me out of the courtroom. He releases me as soon as we make it to the hallway, but I can't shake the feeling that something isn't right, and the concern on Blake's face only solidifies my theory.

"Don't panic," he says softly, raising his hands in an attempt to placate me. "It's honestly not the best-case scenario, but it's nothing we can't fix by the next court date, okay?"

"I wasn't panicking until you said that," I spit out. I glance over at Ethan, and he forces a smile.

Blake huffs at me impatiently, but JD comes over and cups a hand over my arm, rubbing softly until I take a deep, calming breath. His eyes meet mine with a questioning look, wordlessly asking me whether I'm okay, and I nod.

"Come on," Blake says after a second, glancing between us. "We've got papers to sign, and then you guys are good to go."

We follow him into a clerk's office, where I scribble my name on a handful of documents. "The judge will sign these and make them official, and I'll have the notarized copies for you by tomorrow," Blake explains. "In the meantime, you're allowed to celebrate. Ethan is officially and legally yours, albeit temporarily." He adds a warm smile at the end, but it's a little late to change the mood.

I reach out to embrace Ethan anyway. "I love you, kid," I tell him, my eyes beginning to water.

"Thank you, Aunt Ten. I love you, too," he says in return, his voice thick with emotion.

He pulls away and reaches out to Blake for a handshake. "Thanks, Coach Blake."

"My pleasure, Big E," Blake replies, his own eyes looking slightly misty.

"Yes, thank you, Blake," I echo.

He nods in response. "Well, I've got to file all this now if I want to make it out in time for practice this afternoon. But you three go on and get out of here. I'll see you guys later."

JD locks hands with his brother next, pulling him in for an unexpected hug and whispering something near his ear. Blake slaps him on the back before they separate, his smile looking a little more genuine now.

Then I watch carefully as JD strides over to me in that suit, and I get unnaturally hot all over again.

CHAPTER 20
JD

We walk out of the courthouse in silence, still reeling from the last few minutes, and my palm rests on the small of Tenley's back as I lead them over to her car.

"Thanks for coming, Coach," Ethan says. I let go of her to clasp his hand and pull him in for a pat on the back. "It means a lot to both of us," he adds over my shoulder.

"I was happy to do it," I return.

Then he ducks into the passenger seat, leaving me and Tenley alone on the sidewalk. I take a step toward her, but she keeps her eyes trained on the ground, pressing her lips into a hard line. "You okay, Ten?" I ask tentatively, nudging her fingertips with mine. I know I'm being presumptuous by touching her as much as I have today, especially in public, but she seems okay with it. Maybe it's because we're away from the prying eyes of everyone in Camellia, though I hope it's because she finds it comforting.

To my surprise, she clutches my hand tightly and glances up at me. Her eyes are filled with tears, threatening to spill over any second, and my heart aches to see her so upset.

"Come here," I say softly and envelop her in a hug. She buries her face in my chest as soon as I wrap my arms around her. I can hear her sniffling quietly, as if she's trying to hide that she's crying, because God forbid anyone spot a chink in her armor.

"I'm sorry. I'm just disappointed because I thought everything would be resolved after today," she explains, her voice muffled. "And now we have to go looking for Ethan's dad instead."

"Hey, it'll be okay. Like Blake said, this is all just part of the process." I vaguely remember Ethan telling me about his father contacting him the other night, but I'm not sure what Tenley knows, and this doesn't seem like the right time to bring it up.

"I hope you're right," she answers. I don't think she wants another verbal response, so I continue holding her and rubbing her back, expecting her to pull away any second. But she doesn't. I wish I could revel in the fact that I finally have her in my arms, but I can't be happy as long as she's hurting. Instead, I settle for savoring her warmth and her floral-and-citrus scent while I can.

Eventually, she pushes back against my chest and fixes her gaze on me, her eyes looking a deeper blue than usual and her cheeks still damp. "I don't know how to thank you for everything you said in there today."

"I only told the judge what I already knew to be true." Without thinking, I bring my thumbs up to gently wipe some of the moisture from her face.

"No, Ethan's right. This means more to both of us than you know."

I gulp as she continues staring at me with an intensity I haven't seen from her before now. "We're friends. It was nothing," I reply, my voice catching.

She shakes her head slowly. "You've been so much more than a friend to me, JD."

There's a change in her as soon as she says it, and she reaches up to cup my cheek and stroke my face gently, sending a chill all the way down. This isn't like the other night, when I initiated the kiss and she was simply a willing participant. She steps closer and presses the full length of her body against mine, making it harder for me to breathe by the second, and her eyelashes flutter as she darts her eyes down to my mouth.

Shit, it's really happening.

My heartbeat drums loudly in my ears once I fully grasp her intent. She's throwing me a line, extending an invitation out of the friend zone. Hell, she might be hauling me across the border at this point.

I hear a faint sigh when she tips her chin up slightly, closing her eyes and waiting patiently for me to meet her halfway. She's probably expecting me to kiss her with same poise and restraint I feigned before. But Tenley is finally making a move *on me*, and I'm not strong enough to hold back this time.

I lean down and tilt my head to the side as I close the last bit of space between us. Our lips meet for a second before she drags her hand down my neck and interlaces it with my tie, pulling me closer and making me feel like my body is on fire. Her mouth parts eagerly, and I enthusiastically take my cue to deepen the kiss. She tastes even better than I remember, a combination of cinnamon and sweet mint. And when she slips her tongue in between my lips, it takes every ounce of restraint not to let my palms inch down to her backside.

Because, you know, that's usually what happens next in nearly every one of my dreams over the past few months.

Instead, I bring my hands up to cradle the back of her neck as I allow myself to indulge in her, exploring her mouth and savoring her lips, lush and pliant against mine. I'm lost within seconds, kissing her like we're all alone—until I'm reminded that we aren't. We both jump back at the sound of a car horn blaring a few feet away.

"Son-of-a—" I spit out, turning my eyes to shoot daggers at the culprit.

And there's Ethan, sitting in the front seat with an annoyingly huge grin, pointing to the phone he's holding up. If looks could kill, I'd have burned a hole right through him.

"That little …" Tenley trails off once she realizes he's filming us.

I can't help but laugh at this point. "You know we're just his puppets, right? He's been orchestrating this for months."

She throws her head back and groans, so I take advantage by pulling her in and planting a few kisses down her neck before she has the chance to straighten up.

"JD." She giggles. "He's still recording us!"

"Hey, you started it," I murmur against her skin. But, sure enough, I look up from my spot beneath her right ear to see the kid wagging his eyebrows suggestively in our direction. I growl and wrap her tightly in my arms before picking her up, making her squeal as I lift her feet just high enough to spin us around. Then I use my body to block Ethan's view of the rest of our make out session.

She taps me on the chest after a while. "Come on. Don't you think we ought to go?"

"No, never," I reply, pressing my hungry mouth back to hers. This time, I let my hand skate down her fitted skirt and give her a light squeeze. A soft moan escapes her throat, nearly costing me my last bit of self-control. I've waited so long for this to happen that I don't give a damn who's watching at this point. Hell, Ethan could post a video on every one of the Camellia High School social media accounts, and I'd still show up to practice later with the world's cheesiest smile.

She pulls away again, panting. I bite my lip in an attempt to restrain myself, because knowing that I'm the reason she's out of breath nearly does me in all over again.

"JD," she repeats, shaking her head and blinking as if she's lost. "We can't stay here forever."

I give her my best puppy-dog look. "I'm not leaving until you tell me this was more than just a reward for helping you today. I want a promise that I'll get to kiss you again."

She sighs, her eyes filled with amusement. "I promise, okay? I think ... I'm tired of pretending I don't like you. What are the chances you still want to go out with me?"

"Like, right now? Can we go somewhere else and make out some more?" I ask playfully.

"Maybe we could start with a celebratory lunch, just the three of us. That is, if you don't have to rush back to school today," she suggests, though she looks like she wants to say yes to my first offer.

"That would be great, especially now that I don't have to rely on Ethan for an invitation," I answer with a wink, making her laugh again. We walk over to her car, and I block her passage when I open the door so I can address Ethan first.

"Hey, kid."

"Hey, Coach Thirsty. I mean, *Uncle* Thirsty."

I clench my jaw as I try to decide whether I want to grab him by the collar and slug him in the nose or to laugh at him. "We're all going to lunch together, just down the road. Follow us in the car."

"Yes, sir," he agrees with a smug look.

I start to back out but lean in on second thought. "Send me that video. Then delete it," I order gruffly. "Got it?"

He glares at me as he climbs across the center console to the driver's seat. "Did you think I'd actually film *that*? Come on. It's disgusting. You're both so ... old."

"You really make me want to say bad words, you know that?"

"Wow, you're taking to parenting really well already, *N'oncle*."

I grind my teeth together and slam the door on his smiling face. "Come on, we're going in my truck."

Tenley's eyes widen as I grab her hand and drag her along. "Okay, then."

I walk around and open the passenger door for her first, and I feel her staring at me from her seat as soon as I climb in on the other side.

"JD," she begins as I crank the truck. "Don't take this the wrong way. But ..." She clears her throat. "Just humor me for a second?"

"You want me to put the Jonas Brothers on again?"

She chuckles. "No, but would you mind taking off that jacket?"

I cock an eyebrow at her but obey her request, tossing the jacket into the back seat. "Can I lose the tie, too?"

"Sure, whatever," she says, waving her hand. I discard the neck trap before I turn back to her expectantly. "Do you have any idea how much ..." Her chest heaves as she trails off. "Hell, could you please just kiss me again?"

I willingly oblige, leaning over the center console to meet her half-way, and that wave of heat begins burning up my insides the second I press my lips to hers. Her left hand crawls over my right bicep until she rakes her nails over the thin fabric of my dress shirt, and I understand what she was too embarrassed to admit a second ago. I smile against her lips and flex for her, and she whimpers into my mouth, clutching at my arm tightly.

So. Damn. Hot.

This time I have to pull away before I get myself into a bind.

"Tenley Robin, you're going to be the death of me," I whisper, resting my forehead against hers and grinning broadly.

Then the car behind us lays on the horn while a text simultaneously comes through my phone. "You have two new messages from Big E," announces my truck's audio system. "Would you like me to read them?"

"Yes," I answer as Tenley scoots back to her side of the truck, to my dismay. I sigh and drive away from the parking lot, eager for a distraction.

"Big E said, 'Wait, why are you taking your clothes off? Ew. Gross. I don't think I like this anymore,' and 'Can we go now? I'm really hungry. You can molest each other later.' Would you like to reply?"

I snort and Tenley shakes her head, her cheeks reddening. "Yes," I say. "Text Big E: But this was all your idea, remember?"

"Okay, message sent. Anything else?"

"Text Big E: Also, I am now going to be the king of *that's not what your mom said last night* jokes."

"Message sent."

Tenley looks over at me, attempting an angry glare but failing. "I can't even with the two of you."

I shrug innocently. "You don't get good at teaching high schoolers without fostering your inner fifteen-year-old boy."

"Hmm, that's funny," she remarks, her hand traveling back over to my right shoulder, then running down my arm slowly. "These feel more like grown-man arms."

I shake my head, growling as I try to focus on the road.

"Okay, I'm sorry, I'll stop," she concedes, grabbing my hand and lacing her fingers through mine instead. "But you've been teasing me with those guns for months."

I glare at her in disbelief. "Me ... teasing *you*? You've got to be kidding me, woman."

She laughs softly. "I'm sorry for turning you down before. It's not that I couldn't see how great you are. I've just been trying to keep one aspect of my life simple while everything else feels so complicated." She looks down, and I squeeze her hand gently. "And to be fair, I wasn't sure if you really liked me or were just a big flirt, at least in the beginning."

"The most nervous and awkward flirt in history, you mean?" I offer with a self-deprecating smile.

"Well, yes, but apparently I find 'dorky with big muscles' cute," she reassures me. "Thank you again for not giving up on me and for being here with me today. You know that things with Ethan still aren't completely settled, that we'll be grieving my dad any day now, and that I have a demanding career that sometimes pulls me out of bed in the middle of the night. And I just want to make sure that you're okay with all my baggage, because there's probably more to come."

I do my best to ignore the implications of her warning me about her bedtime habits as I bring her hand up and kiss the inside of her wrist. Her lips part as she releases a shuddery breath, and I make a mental note of her reaction.

"Tenley, you couldn't chase me away if you tried. I'm here for all of it. The good, the sad, the tough ... I want to be the friend you can count on *and* the man who makes you feel loved at the end of the day. I've just been waiting for you to want it, too."

I hope I'm not scaring her off with my mention of the L-word, but it's not like I'm proclaiming actual feelings—only goals, right?

"Okay," she says meekly, her eyes watering again.

"And we're going to get through this stuff with Ethan together. I promise."

She nods. "Do you think he'll really be okay with this?"

I consider it for a second before I answer, because I'm all too aware that the teenage brain is a complex and unpredictable minefield. "I do. But, as much as it pains me to suggest it, maybe we should keep things quiet for a while—you know, lie low in public, for Ethan's sake. I can't imagine that the rest of the team wouldn't give him a hard time."

"That's probably for the best," she agrees. "At least until football season is over and our custody arrangement is settled."

I can't help but smile when she implies that there will be an "us" in a month from now, since I'm still in disbelief that I've gone from nursing an unrequited crush to kissing Tenley in a parking lot within the last half-hour. "But after that, plan on embarrassing the hell out of him with our PDA."

She rolls her eyes and nudges me, but I see the corners of her mouth curling up.

I drive up to the restaurant and give the back of her hand another kiss, noticing the worry returning to her face. She's probably drifting back to the logistics of Ethan's situation again. "Are you okay? Maybe a little overwhelmed?" I ask.

"Maybe a little," she admits with a half-smile.

"Hey, you know how I feel about Ethan. We're on the same page. His needs will always be our priority, right? But we can do both. There can be an us-two *and* a we-three."

"Thank you," she says, her voice thick and tears threatening to spill over again. I figure she needs a second, so I take my time going around to open her door.

"Are you going to do this every time?" she asks. I offer my hand, and she takes it as she steps out.

"I might. As long as you let me."

Ethan meets us at the front door, handing Tenley the keys. "Finally. You'd think the adults who take you to court to stake their claim would want to feed you, but you two would just as soon get a room and leave me to starve."

I shove him back behind me, making him stumble and raise a few more complaints, but he catches up to us in time to pull out a chair for his aunt before I can. It's likely done out of habit, but the gesture isn't lost on me.

The waitress comes over, and I clear my throat after we're left with our menus. "So, this"—I draw an imaginary line between Tenley and me—"is finally happening. But we're not going to talk about it at school for now, right, E?"

He smirks at her. She says nothing when their eyes meet, but she does blush a little. "Cool," he replies after a second. "And don't worry, I'm not going to bring it up. Although the entire football team has been rooting for you to get together all this time."

Tenley cringes. "What do you mean? How do they even know who I am?"

We both shrug guiltily. "They may have caught me waiting for you to show up at the end of practice or staring a little too hard, just once or twice," I admit.

She glances at Ethan for backup, her jaw slack.

"Oh, come on. The dude's been a total simp since the day you got here. It's pathetic how hard he's been Stanning you," he clarifies dryly. Thankfully, it looks like Tenley needs a second to decode what he's saying.

"You talk a lot of mess for someone who has laps to run at practice this afternoon, kid," I warn him. He sighs and signals that his lips are locked, then picks up his phone to occupy himself.

By the time the waitress returns, I hear my phone chime and fetch it from my pocket. My eyes dart to Ethan when I realize the message is from him. Then they narrow at the screen once I see the video he's sent me—the one he claimed he hadn't recorded. I hit play, lowering the volume and tilting the screen away from Tenley. My stomach flips as I watch our lips meet before she pulls me in by my tie.

Wow. That's ... a lot of tongue for the parking lot of a government building. And my hands probably shouldn't be on her—

I cough awkwardly, hoping my face isn't as flushed as it feels, and stop the video before texting Ethan.

JD

I thought you said you weren't filming us, you little creep.

BIG E

gif of Maui singing "You're Welcome"

i figured you'd want evidence of your first kiss for coach blake

or for yourself 😉

JD

Okay, it is pretty hot … even though it wasn't our first kiss. 😏

I have more swag than you give me credit for, just sayin'.

But thanks, wingman. 🏈

BIG E

ignoring the tmi part of all that

so when can i start calling you uncle jd in public?

or how about uncle coach?

n'oncle thirsty?

just lmk your preference

"How long are you going to continue texting one another while we're all sitting at the same table?" Tenley finally asks while Ethan and I are grinning at our screens like idiots. I set my phone down sheepishly. "If either of you have something to say that involves me, I think I deserve to hear it," she adds.

"You don't want that, babe, trust me," I say, attempting to placate her. I hear my phone buzz and glance down instinctively.

BIG E

ew you're already calling her babe? 🙄

"You know you're just setting yourself up right now, don't you?" I reply out loud.

"Yeah?" he retorts, his face mocking before he picks up his drink.

I lean back, stretching my arm over the back of Tenley's seat. "Oh, yeah. Just wait. I'll have her calling me all kinds of names later."

"JD!" she shrieks, slapping me on the chest, and Ethan chokes mid-sip of his soda.

I calmly lift my shoulder in a shrug. "I meant pet names. You know, 'honey,' 'sweetie,' 'baby.' Get your mind out of the gutter, woman. I'd never imply something like that in front of the kid."

Then I wink at Ethan and try not to laugh while he glares as menacingly as possible.

CHAPTER 21
TENLEY

ETHAN AND I CLOSE THE DOORS TO MY CAR AT THE SAME time and turn to face one another.

"Well, this has been an eventful day," he remarks.

"No kidding." I reach over and grab his hand, giving it a squeeze. "I guess you're officially stuck with me now, for better or worse."

"Are you sure it isn't the other way around?" he asks with a smirk.

"Definitely not."

"So?" he begins.

"I guess this conversation is inevitable."

"Was it the suit?" he asks, grinning.

I roll my eyes and playfully smack him in the chest. "I'd like to think it was the flattering speech about my character, but the suit didn't hurt," I concede.

He chuckles. "We all knew it was only a matter of time. Mawmaw, Pop, and I had our own bets going."

I cringe. "I forgot about having to admit they were right."

"Oh, I already texted them. I don't know if Mawmaw's more excited to hear that you got custody of me or that you and Coach were making out in the back of the parking lot."

My eyes widen. "Ethan, please tell me you haven't been sending out that video."

"What video?" I glare at him. "Okay, I only sent it to JD."

"I don't know if I believe you."

"You probably shouldn't," he affirms.

I snort. "Are you sure you're okay with this, though? You know I never intended on seeing anyone out here."

"I'm more than okay with it. JD is probably the only guy I'd trust with you, to be honest. But I don't want you to feel like you have to start dating him for me."

I pause for a moment, impressed with his maturity. "Although I'd do just about anything to make you happy, I don't think I'd force or fake a relationship with someone. And I could never do that to JD."

"Good, because I don't want either of you to get hurt," he says quietly.

"And we don't want *you* to get hurt." I sigh. "The truth is ... I've been afraid. I thought I was protecting all three of us by ignoring my feelings for JD. As it is, I have no idea what I'm doing as a parent, and now I'll have to be careful not to jeopardize your relationship with him. The last thing I want is to make your life any more complicated than it needs to be."

He shrugs. "My life has always been complicated, Aunt Ten, and none of that is your fault. I'm really grateful you're willing to be my guardian, but you still need to have a life of your own. I'd rather see you take some risks and be happy than miss out because you're being overprotective of me. I can handle more than you think."

I smile. "You never cease to amaze me."

"Maybe you're just easily impressed. I mean, look at your dorky boyfriend," he replies, and I nudge him again.

I purposefully ignore his assumption since I don't have the emotional capacity to add another official title today. "Temporary custodian" and "more than friends" are enough for now.

"Did you even know he was coming today?" I ask, redirecting the conversation.

"Not exactly," Ethan says hesitantly. "Yesterday morning he made a joke about following me into court to make sure the judge knew the homecoming incident wasn't your fault, but I didn't think he was serious."

It takes me a second to realize that Blake must have encouraged JD to show up this morning. While I'd doubted JD's claims about his brother trying to push us together before, it makes more sense in hindsight.

"And then he made me promise never to scare you like that again or I'd have to get someone to pour my next drink down a feeding tube, right before we caught an early Mass," Ethan says, sighing.

I chuckle lightly to downplay how much I'm feeling JD's tough-dad vibe. "I suppose you learned your lesson, then?"

"Yes, ma'am."

"Have you spoken to Caidence?"

He nods. "She said we were cool, but I can tell she's still really upset with me." I notice a blush creeping up his face as he continues. "Coach also had me drive to her house and apologize to her in person, in front of her parents."

I smile to myself because JD *is* pretty freaking amazing. Maybe I'm not exactly prepared or even built for parenting a teenager, but at least I'm lucky enough to have good help.

"You do realize he's only being this tough because he cares so much about you, right?"

"Yeah, I know," he returns shyly.

We get home to find my parents waiting to congratulate us on the results of the hearing before launching into their relentless teasing. And it's only going to get worse, since my mom is insisting on having JD over for dinner.

"You know how much I love saying 'I told you so,' " she announces with a satisfied smile.

I sigh, taking my lick. "Yeah, yeah. You all called it."

"This could have gone a lot easier if you hadn't been so stubborn," my dad explains, grinning widely. "And you can't blame me for being excited about your draft pick, especially since I was afraid I'd miss out on actually getting to see the two of you together."

"Daddy, could you please stop being so morbid?" I grumble, secretly pleased with his approval.

"Well, then, you should probably move this along, because I'm planning to remind you every day from here on out that I want another grandkid before I kick the bucket," he replies dryly, eliciting a gasp from me, a nudge from my mom, and a laugh from Ethan.

My cheeks are on fire, and I cover my face with my hands. "I knew I should have gotten my own place."

"I bet JD has plenty of room," my dad offers. "He looks like a king-sized bed kind of guy."

"Dad!" I squeal, my eyes widening.

He shrugs while the others laugh. "What? Don't you have a degree proving you know how all that stuff works, anyway?"

"Well, yeah, but you could at least let us go on a few dates first."

"Last I heard, you didn't have time for dating," he retorts with a smirk.

I shake my head and mumble a "*pas bon*" at him, then my phone chimes. I'm needed at the clinic while Dr. Simms goes in for a C-section, so I change into my scrubs before driving to work and slipping in through the back, hoping to get done as quickly as possible.

Okay, so I'm admittedly eager to see JD again. Looking forward to going home is new for me, but I'm starting to like the idea of having a life outside of work, especially if it means spending more time with him.

And if getting to know JD better means that we happen to engage in the occasional make out session, so be it, right?

Another text alert brings me back from daydreaming about kissing JD while he flexes his arm muscles for me. It's Loren, checking to see how the hearing went. We've been talking regularly since we met for coffee a couple of weeks ago, when she graciously accepted my long-overdue apology for mishandling things when we were kids. But I'd held off on giving her an update after JD finally made his move the other night—I guess because I was afraid I'd accidentally fess up to something I wasn't ready to admit.

I explain everything that happened with Ethan, and she asks how things are going with JD. I bite my lip as I brief her on the latest developments. It only takes a second for her to reply with a list of questions. The next thing I know, I'm hiding in a corner and twirling my hair around my finger as I gush about JD and his amazing kissing skills.

One of the medical assistants calls for me, so I reluctantly put my phone away and try to school my expression before emerging from my hiding spot. I'm just glad it isn't Mackenzie handing me a chart this time, because she'd undoubtedly read me all too well. I glance through the file as I slip into the first exam room, pleased to find one of my favorite patients awaiting me.

"Good afternoon, Mrs. Thibodeaux. How are you today?"

"Besides feeling like a whale already, I'm great, Nurse Tenley," she answers, groaning as she shifts on the exam table. "But I'd be better if you'd just call me Sybil."

I laugh politely and pretend to study her chart in an attempt to hide my giddiness.

"You seem quite chipper this afternoon."

"Do I?" My voice sounds abnormally high.

She smirks. "You certainly do."

I shrug noncommittally as I take a seat. "Well, I sort of adopted my nephew today, so there's that."

"Did you really? Wow, congratulations," she says.

"Thanks."

"And has Mr. Right come along to sweep you off your feet yet?"

I gulp. "Ah, no. Sorry to disappoint you, but both of my feet are still ..." I glance down and realize that I'm sitting with my left ankle tucked under my butt.

"Firmly planted on the ground, right?" she finishes for me, one of her eyebrows raised in a challenge.

"All right. There's ... a candidate," I concede after a second, standing to examine her. "And I imagine he's very capable of a grand sweeping, but I'm holding steady as of now."

"Are you?" she returns, leaning back on the exam table.

"Barely," I say with a sigh.

"So," she begins again as I lift her shirt and place my hands on her belly. "I'm not just here to tease you while you check on the baby. I'm also looking for a favor."

"Oh?"

"I've been teaching natural family planning classes to engaged couples in our church parish for the past few years, but I'm going to need a break after this. I was hoping you'd be willing to offer your services in my place for a while."

"Oh," I repeat. "I've never really studied NFP, only fertility aware-ness. I don't really know the religious aspect as well as the biological."

"Tenley, you're a smart woman. I think it'll click pretty easily for you," she assures me. "Father Conrad's a great resource, and I can send you all the information you need to get certified, if you're interested."

I consider her proposal as I run the Doppler over her stomach. We're both quiet as the sound of her baby's steady heartbeat fills the room. "Sounds good," I say after a minute.

"So you'll teach the classes?" she asks cheerfully.

"I meant, your baby sounds good," I correct her with a mirthful smile. "I'll think about the NFP stuff."

"Great," she confirms. "And you never know, maybe you'll find the information useful for yourself ... if your feet ever do leave the ground."

CHAPTER 22
JD

"Hot damn, Coach Thirsty. That's a lot of tongue," my brother congratulates me over the phone. "So, what happens now?"

It only took a few seconds for Blake to call me after I texted him that video, and now I'm sitting inside my truck, listening to his live reaction. But the smug look I've been wearing for the past couple of hours softens once I realize I've made a mistake by sharing the video without any regard for Tenley's feelings. And it's not going to get any better now that Blake is transitioning to his usual line of questioning regarding my love life.

"We're, um, dating, I guess. And we're kind of keeping it quiet, at least during football season. We don't want anyone giving Ethan a hard time."

"And what's included in 'dating'?"

"I don't know, man. We barely got the chance to discuss the general idea of becoming an *us*, and it didn't seem like the right time to put any more pressure on her," I say in my defense.

"Well, seeing as though you and Tenley look like you're about to swallow each other whole, I imagine you'll want to figure that out pretty soon."

I cringe, because I hate admitting when Blake is right. I've been so intent on getting Tenley to like me that I'm not even sure what to do with her now. But I probably *should* initiate a conversation to define the specifics of whatever this is as soon as possible, because there's already a desperate need for physical boundaries.

Like, *really* desperate

I'm also starting to second guess my suggestion to hide our relationship status. I don't want Tenley to think I'm anything less than thrilled about us, but people in a town this small have nothing better to do than gossip. And I can't risk letting anyone make Ethan feel bad, not with everything else he's got to deal with.

"Oh, shit, are you …" Blake continues, his voice tinged with amusement. "You're really going for it, kid."

My phone buzzes as he texts me a zoomed-in screenshot. I grunt, disappointed in myself and feeling even more guilty about sharing the video in the first place, even if I'm only bragging in front of my brother.

"It's a little weird that you're enjoying this as much as I was," I say dryly.

"I guess I'm just proud of my baby bro, for once," he mocks me. "I mean, I figured Tenley really was into you, but I'm still pleasantly surprised she's letting you grope her behind the courthouse. And to be honest, I was starting to worry you didn't have it in you."

"All right, that's enough," I growl. I may have let my enthusiasm get the best of me for a minute, but I already sense the need to shield Tenley from Blake's teasing.

"I'm just saying, man—this looks pretty hot for casual dating. We both know sex means something to you, so you'd better make sure you and Tenley are on the same wavelength."

"Yeah, I know," I say on an exhale. He's right. But I don't bother explaining that casual dating isn't a possibility because of Ethan, or that I'd rather dive straight into the deep end, anyway, since I've felt such a strong attachment to both Tenley and Ethan for a while.

Besides, unlike my older brother, I don't just sleep with every woman I date. It hasn't been easy balancing my reputation as a former D-I college football player with my personal values and my Catholic faith, especially my belief that physical intimacy should be secondary to an emotional connection. Still, despite being unable to resist a good "that's what she said" joke and inevitably making a few poor decisions over the years, I've always tried to prioritize morality over getting laid or looking cool.

Which means I've been celibate for a while—a *long* while—so I shouldn't have any trouble continuing to exercise the same degree of patience until Tenley and I are both ready.

"Of course, I'm not just going to jump into bed with her. I need to make sure she knows how much I admire and respect her before we get to the physical stuff, because it *should* mean something ... to both of us. And even though my feelings for Tenley are already pretty intense, I'd rather set a slower pace for now if it makes our relationship stronger in the long run," I declare.

He laughs louder this time. "Really, bruh? You're gonna take it slow after all this?"

Dammit. He's right again. I swallow hard as I acknowledge the fact that I've never wanted another woman as much as I want Tenley. It's as if every cell in my body craves a connection to hers, and if she does give me the green light any time soon, I don't know that I'll be able to resist acting on that attraction.

I clear my throat before I answer him. "I should. I mean, we should—we will."

He snorts. "Yeah. Let me know how that works out for you."

"Do me a favor and make sure I don't get too dehydrated," I tell him, prompting one more laugh before we hang up the phone.

I finally make my way into school, stopping by the teachers' lounge first. A text comes through from Ethan, and I smile to myself as I accept his dinner invitation. I know I'll be walking headfirst into the butt of every joke at the Robin house tonight, but I can't bring myself to care. And besides being overeager for any opportunity to see Tenley and hang out with their family, I'd never turn down a bowl of Mrs. T's gumbo.

"What's with the cheese, Coach?" Loren asks and gestures to my smile when she walks into the lounge.

"Who, me?"

"No, the other six-and-a-half-foot tall dork grinning at the vending machine," she replies dryly.

I shrug as I retrieve a drink. "I'm just ... having a good day. And I'm only six-four, for the record."

She narrows her eyes, ignoring the height comment. Since Loren comes in at just over five feet, it's probably all the same to her. "But what has made this day so great among others?"

I bite the inside of my cheek and fight the urge to gush about Tenley again. But I've learned my lesson after my conversation with Blake. "Can't a guy just have a good day?"

"Not one who works with teenagers in the middle of 'too hot for a hoodie but I'm wearing one anyway' season, and not one with a serious unrequited cru—wait a minute!" Loren slams her tiny hand down on the table, and my eyebrows shoot up.

"Hmm?"

She circles me, pretending to scan for—I don't know—changes? She crunches on a chip as she leans closer and studies my face. "Did you ... shave?"

"Uh, yeah. I had to go to court to say some stuff for Ethan today."

"For Ethan, huh?"

"Yep," I fib, popping the *P* sound at the end.

"Anything interesting happen while you were there?" I shake my head, but I can sense my ears turning red. "Aha!" she yells, pointing a chip at me.

I gulp. "What?"

She glances around the room again to make sure we're alone. "You finally kissed Tenley, didn't you?" she accuses in a loud whisper.

My jaw drops. "How can you tell?"

"It's written all over your face," she replies, shaking her head. I press my lips together in an effort not to smile again, but she breaks character and starts giggling uncontrollably.

"I'm just messing with you. Your girlfriend already fessed up," she admits, to my surprise. Then she reaches out to pat my arm softly. "I really am happy for both of you. And don't forget, you promised I could be a bridesmaid."

"A deal's a deal," I grin.

I don't know if Tenley would even consent to being called my girlfriend, much less approve of the marriage jokes, but that doesn't stop me from strutting all the way to the football field.

Practice runs late because of the extra reps we need to prepare for the playoffs, giving Blake and Ethan more time to get in a few good roasts, but I'm invincible today. They could have told me my favorite TV series was cancelled or that I had to clean the boys' locker room myself this weekend, and I'd still be sporting my corny Tenley-likes-me smile.

I follow Ethan home after practice, opting to forego the shower since it's almost dinnertime, but I notice Tenley's car is missing from the driveway when I pull up behind him. He's already laughing as he steps out of his truck. "Looks like you're getting the official welcome today, Coach," he says, nodding his head toward the front porch, where his grandfather is sitting patiently in a wheelchair with his oxygen tank beside him.

"I guess I should've expected this." While I'm confident Tenley's dad approves of us dating, she *is* his only living daughter. At least he doesn't have a gun in his lap, though I imagine he would if he were in better health.

"Hey, Pop," Ethan says once he passes by, slapping a gentle hand against Mr. Jude's.

"Ethan, why don't you go on inside so JD and I can have a little talk?"

Ethan turns and mouths, "Good luck," before passing through the front door.

"Good afternoon, Mr. Jude," I greet Tenley's dad as I climb the steps, figuring it's best to humor him. Even though his physical and mental strength are on a sharp decline, I still have a lot of respect for him.

"Afternoon, JD. Have a seat, will you?"

"Thank you, sir," I reply, stopping to shake his hand before I sit across from him on the porch swing.

"I hear congratulations are in order," he begins, eliciting a smile from me.

"And I hear I owe you my gratitude for putting in a good word."

He tries to laugh, but it triggers a coughing fit, and my heart aches as I wait patiently for him to catch his breath again.

"I figured it was time I made sure you and I are on the same page, you know, with your intentions," he says after he settles down and adjusts his oxygen supply.

"Yes, sir, I can respect that. Although I'm a little surprised to see that none of your guns needed cleaning this afternoon."

He shakes his head, amused by my reply. "You can't keep making me laugh if you want me to live past the end of this conversation, son."

I grin back at him. "Does that mean we can skip the part where I get grilled?"

"Actually, JD, I want to tell you how much I appreciate everything you've done for Ethan. I hope he'll still be able to depend on you once I'm gone."

I furrow my brow and swallow hard. This is unexpected, and I'm going to have to work to keep my composure. I blink away the moisture pooling in my eyes as I nod. "I'd do anything for Ethan, and I'll make sure he knows that," I answer after I'm sure my voice will hold up.

"I know you will. And I hope you and Tenley will stay together for the right reasons in the long run—for love, and not just because you think you owe it to Ethan to stick around."

I shake my head quickly after he catches me off guard again. "As much as I care about him, sir, I could never do that to Tenley. I promise, my feelings for her are very real."

He nods. "And you're sure you'll be able to hold your own? She can be ... *tête dure*."

"Yeah, it hasn't been easy getting her to admit she likes me," I say with a soft laugh. "But I'm pretty stubborn, too."

"Good, since I assume the only reason you'd stick it out this long is because you intend to marry my daughter one day. I'm sorry for bringing up the big stuff now, but I can't exactly afford to procrastinate."

I keep my expression serious despite enjoying his humor. "I think you know I'd like to have a family of my own, and that I wouldn't have pursued Tenley if I couldn't see that possibility with her," I reassure him. "Or that I didn't feel like this is the path God intended for the three of us. And although I'm not sure how long it'll take to get there, I definitely want marriage ... eventually, if she'll have me."

"Then there's one more thing I'll ask of you," he says. "Promise me that if it works out between you and Tenley, you'll convince her to at least try for a baby. She's always wanted to be a mother, but after everything that happened with her sister, I think she's talked herself out of having kids of her own."

I gulp, my eyes feeling misty again. "Nothing would make me happier."

"I'm glad to hear it. Thank you, JD. Take care of them for me." He holds out a hand, and I clasp it.

"Thank you for trusting me with your family. And don't forget about me down here. I'm probably going to need your intercession later."

"You'll have to make sure I get enough prayers to make it there first." He chuckles again, just as Tenley's car pulls into the driveway. "She had a few patients to see this afternoon," he explains once the coughing subsides.

I nod knowingly as I lean back on the swing and watch her walk over to us with a wary smile.

"What's this about?" she asks, leaning down to kiss her dad's cheek before sitting beside me on the swing.

I reach over and drape my arm behind her, intending to pull her closer. But she surprises me by drawing her legs up and scooting in so that our sides are touching. I inhale deeply, willing my heart to stop beating like it's going to explode.

"Oh, JD and I were just talking about his long-term game plan."

"Mm-hmm," she responds, eyeing me as if she doesn't believe him.

I wink. "Next year will probably have to be a rebuilding year, but I think we'll manage."

CHAPTER 23
JD

"I SEE YOU CAME WITH A GAME PLAN, COACH." MRS. T smirks at me when I hand her a small bouquet of flowers and lets me into the house.

"I need all the help I can get."

She chuckles and leans in for one of her signature cheek kisses. "Good luck. She's in her room, probably still fussing over what to wear."

I smile and think back to one of our numerous text exchanges earlier this week, when I asked Tenley out on an official date and she *finally* accepted. Then she threatened to take back her "yes" once I told her our destination would be a surprise.

"You'd better go reassure her that she's dressed for the right occasion, or you might never leave," she says, gesturing toward the door I've always presumed led to Tenley's bedroom. "Ethan's out with Caidence, and Jude's asleep, so don't worry about having to suck up to either of them tonight."

I laugh before knocking. "Hey, it's me. Your mom said you—"

The door swings open, and Tenley stands before me in her Saints pajamas, one hand resting on her hip. "How the heck am I supposed to know what to wear if you won't even tell me where we're going?"

I blink at her a few times, trying to force my brain to catch up. "Uh, these are for you." I hold out another slightly bigger bouquet.

"Thanks," she mutters, hesitating for a second before taking the bundle and setting it down on her nightstand. "Do you really show up to all of your dates with flowers?"

"You're welcome. And to answer your questions—wear whatever you want, but my vote is your Aunt Tenley shirt, and no, at least not since I brought a corsage to my senior prom date."

She rolls her eyes and turns to her closet without another word, so I step inside. There's a growing mountain of clothes on her bed, and suddenly, the fact that she's worried about picking the right outfit is making me nervous all over again.

"What kind of activities are there on our itinerary?"

My eyebrows shoot up. There are plenty of activities I want to do with Tenley, including the kind that don't require her to be dressed. But that's not what she meant. I scold myself and shove those thoughts to the back.

"Just dinner for tonight. I suspect we're both too competitive to risk the batting cages or mini golf before the third date."

"Hmm," is all she says. Then she turns and glares at me, her eyes roaming over my body in a way that makes me want to suggest ditching the whole idea of going out and wearing clothes in lieu of finding something else better to do.

In fact, we wouldn't even have to leave this roo—

"I'm guessing we aren't just hitting up a Walk-On's, either, or you'd be wearing a polo instead of that dress shirt."

Oh, right. She's checking out my outfit and not necessarily me. I sniff, surprised and even slightly offended by her sarcastic tone. I guess it's a good thing I planned to take her somewhere nicer than a sports bar.

"Yep."

She frowns and returns to her task, and I sigh, feeling guilty about my short response when she's obviously trying to make an effort. I have really got to get a handle on my spicy thoughts, too.

Tenley continues flipping through the hangers in her closet, so I take a second to inventory the room. It's mostly neat besides the piles of the clothes and shoes, and not quite as girly as I imagined. I walk around, spotting some fan gear and trying not to let my mind drift at the sight of Tenley's bed again.

After a while, my feet involuntarily lead me over to her, and I finally satisfy that urge to wrap my arms around her from behind. I gently press my lips to the back of her neck, relishing this moment after dreaming about it for the past couple of months. Her chest expands as she inhales shakily.

"Tenley, it doesn't matter what you wear," I murmur against her skin. "I'm just looking forward to staring at you all night." Then I brush a couple more kisses over the spot beneath her left ear before loosening my grip.

She clears her throat as I back away, and I can't tell whether my embrace has bothered her in a good or a bad way. "If you, um, don't mind giving me some privacy, I promise I'll be out in a minute."

"Yeah, sure," I reply, slightly discouraged by her lack of enthusiasm. I guess after finally hearing her admit that she likes me, too, I expected at least a little more excitement from her tonight. But she doesn't even bother turning around as I walk out and shut the door behind me.

Back in the living room, Mr. Jude is awake and watching college football. If Tenley won't acknowledge me, maybe he will.

We're just getting into the Bama and Ole Miss game when she finally emerges, her flowers in hand. "I'm just going to put these in a vase so we can go," she announces.

"Cool," I reply, barely glancing away from the TV.

I feel her foot nudging mine a minute later. "Are you sure you don't want to stay here instead?" she asks with her hands on her hips.

"Uh, one second, babe. I just need to see this next play," I say distractedly. She hasn't exactly been responding well to me so far, so maybe I'll test Blake's theory and play hard to get, just a little.

She grumbles something under her breath, and I suppress a smile. Though I'd never willingly admit it to him, my brother has been right about at least one thing: Tenley seems much more interested when I give her a reason to think I'm not. I hear her dad laughing at us when I reach out and yank her arm until she plops down beside me on the couch. Alabama scores on the next play, and I slap my hands down onto my lap.

"All right, ready?" I finally turn to face her, immediately blowing my cover because she looks so beautiful. She rolls her eyes at my goofy expression and places her hand in mine when I stand and offer to pull her upright.

"How tall are you, anyway, JD?" Mr. Jude asks as Tenley smooths out the skirt of the relatively modest dress she's changed into. But I'm too busy appreciating the way it outlines her curves and hangs so perfectly over her hips to answer him. And now all I can think about is how desperately I want to put my hands on the narrow part of her waist and pull her closer.

I clear my throat once I realize I'm guilty of staring too hard again. "Sir?"

"I bet you've got to sleep in a king-sized bed, don't you?"

Tenley glares at him, oblivious to the way I'm still gaping at her. "Daddy, please don't start."

I hesitate, glancing back and forth between the two of them, though Mr. Jude continues watching me expectantly. "California king," I finally reply. "I need the extra legroom."

He grins at Tenley, who stands with her arms crossed, looking irresistibly *fâché*. Her expression softens when her eyes meet mine, and I can tell I've accidentally made things worse for her as her cheeks darken.

"There's still plenty of space beside me, though," I add with a wink, hoping to lighten the mood. She shakes her head and tries not to smile, and Mr. Jude laughs so hard that Mrs. Therese rushes in to check on him.

"Right," Tenley returns after a while. "Good to know."

"Are you teasing them again?" Tenley's mom clicks her tongue as she adjusts her husband's cannula.

"*Mais*, I'm just trying to secure my daughter's ticket to the genetic lottery while I still can," he admits after catching his breath.

"Now, Jude," Mrs. T fusses. "I'm sure you'd love all your grand-kids to be ballplayers, but this ain't a stud service."

I cringe and scratch the back of my head, somewhat flattered and fairly embarrassed, though I imagine Tenley is ready to hide away forever. "Look, I make no guarantees, but I do come with a 'third' at the end of my name. That ought to signify something, right?"

Tenley groans when her parents chuckle, but she glances at me with a hint of appreciation in her eyes. She mouths, "I'm sorry," and I smile as I gesture to the door.

"We should probably head out if we want to make our reservation," I declare.

"Well, you heard him. Good night," Tenley says, grabbing my hand and hauling me forward. I think I hear her dad cracking another joke about not waiting up for us and her mom scolding him and calling him an "old *couillon*" as we make our escape.

I stop abruptly on the front porch as the door slams behind us, surprising Tenley by turning her around and grasping her by the hips. Her eyes are wide when I lean in for a kiss, which, unsurprisingly, gets a little hotter than I intend.

"Um, okay, what was that for?" she asks once I back away, looking just flustered enough to imply that she enjoyed it.

"For our fan base," I reply, waving at the security camera over her shoulder. It's a lie, of course, but she buys it. She snorts and shoves me playfully, and I clasp her hand as we walk to my truck before helping her into the passenger seat.

"When will I know where we're going?" she asks once I pull out of the driveway.

"When we get there." I glance over to find her looking annoyed, which makes me laugh. "You don't like surprises, do you?"

"Nope."

"Fine. I made a reservation at this place called Gusto in Lafayette. It's a paleo restaurant where they curate a different menu each night with a bunch of tiny courses and specialty paired wines. Ethan mentioned you like to eat healthy. And Blake recommended it."

"Oh. Okay. That sounds ... nice." But it comes across as though she means to say "disappointing" instead.

I clear my throat as the silence grows. "Tenley, is everything all right?"

"Of course. Why?"

"Well, to be honest, it doesn't really feel like you're into this."

She turns and stares out the window. "I'm sorry. I didn't mean to give you that impression."

"Are you having second thoughts?"

Then I start to panic. What if she's only doing this because I made her feel guilty with my stupid quid pro quo jokes?

"You know I was kidding about trading dates for helping with Ethan, right? You're not obligated to go out with me."

"I wouldn't be here if I didn't want to, JD. I'm not *that* nice." She tucks her hair behind her ears before she turns back to me, looking slightly bashful. "I guess I'm feeling a little anxious about our first real date." My breath catches in my throat as she continues. "More like ridiculously nervous, actually."

She's nervous? Seriously? I can't help but smile.

"Yeah, same," I tell her. "But you don't need to worry about impressing me. I'm already pretty convinced."

She ignores my flirty response. "It's just ... There's something I need to get off my chest. Keep in mind my line of work, all right?"

"Okay," I reply cautiously, hoping I'm not looking at her stupidly after she references her chest.

"I don't really trust any kind of artificial or hormonal birth control."

"Okay," I repeat, my eyes widening.

"Instead, I use a fertility awareness method to track my cycles very carefully. I monitor all these different symptoms and plot them in a chart, and it helps me to figure out what's going on. You know, whether I'm fertile or not, and when to expect my period. It's basically the biological element of what married women do for natural family planning."

I nod calmly, even though I'm dying on the inside because *Tenley is talking about—*

"And, um, you wanted me to know about this because ..." I have to cut off my inner dialogue before I get myself into trouble.

"Well, I thought about it ..."

She's been thinking about it?

"And it only seems fair for me to tell you up front that I don't really trust contraception, which also means I take the physical intimacy part of dating very seriously ... and slowly."

"Oh," I respond, swallowing hard. "Because you don't want to get pregnant?"

She sighs, probably in disbelief at my lack of maturity. "Yes, that's one of the reasons."

"And you're worrying about me stealing home on the first date?" I ask with a smirk, finally garnering some confidence.

Her face flushes. "Of course not. And this whole conversation wasn't necessary, because you probably weren't even thinking about that yet." Then she turns back to the window and cringes while she quietly scolds herself.

"Tenley, with all due respect, I don't know if I've ever stopped thinking about *that*—with you—for the past few months," I correct her. "Especially since the bra incident. I'm just trying not to sound like a total creep."

She faces me again and smiles, looking more timid than embarrassed this time. "So, I wasn't being too presumptuous by initiating this talk now?"

"Definitely not," I answer, grinning. "I'm actually relieved to hear you bring it up. And while I am completely on board with taking it slow, you should never doubt my attraction to you. So it's probably best if you set the pace, you know. Don't be afraid to tell me exactly what you want and when you want it to happen."

"Well, this'll be a disaster," I think I hear her mutter under her breath.

"What?"

She shakes her head quickly. "Nothing. I'll explain the rest later.

I'm so used to talking about women's health and bodily functions all day that I forget it makes most people feel uncomfortable."

"I've studied my fair share of anatomy and physiology in college. That stuff doesn't bother me," I reassure her. "And I actually like that you're so knowledgeable. It's one of the first things I noticed about you."

"I don't know, you seemed pretty *honte* when we were perusing the feminine-hygiene department together a while back," she replies with a smirk, downplaying my compliments again.

I scrunch up my nose. "Yeah, that had a lot more to do with the tight leggings you were wearing that day and a lot less with the tampon aisle," I admit. She giggles, making my insides feel all warm and gooey, and I continue. "Seriously, though, I was crushing so hard by then that I was willing to do anything to spend time with you. In fact, I literally used a charity case to my advantage."

I look over, expecting her to laugh again, but she's blushing instead. "Because of the leggings?" she asks shyly.

"Because of the lab coat ... and the Aunt Tenley shirt, and the Saints pajamas." Her expression falls, so I hurry to explain. "It all made me desperate to find out more and to confirm everything I'd started to suspect about you, that you're interesting and smart, but also caring and devoted to your family ... and your football team."

"So you *do* like me for more than my bra size, then?" she poses, her lip twitching when she tries to hide her amusement.

"Of course," I confirm, resting my hand palm-up between us. She hesitates for a second before dropping her hand in mine. "There's also your cooking."

She laughs. "Right."

"Seriously, Ten, I'm sorry if I ever made it seem as if I only appreciate the way you look. The more I get to know you, the more I like you. The fact that you're this hot is just a bonus."

"And I'm sorry about reacting defensively to your compliments. It's just a reflex, I guess, but you haven't made me feel objectified or anything, only ... admired." She pauses and sighs. "I wasn't kidding before when I said I was really bad at this."

I can't help but laugh at the notion that she's the awkward one here. "I'm pretty sure I've set a record with the number of times I've made myself look and sound stupid in front of you."

"That's probably my fault. I'm kind of a jerk," she explains. "I don't even do well with making friends because I usually end up pushing people away. I'm too serious and too blunt. And it obviously takes me a while to open up."

I shake my head as I keep my eyes on the road. "Nah, I'm going to have to disagree with that. I know exactly what it is about you that makes me nervous. I think you have a great sense of humor, and I also like that you don't fake it or sugarcoat what you're thinking most of the time." She squeezes my hand a little tighter. "With the exception of the past few months while you were pretending you didn't like it when I flirted with you or that you weren't watching every time I flexed my arms just for you," I add after a while, making her smile.

"While we're being honest, I hope you don't think you need to take me to a fancy restaurant or go out of your way to impress me," Tenley says. "I'm already pretty convinced, too."

I glance at her before I answer, and she's staring as if she's reading my expression. "Truth be told, having burgers and beer in front of a wall of TVs playing live sports does sound more enticing than sipping wine and pretending to enjoy a tiny plate full of weird garnishes," I admit. "I like the idea of picking up a pizza and bringing you back to my place to watch football and chill even better. And by *chill*, I mean make out. But I wanted to take you somewhere special, something closer to what you're used to, and I'm down for anything so long as I'm with you."

She sighs, her cheeks turning pink. "That actually sounds kind of perfect to me."

"Which part?" I ask, raising an eyebrow.

"Cheat day with burgers and beer, watching football and hanging out ..."

I blow out a breath, realizing I'm dangerously close to blurting out some embarrassing declaration like "I love you" or "I want you to be the mother of my children." It takes me a second to get myself back in check.

"While I appreciate the thought you put into this, I don't need fancy and cultured," she repeats. "I like low-key and comfortable. And I like being with you."

I turn my eyes back to her when I reach the next red light. "Tenley, I know we might be slightly overdressed, but how do you feel about Walk-On's?"

She grins. "It's my favorite restaurant. How'd you guess?"

Tenley and I settle into an easy conversation for the rest of the drive.

"Can I ask what happened? With your football career, I mean," she ventures after a while, surprising me.

I purse my lips. "Well ..."

"It's okay if you don't want to talk about it," she adds when she senses my hesitation.

I smile and rub the back of her hand with my thumb, amused that she still can't tell I'm incapable of refusing her. "I don't mind. I'm just not sure where to pick up the story."

"You got hurt at LSU, right?"

"Yeah. I blew out my knee a couple of games before the end of my senior season, passed on physical therapy school when I got drafted late, and came back the next year on the practice squad after rehabbing the knee. Then I tore up my shoulder before the season even started, got cut, and decided against free agency. It was around the same time we lost my mom to early-onset Alzheimer's and my dad not long after to a heart attack, and I figured it wasn't wise to rack up any more concussions or overwork my body with those genetic predispositions. So, I came back to Camellia when I heard Coach Reed was retiring, and here we are."

"Wow," she says. "How did you stay so positive through all of that?"

I shrug. "Don't get me wrong, I have my bad days. But I'm not owed anything, and I try to see every opportunity as a gift. I can't be angry or disappointed about losing something that was never mine to begin with."

"Do you ever think about going back?"

"Not really. I loved playing football but didn't care for the lifestyle, and I missed living in Camellia. Lucky for me, I found a career that incorporates both."

"I know everyone is really grateful for your work with the kids and the community," she tells me.

"Eh, it's the least I can do for the people who supported me growing up, don't you think? Plus, it's not like I don't get paid," I whisper the last part conspiratorially, making her laugh.

"Do you plan to spend your whole coaching career at Camellia?" she ventures. "I can't imagine that some fancy private school or college won't try to scoop you up after a few winning seasons."

It feels like another test, but she deserves my honesty. "I don't know what the future holds," I begin as I pull into the parking lot. "But I'm not interested in coaching anywhere else right now. I'm very, *very* happy here." I meet her gaze as I say the last part, and she looks pleased.

Tenley lets me get all the doors for her as we make our way into the restaurant and excuses herself to visit the ladies' room after hearing there'll be a short wait for our table. I attempt to work through some of my nerves by playing an arcade game in the lobby while she's gone, and I'm still shooting free throws when she returns with her expression looking downcast again.

She smiles and shakes her head when I offer her the ball. "No, thanks. I'm terrible."

"Basketball's never been my sport, either," I say as I toss the ball away without looking, scrunching my nose in an apology when the jingling of the chain-link net contradicts me.

"Cool story, bro," she retorts, but her smile fades again.

What if she thinks I'm just an annoying show-off? Has she been trying to tell me that all this time?

She sighs wearily and shifts her weight to one side, and it's obvious something's still bothering her.

"Are you sure everything's okay?" I whisper.

She shrugs apologetically. "I'm fine. I just started my period a little early. But at least I have an explanation for all the mood fluctuations, right?"

"Oh," I reply, surprised to hear her admit the correlation between her hormones and her emotional state. "Do you have everything you need? Should we go?"

"I'm good, really." She taps her purse to reassure me.

"Tenley, if you'd rather try this again later—"

She cuts me off by bumping her shoulder into mine. "Nah, I think I'll stay, especially with all the comfort food and compliments you're bound to feed me tonight."

I'm still grinning at her when the hostess comes around to lead us to a cozy booth.

"Hi, I'm Cara, and I'll be your server for tonight," the waitress greets us next. "Can I get you guys anything to drink?"

Tenley glances up at me before she requests a draught beer. "I'll have the same, please," I add, scolding myself for thinking she'd prefer something fussier when everything I've seen from her so far suggests the opposite.

Our waitress's eyes dart around nervously as she scribbles on a notepad. "Great, I'll be back as soon as I get your order in at the bar." I track her for a second, trying to figure out why she's so antsy. Then I curse under my breath when I recognize the photo and the jersey hanging on the wall beside our booth.

"Is something wrong?" Tenley asks.

"Oh, no, not at all," I say, shaking my head.

"Then why is your face suddenly so red?" She narrows her eyes and peers at me from across the table. "You look a little flustered, Coach."

I scratch my chin as I debate whether to risk making Tenley feel uncomfortable after I've finally gotten her to loosen up. My eyes betray me when I cast an anxious glance over at the jersey, but she continues staring me down and presses her lips together to stifle a laugh.

"It's yours, isn't it?" Her voice is surprisingly sultry when she poses the question.

I cringe as I turn to look up at the framed jersey with my signature scribbled across the left shoulder, right above the "BOUR-GEOIS III" patch. It's not really a surprise, since this is the type of place that embraces sports memorabilia in the decor, and I've eaten here enough times to know that being born and raised in the Acadiana area and playing for an in-state college have earned me a spot on their wall. I'm just kicking myself for having forgotten about it.

"Yeah," I admit reluctantly. "It's mine."

"Does it freak you out?"

"Not really. But if it bothers you ..." I abandon what I was saying when her hand slides over mine.

"I noticed it as soon as we rounded the corner. And unless you were tacky enough to request this booth specifically, why wouldn't I be impressed?"

"Wait. You ... like it?" I ask, studying her reaction. She shrugs, but the way her cheeks flush and her tongue darts out to wet her lips says she likes it a whole lot more than she's letting on.

I feel the corners of my mouth turning up when I remember the way my brother kept hinting about Tenley's reaction to the collection in his office. "So, would it be safe to say that you're into football players?"

"I suppose that's a reasonable assumption, regarding my physical preferences, at least." She stares down at our hands while I begin rubbing the side of her thumb with mine.

"Well, then. Since we happen to have very compelling evidence that I have, in fact, at one point, fit the description of a football play-er," I explain, gesturing toward the jersey, "I could reasonably reduce that claim to 'Tenley thinks JD is hot.' Am I wrong?"

She smirks at me. "You would be right, except I only like my football players to sound that cocky on the field."

"You've had other football players?" I blurt out, blinking in surprise.

"Oh, are we doing the whole dating history thing now?" She looks so coy that I'm fighting the urge to jump over the table to get to her. "It won't take me very long."

"I think you're evading the question."

"Fine. There was a linebacker in college," she admits after a second. "I doubt you ever played one another," she adds, but it does nothing to calm my raging jealousy. I let go of her hand and lean back in the booth when the waitress returns with our drinks.

"A linebacker, huh? You weren't kidding about having a type," I venture after we're alone again. The fact that she even bothered to mention that her ex played a position which lined up across the field from mine tells me she understands exactly what she's implying, since we most likely shared a similar build.

"Does that bother you?"

Of course it does. I want you to like me and only me, and I'd rather pretend that there was no one else before me.

"It's not like I expected to hear you've never been in a relationship before," I reply instead.

"Hmm. Who's evading the question now?" she returns, glaring at me before lifting a glass to her lips.

I gulp as I watch her swallow. "Maybe it does bother me, just a little," I divulge, since my brain never seems to function in her presence.

Tenley sets her glass down and folds her hands over the table. "Then allow me to reassure you with another confession," she begins, taking a fortifying breath. "Ethan isn't the only reason I've been trying so hard to keep my distance. The truth is that I don't think I can trust myself with you. If I were to make a list, you'd literally check every box. And that scares the hell out of me."

My pulse quickens. "So, you repeatedly shot me down because

I'm *exactly* your type? And the last guy only checked, what, the 'built like a football player' box?"

"Basically."

"Hmm. What else is on this list?"

She hesitates for a second. "Shared values, I suppose."

"And you've never found that with anyone else?" I take a sip of my beer to slow my pace.

"No. That's exactly what makes this so scary," she replies, her voice barely above a whisper, and I can tell she needs me to lighten the mood.

"Plus, I'm a better kisser, right?"

She bites her lip. "Among other things."

"We can test that theory whenever you're ready," I offer, shooting her a wide grin. I know I'm pushing my luck, but I can't help myself.

She shakes her head. "And I never thought 'shameless flirt' was on my list, but here we are."

I laugh softly before adopting a more serious tone again. "You bring it out of me. I've never been drawn to anyone the way I am with you." She's quiet as I continue. "The more I learn about you, the more I want from you. So, believe me when I say, this is just as terrifying for me."

"At least you know what you're doing. I'm sure you have more dating experience than I do," she says after a while.

"I've forced myself to go on first dates here and there, just to keep up appearances, but I haven't gotten past that with anyone in a couple of years, at least." I cough over that last part, realizing how desperate I sound. Now she's probably thinking I'm pathetic, even though 'a couple of years' is still generous.

"I honestly can't remember my last date," she admits, looking embarrassed. "I guess that means we're both a little out of practice ... I mean, with relationships in general," she adds quickly before taking another sip of her beer.

"I guess we are." I mean to say that I don't want to refer to this as practice, but I'm distracted by her dropping the R-word. "And just to clarify, we are actually *in* one of those, right?"

This time, she coughs and chokes on her drink before she ends up emptying her glass in an attempt to clear her throat. "Sorry, that went down wrong," she says breathlessly.

"Tenley, I meant every word I've ever said about you being the only woman I want," I tell her, amused by her awkwardness. "Look, I know we're technically still brand new and that we agreed to keep this quiet for now, but our situation is anything but typical. I don't see the point in wasting time and going through the motions of conventional dating if we both know we want more."

I hold my breath while she stares down at the table quietly as if she's mulling it over, until our waitress interrupts us again.

"Hi, I took the liberty of bringing refills," Cara drawls, setting the glasses down. "So, um, can I get you any appetizers?" The poor girl obviously cannot read the room, probably because she's too busy trying to avoid the elephant on the wall by pretending to study her notepad.

I glance over at Tenley and notice her eyes looking a bit glossy after downing that first beer. "We could use a couple glasses of water ... and maybe something with carbs," I mumble. "How about some chips and queso?"

Tenley nods, then stops and blinks a few times, as if her head has gotten too thick. I suppress a smile, thinking I might enjoy seeing her tipsy.

"Sure, I'll put that right in," Cara replies before her eyes flicker to the photo on the wall and back down to me. She recoils when she realizes I'm staring at her expectantly. "I'm sorry, this is going to sound crazy, but—"

"Oh, it's him," Tenley finishes for her in a surprisingly stern tone. "Your hostess really sat a guy directly below his own freaking jersey without realizing it. Unless y'all did it on purpose just so you could have an excuse to ask him about it, despite the fact that he's *clearly* on a date."

Well, okay, then.

I shoot Tenley a heated look across the table as I formulate a new game plan. Hearing her get all worked up and stake her claim is absolutely turning me on. "I'm sure it was just a coincidence, though. Right, babe?"

Tenley forces an apologetic smile, seemingly reassured by that small declaration of attachment, and I turn back to the waitress. "Would it be too much trouble for you to box up a couple burgers to-go while we wait on that appetizer? Oh, and something with chocolate." I figure it can't hurt, given Tenley's current state.

"Um, sure, of course. Anything else?" Cara nods quickly as she looks back at Tenley, who has already resigned herself to the fresh beer at the table, presumably because she's planning to drink away her shame.

"Just the water," I say, keeping my eyes locked onto Tenley this time. Our waitress finally gets the hint and shuffles away.

I reach over and slide Tenley's glass beyond her reach. "You good over there, *date*?"

She cringes. "I might have accidentally shotgunned that first beer on an empty stomach, so—no, not really. I'm sorry." Her cheeks are red as she covers her mouth to stifle a hiccup, and I laugh at her again.

"You're a cute drunk, aren't you?" I ask, reaching over to pull her hand away from her face and interlace our fingers.

"I *am* more fun, or so I'm told," she replies, then bites her lip once she realizes she probably shouldn't have shared that much information. I say nothing but slide the glass back to her with my free hand, making her giggle. "Not *that* kind of fun."

I give her that same smolder from before, and the way her chest heaves tells me she's lying. I get the feeling that drunk Tenley is extra friendly.

"Hmm," I begin, adding a growl to my voice. "Speaking of fun, do you think you'd be okay with finishing off the burgers at my place, so we can make my whole 'getting cozy and watching football' fantasy come true? I could bring you home, though, if you're not up for it."

She shrugs. "I'm sure I'll be fine once I get something in my stomach." I beam at her as I continue playing with her fingers.

Cara returns with two glasses of water, a platter of chips and queso dip, an awkward apology, and a promise that our order will be ready within minutes. I shoo her away as quickly as I can and coax Tenley into getting a bit of water and some of the chips down, but she still manages to finish off that second beer by the time our takeout arrives.

"I'm okay, I promise," Tenley swears as she scoots out of the booth, but she's a little wobbly on her feet. I make sure to leave our waitress a decent tip before helping my adorably tipsy date out to the truck.

The conversation is a lot sillier on the way back, especially once Tenley gets the giggles, and we entertain each other with funny Ethan stories. She seems to have sobered up by the time we get back to my house, protesting when I scoop her up and carry her to the front porch. But she takes her time unwrapping her arms from my neck and getting back to her own feet.

I sigh after setting her down to open the door, already missing her warmth against me. She peers around as she steps inside and kicks off her shoes, and I immediately love the way she looks at ease being barefoot in my house. I consider skipping the burgers and going straight for the "football and chill" part, but I ultimately go into the kitchen to plate our food because I'm actually starving.

"Want to grab us a couple of drinks?" I ask her.

"Sure," she answers, and I hear when she opens the refrigerator.

"Is the couch still okay, or would you rather eat at the table in here?"

"You made that couch sound pretty nice earlier," she replies as she joins me at the counter.

I smile and gesture toward the living room, and by the time I set our food down on the coffee table, Tenley's already sitting with a throw blanket in her lap, reaching up to offer me a beer. I press my lips together to suppress a grin.

Okay, maybe it's a sob.

"Uh, thanks," I reply, my voice thick. Then I twist off the cap and take a sip before plopping down beside her on the couch.

This might very well be the greatest moment ever.

She snuggles closer to me, and I reach over to open her beer bottle, despite being a little concerned about her tolerance level. "Don't worry," she says, apparently sensing my hesitation. "I'm a lightweight, but not *that* light."

"Yes, ma'am," I agree, even though she's still speaking slower than usual. I offer to say grace, and she joins me, then I switch on the TV before I proceed to inhale my burger. Tenley gets through half of hers before she calls it quits and asks where she can find the bathroom.

I think briefly about sending her through my bedroom to the en suite, because I want her to get *all* kinds of ideas, but I reprimand myself and lead her to the tidier guest bath instead. While she's away, I pick up our dinner and make a fast dash to brush my teeth and freshen up. I stop in the kitchen to grab dessert, another beer for myself, and a water for Tenley before I return to find her on the sofa, watching football intently. I put the Baylor game on for her earlier, and although we agreed to switch to the LSU game after a while, I can't bring myself to change it yet. I set everything down and sit beside her, then reach out to pull her legs into my lap.

"Thanks for the chocolate. It was very thoughtful of you," she says through a mouthful of brownie and sets the box down. "And too tempting to pass up."

"It's cheat night," I remind her, and she laughs. I automatically wrap my hands around her right foot and begin massaging it gently, and she sighs contentedly, shifting her position until she's facing me. "Is this okay?" I realize too late that I probably should have asked permission before touching her, though she doesn't seem to mind.

"Mm-hmm," she returns, her eyelids fluttering closed as she lets her head fall to the side and rest on the back of the couch. The noise she makes on the next exhale is dangerously close to a moan, and I'm forced to take a few measured breaths of my own. I switch to her left foot and attempt to concentrate on my task, but my hands involuntarily begin trekking up her calves.

I turn to face her, hoping she's okay with skipping ahead to the next item on our agenda for the evening. "Tenley," I whisper as I gravitate closer. "What's your policy regarding kissing on the first date?"

She opens her eyes and stares back at me. "I only consider it when the date goes really well and I suspect he might be a good kisser."

"And how are my chances looking?" I reply, already closing the distance.

"Since I've already confirmed the second part, and you kind of flexed on me with the PMS brownies and the foot massage, I'd say pretty damn good." She grabs a fistful of my shirt, and I lurch forward, our lips crushing together.

My tongue glides over hers as soon as she opens her mouth for me, and I hum when I realize she tastes like chocolate. I lean in after a minute, cradling her as she lies back and shifting my weight to hover above her. My right hand roams over her body while I continue kissing her, and she clutches at my back and digs her fingertips into the muscles there and behind my arms.

After a bit, she hitches her leg up and hooks it over my hip, making me groan. No doubt the amount of time since I've last been this close to a woman is a contributing factor, but the feeling of Tenley's body beneath mine is even hotter than I imagined, and I'm dying to use my considerably large handspan for gripping something better than a football for once.

I barely manage to remind myself that this can't go any further tonight, despite the overwhelming temptation. But the way she keeps responding so encouragingly isn't making it any easier to tap the brakes, especially once she tugs me down and arches her back to press her chest against mine. My thoughts flash to that lacy black bra, and I have to pull away because I'm smiling too hard.

"I wore it tonight," she says breathlessly. "Your favorite bra—the itchy one."

Holy cow. She can read my mind now?

Then she shoots me a smirk so sexy that I doubt I'll survive the night. I stare down at her in appreciation for a second longer before bringing my lips to her neck and my hand down to her butt.

"Mm, Tenley. I've wanted to do this with you for so long," I murmur over her ear before I give it a light nibble. "And you feel even better than I—"

Oh, no, not now...

I panic as I feel a rumble in my chest, suddenly regretting the speed at which I consumed that burger in conjunction with the beer, but it's too late. The loudest burp in history is already making its way up from deep in my gut and bellowing out right over Tenley's ear. Though, I suppose this kind of gas is better than the alternative, and at least I'm not kissing her on the mouth when it happens.

I rock back to sit on my heels, and the movement brings another huge gas bubble to the surface. I cover my face and turn my head to the side to belt out another deafening burp. "I am so, so sorry," I attempt to apologize, my eyes wide. "I swear I didn't mean to do that."

But I'm surprised to find her stifling a giggle when I glance down, and then she hiccups. "It's okay," she replies, just before her body twitches again. "Ugh! I hate having the hic-cups."

I chuckle and help her up to a seated position before handing her some water. She settles into my side and continues to flinch every ten seconds or so for the next few minutes, cursing adorably under her breath each time. We sit that way comfortably for another hour, each of us offering our commentary on the game. I eventually switch to the LSU-Florida matchup, and she humors me by rooting for the home team.

And even though we don't spend any more time kissing—at least, until I make sure to plant one on her in front of the security camera when I walk her back to her door—it's absolutely the best first date I've ever had, and hopefully my last.

CHAPTER 25
TENLEY

"We really appreciate everyone in Camellia for coming out to support us tomorrow night, and we hope to make y'all proud," JD calls out over the large crowd in the hotel lobby and receives an enthusiastic response.

I bite my lip and smile coyly when our eyes meet across the room. He grins back, his dimples barely visible now that his beard has filled in again. "The team will be going out for a quiet buffet dinner later tonight, and while everyone is invited, we ask that you allow the guys to sit together in preparation for game day. Boys, I'll give you a half-hour to get settled in. The bus leaves for the Bossier State University practice field at two o'clock sharp."

There's another rumble of excited chatter while everyone disperses, and some of the assistant coaches help JD hand out room keys to the players while fans continue checking in. I sense him glancing my way again, and I turn in time to see him elbow his brother in the ribs. Blake laughs heartily, and whatever he's saying makes JD's ears turn red.

I walk over just as Ethan makes it to the front of the line, giving me a good excuse to approach them. "Why do I get the feeling I was just the punchline of an inappropriate joke?" I whisper loudly.

"Because you've already met my brother," JD retorts, shooting Blake a warning glare.

"I was just encouraging Coach Thirsty here to ask for your spare key—you know, so he can stop by later tonight," Blake explains. "He's got us sharing a room, and I feel like we're too mature for the whole 'sock on the doorknob' game."

I watch JD roll his eyes and shove Blake back with his shoulder. "How about you grow up and quit saying that crap in front of everyone," he demands gruffly, gesturing toward Ethan.

"Whatever you say, boss." Blake grins, making JD's jaw twitch.

"It's fine, Coach. I've gotten used to being grossed out by you guys. But could you at least try to control yourselves this weekend?" Ethan grumbles before he takes his key card and walks off.

To be fair, our affection probably does seem excessive from Ethan's point of view. JD and I have been spending practically all of our free time together since we started dating about a month ago, right around the same time my dad's health took a turn for the worse. And since we obviously can't go out together around Camellia, we've mostly been relegated to my parents' house, save for a few Saturday-night dates out of town.

This means Ethan's had the unfortunate (and allegedly scarring) experience of interrupting us every time we disappear down the hallway or sneak out to JD's truck for a minute of privacy. I imagine the kid has also had his fill of JD's tendency to maintain constant physical contact or flirt with me from across the room, even though I surprisingly can't get enough of it.

JD glances at Ethan's retreating form before looking up at me apologetically. "Ignore Blake. He's just pissy because I'm making him share a room with me to give the fans more space."

I'm not exactly sure what comes over me, but I'm suddenly determined to help JD get the best of his brother this time. "I happen to think that's really sweet of you, Coach," I declare, reaching out to hand him a sheet of paper. "Oh, and here's that permission slip for Ethan. I'm sorry I forgot to turn it in earlier."

He furrows his brow, obviously confused, but takes the hotel receipt tentatively. "Thanks, I guess," he murmurs. But his posture straightens as soon as his fingers connect with the plastic card beneath the decoy paper. He clears his throat awkwardly as he folds the receipt and tucks it into his back pocket.

"Have a good night, Ms. Tenley. Maybe I'll see you around." His tone immediately shifts to sound more suggestive, and he presses his lips together to keep himself from smiling.

"Maybe you will," I turn and glare at Blake, and I can tell he's dying to add his own saucy commentary. Then I wheel my suitcase around toward the elevators, swaying my hips as I walk away.

I shake my head as soon as the elevator doors close, still a little stunned at myself. I didn't mean to give JD the impression that he's actually going to score tonight, but I realize that's exactly what I've done with my uncharacteristically bold gesture, and a shiver runs down my spine.

While I'd been able to hold my feelings for JD at bay for a while, since allowing myself to like him—and kiss him—my willpower has become practically nonexistent. It's probably lucky for me that we're so rarely unchaperoned at home, because the more I get to know him, the harder it becomes to keep things casual. And since we haven't had much practice enforcing our boundaries due to the lack of opportunity, I'm not sure I trust myself to maintain propriety if he shows up at my room later.

The elevator dings as the doors open again, and a group of boys trickles out, whispering and smirking at me. "Bye, Ms. Tenley," one of them drawls. I flash them an embarrassed smile, still floored by the idea that most of Ethan's teammates knew about JD's crush on me before I did.

I continue to the fifth floor, stepping out into a hallway already teeming with Camellia High parents and fans. I greet a few of them politely as I manage to find my room. Then I immediately pull out my phone to set the record straight.

TENLEY

So … I know that was kind of forward of me just now. But I saw the opportunity to stroke your ego in front of your brother and couldn't help myself.

JD

STROKE MY WHAT?

I just spit water on a kid.

Please stahp texting me while I'm in public. I'm embarrassing myself. I can't keep looking this whipped in front of the team.

TENLEY

Lol. Sorry. It was a figure of speech. My lips are sealed.

JD

gif of "You're killin' me, Smalls" from The Sandlot

Don't talk about your lips either.

But I guess you're trying to tell me that the invitation to use your room key later tonight was part of the act?

TENLEY

As much as I'd enjoy hanging out, this probably isn't the right time or place, don't you think?

JD

Yeah, it wouldn't exactly set the best example for the kids if they saw me sneaking in or out of your room.

Tbh, I'll probably be smelly and exhausted, anyway. And I already planned to eat my body weight in gassy food at the buffet as a special treat for my roomie. Rain check?

TENLEY

Sounds good. See you around, Coach.

He stops responding after that, likely because he's busy getting the team to practice. Once I give up on hearing from JD again, I grab my laptop and opt to get a bit of work done, completing some charting and answering a few patient emails. Pregnant moms always seem to have a million questions, bless their hearts.

I hesitate before I send off the last reply. Sometimes I feel like a fraud, doling out advice to expecting mothers, coaching women in labor, and helping them troubleshoot breastfeeding, all without ever having done any of it myself. There's always been some lingering doubt, my insecurities telling me I don't deserve to be a midwife if I haven't experienced motherhood. But I've managed to convince myself it's better this way. My advice is probably safer from an objective standpoint, and it's easier to remain detached in the case of a medical emergency, especially after what happened with my sister. It's not like I set out to become a labor and delivery nurse because of Tessa's death, but I still feel responsible for preventing it from happening again. And though her condition is relatively uncommon, I always check my patients for the symptoms of peripartum cardiomyopathy, just in case.

I finish the email and open another tab. I've been looking into adding "NFP Instructor" to my list of professional qualifications after Sybil Thibodeaux mentioned it a few weeks back. My initial research led me down a rabbit hole, and it turns out there are only a few minor differences between NFP and FAM, specifically the religious and ethical principles behind them. And although I haven't been as devout in the past, I'm starting to get a better understanding of some of the teachings and doctrines of my Catholic faith through the application of NFP. I can see myself getting behind the whole "open to life" mentality, if I were ever in the position to get married and start a family.

But that is a huge *if*, and one I haven't found a reason to give much consideration to thus far ... well, until now.

We haven't talked about it explicitly, but I know JD wants those things and that I shouldn't be wasting his time if I'm not up for marriage or motherhood. So, for the first time in years, I give my mind permission to wander into some dangerous territory.

What would it be like to "try" for a baby? How would I react when I saw the second line on a pregnancy test? Would I be sick all the time? Would I enjoy feeling those first little flutters I hear so much about? What would I think about my body changing? Am I tough enough to labor naturally? How would I handle it if my baby had trouble latching?

I swallow hard, admitting to myself that a huge part of me has always wanted those questions to be relevant. The truth is that I've been longing for that experience, and since I wasn't going to allow myself to have it, I've poured all my energy into helping other women live out my dreams instead.

Good grief. I'm a hot mess.

Which is exactly why I've avoided relationships and babies until now. But I owe it to myself—and especially to JD—to figure out whether I could even handle a family of my own before I let things go any further.

Then again, if I'm already raising Ethan with JD's help, what does that make the three of us?

CHAPTER 26
JD

"What do you mean, you aren't going up there? She slipped you her freaking room key in front of all of us!"

I heave out a sigh and put a whistle to my lips. Each player on the team shifts to the next warm-up exercise. "It would be completely inappropriate," I finally answer my brother.

"Says who? It's not like she's a student or even one of your coworkers. You're both single adults, and you're not on campus. What's so wrong about it?"

I blow the whistle again. "Don't you think these boys will put Ethan through hell if they hear about me sneaking up to Tenley's room?"

He shrugs, knowing I'm right. "You'll just have to make sure no one finds out, then."

"It's not worth the risk, and I don't like sending the wrong message to the kids. I'm not about the whole 'do as I say, not as I do' teaching style."

Blake rolls his eyes. "You do realize the majority of these kids are already getting more action than you, right?"

I lay on the whistle as hard as I can this time. "Drills. Let's go," I call loudly, glaring at Blake. "Why are you so concerned with my sex life in the first place?" I grumble as we walk to the other side of the BSU Bears' practice field, where the offense is already gathering.

"Because you're not looking out for yourself. Hell, JD, you've been stuck so far up her ass lately that I can't even remember the last time I've seen you outside of football. Tenley's had you wrapped around her little finger for months now, playing you hot and cold, and what do you have to show for it?"

I turn to him, my eyes darting around nervously. "What do you want me to say? I'm pretty sure I'm in love with her, all right? And I know I'm probably going to get hurt at some point, but I can't exactly help myself."

He scratches the back of his head as he looks at me with pity in his eyes. "I still don't see how that's a valid excuse to let her walk all over you."

"No offense, but you wouldn't understand," I mumble and walk away. Sure, I've done some dumb things to get Tenley's attention, and maybe I did go above and beyond the normal bounds of friendship to gain her trust. But I'm still not going to let Blake cut her down and accuse her of using me just because we aren't sleeping together, especially since it's just as much my choice as it is hers.

Okay, yeah. That last part might be a stretch.

Technically, we've met most of the qualifications for that level of intimacy on my end, though this is the first time I've admitted the extent of my feelings for Tenley aloud. And while I don't plan to take the physical stuff any further until she knows how I feel, I can't just spring that kind of declaration on her after only a month of dating in secret and expect her not to freak out.

There's also the matter of the annoying little voice in the back of my head that enjoys reminding me about the chances of Tenley getting pregnant, even if we followed her fertility awareness practices and used protection, and that this is one of the most important reasons sex was ordered for marriage. And although I've been patting myself on the back for using love, trust, and commitment as my prerequisites for physical intimacy, I suppose I'm still ignoring my conscience when I make excuses like "waiting for marriage is an outdated standard" or "it's just an unreasonable expectation" to justify my actions.

Then again, things have felt different with Tenley from the beginning. I'm just not sure whether it all means I'm supposed to exercise more patience or speed things up.

"Ay, what the hell is that supposed to mean?" Blake demands as he follows me over to where the team has assembled into small groups according to their positions. I'm not stupid enough to believe he'd offer any empathy regarding my moral dilemma, either.

I turn abruptly, hoping to finish this conversation before we get close enough for anyone else to hear us. "When was the last time you were in a serious relationship, Blake? Hmm?"

"Hey, I'm single by choice," he retorts, crossing his arms. But I suspect the answer to my question is actually *never*, especially once he rolls his lips in the way he always does when he's lying.

"Exactly. You and I are motivated by completely different things. I have values and end goals, while you have fun. So I don't know what makes you think you're qualified to force-feed me your advice, but I don't need it," I say, stepping forward and poking him lightly in the chest. "And, by the way, 'single by choice' is a bullshit answer." Then I turn to a group of running backs and blow the whistle again. They glare at me as they line up, probably noticing our exchange. All except for Ethan, who keeps his head down.

I continue ignoring my brother after he sulks over to the quarterbacks. A few minutes into our drills, some of the Bears' coaching staff and players join us to give the kids a few tips and offer some encouragement. My guys really eat up the attention, and I feel a surge of pride when I notice Ethan talking with one of their special teams coaches.

"JD, hey!" The offensive coordinator and head coach call me over. We were introduced earlier, though I already knew their HC, Ray Deville, from the time he spent as an assistant while I played at LSU. "Gotta minute?"

"Sure, Coach." I follow them into one of the offices inside their fancy practice facility.

"You've done a pretty good job out there, JD," says Ray. "I'm impressed. Those kids are well disciplined, which isn't something we see too often."

"Thanks," I reply, pleasantly surprised by his compliments. "We work hard, and I've been blessed with a ton of support from the community. It's a lot easier when you have great kids and everyone buys in."

"Sure, it is. But I know you, JD, and I don't doubt that you're the reason for the buy-in," he declares.

I shrug. "I'd like to take all the credit, but I have an awesome staff as well."

He laughs lightly and nods. "I figured you'd say something like that." Then he glances over and makes a wordless exchange with the OC. "Coach Cliff and I will be looking to fill a position on our staff this spring. Our tight ends coach is moving on to another program, and we think you could be a great asset to the BSU family."

I blink a few times, utterly shocked by their offer. "Oh, wow. You're serious? That's ... I'm flattered."

"The position won't officially be open for a few months, but I'd really like to see you throw your name in the hat. I might even be able to pull a few strings," Ray adds with a knowing smile. "What do you say, JD?"

"I guess I'd have to give it some thought. I haven't considered coaching anywhere else, but it sounds like a great opportunity," I reply, fishing for something polite to say. But the truth is that I have no intention of applying for the job, because I have no desire to leave Camellia, at least not as long as Tenley and Ethan are there.

Cliff speaks up this time. "Are you married, JD?"

"Ah, no, sir." It seems like everyone is worried about my love life today.

"Hmm. Gotta girlfriend back home?"

I half-shrug, trying to play it cool, though I know I'll start gushing about Tenley if they give me an opening. "Yes, sir," is all I allow myself.

"Any kids yet?"

I scratch my chin. "My girlfriend is fostering her teenage nephew." It's the first time I've ever referred to Tenley as my girlfriend in public, and although I'm not sure she'd be willing to own up to it, she certainly fits the definition. Either way, it gives me a small thrill.

"Does he play for you?" Ray asks this time.

I grin and nod proudly. "Yeah, he's a great kid, currently my RB2." Then I remember I'm supposed to be protecting Ethan, not bragging about him. "But, uh, we've been keeping our relationship quiet while they finalize a new custody arrangement." They both look confused. "It's complicated," I add with an awkward laugh at the end.

"Right. Well, keep in mind that a place like this can afford a lot more opportunities for your, uh, nephew. Not to mention you wouldn't have to worry about small-town gossip," Cliff explains, making me frown.

I'm not that naive. I've had my share of dealing with people who only pretend to care about my well-being for their own benefit, and I don't appreciate the way these guys are playing the "what's best for your family" card, much less cutting down my hometown, school, and football program in the process.

"I'll certainly keep all of that in mind," I say dryly.

"Great." Ray and Cliff both rise from their seats, signaling the end of our meeting. "I'll have one of my guys reach out to you when the position officially opens."

"Sure, Coach. And thanks again for letting us use the facilities here. My boys are having the time of their lives." I stand to shake each of their hands. "We really appreciate it, you know, especially coming from such a small town." I can't help myself as I throw that last bit of shade in, maybe because I'm still salty after that fight with Blake, but it seems to fly under their radar.

We exchange a few more pleasantries on the way out, though I'm eager to get back to my team. I return to find Blake giving Ethan and another running back a lesson on ball security, which isn't a promising sign at this point in the season. Now I'm worrying about Ethan fumbling the ball, not only because we can't afford any turnovers tomorrow night, but also because he'd be upset with himself if he lost the ball during a game. And these days, my stomach turns at the mere possibility of having to watch Ethan endure any kind of disappointment.

I begin walking toward them, watching as Ethan tries the move Blake's just shown him. Then Blake grabs him by the face mask and tells him something before tapping on the top of his helmet. I've probably imitated that same attaboy gesture hundreds of times after seeing my brother do it first. I sigh heavily, realizing I owe Blake an apology. He may have been a jerk in the delivery, but he only meant to ensure I'm looking out for myself. I lift my whistle and give it a few quick bleats before allowing the team some free time to check out the rest of the facilities.

"Yo, Blake," I holler. He presses his lips together as he walks toward me, though he doesn't turn to face me until we're standing in front of one another.

"Back from rubbing elbows with your old friends, boss?" he asks, his voice dripping with resentment. This probably isn't the best time to mention that job offer.

"Someone has to suck up so they'll invite us back," I reply, and he grunts in response. "Listen, man, that was my bad earlier. I passed judgment on your lifestyle, right after getting pissed at you for thinking you were doing the same to me. I'm sorry."

He nods and finally allows his expression to soften. "Yeah. And I might have gone too far. I just want you to be careful. You're too good sometimes, JD, and I can't allow anyone else to take advantage of you, because that's my job." He smirks at the end, surprising me by reaching out to offer his hand for a bro hug.

"But if you ever bow up to me in front of the team like that again, you'd better be ready to swing," he grumbles over my shoulder, making me laugh. We both know I'd kick Blake's ass in a fight, though size is my only advantage. He's definitely scrappier and angrier, though I've never understood why.

"All right, now that we've gotten that out of the way, I'm ready to accept any wisdom you wish to impart regarding my current situation, so long as you don't accuse my girlfriend of any ill intentions again," I say after we separate.

He raises a brow. "Your *girlfriend*? Are you even allowed to call her that?"

I roll my eyes. "Whatever. We may not be sleeping together or holding hands in public, but she doesn't seem to mind my tongue in her mouth on a daily basis."

He tilts his head back and laughs. "There you go, buddy," he says, slapping me on the back as we walk toward the sidelines. "This is what's been missing. You went from throwing yourself at her when she seemed uninterested to being too chicken to use the hotel room key that she very purposefully slipped you."

"Okay, okay, I get it. Maybe I've been taking it *too* slow with Tenley. But I can't just go all in, either. You know as well as I do that I'll scare her away if I tell her everything."

"JD, don't take this the wrong way, but I think your girl might be a less-talk, more-action kind of woman. Maybe she needs that physical connection to get to the next stage of your relationship, and she's just waiting for you to make a move. She slipped you that key *in front of me*. She freaking stared me down while she did it to make absolutely sure I saw. Do you know why?"

I shake my head and play dumb. I don't think Tenley would appreciate it if I told Blake she only initiated the whole exchange to help me look less pathetic in front of him.

Unless ... What if Tenley was just using that as an excuse to move things forward without having to admit it was her idea?

"So you'd have someone else to hold you accountable, bruh. She knew I'd encourage you to go and keep you from punking out," Blake continues.

"Even if we already discussed the reasons why it would be a bad idea?" I venture.

"If she crawfished on the offer, it's only because she got the vibe that you weren't interested." His rationale makes a little too much sense this time.

"And you really think she wants me to go up there later?"

"Text her again if you don't believe me. If she turns you down, I'll butt out for good, I swear. But if she says yes, you have to use the old hoodie trick on her when you get there and admit I was right when you get back."

I grin and bump my fist against his. "Deal."

CHAPTER 27
TENLEY

My phone chimes and I jump up to grab it, secretly hoping to hear from JD again. But it's my mom, letting me know my dad is having a particularly bad afternoon. I say a quick prayer for his sake before returning to my work.

A minute later, I get the text I've been waiting for, and I can't help beaming down at the phone as soon as I see JD's name at the top of the thread.

JD

Just got done with practice, and it turns out that I'm not as sweaty or tired as predicted. So, if you change your mind about later …

Just lmk if you'd like me to stop by after I put the kids to bed, and I'll make sure I don't go overboard at dinner. 🙂

TENLEY

How … romantic.

gif of Jimmy Fallon saying "Ew!"

JD

Uh, quick, think about my muscles? My butt in a football uniform?

How about … I'm great with kids?

TENLEY

There's that checklist again.

gif of Blanche from The Golden Girls spritzing herself

JD

Does that mean I can see you later tonight, Blanche?

TENLEY

You know, I've always considered myself to be more of a Dorothy …

JD

heart react

Good thing I like my women old and bossy.

I bite my lip, suddenly nervous again. I thought I'd taken care of the JD situation for tonight, but I should've known better than to assume he wouldn't at least *try* to take me up on that offer. I'd dangled the possibility of sex in front of him, after all, even if it was only meant to be a joke.

I know JD isn't going to pressure me into anything before we're both ready. I'm just not sure that one thing won't lead to another, given our … chemistry.

Then the thought occurs to me that the overwhelming attraction might not be coincidental, as well as this afternoon's case of sudden-onset baby fever. I reflect on some of the symptoms I use to track my cycles and open the charting app on my phone.

Bingo. Peak fertility.

Well, that explains a lot. It also means I have no choice but to be responsible this weekend, or JD and I could be in *big* trouble. I need backup—a pep talk, and Loren is the first person who comes to mind. I grab my phone and hope she answers quickly.

TENLEY

Hey … are you busy?

LOREN

Not at all. And Camellia's empty, thanks to your bf, so I don't exactly have any exciting prospects, either.

TENLEY

Also thanks to JD, I might have overdone it with my exciting prospects for tonight.

The thing is, we've agreed to take it slow … but we're all staying in the same hotel … and I might have slipped him my room key in front of his brother as a joke.

LOREN

And now he's offering to keep you warm tonight?

Also, DAMN, GIRL.

TENLEY

Yeah, pretty much.

LOREN

Before we go on, I want to make sure I'm doing my job well. Am I supposed to be encouraging you to smash or pass right now?

TENLEY

Um. The second, I think.

LOREN

Okay, then. Since you mentioned "taking things slow," I'm assuming this is still relevant: I can't imagine JD being the kind of guy who would demand sex or even push for it before you were ready. And from what I gather, he likes you too much to risk making you feel uncomfortable or jeopardizing his chances.

TENLEY

You're absolutely right. He's been super respectful of my boundaries, and I know I can trust him.

Tbh, it's not JD I'm worried about …

I mean, how exactly am I supposed to football-and-chill alone in a hotel room with freaking Thor Lite while he fawns over me and not let things go too far?

Also, sorry, I may be feeling a little hormonal today.

LOREN

Well, my friend, I knew you liked JD before, but I had no idea you rated him at a Hemsworth. Though, I'm totally getting a 'Ragnarok' vibe since you mentioned it.

gif of short-haired Thor

I guess you need to decide what you're really looking for here. Are you ready to take the next step with him? Or do you want to keep stoking that slow burn while you build a strong foundation and a lasting relationship?

(I think we both know how he would answer that.)

TENLEY

Thanks, Lo. That all makes a lot of sense. I just hope I'm able to remember it later.

LOREN

Yeah, that wasn't rhetorical. You're gonna need to pay the bestie tax and tell me how you really feel about him.

TENLEY

I guess I haven't really thought about it.

It took getting to the point where I couldn't ignore how much I liked him before I could even wrap my mind around the idea of dating him … Idk if I can handle love and all that other serious stuff.

LOREN

You sure about that? You didn't object when I called him your boyfriend earlier in this conversation.

Reread your last message from an objective POV.

My pulse begins racing. I've actually spelled out the L-word, which means my subconscious is at least considering the possibility. Then I do that thing where I stretch the rubber band and see how far my heart can reach. It extends much, much further than I'm used to, and it doesn't even snap back on its own this time.

TENLEY

*gif of '*chuckles* I am in danger.'*

LOREN

Does that mean what I think it means?!?

TENLEY

I don't know if I'm there yet. But I just realized I'm much closer than I ever thought I'd be.

But that's crazy, right? People don't really fall this quickly.

LOREN

OF COURSE THEY DO

Come on, Ten. Read a romance novel, watch a rom-com, be a chick …

TENLEY

None of that stuff even remotely resembles real life.

LOREN

Okay, then try one of those exercises where you imagine what your life would be like if you parted ways. How have you changed since you started seeing JD? I bet he's already left his mark on you.

I pause to consider her last message, immediately recognizing that being with JD has already forced me to do some major self-reflection, especially today when I finally owned up to my desire for motherhood.

TENLEY

Gah, what is happening here? I thought I'd limited this to "more than friends."

LOREN

gif of little girl squealing excitedly

You caught all the feelings, didn't you? 😏

TENLEY

Shit. Did I? Maybe?

At least some of the feelings?

Enough to know we shouldn't be using a hotel room to hook up, I suppose.

LOREN

Need me to check on you later tonight?

TENLEY

That would be great, thank you. In exchange, I'll pay your tax with more details when we get back.

LOREN

Deal

I exhale and shove all those thoughts about the extent of my feelings for JD to the back of my mind before I type a quick response, telling him he can only come to visit if he promises to control himself at the buffet. He agrees, adding that he'll be on his best behavior all night, to my relief. Now, if I can only get my own reproductive system on board with that plan.

A little later, I hear a soft knock and a whirring from the card reader. The door opens slowly to reveal JD wearing a ball cap, hoodie, and gym shorts.

"Hey," he greets me awkwardly and shuts the door behind him. "Still up for some company?"

I can't help but allow my gaze to run up and down his body. I've seen him in shorts before, but it isn't often that JD steps out in anything besides his signature khakis-and-a-polo look. He's unbelievably hot right now, even with the socks and slides. I'm grateful he's wearing a bulky jacket to tone down the gun show, at least.

I smile at his expression. He looks nervous, clasping his hands in his front pocket while he waits like a vampire who can't take another step forward without an invitation.

"Sure," I answer eventually, patting the spot beside me. He kicks off his shoes and sets his cap on the desk before joining me on the bed, stretching his long legs out in front of him.

"What's that?" he asks, pointing to the bag of candy in my lap.

"My weakness," I admit.

"Candy?" he asks hesitantly. "I thought you didn't eat that much sugar?"

I cringe. "Cinnamon candy is kind of my guilty pleasure."

He reaches into the pocket of his hoodie and pulls out an identical bag of Red Hots. "I had a feeling," he says with a smirk and hands over his offering.

"Thanks, but ... how did you know?" I stare at the bag, confused. I've eaten brownies and cake in front of him, but never candy.

He lifts my chin before leaning in for a short kiss. "Call it a hunch," he says after he pulls away. I feel my face heating up, because I can't even think about JD noticing the way I *taste*, and I stare down at the candy in my lap while I attempt to regain my self-control. I clear my throat before offering him the open bag. He meets my eyes as he takes a handful of red candies and pops them into his mouth.

"So, um, how was dinner?" I ask, trying to distract myself, because even the way he chews is entirely too sexy right now.

"We survived. I'm not so sure the good folks at the Golden Corral of Shreveport feel the same, though," he says with a grin. "My boys were a little ... hungry."

I chuckle. "I bet."

"Did you get something to eat?"

"I found a salad at the grocery store down the road. As well as this dessert, obviously."

"A salad?" he asks incredulously.

"It was a tradeoff for the candy," I reply, embarrassed again. It's not the first time we've broached the diet topic, though I usually just play it off as though I prefer eating healthy food. But now JD knows the truth—that I actually *like* processed sugar—and I'm sure he won't be willing to let it go.

"You should eat whatever you want," he states matter-of-factly. "Within reason, of course."

"Listen, I wasn't exactly blessed with a great metabolism, and you know cardio and I don't get along, so I have to keep my diet some-what healthy. Not to mention, I really need to watch my weight now that I'm eating like a Cajun again."

He smiles and reaches into my lap for another handful of candy. "For the record, I think your body is perfect," he says before he raises his hand, allowing the red beads to trickle down into his mouth.

I chew on my lip. He's also said this before, but I'm not good with compliments, especially about my appearance. I can appreciate someone praising my work ethic or my brains, but I prefer to blend in and fly under the radar when it comes to looks. I figure it's probably a result of being the first girl in my class to develop.

"Tenley?" His voice brings me back from my thoughts. "You okay?"

"Yeah," I sigh. "I just ... I've always been self-conscious of my curves, I guess."

He furrows his brow and rests his hand on my right leg. "Your curves are amazing. How do you think I earned the nickname 'Coach

Thirsty'?" he admits with a smirk, his hand curling in and his fingers softly raking my bare thigh. My breath catches in my throat and my stomach flips.

Oof. This is going to be harder than I thought. Thankfully, he pulls his hand back after a second of my silence.

"So, uh, whatcha watching, Dorothy?" he asks, trying to lighten the mood.

"Pittsburgh and Cincinnati." I gesture at the TV.

He eyes me suspiciously. "Seriously? You were all alone in a hotel room watching football? Where are the cameras? Is this a prank?" I giggle as he looks around the room, pretending to be searching for evidence of a setup.

"Are you *still* questioning my affinity for football?"

"I have to," he replies, shaking his head. "I can't believe you're real half the time."

I look away, my face heating up again. "How was practice?"

"It was great. The kids really enjoyed hanging out at the field house."

"Did it bring back any memories for you? Or tempt you to go after a college coaching job?" I ask, my tone a little flirtier than intended.

"Well, actually ... I kind of got hit on by the BSU coaching staff today."

Unexpected pangs of jealousy and even fear immediately flood my chest, but I ignore the feelings and force myself to sound excited for him. "Wow, seriously? That's awesome, JD!"

"Like I said before, I'm happy where I am right now." He shrugs and continues staring at me intently, and now I'm not sure whether it's the sense of relief or just the way he's looking at me that's making me all warm and tingly inside. "By the way, I haven't told anyone else about that, so can we keep it between us?"

"Yeah, of course."

I'm reminded of my conversation with Loren as I consider the implications of him confiding in me. Have I become that person for him, the one he trusts with his secrets and considers before making big decisions? Do I even want to be?

I'm afraid my honest answer is that I want to be anything and everything JD needs. And that I also want to fulfill his ... *other* desires.

I'm slowly realizing that I've never felt this way about anyone before.

I sniff to disguise the way I'm breathing so heavily. "Are you nervous about tomorrow?"

He licks his lips, distracting me for a second. "A little. I mean, we're totally preparing for a good old-fashioned ass-whooping," he admits. "But hopefully the kids will at least have some fun and make a few good memories from that time they got far enough into the play-offs that the town threw them a send-off parade."

I squeeze his forearm. "You're definitely giving them that. Those boys are having a blast."

My phone sounds, and he reaches up to tug at the collar of his hoodie. "Man, I'm dying in this thing. It's so much warmer in your room." All I can do is squeak an "mm-hmm" in return.

"You should probably check that, just in case it's your mom or something," he says and shifts around as if he's preparing to remove a layer. I pull out my phone, relieved to see a text from Loren.

LOREN

Wellness check! Is he there? Are you good?

TENLEY

Thanks, we're fine so far.

LOREN

Are you ... clothed? 👀

TENLEY

Yes.

(Unfortunately.)

LOREN

Planning to stay that way?

TENLEY

Yes … I promise.

LOREN

Good girl.

Text me if you need an SOS call.

My phone is just about dead, so I set it down with the intention of looking for my charger. "It was just Lor—" I nearly choke when I turn to find JD sitting beside me in nothing but his shorts.

"Sorry," he says with an apologetic smile. "I didn't think to throw on a T-shirt under my hoodie. You don't mind, right?"

I clear my throat and attempt to regain my composure, accidentally inhaling a lungful of the manly, soapy scent emanating from all that newly exposed skin. "You're fine. I mean—it's fine. You're good."

One side of his mouth turns up in a cocky smirk. "Um, are you?"

I narrow my eyes at him and elbow one of his huge biceps. "And you accused *me* of setting *you* up?"

Whoops.

I really shouldn't be flirting this hard. JD throws his head back and laughs heartily, giving me an even better view of his bare torso. I glance over, taking in the sight of his solid chest, the barely discernible outline of his ab muscles, and the nice bit of skin between his belly button and the waistband of his shorts.

My ovaries ache. They literally *hurt*. The most attractive man I've ever laid eyes upon is sitting next to me, half-naked, and my entire reproductive system has taken notice. In fact, I'm pretty sure my uterus is growing more impatient by the second.

I look up after a while, expecting to see the same smug look on his face. Instead, he's staring back at me with uncertainty in his eyes, as if he can't tell how much I want him. He's letting me set the pace, waiting for my cue before he makes a move.

How can he possibly be so wholesome yet so sexy at the same freaking time?

"JD," I whisper, not intending to sound so breathy and bothered. "I ... I, um ..."

Until this very moment, I'd never really considered myself to be a lustful person. If anything, my career has led me to develop a more scientific and even utilitarian view of sex, ruining most of the magic for me. I've always thought of the act itself as more of a means to an end, only useful for procreation or positive reinforcement in a relationship. And since I never planned on getting married or having kids, long-term celibacy hasn't been a problem for me before now.

However, there's a first time for everything, and being alone, in bed, with shirtless JD has left me so flustered that I'm incapable of stringing together a coherent sentence.

"Can I please kiss you?" he asks after I trail off, still gazing at me as if I don't sound like a total idiot.

This time my ovaries reach around my uterus to high-five one another. I swallow and nod, because that's all I can manage, and he cradles my cheek as he pulls me in. He kisses me slowly and tenderly at first, with just a hint of cinnamon lingering on his tongue, but it isn't long before he deepens the kiss. I feel his other hand creeping around to my lower back, guiding me to turn my body and move closer to him.

A rumble escapes from the back of his throat at the same time I discover that I've been running my hand over his chest, my middle finger tracing the outline of the large, raised vein from his left pec onto his shoulder.

Oops.

I will myself to stop, but before I know it, my fingertips have ventured lower, edging along the waistband of his shorts. He moans again as I trail across his skin before stopping to rest at his hip. He grips my backside in response, pulling me even closer until I hitch one of my legs over so that I'm sitting in his lap.

No, no, no ...

This is a really bad idea, according to my brain. But I'm a literal ovulation station right now, and my hormones are slowly but surely gaining control.

His palms slip around to my hips, steering my body over his. I grasp at the short, damp hair on the back of his head, still wet from his shower, and I let out a pained squeak as he shifts our position until I can tell exactly how much he's enjoying this, too.

To my dismay, he moves his hands up to my shoulders, holding me in place as he falls back just enough to break away from our kiss. "Tenley," he says, his voice strained and his chest heaving. "I'm sorry. I didn't mean for things to get out of hand so fast."

"Hmm?" I ask, still drunk.

"You're just so ..." He sighs, closing his eyes and resting his forehead against mine. "I want you so badly."

My insides are molten lava. "I want you, too," I reply, trying desperately to wake up my brain. I lean back to put at least a few inches of space between us. "But I have to tell you something."

He nods, staring raptly at my mouth as I clumsily blurt out, "JD, I'm ovulating. Like, right now."

CHAPTER 28
TENLEY

JD BLINKS AWAY HIS SURPRISE AFTER MY AWKWARD confession. "Mm-kay."

I cringe as I scoot off the bed, hoping to get some separation. "I'm sorry. That came out weird. I just wanted to explain why we can't ... you know, get carried away. So we'll be on the same page."

"Oh," he says, exhaling as if he's relieved. He leans up and grabs my hand, stopping my pacing. "Hey, you know I didn't come to see you with any expectations, right? Don't get me wrong, there's definitely an open tab in the back of my brain with all of my Tenley fantasies playing on loop, but I wasn't banking on most of that happening tonight."

"Okay, good," I reply, my mind reeling as I try to process what he's saying. "Because, well, even if we were ready for that level of intimacy, other methods of contraception are still significantly less effective during peak fertility, and—"

"Ten," he says as he stands beside me, still gripping my hand in his. "I have a biology degree, too. I get it. Stop worrying. Like I told you, I didn't assume you were inviting me over just for a booty call when you slipped me that room key. Which, by the way, was still *really* freaking hot ..." He pulls me in for another kiss.

"But you don't understand," I protest, pushing off his chest against my own wishes. "When I'm at this point in my cycle ..." I sigh before trying again. "You obviously know about pheromones?" He nods in agreement. "Well, since we're biologically wired to detect the best opportunity to procreate ..." He smirks and distracts me by rubbing his thumb over the skin beneath the hem of my shirt. I huff, annoyed at my own lack of concentration. "Basically, I'm trying to warn you because my stupid hormones are on overdrive tonight, which means you might find me more attractive than usual. Meanwhile, I won't have as much self-control as I should."

He presses his lips together, stifling a laugh. "I need a warning? Tenley, are you planning to take advantage of me?"

"Ugh. You're not taking this seriously!"

"I'm sorry," he says through a chuckle. "I'm just trying to get you to lighten up. You see, I don't know what it's like to have any self-control around you. I already grow more attracted to you each day. And since most of my instincts lean toward reproduction or finding something to eat, and I already know you're good at fulfilling one of those, I can't help but be curious about the other." He barely gets through it without laughing again.

I roll my eyes. "Normally, I'd find that annoying, but today, everything you do is cute and endearing. And ... *really* freaking hot," I mimic his reply from before, and his laughter ends abruptly.

"Wait, this is all turning you on?" His voice deepens as he pulls me closer again.

"Yes. It shouldn't be, but it is," I say, pouting.

"And when I touch you like this, here, does it feel better than it usually does?"

My pulse begins racing as he runs his fingertips lightly down my arm, leaving a tingle where he stops at the edge of my palm. I watch as he brings my hand up to place a few warm kisses on that apparently overly sensitive spot on my wrist.

"Maybe," I breathe, my eyes fluttering closed.

"Hmm," he hums thoughtfully. "What if I tried kissing you here?" He moves his lips over to my neck, and I tilt my head to give him better access.

"It's okay," I reply in a shaky voice.

He stops to whisper into my ear. "Just okay? I'm going to need you to be more specific, in the name of science and all." He punctuates his statement by taking my earlobe between his teeth, and I accidentally moan. "Noted," he adds, stepping back to mime pulling a pencil out from behind his ear and jotting down notes on the invisible pad in his palm.

"Stop making fun of me," I whine, pressing my thighs together to relieve some of the building discomfort.

"I'm just trying to collect some qualitative data and examine the situation objectively, babe. Don't you want me to figure out the most effective way to get you in the mood—you know, in case the day ever comes when you're ready to listen to our biological hardwiring?"

I've forgotten that he's shirtless until one of my hands finds its way to his arm, and then my brain gets all foggy and dense again. "What?"

He flexes for me, and the deliciously hard muscles ripple beneath my fingertips. "I just want to be prepared for the right opportunity," he continues, his lips quivering. "To play my part in evolution ... you know, survival of the fittest ..."

"JD?"

"Yeah?"

"Can you just ... kindly shut up?"

"Mm. Make me," he dares with a cocky smirk.

He growls when I grab his face with both hands and pull him down to meet me, our lips crushing together roughly. It suffices to stop him from verbally teasing me for the next few minutes, at least.

I feel his hands crawling hungrily over my body again. He slips one of them up my shirt, and I whimper in response, cursing my body for being so sensitive to his touch.

"Noted," he says into my mouth as he continues his experiment. Next, he uses his teeth to tug at my bottom lip. My fingers dig deeper into his arms, and he smiles, probably making another mental note about which buttons to push later.

Then he begins trailing kisses back down to my neck. "What else do you like, Tenley? Tell me. I want to learn *everything*." He punctuates the last part with another nibble on my ear, and it's all so hot that I wish I could hate him for making me feel so out of control. Instead, I find myself clenching all my core muscles at once, my toes curling in at the mere sound of his request.

"No more talking," I demand, only because I can't bear it.

He obliges and brings his lips back to mine. I clasp my hands behind his neck as he palms my backside and lifts me up with ease, guiding me to wrap my legs around his waist. He takes a few steps and bumps into something firm, presumably the small desk in the corner of the room. "Mm, too short," he mumbles before effortlessly reabsorbing my weight and turning in a different direction.

Around this time I realize I'm being a little selfish, and my curiosity gets the best of me. I reluctantly free my mouth and take a turn mimicking some of the same moves he's been using on me, paying close attention to his reactions. It turns out that JD simply likes it all, and I *really* enjoy the sounds he makes when he likes something.

None of this is helping our current predicament, and all I can do at this point is hope that he has more willpower than I do in my hormone-induced state. We finally reach another solid surface, this one a little higher than the last. He hitches me up before setting me down on the cool stone of the bathroom counter and taking a step back. Then, he clutches me in both hands and grinds his hips roughly into mine. I gasp and pull away from the spot I've been attending to on his neck.

He doesn't bother to say "noted" this time.

We both look up, staring wide-eyed at one another, chests heaving. He clamps his jaw down tightly, and I can see the muscles flexing. I gulp, my legs involuntarily clenching around him and pulling him closer until all that's left between us is a pathetically inadequate layer of damp fabric.

"Tenley." He says my name breathlessly, his grasp on my thighs so strong that I'm afraid I'll find bruises in the morning. "I'm sorry," he whispers. "I thought I could ... stop. But you were right. You're so ... it's all *so good* ..."

He captures my lips with his again, arching his back slightly. Unfortunately, the effects of that seemingly modest movement are multiplied by the more sizable evidence of his ability to see that whole reproduction thing through if need be. I try desperately to reach my brain again, searching through the fog for some semblance of control.

Think of non-sexy things.

What had he joked about earlier? Sweaty, smelly, exhausted JD?

Nope, still hot.

I recalibrate and try again.

Okay, childbirth and morning sickness and ... babies.

That one backfires, too. My ovaries continue cheering and urging me onward.

Must ... not ... make a baby. Keep pants on ...

Despite my attempts, I can't focus on anything with JD still pressed against me. My heels have even mutinied, digging themselves into his back and encouraging him.

I *have* to do something smart. We're almost past the point of no return, if we aren't there already. I remind myself of what Loren and I talked about earlier—how sleeping with JD this early into our relationship could lead us down the wrong path, especially since we'd be cheapening our first time together by giving into temptation now, in a random hotel room surrounded by the football team and half of Camellia.

Plus ... *ALL THE BABIES.*

(My ovaries supply that one.)

I slip my hand down between us, hoping to get some separation, but I end up conducting a brief investigation of my own instead.

Hey, it's *for science*, okay?

JD flinches and hisses through his teeth. "Please," he begs, resting his forehead on my shoulder, and I can't tell whether he's pleading for me to quit or carry on. I consider initiating some other non-pregnancy–inducing activities for a second, but then I think of the NFP-related stuff I've been reading; I know it'll just feed the flame.

"I'm sorry. We have to stop," I whisper.

He looks up at me with puppy-dog eyes and nods, then shakes his head side to side, making me laugh, and nods again. "I told you you'd be the death of me, Tenley Jean," he mumbles, his lips swollen and still enticing.

"You started it," I complain. "And I warned you, remember?"

He sighs. "I only meant to collect some light field observations, but that admittedly escalated too quickly."

I giggle immaturely. "Oh, it *definitely* escalated." We finally manage to come up for air, and I decide to start cracking suggestive jokes? I knew I couldn't trust myself with him.

He narrows his eyes at me. "Did you just ... No. You can't. Nope."

"What?"

"You can't get all hot and bothered with me, then roast little JD after leaving him high and dry. Uh-uh. I'm the only one who gets to make the jokes after all that."

"What do you mean?" I ask, trying not to laugh.

"None of this is fair. I've got to keep putting myself out there and searching for clues just to figure out whether you find me remotely attractive. In the meantime, I have no way of hiding exactly what *you* do to me," he explains, taking a step closer to demonstrate his point.

I stifle a whimper when he backs away, and he grins. "Noted."

Then I pull a face at him, but he looks even more smug in return. "You sure have been taking a lot of notes," I remark, forgetting again that I'm not supposed to be flirting anymore.

"I plan on needing them, eventually," he says, his voice deep. And he pretends not to notice when I shiver.

After that, he helps me down from the counter and leads me back to bed, which isn't much of a mood-killer, if I'm being honest. But we settle in quietly beside one another, and he grabs the remote to turn up the volume on the game, presumably as a distraction. He leans back against the headboard with one arm raised, an offering for me to tuck myself in against him. I snuggle in nicely and try my best to keep my eyes trained on the screen and not to glance down. A few minutes pass before I hear him exhale loudly as he pulls one of the pillows stacked behind us to hold in his lap.

"Not a word," he warns, and I snicker quietly.

"I'm not doing anything," I say in defense.

"I'm trying to close that Tenley tab in my browser before I have to go back and share a hotel room with my brother. And you have the audacity to squirm around and make noises like you aren't reacting to this game?"

"Sorry." I choke back the rest of my laughter and do my best not to make any sudden movements, though it's a little difficult not to yell at the TV when the refs make a crazy call. By the time the game ends about twenty minutes later, I glance up and notice his eyes are closed, his breathing slow and steady. It isn't even fair how beautiful he is, his long eyelashes curling up from his cheeks and his dimples set back into his stubble. And his nose ... I love that it's just a little too big for the rest of his face.

I watch him for a second longer, drinking in the sight of him as my eyes roam down his neck and torso until they reach the strategically placed pillow. The fact that he's this gorgeous yet attracted to me is quite intimidating, to say the least. I inventory my own physical imperfections, my stomach turning when I consider letting JD see the stretch marks and dimples that accentuate my curves. Despite having a real appreciation for the female body and knowing that there are very few "perfect" ones out there, I'm still self-conscious about mine. The very same attributes I think make other women look distinctive and beautiful make me feel awkward and unworthy. And even though my figure is supposed to be enviable, I hate that I don't have a thigh gap and that my breasts can't hold their own without an underwire. But I will just have to trust that JD really means it when he says that he likes my body the way it is.

I heave out a sigh. I'm overanalyzing everything, just seconds away from convincing myself that he's too good for me—though he definitely is. If I don't get out of my own head, I'll end up sabotaging our relationship. His intentions are obviously honest; he'd have given up on me a long time ago if they weren't, and he certainly wouldn't have given me a pass just now if he were only after sex.

I know what he wants. The only question is whether I'm capable of giving him everything he deserves.

I notice the time and reluctantly reach over to wake him. "Hey, Sleeping Beauty," I say, rubbing his chest softly. "I think you'd better go back to your own room now. We don't need you doing the walk of shame in front of Ethan and his friends in the morning."

His eyelids flutter for a second, but he just shakes his head and tightens his arm around me, mumbling something about not caring. "JD," I start again, this time adding a kiss on his cheek. "It's time for you to go back to your own bed. You've got a big day tomorrow."

His chest expands before he finally opens his eyes. "Okay, okay, I'll go, but only after one more kiss," he agrees sleepily. I happily grant his request, and he eventually pulls away with a groan.

"I should probably make a pass down the team hall on my way back, too. I almost forgot that we might not be the only kids sneaking into one another's rooms tonight."

I cringe at his reminder that Ethan's crush and the rest of the cheer squad traveled with the team. "That's not a bad idea. I don't want to see any new teenage maternity patients in a month."

"Let's hope not, unless we end up winning tomorrow night and getting a bid to the state championship. I mean, you'd consider that adequate cause for celebration, right?" he asks carefully, making me laugh. Then he smiles and stands to yank his hoodie down over his head. (What a travesty, by the way.) "Good night, Tenley Jean."

"Stop calling me that, or I'm going to start using your whole name in public, Joseph Drake Bourgeois the *Third*," I warn him, but he doesn't seem bothered. It's probably the result of growing up with his namesake on law firm billboards and having his full name and stats listed during televised football games.

"Call me anything you want," he replies smugly. "Just remember, we're supposed to be keeping the pet names moderately clean in front of the kid."

Or maybe he's just flirting again.

"How did you find out about my middle name, anyway?" I continue, trying to ignore his smoldering look.

"Ethan, of course," he states as he breaks eye contact to slide into his shoes. He puts his cap on backward this time, which I now understand means he's activating his cocky teenage-boy persona. "Between everything I learned from picking his brain for the past few months, all of the details I've been cataloging since we started dating, and the very valuable qualitative data I've collected tonight, I'm well on my way to becoming a Tenley Jean expert."

Yep, there he is, folks.

"Oh, yeah?" I retort.

He smirks as he steps back toward the exit. "Yep. So, uh, how many more days of this peak fertility stuff, you think?"

I narrow my eyes at him. "Why do you ask?"

"Just wondering whether I'll get 'Friend-Zone Tenley' or 'Thirst-Trap Tenley' if I come knocking on your door again tomorrow night," he says, winking. "It seems as though there's no in-between."

My nostrils flare, and he chuckles as I grab a pillow and chuck it at his head. But he simply dodges it and purses his lips to blow a kiss before sneaking out the door.

As soon as he's gone, I sigh heavily and throw myself back onto the rest of the pillows. I, for one, hope not to see Thirst-Trap Tenley again tomorrow night. Unless, of course, Backward-Cap, Shirtless JD comes knocking.

THAT'S IT. *ÇA C'EST FINI.*

I close the door to Tenley's room behind me, stopping to let my head fall back against the solid surface. I thought I had it bad for her before, but I was wrong. There's no doubt in my mind, after all that positive reinforcement in the form of the hottest pheromone-driven make out session I've ever experienced, that I am completely in love with her. I mean, I am like, cheesy, mushy, whipped, head-over-heels in love with Tenley Robin.

I bite my lip and shake my head, remembering the flustered look on her face when I handed her that bag of Red Hots, and then again as she explained the ins and outs of female fertility, just so she could have an excuse to jump me without looking like a tease. It was almost as hot as when she got so worked up at that bad PI call that she yelled at the TV.

I still don't want to risk ruining anything by rushing the physical aspect of our relationship; it's just that I hadn't realized it was even possible for everything to feel as good as it does with Tenley. Although I know slow and steady is the right pace, I'm going to have to exercise more willpower than it took to recover after my knee surgery to keep myself from giving in to the overwhelming temptation. And I'm almost certain that once we cross that line, we won't be able to stop.

Oh, and there's also that small detail about Tenley not being a fan of contraception. All the more reason to postpone sex, right? Or should I just prepare for the inevitable?

Another fantasy pops into my head: I return home from practice to find Tenley sitting at the kitchen counter with a basketball-shaped belly poking out of her open lab coat. She greets me with a kiss on the cheek as Ethan walks in behind me.

One second of that vision is enough to solidify my end goals, even if it means waiting until the right time.

A noise coming from somewhere down the hallway jolts me back from my thoughts and reminds me I'm not supposed to be out here. I carefully survey the area before darting back to the empty elevator and considering whether I should check the spirit group floor for any suspicious activity. But I reassure myself that Mrs. Rachel, our cheer sponsor, runs a tight ship, and I venture down to the team floor again. Then the elevator doors open to reveal a handful of boys dressed identically to me, all wide-eyed and scared shitless, except for one.

Ethan steps forward from the group, and I cross my arms and stare him down, not saying a word. "And where might you be coming from, *Coach*?" demands the cocky little twerp.

My lip twitches, and I squeeze my arms tighter over my chest. "I'm just returning from none of your damn business," I reply.

"Oh, yeah, and how was your stay?"

"Very nice, actually." I step out into the hall, and the other kids glance at Ethan as if this is the last they'll ever see of him.

"Meet anyone I know there?"

I lean in and lower my voice. "Are we gonna keep playing this little game all night?"

He glares up at me. From the look in his eyes, it's clear that he suspects I've been upstairs with Tenley all this time. And he's pissed about it.

Technically, he's right, even if it isn't quite as bad as he thinks.

"Any of you have a problem with me doing my job and monitoring the girls' floor to make sure you little pervs aren't trying to sneak up there?" I ask after a minute of awkward silence, fighting the smirk that might give me away.

"No, sir," Ethan's entourage answers.

"What about you, E? Anything you wanna get off your chest?" I might be picking a fight, but I also figure this conversation needs to happen, regardless. And I've spent enough time around teenage boys to know if I don't get a jump on the situation, his resentment will only grow.

He blinks a few times, his anger seething. "Do I have a choice?"

"The rest of you, get back to your rooms," I order, making them scatter. I nod for Ethan to follow me, and he obeys. Though he doesn't seem to be in the mood for a heart-to-heart.

"Look," I begin, attempting to soften my tone. "It's not what you think. I mean, it's not like *that*, anyway."

"Isn't it?"

My brow lifts. If I weren't so offended by the audacity of the little punk, I might've been proud of his newfound nerve. But if there's anything I've learned from my time in the classroom, it's that behind every teenage jerk is a kid trying to cover up the fact that he's going through something way too tough for him to handle at his age.

I insert a key into the card reader, but the lock beeps and flashes red. I cringe, realizing I've inadvertently rubbed it in by using Tenley's card instead of my own.

"You've got to be freaking kidding me," Ethan mumbles behind me while I scramble to swap keys and try again. I'm rewarded with a green light this time, and I give Blake a short warning knock before opening the door.

"*Mais*, if it isn't Coach Thirsty," he remarks from his bed. "You've been up there so long I honestly thought you weren't coming back tonight. Did our old 'no shirt under the hoodie' trick work on Tenley, or what?"

I clear my throat, willing him to look up from his phone. "I don't know what you're talking about, man."

"Come on, bruh. Tell me you finally sco—"

"Heyyy, look who I caught trying to sneak up to visit the cheer-leaders!" I drown him out and shove Ethan forward.

"Oh, hey, Big E." Blake sits up quickly. "Didn't see you there at first."

"Nobody ever does," Ethan replies before turning to face me. "And, for the record, I was actually going to check on Aunt Ten because my grandma said she hadn't been able to reach her all night."

I look away, the guilt and shame churning inside my stomach.

"I should probably make another round, just to be sure everyone's back in their own rooms," Blake announces before grabbing his shoes and giving me a pity shoulder pat on his way out the door.

I sigh once we're alone. "I'm sorry, Ethan. Is everything okay back home?"

"Yeah, we just got worried when Aunt Ten quit answering her phone. But I guess she's been too busy for us tonight." His eyes are trained on his feet, and he's obviously not just mad at me for allegedly hooking up with Tenley. He seems anxious and even afraid of something else, and the anger is just a cover-up.

"Would you like to go talk to your aunt?"

He shrugs a shoulder. "I'm sure you already know whether she's okay."

"Yeah. She was fine when I left her room," I admit ruefully. "And you know she'd never ignore you guys on purpose. Her phone must have died or something."

"Cool story, bro. Can I go back to my room now?"

"Not until you tell me what's really bothering you," I demand.

He huffs. "I don't have to tell you shit. You're not my dad, remember?"

Well, here we go. It's the moment we've all been waiting for. He's flipped a switch now, and I have no choice but to respond accordingly.

"All right, then, big man. Either you tell me what the hell is going on with you, or we take this outside, and you get your disrespectful ass handed to you. So, what's it gonna be?" I lean back on my heels, crossing my arms over my chest again and eliciting a loud gulp from Ethan.

Okay, so I'm not *really* going to lay a hand on him. But sometimes coaching requires me to metaphorically knock a kid further down before I build him back up, and it works, so I figure it'll have to do for my foster-step-uncle approach, too.

"You wouldn't actually fight me," he says with an eye roll.

"You sure about that? I'll even let you get in one good lick first, if it'll make you feel better." I take a step closer and spread my arms out, leaving my chest open.

"No." He shuffles back.

"But this is what you want, right? What if I made you really mad? You man enough to hit me then?"

"You're already making me mad," he growls through his teeth.

"I can do better. Want me to tell you why I went upstairs?" He glares at me and shakes his head. I move close enough for his face to be even with my chest and stare down at him. "Either you start talking or I do. And you won't enjoy hearing what I've been up to."

"Just ... *stop*," Ethan yells, covering his ears.

Immediately, I drop my guise and reach an arm around to trap him against my side in a light embrace. He stands there stiffly for a second before finally leaning in and allowing me to support his weight. Then he brings his fists down and rests them on my shoulder, and I place my other hand on his back. He lets me hold him that way for a while, the only sound being his ragged breathing.

"I'm sorry, Coach," he says after a minute, his voice thick.

"I know," I reply. "So am I."

Ethan turns away to wipe his face and moves to sit at the edge of the bed. "I honestly don't know what my problem is," he begins as I settle beside him. "Maybe it's just a little bit of everything."

"Then start by telling me about just one thing." I want to give him the space to explain himself now and encourage him to do most of the talking.

He sighs wearily before he speaks again. "Don't get me wrong, I'm grateful for my family. But being a sixteen-year-old orphan still sucks. I never got to meet my mom, and I'm about to lose the only dad I've ever known. I mean, it's not like Pop can help it. I'm just sick of being abandoned."

My chest aches for him. I've only experienced a touch of what Ethan's going through, but losing my parents as an adult pales in comparison. And although I'd do anything to spare him this pain, especially at his age, a vain offer to fix everything isn't what he needs to hear right now.

"I'm sorry, E. I can't imagine how hard this is for you," I say.

"He's been calling me, you know? He found me."

I gulp, remembering what he'd let slip at homecoming. "Your biological father?"

He nods. "Yeah. He seems nice, for the most part, but he's already trying too hard."

My protective instincts flare. "Has he made you uncomfortable? He's not forcing you to do anything you don't want to do, right?"

"No, it's just awkward, I guess. He really wants to get to know me, but I'd honestly rather spend time with Pop while I still can."

"That's fair," I tell him.

He chews on his lip and stares down at the floor. "Also, I shouldn't have said most of that stuff to you just now."

"And I never should have gone to Tenley's room. I wasn't setting a good example."

"No, you both deserve to be happy, and I'm still glad you're together." He pauses for a second before he continues. "I think I'm just afraid if something goes wrong and you break up now that I'll lose one of you. Like, things would become weird between us, or Aunt Ten might leave again. And you're kind of all I have left."

"Ethan ..." My heart sinks to my feet. "I'm sorry. I hadn't realized you've been worrying about that. But I hope you know we both want what's best for you, first and foremost. Even if things don't work out between Tenley and me, I'll always have your back."

"Okay, but what if you eventually get married and have kids of your own? I'll just be in the way."

"You could never be in the way, man. That's not how any of this works, anyway. You don't suddenly forget about your older kids once you have new ones. If anything, you'll always know that we *chose* you before we elected to make second-rate replicas." I lean over and bump his shoulder playfully, and he rewards me with a halfhearted laugh.

"And listen, if your aunt is willing to put up with me for that long, I'll be thrilled to play whatever role you want in your life. But I think we're getting ahead of ourselves. You'd better not let Tenley hear all this talk about marriage and babies. I'm not even sure she likes me all that much," I chuckle.

He glares at me from the side. "Hold on. I thought you just said—"

"All I said is that it wasn't like that."

"So, you mean to tell me—"

"I don't mean to tell you a damn thing about my sex life," I bark out defensively. Then I remember I'm supposed to be working on leading by example, so I soften my tone. "Look, I'm assuming you've at least gotten the chastity talk in confirmation class by now?"

He nods. "Then I'd like to reinforce the importance of building emotional intimacy with someone instead of rushing into the physical stuff," I continue. "For many different reasons, most of which justify waiting for marriage."

That last bit stings a little after saying it out loud.

"Yeah, like you've never—"

I cut him off again, trying to redirect the conversation. "Hey, my dad taught me to respect women, just like I'm sure your Pop did with you, and I care entirely too much about Tenley to risk doing things out of order. Did you really think I was desperate enough to use a trip with the team for *that*, anyway?"

"I mean ... yeah."

I elbow him and scowl. "Okay, *desperate* isn't the word I'm trying to emphasize here. But I am offended, since you apparently assumed I've just been trying to hook up with her."

He sighs. "I know you're not that kind of guy. But they were roasting you at practice earlier and ..." He cringes and shakes his head, as if he can't bear to repeat what he heard. "I'm sure it was meant to be a joke, but one of the guys said I'd get more playing time if I sent Aunt Ten to your hotel room. That's why I assumed the worst when I saw you coming downstairs."

"Ignore them. They're just jealous because they think I'm getting laid and they're not."

He laughs. "So, nothing actually happened up there?"

"You don't really want me to answer that, do you?" I ask with a cocky grin.

He rolls his eyes before turning to face me directly. "No, but can I tell you something off the record? Like, you can't review the catch anymore because we've already run the next play?"

"I guess I can grant you a free pass tonight, within reason."

"By the time you caught us in the hallway, I'd already been to Caidence's room and back," he admits with a smirk.

"You little ..." I clench my jaw and knock him in the shoulder, and he winces as he rubs the sore spot. "I'll make you regret it if I find out you even *tried* anything with that girl. I mean it."

"It wasn't like that," he says mockingly. "We just hung out for a bit." His face reddens, spoiling his efforts to sound nonchalant.

"In a hotel-room bed?"

"All of our clothes stayed on, I swear," he squeals defensively.

"You shouldn't be putting yourselves in that situation in the first place. There's too much temptation." He raises an eyebrow, silently pointing out that I sound like a big, fat, hypocrite again. "No more hotel-room visits ... for either of us. And you'd better make sure you haven't damaged Caidence's reputation, either," I continue scolding him. But I can't help it when my scowl fades into a smile, which he returns. And we just sit there for a while, both of us wearing the same silly, lovesick look on our faces.

We're interrupted a minute later when Blake knocks and cracks the door open. "All clear?"

"Yeah," I call, glancing down at Ethan. "Everyone's still alive. Although, it was touch-and-go for a while, there."

"All right," Blake says cheerfully, letting himself in. "Did I miss all the gory details from your trip upstairs?"

"What was I thinking when I offered you a job around kids?" I say through my teeth, standing and urging Ethan out of the room before Blake can add anything else.

Ethan snorts. "Good night, Coach Thirsty," he has the nerve to say as our handshake ends in a bro hug.

"Keep calling me that, and I'll make you a little cousin next time."

He rolls his eyes on his way out, blissfully ignorant as to how close I came to making that last threat a reality. I step out into the hallway to make sure he's back in his own room for the night before changing out of my sweaty hoodie.

"So?" Blake inquires again from his bed, implying that I have something more to say now that we're alone.

I sigh, knowing that he won't let up until he gets the truth out of me. "Sorry to disappoint you, man. But I didn't need the protection you so thoughtfully slipped into my pocket," I remark as I lie back in my own bed.

He grunts. "Did you at least get a little action?"

"Yep." He looks over at me expectantly, waving his hand for me to continue, and I can't help but smile again. "When I walked in, she was just sitting there, watching football."

"Like, on purpose?" I nod and he raises his eyebrows, knowing how much that would drive me crazy. "Then you came up with a pretty quick excuse to get out of that hoodie, didn't you?"

"Damn right, I did."

He laughs. "And?"

I shrug nonchalantly. "Some really, *really* hot messing around."

"How hot, exactly?"

"Like I'm going to embarrass both of us with my reaction if you keep making me think about it," I return, narrowing my eyes at him.

"Hold up. You're telling me the girl of your dreams invited you over to her hotel room to watch football and chill, then you took off your clothes and messed around, but you didn't actually have sex?" he asks, squinting at me. "What am I missing?"

I swallow hard, unsure of whether it's worth trying to explain the fertility stuff to Blake right now. "It just wasn't the right time," I tell him. "And I'm not going to rush it, because I'm very confident it's going to be worth the wait when we do get there."

"Good for you, then," he says, surprising me with his sincerity. He's quiet for a while before he speaks up again. "JD?"

"Yeah?"

I turn to face him, but he's looking up, his expression thoughtful, as if he's reading a script on the ceiling. "Your feelings for Tenley aside, are you sure this is what you really want? I know we've talked about the whole instant-family situation before, but it seems like your relationship is on a pretty fast track. And you're already having to deal with some backlash from Ethan."

"This stuff with Ethan was my own fault, really, and the exact reason I hesitated to visit Tenley in the first place." He rolls his eyes when I pause to shoot him an I-told-you-so glare. "And although I appreciate your concern, honestly, this is *all* I want, now. Being with Tenley and Ethan, it just ... fits."

"Then I'm happy for you, bro."

He does look happy, but there's something else there—sadness, jealousy, maybe even loneliness. I'm not used to seeing this much emotion from Blake. He's always been so good at keeping his true feelings hidden, and it makes me wonder whether he needs me to question some of his self-imposed lifestyle choices so he'll have an excuse to change them.

"Thanks, man. That means a lot," I reply after a while, resolving to revisit those thoughts.

We say good night, and I roll over to grab my phone from the nightstand.

JD

Hey. You still up?

TENLEY

Sort of. What's up?

JD

Just checking in. I heard your mom was having trouble getting through to your phone.

TENLEY

Yeah, I accidentally let it die earlier, but I've spoken to her since then.

JD

like react

So, I've been thinking … Football season is almost over. Maybe we could go out together in town … or even try a little PDA since we won't need to worry about hiding out anymore.

TENLEY

We should wait until after the custody hearing, don't you think? Besides, I don't mind keeping you all to myself. Sneaking around can be kind of hot, right?

JD

NOTED

TENLEY

Good night, Coach.

JD

Good night, Dorothy.

Although I'm growing more desperate by the minute to tell Tenley I'm in love with her, her hesitance to go public with our relationship makes it clear that she isn't there yet.

Unless Blake really was onto something before—except it's not the physical connection she needs to allow herself to fall for me. Maybe she's actually waiting to hear me say those three little words before she can go all in.

I guess there's only one way to find out.

CHAPTER 30
TENLEY

Camellia High: 2, Buffets: 0

THE HOTEL LOBBY IS PACKED THE NEXT MORNING. THAT poor buffet spread doesn't stand a chance against our football team.

Normally, I'd skip the heavy breakfast, especially with a crowd this size, but the waffle-making station calls for an indulgence. I'm pouring batter into one of the irons when I hear JD's voice rumbling over my shoulder.

"Good morning, Ms. Tenley."

"Morning," I reply, already cursing my body's reaction. My heart shouldn't be racing like this before I've even gotten the chance to look at him, should it?

He turns and leans back against the counter with his hands in his pockets, positioning himself just a few inches closer than proper, and my stomach dips. "Mind making another one of those for me?"

"Okay." I scoop more batter and shut the other waffle iron.

"Slept well?"

"Mostly." It's not true, though. I tossed and turned all night, recalling the way he'd made me feel earlier that evening and wishing I'd let him stay. He nods, and his eyes roam over me as if I'm another item on the buffet. I swallow hard, pretending to focus on making our breakfast.

"Hey, Coach, you're looking a little dehydrated this morning. You know, they have drinks if you're feeling thirsty," one of Ethan's teammates calls as he passes us with his plate piled high, his friends laughing at JD's expense.

I instinctively scoot over to put some space between us. JD, on the other hand, calmly extends a foot the size of a water ski and trips his offender, who in turn loses half his breakfast haul. His friends snicker even louder as bacon and biscuits tumble off his plate while he tries to regain his balance.

"Watch where you're going, Damien. And clean that up," JD commands gruffly, sufficiently reasserting his alpha status.

"Yes, sir," the kid grumbles as he scurries away.

"So, uh, have you talked to Ethan this morning?" JD asks, turning back to me.

I shrug, trying not to smirk. I think I'm developing an appreciation for the way he handles teenagers so smoothly. "Not yet. Why?" The first iron beeps, so I open it up.

"Let's just say I'm glad I got that power nap during the fourth quarter last night."

"Did something happen?"

I hand him the plated waffle, and he thanks me before drowning it in syrup and chocolate chips. It's hard not to be jealous of the amount of calories the man consumes every day.

"We had a temporary hiccup. But we were able to talk it out."

"What do you mean?" I furrow my brow, taking the second waffle for myself, and JD automatically reaches over to pour syrup over it for me.

"I ran into him on the way back to my room. Apparently, he was going up to check on you because you weren't answering your phone."

I sigh. "And he was upset about us ... being together?"

He pauses and licks his lips. "He was."

"Oh. I wouldn't have expected that."

"It sounds like a few of the guys figured out something's going on and started teasing him about it," JD replies. "Honestly, I've been waiting for this to happen. But I think he only acted out last night because he's having a hard time dealing with everything else going on." He turns and glances around, quietly motioning toward the side where Ethan is walking into the lobby with a group of friends. "Look, I don't want to betray his confidence, but I think it's important for you to know that he's a lot more insecure about the custody situation than he's been letting on. And that he's not going to take it very well when ..." He meets my eyes with a sympathetic look.

I nod, pressing my lips together. "Thanks for the heads-up. And thank you for talking to him last night."

"Anytime." He hesitates for a second, probably trying to decide whether it's worth having breakfast together in public. "Do you have any plans today?"

I shrug, then I follow Ethan's expression as he notices the two of us together. He looks a little more downcast than usual at first, but he forces a smile and heads my way. "Probably just going to check out the mall and do some Christmas shopping." I clear my throat as Ethan approaches.

"Have fun, then. I'll text you later?"

I pout inwardly. I guess I'd expected a little more flirting or at least some teasing after our "date" last night, but JD almost seems distant. And I've gotten so used to his relentless pursuit that I'm slightly disappointed he isn't at least *asking* me to sneak away with him.

"Yeah. Good luck, if I don't see you before the game."

He smiles and turns to walk away, wordlessly trading fist bumps with Ethan. Their familiarity makes my heart swell, and I'm even more curious about what went down last night.

"Morning, Aunt Ten," Ethan greets me. "How are the waffles?"

"Not sure yet, but they smell good. Would you like one?"

"Yeah, thanks. Two?"

"Ready for the game?" I attempt to make small talk while I restart the irons. I may as well be wearing a Waffle House visor this morning.

"Oh, for sure."

"That's good." We stand there in a cloud of awkward silence until the machines beep again.

He sighs as I hand him a plate. "I guess Coach JD briefed you on what happened last night."

"He mentioned running into you and that you were upset because I hadn't been answering my phone, which I'm really sorry about."

"It's fine." He clears his throat. "He told me he'd talked to you and that you were okay."

I nod, neither of us willing to admit that we know more than that. "Do you need anything today?"

"Uh, no, I'm good. I think we're supposed to go back to BSU for practice, then get some lunch and hang out here at the hotel for the afternoon."

"Oh, okay. Cool. Well, let me know when you make it back. I planned on going shopping to pass the time, so I can pick up some snacks or something for you and your friends, if you'd like."

"Thanks." He smiles warmly and turns toward the others.

"Ethan, wait," I call.

"Yes, ma'am?"

I take a few steps over and place my hand on his arm. "Look, I know we've talked about it before, but you'd tell me if I ever made you feel uncomfortable—you know, with JD—right?"

He snorts. "Is that a trick question? Everyone in the room is probably laughing at him right now. I don't even have to turn around to know he's staring at you like a heart-eyed emoji."

I look away, feeling my face heat up. "Might I remind you that you knew he was this corny before you practically begged me to give him a chance?"

"Yeah, that's on me."

We both laugh softly. "I mean it, though, Ethan. You've got enough going on. The last thing I want is to make things harder for you."

"I know," he replies. "And I don't regret encouraging you to get together. I've just been worried about some other stuff, like what would happen if you broke up."

"Oh, well, that's understandable." I'm surprised he's willing to admit what's been bothering him, but it's likely because JD already talked things through with him last night. Then it registers that I may not be able to do this parenting stuff without JD. I probably need him more than I've been willing to admit, and Ethan must realize that, too.

"I can't say for sure what's going to happen with JD and me, but I will always put you first, Ethan. You know that, right?"

He nods. "I do."

"Good, because I love you, kid," I add, giving his arm a light squeeze. "Now, go eat your waffles before they get cold."

"Love you, too, Aunt Ten." He rewards me with a wide smile before wandering off to sit with Caidence and some friends.

I search for an empty table so I can finally get around to eating my own breakfast, purposefully sitting behind JD to avoid drawing attention to myself (and only a little because I want to check out his back muscles). However, I find myself meeting his brother's gaze as soon as I glance up. Blake smirks at me over his plate of eggs and bacon, that knowing look on his face most likely the result of the room-key stunt I pulled in front of him yesterday and the assumptions he's made about last night.

What if JD told him that I was so … easy? No, he wouldn't, right? Do guys even talk about that stuff as much as women do?

Before I can finish my thought, JD rises from his seat across from Blake, turns to wink at me as he slides his chair back under the table, and saunters off. I think I'm finally safe, until Blake struts over and plops down into the chair across from me.

What is it with these Bourgeois men and their walking?

"Um, hi?"

"Hey," he replies, as if it isn't weird that he's invited himself to join me. "Look, I don't want to make a scene, but I need a favor."

"Okay." I eye him suspiciously.

"Tenley, my brother is literally the best person in the world. And you should know this isn't just a casual fling for him. He really likes you, and he's probably holding back because he's afraid to scare you off. So I just want to make sure you're somewhat on the same page. I don't want to see him get hurt."

I chew on my lip, digesting everything Blake is saying. "And you think I'm going to hurt him?"

He shrugs. "I hope you won't. But I'd rather not watch him get any more invested with you and Ethan than he already is if you're only interested in messing around while you're here, especially if you plan to leave again."

"You know I don't have any room in my life for messing around. In fact, that's exactly why it took me a while to even consider dating JD," I say defensively.

He stares at me for a second before replying, one corner of his mouth turning up slightly. "That's what I figured. I just wanted to make sure that you understood his ... intentions."

"Okay."

"And to warn you that he might come on a little strong."

"Oh." I swallow hard. "Does he do this often?"

"Fall for someone and go all in right away, you mean?"

"Yeah, I guess," I answer, my voice almost squeaky. Did someone turn up the heat in this area of the hotel? It's certainly feeling stuffy in here.

"JD has always been kind and generous to a fault," he says. "But I honestly can't remember the last time he went on a second date with anyone, and I've never seen him as nervous and giddy as he is around you ... or as happy. Hence, this little injunction."

I stare down at the table, trying to process. What has JD been telling his brother about us?

Blake stands and scoots his chair in. "Just be careful, would you?"

I press my lips together in a hard line. "I will."

He walks away, leaving me to consider my own intentions. I glance down at my breakfast, but I've lost my appetite. There have been too many heavy conversations already today, leaving me emotionally drained before nine in the morning. The stress over the physical aspect of my relationship with JD, my self-doubt regarding our future, the conflict with Ethan, and now this tension with Blake are all getting to be too much, the pressure building as soon as I realize there was never really any chance for JD and me to just *date*. Given the circumstances, we've basically signed up for a semi-serious relationship by default. And JD's probably been trying to tell me he's on board for the past month or so, while I've been hesitant to label us as anything but "more than friends."

This is also why I avoided dating in the first place. I still don't trust myself to have the mental and emotional capacity to handle losing my dad, becoming a parent, rebuilding my career, and maintaining a relationship, all at the same time. Unfortunately, that means some of Blake's concerns are valid. My first instinct is to brush my love life aside once I get overwhelmed, and JD deserves so much better.

Although, so far, I guess JD *has* been getting a whole lot of my time and attention. I wonder what it signifies after I tally up the unconscious energy I've been devoting so far to thinking about him and being with him.

It's all too much to wrap my mind around.

I give up on eating and stop at Ethan's table to hand him my mostly untouched food, which he gladly accepts. Then my phone chimes, so I reach into my pocket to retrieve it as I leave the lobby.

JD

So, idk if you're aware, but there's this really great stairwell here.

And taking the stairs instead of the elevator is a great way to incorporate cardio into your daily schedule.

TENLEY

Is that so?

JD

Yep. I know you don't care for exercise, but it's good for your heart.

And you're worried about my heart?

Way more than I should admit. 

I look up from my phone to find myself staring at the elevators, the door leading to the stairs just off to the side.

Elevators are quick and efficient, while stairs require more work but are better for the heart. But then again, it takes time to wait on the elevator to come back down, and the stairs are always readily available. They also don't break down. I fiddle with my bottom lip. This decision shouldn't feel so symbolic.

I sigh, deciding my heart could use the workout. I reluctantly open the door to the stairwell, grateful to find it empty and without witnesses as I set out to climb the four flights to my room. But once I reach the second floor, I'm surprised to see JD sitting on the stairs, fidgeting with his phone. He stands as soon as he spots me, a smile spreading over his entire face and melting me from the inside out.

"I was hoping you'd get the hint," he says shyly, reaching out to grab my hand and pull me closer. I realize he was just trying to get me to sneak away with him, but the fact that I took his advice without knowing he'd be waiting for me registers in the back of my mind. And then all that serious cognitive stuff ceases once his lips brush the inside of my wrist.

"I suppose you're hoping to convince me you just need a quick kiss for luck?" I ask, since my body seems to have its own ideas again.

"Nope. I wasn't planning on asking for anything quick."

I don't even notice that he's slowly backed me up against the wall until he plants his feet and reaches a hand over my head to brace himself. Then he leans in and presses his lips to mine. He inhales deeply, as if he's been underwater and I'm the first breath of air on the surface.

My hands fly up to his collar as he deepens the kiss. I'm surprised at his urgency, and of course my body reacts by upping the ante, my hips rolling away from the safety of the wall as if they're magnetically drawn to his. He groans and uses his free hand to palm my backside and pull me even closer against him, and his mouth begins trekking down my neck. The way he's able to handle me so easily with his super strength makes me shiver. But then again, there isn't much about him that wouldn't turn me on in my current state.

"Tenley," he rasps. "I don't think it's the pheromones."

"Hmm?" I ask, dazed. I glance up at his arm, and the way it's straining against his weight as if he's struggling to hold himself back is quite possibly the sexiest thing I've ever seen in my life. How can I tell JD that I need him to slow down when being with him makes me want to forego all sense of decency and throw down in a hotel stairwell?

"You are just ... so ... damn ... beautiful," he replies, punctuating each word with another kiss on my shoulder, then he straightens up and locks his eyes onto mine. "The hormones don't matter. I want you all the time. You're all I ever think about since the day you came home."

I'm so drunk that I can't even open my eyelids completely. I try to say something back, but it only comes out as a stutter. He must not care, because he responds by crushing his mouth into mine again.

Screw being responsible and emotionally stable. If this is how JD makes me act, then I don't even care about the rest. I'll figure it out at some point, when I'm not hyper-focused on how nice the full length of his body feels pressed against mine or whether I could actually swallow his tongue if I try hard enough.

But ... what if being with JD is more responsible than being without him? What if he makes me feel this way for a good reason? Maybe the physical attraction only seems so strong because of my emotional attachment to him? I've never experienced this connection with anyone else before, and so far, I've been chalking it up to chemistry and hormones. But maybe there's more to it?

He pulls away, bringing me back from my thoughts. "I'm sorry," he whispers. "I know it's too much. I don't mean to overwhelm you. It's just that my feelings for you are sort of like that." He gives me a sad smile.

"Overwhelming?"

"Yes, but in a good way."

I nod. "I get it."

"You do?" He looks surprised to hear I might feel the same.

"Honestly, I don't understand what's going on in my brain or what's happening between us most of the time, and I still want more of it. So, yeah, I know what you mean," I confess with a short laugh.

He closes his eyes and shakes his head, as if he's holding an internal debate. "It's actually a huge relief to hear you say that," he begins, his eyes opening again. "Because I'm about to tell you something that might sound kind of crazy."

"Crazy?" I ask.

"Yeah." He takes another fortifying breath. "Maybe it hasn't been the same for you, but I swear I've felt something calling me to you since the day you got back, maybe even before then. It's like everything I've ever wanted was right in front of me, like God was leading me directly toward what I've been praying for, and I immediately knew in my heart that things were meant to be different with you. But I hesitated to make a move because I was terrified of getting shut down. As long as I put off admitting how much I liked you, I could hang on to that little bit of hope, which was enough to keep me from trusting in His will for us the way I should have. But I see that now, because it only seems to complicate things when I hold back. So I want to make my feelings clear this time, even if that means taking a huge risk."

"Okay," I reply carefully, my mind reeling. He reaches up and strokes my cheek softly, staring at me in that way that melts my insides again.

"Tenley, I am so very much in love with you."

I blink a few times, and it takes reaching the point when my lungs start to burn for me to realize I've been holding my breath. "You *are*?"

He nods, furrowing his brow. "I really am."

"Oh," I say on a shaky exhale.

"I know you might not be ready for that, but I can't help myself."

I gulp, preparing to feel the walls closing in around me. "JD ... I ..."

"Please don't let it scare you away," he adds quickly. "I just think you deserve to know where I am, why I'm so drawn to you, why every little thing you do is such a turn on for me."

I shake my head. "I'm not scared. Well, maybe I am, but you're not scaring me *away*."

"I'm not?"

"The old me might have been making an escape plan as we speak, but right now, I just feel warm ... and *happy*," I reply, to my own surprise. Maybe it's because last night's conversation with Loren and the timely warning from Blake both prompted me to do my over-thinking and panicking beforehand, but I'm handling this way better than I expected. Then again, it could be all the spicy hormones clouding my judgement, too.

JD smiles at my answer, relief washing over his face, and he leans in for a short kiss. "Good. Because I was really hoping you wanted to hear me say it."

"I don't know if I've ever wanted to hear those words until you said them," I admit. "But, coming from you, I like it even more than I thought I could."

He hums and kisses me again. "I love you, Tenley Jean," he says once more as he pulls away.

"I think ..." I inhale sharply, deciding to go for it. "I think I love you, too, JD."

And the second I say it out loud, I'm absolutely sure it's true. That's what this feeling is—the intense connection we share, this incessant need to be around him. Of course I'm in love with JD. How the heck wouldn't I be?

"Come again?" He rears back in shock.

I scrunch up my nose in embarrassment, but I know I've earned that look from him. "I love you, too," I repeat, my voice barely above a whisper.

He groans as if he's in pain. "And I'm supposed to leave you alone now? Just hearing you say that aloud feels so good that I can't even imagine what it would be like to show you."

"Show me?" I squeak.

He nods slowly before bringing his lips down to my jawline. "I want to show you I love you ... without words." His voice grows huskier as he speaks against my skin. "Even though I'll still be using my tongue."

Good. Night.

He literally knocks the wind out of me with that one.

"Oh," I breathe ... and breathe some more. "Uh, let's do that some other time, though. Later, and not during prime baby time."

He throws his head back and laughs heartily, breaking the spell. "Prime baby time?"

"Shut up," I whine. "Don't make me take my L-word back."

"You can't." He grins. "It's too late. You totally meant it."

I nod. "I did. And I've never said it and meant it this way before."

"Mm," he growls. "You'd better get your room key changed before tonight."

I laugh until he brings his lips back to mine, but then there's nothing funny about the way he's kissing me. There is desperation, need, reverence, all of it. I've never imagined finding a man who could make the physical aspect of our relationship this good for me, but JD seems to be managing it just fine, even fully clothed.

He pulls back abruptly, his eyes wide, then pushes himself away from his brace against the wall. "Someone's coming," he pants.

"No," I protest, attempting to collect myself but failing miserably.

His mouth turns up on one side, then he leans in for a short kiss and one last squeeze of my butt before backing away. I can hear someone approaching as laughter echoes up the stairwell, but I'm slow to move. My brain is still trying to catch up after having been kidnapped and stuffed in the back of a closet.

"Don't take this the wrong way, babe, but you'd better get to work on that cardio." He winks and gestures toward the next set of stairs before darting out into the hallway.

I whine again as I gaze at the stairwell. I'm not sure my heart is built for this.

CHAPTER 31
TENLEY

My mom ends our call, and I immediately begin searching for Ethan. I have to get us home before it's too late.

I spot him on the sideline, talking to another running back, so I quickly trek down the bleachers. But as soon as I make it to the bottom, I realize there's no easy way to get to him with the tall fence that surrounds the field, and there doesn't seem to be an opening on the visitors' side.

Crap.

How am I going to get down there fast enough to grab Ethan before the game starts? My eyes follow JD as he walks over to join the other coaches, and I figure I'll start with him, since I probably need to explain what's going on before pulling Ethan away.

I guess he might want to know that my dad is dying, too.

I lean over the railing and shout his name, my eyes darting around nervously when I catch myself calling out for "JD" and not "Coach." He doesn't hear me, anyway, so I pull out my phone and attempt to text him. No luck—his phone's probably set on silent mode.

I sigh and holler for him one more time. Someone finally nudges JD in the shoulder and points in my direction. He turns toward me with a confused smile, until he sees my expression. Concern grows on his face as he hands off his clipboard and jogs to the stands.

"Hey, what's up? Everything okay?" He must think I'm crazy for calling him over in public, especially with only minutes until kickoff.

The band begins playing our fight song just then, triggering a domino effect that includes the cheerleaders carrying a giant Camellia High flag down the sideline and the crowd rising to its feet to yell enthusiastically. I try explaining myself to JD, but it's impossible with the noise level.

"How do I get down there?" I shout.

"Just … jump, I'll catch you!"

Just jump? Seriously?

I glare at him, his face stationed well below my feet. There's no way to make that drop on my own. I've never been under the impression that I'm athletically inclined enough to do any jumping of any kind, and having big boobs means I've never even bothered to try. But I remind myself that this is literally a life-and-death situation. I nod briefly, and he positions himself nearby with his arms ready. I squat and attempt to hop down gracefully, but I end up panicking and grabbing the bottom railing, stranding myself a few feet off the ground.

JD chuckles and steps over to wrap his arms around my thighs. "I've got you. Just, let go," he yells.

I finally comply and latch onto his shoulders, and he loosens his grip just enough to allow me to slip down within the security of his arms. I hold my breath, feeling his capable hands moving up my backside and locking eyes with him as the front of my body slides over his. This is certainly *not* the time for a steamy interaction—in public, nonetheless. He gulps without breaking his gaze, his hands stopping at the small of my back while my toes hover just above the turf.

"Um, thanks. You can put me down now," I mumble. But it takes him another second to snap out of his trance and help me to my feet.

I glance around and realize we've garnered attention now, the band having stopped and the cheer squad and half of the football team watching. Ethan glares at us with an unreadable expression, his helmet tucked under his arm. Hopefully the fans in the bleachers are at least too high up to have seen us inadvertently groping each other.

JD clears his throat, bringing me back from my thoughts. "Are you all right?" he asks again.

I sigh. "Mom called. Dad took a turn for the worse this afternoon. They're not sure he'll make it through the night."

"Dang, Ten. I'm so sorry." He grabs my hand and squeezes. "Are you leaving for home right now?"

I nod solemnly. "I think I need to take Ethan back, too. I know this is a big deal, this game, but he'll never get another chance to say goodbye," I say softly, my voice breaking at the end once the realization hits me. I'm talking about whether we're going to spend my dad's last minutes together.

"Absolutely," he agrees. "I'm just worried about how he's going to take the news."

We both turn and look at Ethan expectantly, and he gives his helmet to a teammate before taking off in our direction. JD releases my hand as he approaches.

"What's going on?" he asks gruffly once he's close enough for us to hear.

"Ethan, Mawmaw just called," I begin. He drops his gaze to his feet, probably preparing for the worst. "She doesn't think there's much time left. Tonight may be it."

He's quiet for a minute. JD places a comforting hand on his shoulder, and Ethan leans into his touch. "I should go." It's a statement, but his eyes are questioning, looking for confirmation from JD.

"I think so too, man." JD gives his shoulder a slight squeeze before he turns to me. "Can I drive you home?"

I furrow my brow. "You can't leave the team."

"That's not what I asked you," he replies sternly.

I'm not surprised he's willing to drop everything to take care of Ethan and me. That's the only version of JD I've seen so far, and I know he wouldn't hesitate to cut a playoff game and drive over three hours to get us home in time. It's my own impulse to take him up on his offer and the sudden dread of having to go through this without him that shocks me.

"No, thank you," I tell him, ignoring those feelings. "I think the drive might actually help occupy my mind. And if I get upset or tired, I'll pull over and take a break."

"Are you sure?" he asks, glancing back and forth between Ethan and me.

"Yeah, we'll be good, Coach. But thanks," Ethan answers. "Just … can you tell the guys I left for a good reason? I don't want them to worry or anything."

"Of course, bud. Why don't you grab your things from the locker room and leave your helmet back there?"

"All right, I'll meet you in the car," he declares before exchanging a handshake-half-hug with JD and jogging off.

"Keep me updated?" JD asks after a second.

"Yes. Maybe you could ask someone to text us game updates, for Ethan?"

"I will." He stares at me until Blake calls out for him with a reminder that they're a minute away from kickoff. "I'm sorry, I have to go. But I'll be there with y'all tomorrow, I promise."

"Don't worry about us. We'll be okay," I reassure him. "Good luck."

He catches me off guard when he grabs my arm to draw me in for a hug and whispers over my shoulder that he loves me. I guess we're breaking the rules tonight. I inhale deeply as I allow myself to indulge in the comfort of his embrace, just for a second. Then we pull away, and he turns back toward the sideline.

Caidence comes over a second later, her ponytail bouncing. "Is it Mr. Jude?" she asks as soon as she sees my expression.

"Yeah," I answer quietly. "He's gotten worse since this afternoon, so we're going back, just in case."

She reaches out and places her hand on my forearm, offering me a small bit of comfort. "I'll be praying for y'all. We all will."

"Thank you, I appreciate that. I'll have Ethan send you an update when we can."

She nods and gives me a sympathetic smile before returning to her squad, and I reflect on how much I like Ethan's girlfriend as I walk off to join him at the gate.

"I told Caidence we were leaving," I inform him on our way out of the stadium.

"Thank you," he says.

We hurry to my car, and he finally speaks again once we're on the road. "So, um, speaking of Caidence ..."

"Yeah?"

"She mentioned seeing you and JD together today."

I open my mouth to speak but think better of it when I remember that JD and I were interrupted in the stairwell earlier. She must have walked in on us. "Oh," is all I say.

"Oh?" He huffs. "So much for not embarrassing me."

"I'm sorry, we didn't think anyone would see us. But people will find out eventually," I explain in my defense.

"Yeah, especially now that you're *serious*."

"What do you mean by that?" I ask, my heart rate quickening.

"I read his lips just now, when you guys were hugging in front of everyone. I came back to remind Coach about something I'd seen in the game film, and it looked like he was saying 'I love you.' " My face flushes. "That's what Caidence overheard, too, isn't it?"

I can't help but smile. "Probably." But when I glance at him again, he looks much more sullen than I expect. "You don't seem happy about it."

"It's none of my business, I guess," he says, crossing his arms.

"I didn't think either of us needed to get your permission to make that declaration, but I suppose it's still somewhat your business," I clarify. His only response is a grunt. "Okay. Want to tell me why you're so upset, then? Because I could have sworn you wanted us to be together, last I checked, which was—oh, yeah, this morning."

"Well, I did. I mean, I do."

"Then what's the problem with us being ... serious?" It's still hard for me to get that last part out.

"I guess I don't understand how you were afraid to date him up until a month ago, but you're already cool with all this emotional intimacy," he says sarcastically. "And you're actually in love with him, too?"

I bite my lip and take a deep breath before I confess. "It sounds crazy, but I think I am. Does that bother you?"

"I don't know. Maybe. It's just that everything is changing, and it's all happening really fast," he rambles.

"You're not wrong. It feels that way for me, too, bud." I stare at the road for a while. "But Ethan, even if some of these changes are sad ones, there are still some good things happening, right?"

"Yeah, I guess," he reluctantly concedes. "Could you take the PDA down a notch, though?"

"Seriously? The stairwell thing was a fluke. And we literally *just* hugged in public for the first time," I protest.

"Okay, then how about the in-front-of-E-DA?"

I turn to him, ready to defend myself again, but he's smiling. "And you mean to tell me that you and Caidence haven't kissed yet?"

He licks his lips as his ears turn red. "That's different."

"Oh, is it?"

"Yeah. We're—"

"Young? And what, JD and I are too mature for that at the ripe old age of thirty?"

He shrugs. "Maybe."

I reach over and whack him in the arm with the back of my hand. "For the record, we're adults. You and Caidence, on the other hand, are not. That means JD and I have the right to do whatever adults do. And you and Caidence do *not*. Got it?"

"But Coach said ..." he begins, trailing off as soon as he realizes he's revealed too much.

"Coach said what?"

"That it wasn't like that."

I frown. "What does that even mean?"

"That you guys were waiting to ... you know ..."

"He told you that?" I'm surprised to hear that JD's been talking about this part of our relationship with Ethan, though I suppose it could have come up in their discussion last night, especially under the circumstances.

"I mean, sort of. Ugh, why are we still talking about this?"

"What? Sex?" I ask brightly, just to watch him squirm.

He cringes. "Gah, do you have to do that?"

"Technically, it's how I make my living, you know," I retort, holding back a smirk.

"Now I know you've been spending too much time around JD, because that's like the worst dad joke in history."

"Ethan, you do realize that someone has to make the babies before I deliver them, right?" I say in an exaggerated whisper.

"Yes. Pop gave me the talk a few years ago, okay? And I basically got round two from Coach last night."

We both quiet after his mention of my dad, the awkward conversation we've been using to avoid the inevitable finally outliving its utility. I reach over after a minute and grip his hand in mine.

"It's not fair, you know," he murmurs.

"I know."

He sniffles and lets go of my hand to wipe his face. "I guess I should get this out now. I'm sure we're supposed to be strong or whatever once we get back."

"That's a load of crap," I say. "Pop won't want us to cry over him forever, but I'm sure he'd like a little reassurance that we'll miss him, right?"

He laughs through his tears. "Yeah, maybe."

My phone chimes, so I snatch it up before Ethan can see the message, praying it isn't a sign that we'll be too late. To my relief, it's just my mom asking us to be careful on the road.

"Do you think he'll be awake when we get there? That we'll be able to talk to him?" Ethan asks after a minute.

"I hope so. But even if he doesn't respond, he might still be able to hear us. And if we don't make it back in time for that, at least we've been making sure he knows how we feel about him, right?"

He swallows hard. "Yeah. But I'd still like to tell him again."

"Me, too."

CHAPTER 32
JD

"Coach JD, Principal Soileau would like to see you in his office during your planning."

I shoot my class a dirty look when they all *ooh* at my intercom court summons. "What did ya do, Coach?" asks one particularly annoying sophomore boy.

"Nothing ... yet," I grumble. I cross my arms over my chest and stare at him a second longer. He quickly turns his attention back to his work until the bell rings, as do the rest of them.

The truth is that getting called to the principal's office is even scarier for a teacher than it is for a student. It usually results in one of two things: a reprimand because of a parent complaint or an added duty because no one else can be trusted to do it. And even though I doubt I'm *really* in trouble, the invitation still feels like blue lights in the rearview mirror.

"Hey, E," I call as the class files out. Ethan reluctantly turns and waits for the rest of them to leave. "You okay?"

He shrugs as he looks down at his feet, shifting them around.

"What's wrong?" I ask, but I know it's a loaded question. He's been struggling since his grandfather passed away a few weeks ago, just as I feared he would. On top of that, his first real girlfriend has apparently dumped him, though he won't share much about it.

"Everything," Ethan answers quietly, making my heart ache. I reach out and pat his shoulder, wishing I could take up some of his burdens.

"I'm sorry, man. Is there anything I can do to make you feel better?"

"I'll be fine," he mumbles. "But thanks, Coach."

"Why don't I ask Tenley if I can help her make your favorite stew for dinner? I was planning on coming over to watch football, anyway."

"Sure, that'd be cool," he replies, his voice still flat. "As long as you don't put on a show again, like you did for my birthday." He attempts a smile and reaches out for a fist bump, but he's obviously making an effort for my sake.

"I can't make any promises when it involves Tenley's corn bread," I say, trying unsuccessfully to get a laugh out of him. I watch him go before I text Tenley about my plans for dinner, just as the tardy bell rings for my off hour. She goes for it, even though she adds a line about wanting to turn in early tonight.

I purse my lips as I stare down at her last message. Things have been going fine for us, but that's also sort of the problem. I guess I'd expected our relationship to progress after we both declared our feelings a few weeks ago, but it almost seems like Tenley's been tapping the brakes since then. Well, maybe not the brakes—we're still spending all of our free time together and getting to know one another, and she certainly doesn't seem to mind kissing me. But she always pulls back once things get really heated or when the conversation gets too serious, especially when it's time for her to use the word "love" again. Unfortunately, that means I haven't been able to continue moving things forward at the speed I'd hoped for.

In other words, I'm getting really, *really* thirsty.

It turns out that I'm no less attracted to Tenley on any given day, despite her theories about fertility and pheromones. In fact, I've formed my own hypothesis and concluded my infatuation with her must be a sign or even a gift, because I can't imagine a desire this strong wasn't meant to last a lifetime. And although I'd love to present my ideas about the Holy Spirit not only leading me to her but also gifting us with this crazy chemistry as a means of reinforcing our call to forming our own family together, I'm also afraid to overwhelm her again. Her feelings already seem to be wavering, and I can't bring myself to push her out of her comfort zone, at least not right now. In the meantime, while her desire for me changes from day to day, I want her all the time, think about her constantly, and have reached the point where I'd do just about anything to take our relationship to the next level, permanently. But I've settled for working off my frustration in the gym and started attending an extra weekday Mass instead.

I'm sure some of Tenley's hesitation comes from the loss of her dad, not only because she's still mourning, but also because she's concerned about Ethan. By the time I made it home the morning after that playoff game, Father Conrad was already there to anoint Mr. Jude. I stayed with them until well after it was all over, despite it being such an intimate family moment. I couldn't imagine leaving Tenley, Ethan, or Mrs. Therese after having promised Mr. Jude that I'd take care of his family. So I lingered and waited patiently in the background for any opportunity to be helpful.

Tenley actually embraced me for a while, finding comfort in my arms for that first day or so until flipping a switch and becoming distant and withdrawn during her father's funeral. I wasn't sure if it was the presence of Ethan's friends, since the whole football team showed up for the wake and burial Mass, or maybe just part of her grieving, but she avoided me the entire time. And it's not like I was upset with her for refusing to hold my hand or sit beside me, except that I could tell she wanted me to comfort her and couldn't understand why she wouldn't let me.

Since then, I've been carefully dropping hints about going public with our relationship, mostly because I'm too much of a chicken to suggest getting engaged or even living together. But Tenley's still adamant about not wanting to pile anything else on Ethan's shoulders and needing to make sure the second custody hearing goes well before purposefully outing ourselves. If it were up to me, I'd happily move all of Ethan and Tenley's things into my house before supper tonight and equip her with a new last name or at least an engagement ring by the time she has to face the judge again.

Yet, here we are, unable to sit together in church or go out to dinner around town, basically dating in neutral. I'm still unsure of how to convey the extent of my feelings for her and my vision for our future together without spooking her, and as desperate as I've become, a large part of me is hesitant to initiate the next level of physical intimacy while she's worried about being seen in public with me.

I redirect my attention to the stack of ungraded tests on my desk until I receive another text from Tenley.

TENLEY

> Do you know a Ryan Jameson?

JD

> I know of him. We used to play against each other in high school, but he's a bit older than us. I think he became a lawyer and a wannabe politician. Why?

TENLEY

> He's Ethan's biological father. And he's filing for custody.

I'm instantly overcome with guilt as I remember fragments of conversation in which Ethan mentioned his father reaching out to him. But to be fair, I didn't realize it had gone this far. I tap her contact to continue the conversation over the phone, thinking this seems too important to process over a text thread.

"Hey," she answers, her voice weak.

"Hey, are you all right? What's going on?"

She sniffles. "Your brother just warned me. Ryan recognized Ethan in the newspaper a while back and sent a private investigator to find out more about him. And Blake just heard that he's suing me for custody."

I brush aside a pang of jealousy, not only because Blake and Tenley have a working relationship, but because they haven't involved me. It's a disappointing reminder that I'm not important enough to warrant the same notification or to have a say in what happens to Ethan.

"Isn't it too late for him to do anything?" I ask, swallowing my pride.

"Apparently not. He's also been communicating with Ethan for a while now, at least for the past couple of months."

And now I know I've screwed up by keeping what Ethan confided in me to myself. All I can think about is how grateful I am that things didn't turn out worse.

"I'm so sorry, Ten," is all I can offer as I swallow hard.

She sighs. "I know it's not Ethan's fault that things happened this way, but I can't believe he'd let us go forward with the custody hearing without saying anything about talking to Ryan. It's so unlike him to sneak around like this."

"He's going through a lot, babe. I'm sure he didn't mean to hurt you. He's just a kid trying to figure out who he is, and the opportunity to meet his biological dad must have been too tempting to pass up." She doesn't say anything in return, but I can hear her crying softly on the other end of the phone, and it takes all I have not to walk out of my classroom and drive over to see her at work. "Hey, I know this is a lot, but it's all going to work out. I'll be there for support if you want to talk to him about it tonight, and I'll do everything I can to make this easier for you guys."

"I know. Thank you."

"Are you going to be okay?"

She exhales again. "Mostly."

"See you in a few hours?"

"Yeah."

"I love you, Ten."

"You, too. Bye."

I run my hand through my hair and scratch the back of my head as I try to process. I know I don't have the right to feel slighted at the moment, but Tenley's curt reply still has me worried. The last thing I need is for her to panic and distance herself from me even more, especially when we're better off handling this situation together. All I want is for her to trust me enough to let me help her and to keep Ethan safe.

The secretary's voice blares over the intercom and interrupts my thoughts, politely informing me that my principal is waiting. I'd forgotten about our meeting. I walk over to his office on autopilot, my mind still reeling from that phone call.

"We just found out that James isn't returning after his extended leave. He's decided to retire," Mr. Soileau explains from behind his desk, referring to our assistant principal. "And I'm not far behind. I'd like to leave Camellia High and our kids in good hands, and I can't think of anyone I'd trust more than you, JD."

I clear my throat. "Sir?"

"You are certified in administration, right?"

"I am. I got my master's while I earned my alt-teaching cert."

"Thought so. I was hoping you'd be interested in taking the open assistant principal position for now and letting me prepare you to become the next principal of Camellia High."

I blink away my surprise. "Oh. Well, uh, wow. I'm flattered."

"I've already brought it before the school board, and they were all very enthusiastic and supportive of the move. Of course, the decision is yours, but if you want to at least give admin a try, you have the summer to figure out whether you want to keep working as head football coach and athletic director, as well."

"That's ... great."

He chuckles softly. "Why don't you take a day or so to think it over and let me know once you've made up your mind?"

"I will, thank you," I say, still trying to process his offer. I rise and turn for the door, but I hear him call my name again.

"Is everything all right, son?"

I look down at my feet, hoping he can't see the concern for Tenley and Ethan written on my face. "Yeah, I'm fine. I'm just surprised." Then I glance up and paste on a happy face for him. "And I guess I'm a little sad to hear that you and Mr. James will be moving on to greener pastures, specifically golf greens, even though it's well deserved."

"Oh, I don't doubt you'll survive without us. Leadership comes naturally to you, and you'll have the support of the community," he replies, eyeing me shrewdly. "Unless you're worried about what your girlfriend will think?"

"Uh, well, I don't ..."

"Camellia is a small town, and you don't exactly have the best poker face. Not to mention, the office staff keeps a running count of how often they spot your truck at the Robins'."

I shrug and try to hide my smirk. "Right."

"JD, you don't have to hide your relationship because of Ethan. In fact, getting to teach and coach our own kids is a career perk. Although, in my experience, it's easier being their principal than their teacher," he tells me with an amused smile.

I nod again, reflecting on the differences between this conversation and my last job offer. "Thanks, Mr. Soileau. I'll definitely take that into account."

CHAPTER 33
JD

THE REST OF THE SCHOOL DAY GOES BY IN A BLUR BEFORE I stop at home to shower and change into a Saints football jersey, thinking maybe it'll cheer Tenley up, but no one seems to notice my arrival when I let myself into the Robin house.

"Wait, you've met him? In person? What were you thinking, Ethan?" I hear Tenley's raised voice as I walk into the kitchen. "We don't know anything about this guy. He could be a jerk, or even worse, dangerous!"

It doesn't sound like the best time to intrude, but they've already spotted me, so I'll only make things more awkward by leaving now. I'm quiet as I move to lean against the counter.

"But he's not," Ethan replies in his defense. "Well, he's not dangerous, anyway. He's got a wife and kids, and he's actually nice to me."

Tenley rocks back on her heels, absorbing the blow. "You ... you have siblings?"

He smiles. "Two little sisters, Kaylie and Kirsten."

"Have you met them?" she ventures.

"Not yet. Kirsten has called a few times, but I've only met Ryan so far."

She crosses her arms and looks down. "That's great, E. I'm really happy for you. And of course, I want you to spend time getting to know your ... family. I just wish you'd told me so we could have gone about all this differently."

He sighs. "I'm sorry. I know I should have said something to you. It's just that you already worry so much, and this is *my* problem, not yours. I figured you'd be upset if you found out about Ryan, and now you are."

"Ethan." She softens. "I'm not angry with you for wanting to meet your dad and your sisters. I could never be mad about something like that. I'm upset because you've been sneaking around, and because you could have gotten hurt. I don't even want to imagine what might have happened if something had gone wrong when you met him, and none of us would have even known where to begin looking for you. Not to mention how this will affect the next custody hearing."

"Well, it wasn't *exactly* a secret," he mumbles after a while, glancing up at me.

Oh, no.

"JD knew about it."

Tenley blinks a few times and turns to face me, her hands on her hips now. "You knew?"

I clear my throat, reminding myself that this isn't a good time to consider how attractive she looks. "Sort of. He didn't give me any details, or even the guy's name, but Ethan did mention to me that he'd been in contact with his biological dad."

"And you didn't think this was something I needed to know?"

"I asked him if everything was okay, made sure the guy wasn't a creep, but it wasn't my story to tell. And I had no idea he'd been meeting him in person," I say, splaying my hands in front of me.

She narrows her eyes and shakes her head slowly. "Why didn't you say anything when we spoke on the phone earlier? What else have you been keeping from me on Ethan's behalf?"

"Tenley," I say, stepping forward. But she tightens her posture, glaring at me with an expression that says, *don't you dare.*

"Ugh … of course you're going to fight over this, now," Ethan comments sarcastically.

"What?" Tenley asks.

"Instead of just punishing me, you're going to take it out on JD for being loyal, aren't you?" He shoots her a disgusted look.

She stares incredulously as she speaks. "You think that's what this is about? That I'm jealous of your relationship?"

"He was my friend first," Ethan mutters.

My eyes dart back and forth between them. "I'm still everyone's friend, for the record."

He huffs. "Sure, *friends*. You know, if I'd have guessed you two would start ignoring everyone else so you could spend every waking minute together doing God knows what, I'd never have tried to set you up in the first place."

"You feel like we've been ignoring you?" Tenley asks.

"We're not doing anything, I swear," I blurt out at the same time.

I guess our priorities are made clear in that moment, and her eyes flash to mine, letting me know she doesn't appreciate where my mind jumps first.

"It's none of my business, anyway, like you both said before," he grumbles. He picks up a duffle bag and slips it over his shoulder. "I'm going to the gym," he announces, stomping out of the room.

"The hell you are," Tenley yells. "You're staying right here until we figure this out."

"Maybe we could all use some time to cool off," I offer, trying to placate her again.

"Oh, now you have something to contribute?" she fires back at me.

I furrow my brow, my own temper flaring. "I get that you're angry. But you and I can discuss it later, in private—once you're calm enough to speak *to* me and not just *at* me, since I'm not a kid."

"Could've fooled me." She rolls her eyes.

"What's that supposed to mean?"

"How can I trust you to help me raise Ethan if you're going to cover for him every time he messes up?"

"Wow, if this has been you 'trusting me to help,' then I guess we'd have to be married before you'd even consider my advice to lay off when he's legit having a hard time," I say without thinking.

"Who said anything about getting married?" she cries, her face flushing. I feel my own ears burning up as soon as the words leave my mouth.

"Wait, you're getting *married*?" Ethan chimes in.

I groan. "It was a figure of speech. You're both missing my point."

"You can't get married if you're just going to fight all the time, especially about me," Ethan continues, shaking his head as if he's imagining it.

"When do we ever argue?" I ask.

"And who said anything about getting married?" Tenley repeats. She turns to look at Ethan. "You told me it was too much, too fast. So I slowed everything down, for you," she explains, lowering her voice. "But now I see that it wasn't really my relationship with JD that was bothering you, was it? The changes you were talking about had more to do with you meeting Ryan."

Suddenly, everything makes so much sense.

"Wait, is *that* why you've been so distant? You stalled our relationship without telling me?" I ask her.

"Hey, if you don't like my tone, then don't engage me in conversation right now," she says, holding out a hand to block me. I clench my jaw and grunt in response.

"Oh, right, so now it's *my* fault you still haven't managed to get into her pants," Ethan grumbles at me, lighting a spark at the very end of my fuse.

"HEY!" I boom, making both of them flinch. "Listen, kid. We've been through this already, but maybe you need a reminder. If you want to talk like a grown man, then you'd better be ready to back it up. Because I'll be damned if I let you say another disrespectful word about your aunt, much less in front of her."

"Sorry," he whispers. His lip twitches as he stares at his feet, and he swipes at the moisture accruing on his cheek.

"Now, I'll say it again: Let's all take some time to cool down and come back to this conversation later with clearer heads, hmm?"

"Works for me." Ethan turns and walks out of the house, leaving Tenley and me in a tense silence.

"I'm sorry I yelled," I began. "But—"

"I thought you were leaving?" she asks, cutting me off.

I scoff. "I know you're upset about this whole situation, but don't take it out on me, all right?"

Her brow lifts. "You don't think I have the right to be mad after what you kept from me?"

"It wasn't my place to say anything," I repeat in my defense. "And if I'd have known that he was meeting the guy in person, I would have done something, tried to go with him, tried to stop him, anything. I'd never knowingly let Ethan put himself in danger, and the last thing I want is to risk hurting either of you."

She's silent as I continue. "Tenley, you understand how much I care about him, right? You are the most important people in my life," I explain, my voice thick with emotion. "I love you."

"You don't keep secrets like this from the people you love, JD. Especially not after begging them to open up and face their commitment issues."

I sigh. "It's not as black and white as you think. I didn't have all the details, and until this afternoon, I wasn't sure whether you knew."

"This is exactly why I didn't want to start anything in the first place," she says to herself. "It was bound to get too complicated at some point."

"Come on, Ten, you don't have to do this. Don't make this out to be a big deal."

"I gave up my very comfortable life to come here and take on Ethan, then braved some of my biggest fears for you, and you didn't think I'd feel betrayed when I found out you helped Ethan go behind my back to meet the one person who could take him away? How am I going to show up to the custody hearing and ask for full guardianship after this, JD? The judge is never going to let me keep Ethan now that he's gotten a half-decent response from his father, remember? And

I'm not even sure I deserve to be his guardian anyway, since I've been doing such a crappy job that I had no clue he was talking to Ryan this whole time."

"I'm sorry," I repeat. "I wasn't thinking about that."

She glares at me. "Right, because you had more important things on your mind."

"Well, can you blame me for having a hard time sorting through all the mixed signals? You're angry with me for keeping something to myself on Ethan's behalf, but I'm just finding out that the two of you have been making decisions about *our* relationship without bothering to include me."

She frowns, but she doesn't fold. "And you've known from the beginning that he has to be my priority, over everything and everyone else."

"Okay, but could you freaking clue me in?" I notice my voice getting louder. "One day you love me, the next day you don't. Sometimes you're all over me, and others, you won't let me touch you." I stop and take a deep breath, trying to settle myself. "You know, you're not the only one with a lot invested here. I told you from the start that I was willing to put Ethan's needs first. I fully understood the weight of that, and I'd like to think I've been upholding my promise. The problem is that you're using Ethan's situation as an excuse to pull away from me again. If our relationship was getting to be too much for you, then all you had to do was tell me."

Her eyes are trained on the ground when she answers. "Okay, then. It's too much. I'm sorry I didn't say anything before, but I'm saying it now. Maybe we should take some time to think about all this, to figure out what's best for everyone."

My heart constricts, and my vision for our future together starts to fade. "Time apart, you mean?"

She shrugs. "I think we could both use the space."

"I wish you'd stop telling me what you think I need all the time, because I'm pretty sure I know better. But if *you* want space, I'll respect your wishes."

"Fine. I need space," she chokes out, her chin trembling. And I can tell it's a lie because she's doing a poor job of convincing herself that it's true.

I shake my head. "You're so damned stubborn. He warned me you'd be like this, you know." She looks at me questioningly. "Your dad. He said you'd get in your own way, and he made me promise I wouldn't back down when you did. So, yeah. You can have your space, but I'm not giving up that easily."

She stands there quietly, swiping at her cheeks, and her phone buzzes. Then she glances down and covers her mouth as a sob escapes. I rush over to her, afraid to ask what has her so shaken up.

"It's Ethan. He says he's sorry he's been a burden to both of us, and that he's going to try living with Ryan for a while so they can get to know one another. He asked me not to come after him," she explains through her tears.

And my heart breaks as I watch what I thought was my one chance at a family slipping away.

CHAPTER 34
TENLEY

"Rumor is he's got his sights on becoming the next assistant DA," Blake explains over the phone.

"What does that have to do with Ethan?" I demand. I'm sitting in my car after work, wiping my nose on the inside of my lab coat after big-crying over the papers I was served a few minutes earlier.

"My guess is that after your mom sent that letter, Ryan hired a private investigator and did some digging. If there was any chance Ethan was his, he'd want to get ahead of the situation and use it to make himself look good. Nobody wants to vote for a deadbeat dad, but they love a family man, right? E is literally every parent's dream— good grades, decent athlete, well-mannered with a nice smile. Ryan would be crazy not to capitalize on that and use Ethan to his advantage before anyone found out the whole truth."

"Can he really get away with this?"

Blake sighs. "Unfortunately, he can. Especially if Ethan continues going along with it."

"Even though Ryan's basically just a sperm donor."

"He's got a few other things going for him, too, Tenley. He's married, well established in his community, and can prove that he's been a decent father to his other kids. There's no evidence he knew anything about Ethan's existence until now, so he can't be faulted for his absence if he allegedly stepped up as soon as he found out."

"So what do we do?"

My instincts tell me that having a guy like JD for a boyfriend has to carry some weight, right? Although at the first hearing, the judge hadn't exactly seemed thrilled at the prospect of JD and me living together unmarried. And I suppose I'd have to actually claim JD as my boyfriend in public for his reputation to help, which I've ironically been avoiding all this time for Ethan's sake.

Then again, none of this matters anymore since I pushed JD out last night.

Blake clears his throat as I choke back another sob. "You can continue showing the court that you're putting down roots in Camellia and hope Ethan chooses you at the hearing. But that's about it."

"Can't we at least make him come home for now?"

"Technically, you do still hold temporary custody. But I don't recommend exercising those rights unless Ethan is in danger. Removing a kid from their home when they don't want to leave can be traumatic, regardless of age. And I don't doubt Ryan would resort to throwing around his influence and start fighting dirty if you got the police involved."

"Oh. So ... all I can do is wait?" My heart sinks again.

"Basically. And since the judge warned you he wouldn't make your arrangement permanent if there was any chance of Ethan being reunited with his father, I'm afraid your next hearing will be pointless. We'll likely be settling things on the date set in these papers instead, which is over a month away."

"That sneaky son-of-a ... He did this on purpose, to buy enough time to make himself look like the perfect father and to trick Ethan into staying, didn't he?"

He sighs. "I'm afraid so. Look, Tenley, I'm sorry I didn't pick up on all this sooner, and I know it seems hopeless, but I'm sure you'll at least get some visitation rights if you don't buck him now. And who knows? Maybe E will be happy there. I mean, Ryan may be a prick, but he's not out to hurt his own kid. He'll spoil Ethan with gifts and private-school tuition, and you'll still get to see him here and there without having to sacrifice your lifestyle for the next few years. Maybe it's all for the best."

I huff. "Am I supposed to be relieved by that, like I'm off the hook now?"

"Isn't that what you want? To go back to your old life in Texas?"

What I want right now is to call Blake a few choice names and hang up on him, but I still need his help. And I suspect he's only being this pissy because he found out about the way I left things with JD.

"I'm sorry if I ever gave anyone that impression, but nothing could be further from the truth. I want Ethan back here with me more than anything, and I have no intention of leaving Camellia any time soon."

He sounds tired as he speaks again. "Then your best bet is to build your reputation as a stable parent and establish a role within the community. Like I said before, I'm sure I can get you some visitation, at least. But ultimately, it'll come down to Ethan's wishes at the hearing, unless one of you can prove your household is more fit than the other. And Ryan's already winning."

I bite my lip as I try to keep myself from breaking down again. "Okay. Well, thanks. I appreciate all your help." It probably sounds more sarcastic than I intend, since I'm only seconds away from a complete meltdown.

Blake bids me a curt goodbye, and I throw my phone down as soon as the call is over. I cover my face with my hands and let the feelings of helplessness overwhelm me for a few minutes. I want to wallow for a while longer, but I remember that my patients are waiting at the hospital, so I pull myself together before spending the rest of my Friday afternoon in the L&D ward.

By the time I get home that evening, I can barely keep my eyes open. I throw on an oversized gray hoodie and leggings after having another good cry in the shower, then stagger to my bed before falling asleep face down.

I WAKE THE NEXT MORNING TO A BARRAGE OF MISSED texts, most of them from Loren, one from JD, and none of them from Ethan, though I can't bring myself to check any of them.

I wipe my cheeks with the heel of my hand. It seems like crying is the only thing I can do well anymore. Then I stumble into the kitchen, my hands trembling as I try to pour myself a cup of coffee, replaying everything in my mind for the thousandth time in the past forty-eight hours.

Is this really it? After being so terrified of failure that I avoided relationships for the better part of my life, have I really managed to become a self-fulfilling prophecy this quickly?

In hindsight, it feels like I've unfairly taken out some of my anger on JD. I'd been so stunned to learn he was capable of betraying me that I couldn't rationalize what he'd actually done (or not done), and lashing out was more of a reflex than anything. And aside from sabotaging my only shot at a real relationship, I'm afraid I've caused irreparable damage to JD and Ethan's bond, too.

Then again, according to Blake, I don't even stand a chance at getting Ethan back without JD's help. I've certainly proven I'm unqualified to parent on my own. Hell, I barely even managed as long as I have because I've been letting JD do all the heavy lifting, yet I called him out at the first mistake.

My mom walks into the kitchen. I wipe my nose and attempt to cover up the evidence of my latest emotional breakdown, probably the first of many that will happen by the end of the day.

"Morning." I force a pathetic smile as I greet her, and she's quiet when she sits across from me with her mug and a concerned frown. She hasn't been around as much since starting her new job as a hospice nurse, so I've been fortunate enough to avoid her pity until now.

"Tenley," she begins. "I hate seeing you like this."

I shake my head. "I'm fine. I'm just upset about Ethan."

"Only Ethan?" she ventures, taking a sip of her coffee.

I stare down at my cup in silence, unable to answer without risking another full-on sob fest. I'd mentioned JD and I had a disagreement when I told her about Ethan leaving the other night. It was an understatement, but I couldn't bear to say anything else without falling apart again.

"Do you want to talk about it?" she offers.

"I don't think I can," I reply, my voice strained.

She furrows her brow. "Can you at least tell me whether I'm supposed to be mad at JD or feel sorry for him?"

I smile meekly. "Both."

"Then you're going to have to give me more than that," she says and takes another drink.

I heave out a deep sigh. "He knew Ethan had been talking to Ryan, and he kept it from me. I was really upset, and rightfully so, but I overreacted and projected some of my insecurities onto him. I haven't been doing the whole serious-relationship thing all that well, anyway, and he deserves better. But I knew I'd never be able to handle all of this in the first place."

"What are you even talking about?" she asks, her eyes flashing.

I tick off my mistakes on my fingers. "I made Ethan feel like he was a burden and drove him away. I let JD chase me for months before I even considered dating him, and now I've ruined everything because I couldn't learn to trust him."

She turns her mouth to the side as she considers everything. "First of all, you didn't drive Ethan away. He's a teenage boy facing some difficult and unfair circumstances, some of which are a result of the decisions your dad and I made. Don't you dare put that blame on yourself."

"Okay," I concede. "But I did a terrible job of dealing with him the other night, and I haven't been fair to JD."

She regards me quietly for a minute before she speaks again. "Tenley, you haven't really been afraid of getting stuck in Camellia all this time, have you?" I shake my head. "Then what?"

I look down as the tears begin flowing again. "I've always figured that it's safer to keep my distance than to fail at making a family of my own ... because I'm not capable of caring for anyone," I divulge, my heart beating faster as I finally say the words aloud. "I don't have it in me to be as selfless as you. I'm just not cut out to be a wife or a mother."

She narrows her eyes. "But you've always been selfless. You dedicated yourself to a career in which you serve women when they're most vulnerable. You gave up your social life as a teenager to help me take care of Jude and Ethan. Even as a little girl, you learned to love football so your daddy could have someone to share that with. You dropped everything in Texas as soon as I called, resetting your entire life and agreeing to take custody of Ethan without question."

"You had to ask me, though. I should have been here all that time, but I was so wrapped up in myself that I never considered you might need me. Better yet, I refused to even acknowledge the situation, just so I wouldn't have to live with the guilt."

"That's not completely true. You were just needed elsewhere for a while," she corrects me. She pauses before she begins again. "Tenley, you understand I didn't just ask you to take on Ethan because I was tired of doing it myself, right? Your dad and I were worried you were missing out, and we wanted you to experience that kind of love."

I'm silent as I grasp the significance of what she's just said. The last few months of my life begin to make so much more sense. Ethan was a *gift*, and I'm an idiot for not seeing that. But my parents' love for me doesn't completely fix the lack of confidence I have in myself.

"You've already done such a good job raising Ethan. Picking up where you left off doesn't prove I have the right disposition for motherhood," I say after a while.

"From what I hear, you have a wonderful bedside manner, and we both know how much you love babies. Try again."

"That's different. I can be that way with my patients, but I'm obviously not empathetic enough for my own family."

"Nope, I'm not buying that one either, because it's natural to care and provide for the people you love most without even realizing you're doing it," she continues. "Look how easily you slipped into that role for Ethan."

I sigh, because even though she's got a point, I'm still not fully convinced. "But you made all the sacrifices, you did everything so well, and you still lost Tessa and Dad."

"Not everything." She huffs. "I've made my share of bad choices and gone through some very dark times, especially after Tessa died. But luckily, you guys didn't need me to be perfect. You only needed me to love you." She pauses before she adds, "I was also smart enough to marry a man with infinite patience and who loved me beyond all reason, even when I did screw up, which happened a lot more often than you know."

I think about my dad and the way he adored my mom, and I can't help smiling when JD's face materializes in my mind. My mom grins as she continues. "Jude Robin was a great husband, an amazing father, and a damned good electrician. But accepting apologies was probably what he did best."

"He would've said that being a Saints fan taught him about perseverance," I remark, making her laugh.

"JD is a lot like him, you know," she says, reading my thoughts. "Very patient. I bet he's good at making up, too."

"I guess there's only one way to find out," I concede with a sigh. Then I dry my face again before walking around to kiss her cheek. "Thank you, Mom, for all of it. I love you."

She beams up at me. "I love you, too, Tenley Jean."

After that, I take a fortifying refill of coffee back to my room to begin making amends with new conviction. I text Loren first, since I know she'll be the easiest, and she readily accepts my invitation to meet for lunch tomorrow. I also vow to myself to treasure her friendship this time around. Loren is amazing, and I've realized how much I've been missing her all these years.

I work up the courage to message Ethan next. He answers immediately, to my surprise, and we trade pleasantries before I attempt an apology.

TENLEY

Ethan, I want to make sure you know that you have never been a burden to any of us, especially not to me. You're the greatest gift I've ever received. I love you, and I'm sorry if I ever made you feel unwanted.

ETHAN

yes ma'am

i'm sorry i left the way i did

and i love you too

i promise it wasn't your fault

i've just been feeling like something's off or missing

and I thought maybe meeting my father would help

He may not be angry with me, but my relief is short-lived when he implies that meeting Ryan hasn't helped.

TENLEY

I understand. And I am glad that you're finally getting to know him. So, how has it been?

ETHAN

he's cool i guess

my little sisters are cute

they have a nice house and all

TENLEY

That's great. 😊

I'm sure you're already an amazing big bro.

ETHAN

i really miss you guys though

is mawmaw okay?

TENLEY

She's all right. We all miss you, too, but we want you to be happy. And we'll support you if this is what you want.

ETHAN

and if i want to come back?

TENLEY

You can always come back, no matter what happens.

ETHAN

but will you stay in camellia?

now that pop's gone and i'm out here are you moving back to texas?

or will you stay for jd?

Well, the kid always did know how to get straight to the point. I want to answer him honestly, but I'm still unsure about my future with JD. And then I recall the way I felt the other day, when Blake assumed I'd be running back to my old life, and I know I'll never be able to leave my family again.

TENLEY

I'm not going anywhere, I promise. I'll be around as long as you need me, okay?

ETHAN

heart react

thanks aunt ten

There's only one conversation left after Ethan's. I reluctantly pull up my text thread with JD, afraid of what I might find. There are two messages now, one of them a generic wellness check, but the other is lengthier.

JD

> I'm not trying to impose on your space, but I thought you should know I received a job offer, one that might affect our relationship. I was supposed to bring it up Thursday. But I'd still like to get your input before I make my decision, if you're willing to talk.

My heart drops to my toes. He'd probably been trying to tell me he'd gotten that official coaching offer from BSU, and I hadn't even given him a chance to say anything before jumping his case and burdening him with my problems. He must be debating whether it's even worth sticking around for me since Ethan left.

It's another complication, just minutes after I've promised Ethan I'm not going anywhere. Now I'll have to fight to get Ethan back, convince JD to forgive me, *and* attempt to manage a relationship with JD working three hours away, if I'm lucky.

Will I have to choose between them now? I've been saying all this time that Ethan's needs have to come first, but am I supposed to just let JD get away? Would he even be willing to try the long-distance thing, especially after all this?

The one thing I know for certain is that I can't let JD throw his future away on my account. I can't bear the idea of robbing him of a chance like this or giving him any more reasons to resent me later.

TENLEY

> Hi, I'm okay. I've spoken to Ethan, and he's all right, too.

> Congratulations on the job offer. You deserve every opportunity that comes your way, and while I appreciate that you want to consult me before making your decision, I think you should focus on what's best for your career in the long run. We can always figure out the relationship stuff later.

JD

Glad to hear you and Ethan are good. And thanks for replying, but I've already accepted the offer. I start on Monday.

I gulp as I stare down at the screen. He's leaving? Like, leaving-leaving? *Now?*

It figures that as soon as I allow myself to start dreaming about a happily-ever-after, it would become impossible all over again. I blink back tears as another message appears.

JD

Any new developments in E's situation?

TENLEY

Not really. Blake says all I can do is wait for Ethan to decide whether he wants to come home on his own.

JD

I'm sorry.

TENLEY

Yeah. Me, too. I'd do anything to get him back here with me, where he belongs.

JD

Right. Well, lmk if there's anything you need from me.

I frown as I reread his last reply. He's obviously still upset with me, but I'm unsure whether it's because of the other night or something I just said. I want to ask, to say more, but I'm afraid I'll make things worse, so I leave it alone for now until I can figure out how to make this all up to him.

CHAPTER 35
TENLEY

"Hi, Ms. Reed, Ms. Tenley. Can I get you anything to drink?" Caidence asks Loren and I once we're seated at a table in her family's cafe. It's not her normal bubbly greeting, though, and I suspect she's harboring some misplaced guilt as she avoids my eyes.

Loren orders coffees for both of us, probably noticing the way I can't bring myself to look up, either. Then she waits for Caidence to leave before she reaches over and rests her hand next to mine on the table. "Ten, I'm really sorry about everything. If you want to vent, I'll listen. And if you're not ready to talk about it yet, that's okay, too."

I give her a sad smile. "Thank you." Then I take a deep breath. "I think I probably should get some of this out," I admit, though I'm not sure I'll be able to stop myself from having another breakdown now that JD's leaving town, too. If he hasn't left already, that is.

Loren nods for me to continue, and I explain everything, from the reasons why I squashed my feelings for JD in the beginning, all the way through the half-realized ideas I've been working on over the past couple of days, pausing only when Caidence returns with our drinks. The only thing I don't mention is JD's new job, since I'm not sure who he's shared it with yet. Loren listens carefully and asks nothing, even when I confess to coming down too harshly on JD for being loyal to Ethan.

I release a long exhale once I'm done, feeling slightly better. But the weight of losing all three of the most important men in my life within the last few weeks returns immediately. "So, yeah. I'm basically the worst."

"You're not the worst," she says, smirking. "But you also can't give up on relationships when they get complicated. This isn't a hobby you can quit once you decide it's too hard."

"I know. It just feels like I've been thrown into a tennis match when I'm better equipped and more prepared for football," I explain, making her chuckle. "But I had no idea how much I'd like tennis until after I tried it, and now it's all I can think about, even though I don't understand the rules and I have no idea what I'm doing most of the time."

"So, you'll learn as you go, right? I mean, you literally have an amazing coach at your disposal. I can't imagine that JD wouldn't be happy to hear from you and even more thrilled by all the emotional growth you've made over the past few days."

Caidence interrupts us again by clearing her throat as she sets our plates down on the table. I notice her eyes looking a little misty.

"Ms. Tenley, there's something I think you should know. Is it okay if I sit for a second?"

"Of course," I say, trying to collect myself.

She chews on the inside of her cheek for a second before she begins. "I think I might be one of the reasons why Ethan left. I know he's been dealing with a lot over the past month or so, but he hadn't been acting like himself, and we started arguing about every little thing. I didn't want to break up with him, especially while he seemed so depressed, but he was just so moody that it got to be too much for me."

"Caidence, you're not the reason Ethan left, and you shouldn't excuse his behavior if he's been making you feel bad or uncomfortable." I give her a sad smile and reach out to pat her shoulder. I also make a mental note to talk to Ethan about seeing a therapist or a counselor, something I probably should have done much sooner. "Yes, Ethan has been going through a tough time. But you made the right decision. You've still been a good friend to him, even when you pointed out that he wasn't emotionally ready for more."

She nods and sniffles quietly, trying to hide her tears. "I really miss him. And I'm sorry that I made him feel … you know, unloved. But I'll always love him as a friend, even if he doesn't come home."

My eyes travel up to Loren's, and her expression says that she shares my admiration of Caidence's maturity and honesty. "Have you told him that?" I venture.

She shakes her head. "He hasn't been answering any of my Snaps or texts. He's probably still mad at me."

"I'll bet he's just feeling guilty," I say. "Keep at it. He'll answer eventually. I know he really cares about you, and he's lucky to have you for a friend."

"Thank you, Ms. Tenley." She glances up, and her cheeks turn pink. "I'm sorry about you and Coach JD, too," she adds softly.

"What do you mean?" I ask.

She looks apologetic. "I figured something might have happened between you guys since he seems sort of miserable, but maybe he's just sad about Ethan … or because it was his last day in the classroom."

"Right." My eyes begin watering against my will at the thought of JD leaving, the tears nearly spilling over once I remind myself that I'm the cause of his misery.

"Um, yeah." Loren speaks up. "I wasn't sure if he'd told you about his new position before everything else happened."

I swallow hard and dab at my eyes. "He mentioned it."

Caidence excuses herself to tend to her other tables, and Loren turns to me again. "I'm sorry, Ten. JD made it sound like the assistant-principal offer was a surprise."

I nod and look down, my pulse still racing, and it takes a few seconds before Loren's words actually register. "Wait, assistant principal?"

She regards me strangely. "Well, yeah. Yesterday he announced that he was taking over for Mr. James, starting tomorrow. It's Facebook official and everything."

I drop my head into my hands as I breathe out a huge sigh of relief. I've never been so happy to be wrong. And I realize that means JD has become so much more important to me than I ever expected.

I also recognize that, although I've finally started addressing some of my big, scary issues *for* JD, like tackling my insecurities and admitting to myself that I do actually want marriage and kids, I've skirted thinking about if and when I might want those things *with* JD.

At the risk of looking ridiculous, I leave my head down as I attempt to stretch the rubber band I'd rewrapped tightly around my heart and consider what a long-term plan with JD might look like. The corners of my mouth curl up involuntarily. Try as I might, I can't imagine any tolerable version of the future without him. I've run out of excuses, and I can't come up with a single reason why I should hesitate to commit to JD and eventually start a family with him.

Just like that, the rubber band pops.

I may be stubborn, the kind of overthinker who takes a while to arrive at a conclusion, but once I've seen it, I can't unsee it. And now that I've landed on the truth that I am senselessly in love with JD Bourgeois and that I can't bear the thought of going back to a life without him in it, I know I need to not only earn his forgiveness but to convince him we should do all that forever stuff together, too.

"Are you all right, Tenley?" Loren asks hesitantly.

"Mm-hmm," I return, picking up my head. "I'm just processing. I misunderstood. I thought JD was taking a different job and leaving Camellia."

"You did?"

I nod. "I've been worrying I'd never get to play tennis again, just when I'd figured out how badly I wanted to get better at it."

She chuckles. "Because you love tennis, right?"

"Gah, I do. So much more than I ever thought I could love a sport. And what was I thinking, asking him for space? He's been nothing but amazing so far, and all I've ever done is make him chase me. That seems insane now." I shake my head in disbelief. "Hell, look at the guy! Was I really willing to just let that go?"

She laughs, seemingly entertained by my newfound enthusiasm.

"I mean, he's not my type, but if you're into tall, kindhearted, funny, athletically built, *great* kissers, then ... sure."

I inhale sharply and narrow my eyes at her. "I'm sorry, what?" I don't mean to snap, but I can't help myself. JD and Loren have both maintained that their relationship has always been completely platonic, but my heart is still admittedly sore from having enlarged a few sizes only a minute before.

She throws her head back and laughs loudly. "Your words, Ten, not mine. Like I said, not exactly my thing."

"Oh ... I'm sorry," I mumble, blinking slowly. "It's just ... you've been saying JD's like a brother to you, so that would have made things even more awkward, right?"

She presses her lips together, biting back a smile. "Totally. Even worse than that party in middle school where you ditched me for my actual brother."

I cringe as my face heats up. "I guess I deserve that."

"You know what I think you deserve?" I shake my head and she continues. "A hot make-up session with your amazing boyfriend before you figure out how to get your nephew back."

My stomach flutters, and I bite my lip. "I think I really like the way that sounds," I say, my voice thick. "Thank you for helping me realize that, Lo."

My phone chimes, and I involuntarily glance over to see Ethan's name. I pick it up and apologize to Loren as I reply to his message.

ETHAN

hey

i just wanted to say that i miss you

TENLEY

I miss you, too, kid. How's it going?

ETHAN

ok

TENLEY

Just okay?

ETHAN

i'm really sorry i left the way i did

TENLEY

I know. And I'm sorry for making you feel like you had to leave in the first place.

ETHAN

would it be okay if i came home now?

like for good

i promise i won't run off like that again

My eyes water as I stare down at the words I've been waiting to read. I'm not excited about Ethan being unhappy at Ryan's, of course. But I'm still selfish enough to want him here with me.

Suddenly, I understand JD's reaction to that same phrase yesterday. Because he must be feeling the same way, except he's been praying for Ethan to come home to *us*.

Again, how have I been so thoughtless and insensitive? I suppress the urge to growl at myself as I resolve to make it up to JD, starting with doing whatever it takes to get Ethan back. And the first payment is going to require swallowing my pride. I switch to a new text window and reluctantly pull up Blake's name.

TENLEY

Hey, can we talk? I really need your help with Ethan's situation.

BLAKE

Please make an appointment with my receptionist.

CHAPTER 36
TENLEY

I LET MY FINGERTIP BRUSH OVER THE FUZZY SIDEBURNS OF the newborn baby I'm cradling after having spent most of the previous night helping with his delivery. He grunts in response, puckering his pink lips and nestling his head deeper into the crook of my arm, and I push the miniature "Baby Thibodeaux" hospital bracelet down before it slips up over his little fist.

"He's perfect, Sybil," I say to his mother.

"Hmm," she hums thoughtfully. "Does he know?"

I glance up at her from the chair beside her hospital bed, confused.

"Mr. Right—have you told him about the baby fever?" she asks again with a knowing smile.

I sigh and return to stroking the baby's feather-soft hair. "No."

"And it's bad this time, isn't it?"

"So, so bad," I whisper, my eyes still trained on his tiny features. "But we're not really speaking right now. I've been an idiot lately."

She grins at me. "Then call him. Or, better yet, go to him. I bet he'd be willing to help you out."

I bite my lip, trying not to consider that last bit. "Can I ask you something personal?"

"Sure."

"How did you know?" I look up at her again, hoping to convey what I mean through my expression.

She shrugs. "For me, it was less a conscious revelation and more a lack of desire for anything else. Once I gave Derek a chance, being with him and making babies together was all I wanted. It was unavoidable, and I couldn't bring myself to see the same value in all of the stuff that seemed so important before."

"Stuff like keeping your feet on the ground," I add.

"Exactly," she confirms. "I was afraid I couldn't do it at first, you know. I still am. But, seven years of marriage and four kids later, here we are."

I smile. "Think you'll have any more?"

"Ask me again in a few months," she says in an amused tone. "The beauty of NFP is that Derek and I can discern as we go. We can put off having any more babies indefinitely and still change our minds whenever we want. The problem is he's such a great dad that I can't stop giving him the chance to prove it all over again." She makes me chuckle when she bounces her eyebrows suggestively.

The door opens, and Sybil's husband walks in. "Oh, hey, Nurse Tenley," Derek greets me with a genuine smile, then he turns to his wife. "So, my love, how hungry are you?" He holds up a variety of fast-food bags, and she squeals with delight. As if on cue, their baby twists around in my arms and begins grunting and rooting around, searching for his own dinner.

Sybil groans softly as she sets a box of French fries on the nearby table. "He was talking to me, kid," she calls to the baby, making me laugh again. But she opens her arms anyway, so I bring him over and help her position him for a feeding. Then Derek stations himself beside her and alternates between holding up her box of fries and bringing a straw up to her mouth for a drink. They make it look so natural and routine, wordlessly slipping into their roles and automatically offering small sacrifices for one another.

And all I can think about is how good JD would be at this. Maybe one day, with his help, I could even be good at it, too.

I start to feel like I'm imposing on their private family moment or that I might embarrass myself by ugly crying in front of them, so I offer my congratulations one last time before sneaking out.

My rounds are finished for the day, and I pull out my phone to text JD as I get to my car. I'd hoped to get things more settled with Ethan before reaching out, but I haven't gotten to meet with Blake yet, and I honestly can't take being apart from JD anymore. I've been planning what I want to say all day, even throughout that last delivery, yet my hands are trembling as I begin typing out a message.

TENLEY

Hey. I'm sorry for taking so long to say this, but I've been doing a lot of thinking over the past few days. I understand you were in a difficult position and that it wasn't your intention to hurt me when you hesitated to tell me about Ethan and Ryan.

I also realized I haven't been giving you as much trust or credit as I should. You've only ever been an amazing friend and an even better boyfriend to me, in addition to being a great role model for E, and I've been taking you for granted.

The truth is that I have been holding back, partially because we were making Ethan uncomfortable, but also because I'm still scared I won't be able to do this family and relationship stuff right. And I think I overreacted the other night because all those fears seemed to be coming true at the same time. I'm sorry for taking it out on you and for not being more honest with you about my feelings.

Congratulations on the new job, btw. I'm really proud of you, and I know you're going to be the best assistant principal Camellia's ever had.

I love you, JD.

JD

U use a lot of words 10

but I just need the last few

I furrow my brow. It's unlike him to brush off my heartfelt apology with that kind of reply. I'm not sure whether he's still angry with me or something is up.

TENLEY

Is everything okay?

JD

Ducking autocorrect

I miss u and I might be a lil bit drunk

Maybe

Probably

TENLEY

Are you at home?

JD

Yeah pretty sure I am

TENLEY

Should I come over to check on you?

JD

OK

I'm just so tired

Is a school night

TENLEY

JD, don't go anywhere. Promise?

JD

…

I wait a few seconds for another text to pop up, but I'm more concerned about his well-being than anything else at this point. I stuff my phone into the pocket of the hoodie I'd thrown on over my scrubs earlier before I pull out of the parking lot. I'd taken the jacket from him a couple of weeks back, and I hadn't realized until now that I've been wearing it every day since I last saw him.

To my relief, I find his truck parked in the driveway, and it looks like a few lights are on inside the house. I probably should be satisfied with that, but I can't bear to think of leaving him alone inside, sad and drunk and lonely, especially since it's all my fault. I walk up to the front door and knock softly, then press my ear to the windowpane. I don't hear any movement, so I pull out my phone.

TENLEY

Hey, do you know where JD keeps his spare house key?

ETHAN

why do you ask?

TENLEY

Just tell me where the damned key is.

ETHAN

there's a magnetic box over the window to the right

TENLEY

Thanks. This conversation never happened.

ETHAN

but it totally did

and now i'm saving it for a rainy day 😎

I roll my eyes but follow his directions to find the key box. Then I unlock the door and replace the spare key before letting myself in.

"JD? Are you in here? It's me, Tenley."

A low grunt resonates from the living room, so I venture over to the couch to find him lying face down and fully clothed, with the top portion of his body covered by a throw blanket too short to reach his feet.

"Are you all right?" I pull the blanket back from his head, and he rolls onto his back.

"Tenley?" he asks, squinting at me.

"I'm here. How did you end up drunk?"

He makes a "pfft" sound with his lips. "I only meant to drink enough to help me sleep." I cringe as he points to the empty glass and bottle of whiskey on the side table. JD doesn't normally drink when he's upset, but I guess I've pushed him over the edge.

I kneel beside the couch. "Did you drink that whole bottle tonight?"

"No, no, no. It was only like … half full. Or half empty?" He attempts to explain by using his index finger and thumb to illustrate his measurements, but he can't seem to make up his mind about what a half should look like. I lean in and smell the alcohol on his warm breath. Then I tug his eyelids up and check his pupils, and finally his pulse. He's obviously inebriated, but with his size, it would take a lot more whiskey than that to put him in danger, so long as he doesn't go out on the road.

"Come on, you need to sit up," I say, pulling his arm and immediately regretting my decision to touch my favorite part of his body.

"I don't want to," he mumbles. "I just want to sleep."

"Okay, then, let's get you to bed."

"Will you come with me?" he asks, his hazel eyes wide and glossy. They're a brighter gold than usual tonight.

Yes, please.

"I don't know if that's a good idea. But I'll help you, okay?"

I maneuver him to a seated position. He leans back against the couch, and I fight the urge to climb into his lap and latch onto him forever. "Ten, I'm so sorry I messed up," he whispers. "Can you forgive me?"

I nod. "I already have. And I've been missing you so much."

"And you're sure you really love me this time?"

I sink down in front of him. I can't blame him for asking, since I haven't exactly been as generous with my feelings since first making that proclamation. "Definitely," I say softly. "And I'm so sorry for not telling you I love you as often as I should, but I promise it's true."

He shakes his head. "I hate space."

"I hate it, too."

"Don't leave me," he pleads. "Can we just go to bed? I'm so tired."

"Okay." I stand again and tug his hands, pulling him to his feet. He lurches forward, stumbling a little, but rights himself soon enough and begins dragging me along instead. And as soon as we make it to his bedroom, he starts stripping.

"Oh, no." I panic. "JD, babe, why don't you just leave all that on?" I suggest, stopping his hands as he fumbles with the buttons on his shirt. He's dressed more formally than usual tonight, having upgraded his trademark khakis and black or yellow polo shirt for a button-down and slacks. It's probably because he started his new position today.

"No, I gotta take it off," he whines. "I'm too hot."

I sigh because he's right. "Okay, okay, just ... let me help you." He drops his hands, and I swallow hard as I unbutton his shirt, my stomach clenching when I slowly push the fabric over his shoulders and down his arms.

My eyelids feel heavy as I drink in the sight of him until he distracts me by fumbling with his belt. He shakes his head and lets his arms fall by his sides after a second.

"Help."

I cringe and warily move my hands down to unbuckle his belt and unbutton his dress slacks. I bite my bottom lip hard enough to draw blood as I force myself to drag that zipper down. Then I step back, hoping that his pants will just fall on their own, but he's too caked up. (I'd finally let Ethan explain that expression to me, though I'm not brave enough to try and use it correctly in front of anyone.)

JD's pants stay in place, with the exception of the front folding over at the zipper to uncover the waistband of his boxer briefs. And of course, he refuses to pull his own pants down, raising his hands in the air helplessly and looking at me expectantly. I groan and tug down near the side pockets, uncovering his hips and the length of his muscular thighs before the slacks finally hit the floor with a thud.

Oh, man, is he gorgeous. It's not even peak fertility time, yet my hormones are eating this up.

"Damn you, Joseph Drake Bourgeois," I grumble as I take him in, clad only in a pair of black athletic boxers that fit him like a second skin. My eyes finally meet his again, and he smirks back at me. I gasp. "You little … You're not even drunk, are you?"

"Shhure I am," comes his exaggerated reply. "I doubt I'll remember any of this in the morning. So, if you want to take advantage of me, now's your chance, Tenley Jean," he offers in a singsong voice, using his hands for flair and presenting himself as a game show prize.

I can't help but laugh at him. "Come on, you're going to bed."

"Nuh-uh, not sso fasst, young lady," he says, slurring this time. He reaches out and pulls on the drawstring around my neck. "You're wearing my hoodie."

Busted.

"I stole this hoodie fair and square, and it's not coming off tonight. Now, get into bed."

"Oh, I like it when you … when you boss me around," he says, attempting a sultry look through his half-lidded eyes. It should be funny, but this room is getting warmer by the second.

"Good, then get your ass to bed, Coach Thirsty," I command, placing my hands on his bare back and pushing him along. He giggles and snorts, then stops abruptly before the bed and arches his hip up and to the side. He glances magnanimously over his shoulder, thinking he's doing me a favor with his generous offering.

"You have to do it, or I won't move," he declares.

"JD, you're ridiculous."

"Well, damn, Jackie. I can't control the rules."

"That's not even how that one goes," I point out, trying my hardest to take him seriously. But I don't know which is worse: the bad TV lines or the fact that he's waiting patiently for me to touch his butt.

"Nobody asked you, *Patrice*," he retorts, making me roll my eyes. Then he lifts his chin tauntingly and bounces his eyebrows.

"Come on, Ten. You know you want to," he adds, because we both know I'll inevitably give in to him.

I heave out a loud sigh before I cave and flatten my left hand, using it to softly smack his proffered cheek. Then he throws his head back in a loud guffaw, and I hide my reddened face with both of my hands until he reaches out and pulls them down.

"Babe, I hate to dissa-disappoint you, but I'm not drunk enough" —he stops, hiccups, swallows a burp, and continues—"to forget that part."

"Just ... get your firm butt in bed," I repeat, dropping his hands from mine.

"Only if you'll join me," he says, his tone more solemn.

"I can't. I'm still in my work scrubs."

"Then take them off. Please?"

Heat swirls around in my stomach as he stares at me as if I were the only woman in the world. "Will you behave?"

He grins mischievously. "I'll try."

I attempt to hide my own smile as I pull the jacket up over my head and toss it aside, and JD steps in to tug the waistband of my scrub top.

"Please?" he begs again, impossibly irresistible. Coming from any other man, his request might have seemed pushy or even annoying. Maybe it's because I know he'd be okay if I said no or because I've never had to worry about whether he respected me, but I can't deny that I love the way he makes me feel so desired.

"Can I borrow a T-shirt?" I ask timidly, because I'm still not as brave as I'd like to be, and undressing in front of him with the lights on feels more intimate than actually having sex in the dark.

He pouts for a second before he turns to fetch a shirt from his dresser. But he drops it onto the bed instead of handing it to me.

"I'll go change in the bathroom," I propose, my voice unsteady.

But he keeps his eyes glued to mine as he shakes his head slowly.

Well, if this is going to be the first time I let him see this much of my body, at least he'll be more likely to ignore all of the imperfections with whiskey goggles on, right?

I squeeze my eyes shut for a second, mustering a surge of confidence, then reopen them as I peel away my top. He tugs on the string at my waist until he loosens my pants, sliding them down my hips and leaving me in a bra and a mismatched pair of underwear. But JD's reverent expression says that he's a huge fan of my comfy work drawers, and he devours me with his eyes as he grabs my hand and brings it to his mouth for a kiss.

"So beautiful," he says softly.

I step over my clothes and shake my head, refusing to believe him. But he pulls me closer until our bodies are pressed together, staring me down the whole time.

"You are the sexiest woman I've ever seen."

He doesn't slur that time.

"I am?" I squeak.

He nods intently, as if the sight of me is painful, then reaches back for the shirt before handing it over grudgingly. "Now, will you please come to bed with me?" he asks once I've pulled it down over me like a nightgown.

"Okay." I smile.

He turns the covers and sheets back, allowing me to slide in first before he follows and wraps his arms around me. Then he scoots closer until our faces are nearly touching.

"I love you, Ten. So much."

"I love you, too, JD."

"Please, don't ever push me away again."

"I won't. I promise." And I mean it.

He brings his lips down to meet mine. Relief floods my chest as he kisses me slowly and tenderly, pulling away after a while and tucking me in against him. I feel him kiss the top of my head, then he sighs contentedly.

Despite the strong smell of whiskey on his breath, I realize I don't need to worry about things getting out of hand tonight when he immediately begins snoring. I smile to myself again and turn to assume the position of the smaller spoon before drifting off to sleep in his arms.

CHAPTER 37
JD

"Do. Not. Move." I command Tenley from behind when I sense her waking in the morning, my voice husky. "Just let me have this for a minute."

She breaks out into a fit of immature giggles when I press myself against her, which leads to more of her fidgeting and me muttering a few protests under my breath before being forced to let her go. She flips over to face me.

"I'm sorry," she says, cringing, though I hope she can see the amusement in my eyes.

But then I'm frozen, unable to answer her right away because I'm too busy staring at her. All I've wanted for the past few months is this very moment, the chance to wake up with her in my arms, and it's just as amazing as I dreamed it would be. Sure, the last few days were rough, but this makes up for all that moping. "I'm sorry about last night. I hope I behaved myself," I finally say.

She smiles. "You *were* a bit of a handful."

"Was I?"

"You don't remember?" she asks, her face forlorn.

"I remember what you texted me earlier and that you said you love me again when you came over to beg for my forgiveness ..." I pull her closer as relief settles in her expression. Then I allow my hands to roam, sliding down her shoulders and back until they land on her butt.

Man, is it soft ... and *hot*.

"I also seem to recall you bossing me around, forcing me to strip down to my *caleçons*, then smacking my ass," I ramble on, shooting her a cocky smirk.

She glares at me, trying to maintain a straight face. "Yeah, that's not exactly how all that went down, buddy."

"But some of it went down, apparently."

"More or less," she says with a shrug.

I roll over to my stomach, offering my backside to her. "Well, anytime, baby, just say the word, and it's all yours." She giggles again, but she goes abruptly quiet when I lean over to grab my phone off of the night stand. Then I hear her sigh, and I realize she's checking me out. Maybe all that extra time in the gym wasn't a total waste, after all. I smile to myself and make a show of stretching and flexing my back muscles before turning to face her again.

"It's time to go to work, isn't it?" she laments after a while.

"Yeah, it's about six-thirty."

"How's your head?" she ventures.

"I'm sure it's fine."

"You know, the closer you get to thirty, the rougher the hangover."

I roll my eyes, sitting up in bed to prove she's underestimating me. But there's only about a five-second delay before it feels like someone is beating a drum in the space where my brain used to be. I squint one eye in an attempt to dull the pain before I lie back with a flop.

"Oof."

"Told you so."

"Maybe we should both call in sick," I suggest. "We could spend the day in bed?"

Please say yes...

She gulps. "I can't. My clinic schedule's full today."

"Five more minutes, then?" I can do a lot in five minutes, or at least get a lot of things started.

Huh. Right about now, I'd be lucky if I could last thirty seconds before—

"Five more minutes," she consents with a smile. I scoot over, and she turns automatically so that I can spoon my body around hers again. She's so warm ... and smooth.

"Tenley," I whisper.

She shivers. "Hmm?"

"Do you still want me?"

She draws her shoulders up as if she's fighting against something. "Of course I want you. I love you."

I press my hips into the backs of her thighs, and it feels so nice that I've got no choice but to see this attempt through. "You know what I mean."

"Right now?"

"Mm-hmm," I growl.

"Oh. Don't you have a headache?" she asks, her voice cracking.

"This will cure it," I mumble, brushing my lips over the skin below her ear. "Would we be ... safe?" I slide my hands up the back of her shirt, catching the band of her bra and pinching the fabric so that the clasps separate in one fluid movement. It's probably one of my smoothest moves to date, and hopefully it conveys that I *really* mean business this time.

"Um, I'd have to check my charting app," she says, but her tone is unconvincing. I've started paying attention to this fertility-awareness stuff, doing my own research on the symptoms and charts she's always mentioning, and I'm pretty sure she's not worried about getting pregnant today. I also know that if Tenley were ovulating, she'd already be all over me.

I pull her earlobe into my mouth at the same time my hands travel down to her hips, and I begin steering them in front of me. She takes in a shuddery breath. It feels *so* very good, and I can only hope she's run out of objections to giving in to the overwhelming chemistry we've been fighting for the past few months.

Then that small voice in the back of my head decides to speak up again, telling me I know better, that this isn't how it's supposed to go.

Dammit.

She swallows hard before she finally lets out a hoarse, "JD?"

"Hmm?"

While my conscience is busy with a theology of the body debate, my hands still have a mind of their own, and my fingers edge their way beneath the cup of her bra.

"JD," she whispers again, and I can tell she's into it from the way she's squirming in front of me. And then she lets out the slightest moan, and I'm totally done for.

"Anything you want, Tenley. Just tell me what you want, and I swear I'll do it," I murmur, doing my best to ensure that what she wants is to give herself over to me completely. This desire—no, this *need*—is stronger than anything I've ever felt before, and I'm afraid that this time, the biological instincts I've been joking about have actually managed to override my brain and my heart, both of which were already on the fence.

We're in love. And we're more than likely going to end up married at some point, right?

It's not all that wrong if we—

"I want to wait," she blurts out, seemingly surprised at herself. I whimper, my disappointment manifesting itself in more ways than one. "I think it could be a borderline day ... and I'd just rather be safe than sorry, you know?" she adds meekly.

"You mean, you want to double-check your chart first?" I ask, my voice hopeful.

She twists her body around so she's facing me again and reaches up to cup my cheek. "I have never wanted anyone or anything more than I want you. And I can't imagine I ever will. But we've waited this long. Let's just give it a little more time, please?"

Did she really have to add that bit about wanting me so badly, though? I stick out my bottom lip in a childish pout. "But ... but ... we're finally alone, and we're halfway undressed," I point out.

She only smiles ruefully and continues stroking my face. "I know. But, to be honest, I'm scared."

I shake my head quickly. "You know I would never hurt you. I was really just kidding about the ass-slap stuff, I swear."

She laughs softly. "Not like that. I'm afraid that once we finally start having sex, we won't be able to stop," she admits, her neck flushing and making her look even more irresistible, if that's possible. "Once I get that rush of oxytocin and dopamine, I'm going to have a hard time not coming back for more. We already know that my self-control is nonexistent while I'm ovulating, and everything already feels so good with you. It's all so different when you touch me. I can't trust myself. And I'd rather be married before I'm on kid number two."

My eyebrows shoot up. Did she just say *married*?

Now her face is also turning beet red, so I attempt to defuse the situation before she panics. "Oh. So, um, what does that mean? When will we get to ... you know ... have *intercourse*?" I ask with exaggerated awkwardness, and I'm rewarded with another giggle.

"How about once we decide that we're ready to risk having a baby?"

Did she just say *baby*? I gulp audibly, trying to contort my expression into something resembling disappointment while I continue testing the waters. "So, not until we're married?"

She shrugs. "Maybe."

Don't make it awkward, man. Just let it come out organically.

It's not that getting shut down like this isn't painful for me, both physically and emotionally. I'm just more intrigued by her sudden willingness to discuss, oh, I don't know—*forever*?

"Don't you think we're both a little ... mature for that? I mean, that ship has already sailed for both of us, right?"

"Yes, but like you've been saying, things are different with us. I've been doing some research about natural family planning, and it all just sort of clicked for me. Once I finally made the connection between the theological and biological elements, I realized making this sacrifice now could help ensure we have a successful marriage later. I think I may have subconsciously started pushing you away after that, not only to avoid temptation, but also because I was afraid of having to admit I'd been thinking that far ahead."

Holy cow. My breathing quickens. Hearing her talk about marital chastity is ironically as much of a turn-on as unhooking her bra was a second ago.

"JD, I love you too much to let you compromise your morals. And I don't think we'll regret waiting a little longer," she adds after a while. It's remarkable how calmly she's bringing all this up, as if she's just been waiting for the right time to slip it into conversation.

"A little longer?" I repeat with a hint of sarcasm. "It took me months to get you to kiss me or let me take you out on a date. How long before you can wrap your mind around marrying me?"

"I think I'm over all that commitment-phobia stuff. In fact, I bet I could be very easily persuaded to label this a long-term relationship ... maybe even show you off around town," she says, her lips turning up at the corners. It's so cute that I can't help but mirror her.

"Hmm. I bet I could persuade you to do all kinds of things right now if you gave me half a chance," I say, making my voice deeper and running my fingertips up the back of her thigh before stopping to grab a handful of her again.

She shivers, then pushes against my chest when I laugh at her. "Or maybe you could just keep your hands to yourself," she suggests, her voice betraying her attempts to appear collected. I figure it's difficult enough to bring up the topic of marriage as it is, much less trying to concentrate while I'm teasing her like this. But I also don't care about playing fair.

"Fine. Can I distract you with my lips?"

She pulls a face at me. "It'd be nicer if you didn't."

I grin and kiss her jawline anyway. "And you're absolutely sure you want to wait?" I ask one more time, even though I know she's right.

She sighs wistfully and shifts her hips again, and I'm afraid I may have actually convinced her to change her mind. "I'm sorry," I tell her, even though I can't quit kissing her. "Thank you for being the voice of reason. I'm just struggling to get the rest of my body on board with doing the right thing while also getting really turned on by your insistence that we do the right thing."

"I promise we'll make up for lost time later," she replies with a laugh.

I stop abruptly. Did she just promise to marry me?

"Later?"

"Yes, when the time is right for me to *show* you how much I love you, even though I'll need to use more than just my lips to get my point across," she declares, borrowing one of my lines. And then she leans in for a deep, intense, *desperate* kiss.

This time, I'm the one getting the *frissons* when she finally pulls away. "Tenley Jean, you can't say stuff like that right now, and you can't kiss me like you want me to take the rest of our clothes off, not when we're supposed to be keeping this classy."

"Sorry," she says, giggling again before her tone gets more serious. "It's just ... I thought you were leaving. I didn't know about the assistant-principal offer, so I assumed you were talking about that college coaching job when you texted me last week. And I panicked because I hated every second of being apart from you, but I also couldn't bring myself to hold you back."

I blink at her a few times. "Even if I were interested in that job, I'm always going to choose you and Ethan over work, football, everything. You know that, right?" She nods, her eyes watering. Then I lift her chin and reassure her with a kiss. "When I told you before that I've felt like the Holy Spirit has been leading me to you all this time, I meant it. I'd never leave you, Ten."

"I get it now. And for the record, I'm not going anywhere, either. Not without you."

I lean in for another kiss, because I'm sure it wasn't easy for her to make that declaration. "Besides, I need to help you get our boy back," I tell her once I pull away.

She gives me a sad smile. "As happy as I am to hear you say that, I'm afraid it doesn't look good."

"What do you mean?"

"Blake says it's basically up to Ethan, and either way, I'll never get full custody. Ryan has the advantage. Besides being Ethan's biological dad, he's ... established. He's got his own house and a family, and the courts are always more hesitant to give kids away to single parents."

Don't do it. Don't say it, you idiot. Not yet.

"Well, would it help if you were married, too?" I ask, coughing lightly over the last few words.

She looks at me hesitantly, as if she's trying to read my intent. "I didn't think to ask, since it was a moot point."

I rub a hand over my face, willing myself to think my next few words through before I give in to the urge to get down on one knee like the lovesick dumbass that I am. I can hear my heart thumping loudly.

"Maybe we could beat him at his own game." I swallow hard before I continue. "A month is plenty of time to plan a wedding, isn't it?"

Her eyes are wide, but she doesn't look appalled or even all that shocked. Instead, she bites the corner of her bottom lip, the way she always does when she's really nervous or scared. "JD, I ..." she begins, but then she shuts her eyes tightly. "That's not what I meant. We can't—not like this, anyway."

I shake my head and grab her chin, willing her to open her eyes again. "But marrying you wouldn't be a sacrifice or a favor. You have to know by now how much I want this."

"That's why it wouldn't be fair to you. I can't let you rush into marriage just so you can help me fix things with Ethan. I won't take all that away from you."

A tear rolls down one side of her face, and I bring my thumb up to dry her cheek. "Hmm. You know, you don't have to punish yourself for changing your mind about what kind of life you want, Tenley."

She pulls back slightly and angles her face so that her eyes lock onto mine again. I've definitely hit a nerve. "What do you mean?"

"I haven't missed the hints you've been dropping all morning. I can tell you want all the same things I do. You're just afraid to admit you want it *now*." She exhales as if I've knocked the wind out of her, so I continue. "So what if you used to think you'd never settle down in Camellia? Or that you'd never find someone who could make you want to start a family?"

"You say that like it wouldn't be totally insane for us to get married after, what, three months of dating?" she protests.

"And you say that like you're already considering it," I reply, smirking.

"JD ..." She shakes her head in disbelief. "This is crazy."

But I can already see her resolve fading. I place my hands on both sides of her face and pull her toward me gently. "Just admit you were wrong," I coax. "I won't hold it against you forever if you tell me you love me and want to marry me and have my babies. Hell, I might even say it back and take you up on it."

"But what if I'm bad at all those things?" she asks softly, trying to regulate her breathing. "I don't want to hurt you again."

Wait, so *that's* what this is about? The only thing left standing in my way is her self-doubt? Well, I can work with that.

I shake my head. "Babe, you couldn't be bad at it. I'm sure everything won't be perfect, but we'll figure it out as we go, together." Then I shrug before adding, "There's always make-up sex."

She scrunches up her nose, and a laugh escapes. "Is that where this offer is coming from? Is it because I said we should wait?"

"I'd be lying if I said it's not a factor. But I decided a while back that I wasn't going to stop trying to wifey you up until you gave in. The truth is that I was hoping to ask you and Ethan to move in with me after the custody hearing, before everything got derailed."

"You were?"

I nod, hoping she can sense my sincerity. "I was, and not just because I want to wake up next to you every morning. I want us to be a family, more than anything. And I'd rather do it all in the right order if we can, especially for Ethan's sake."

"But what if it doesn't work, and we can't get him back?"

"Then at least we'll have each other when we're missing him," I reply. "You wouldn't marry me just to beat this guy, would you?"

"Of course not. Even if I hated you, I could never do that."

"I know you couldn't, Ten," I say, running my hands down her back again. "Just like I know you're going to be an amazing wife, and you've already proven you're a great mom."

She continues fumbling with her lip as she considers. "I don't know if you're right, but you make me want to try," she begins, and my heart skips a beat. "Getting married, raising kids, and putting down roots in Camellia may not have been part of the life I thought I'd have, but it's all I want now. Except I only want it with you, and the sooner, the better."

That's it. That's the best thing I've ever heard.

Her declaration is better than seeing my name on the back of an LSU jersey, better than that phone call I got when I was drafted to the NFL, and better than the time they named me Coach of the Year in my district. *This* is what I'm built for, and it feels so right to hear Tenley say that she wants it, too.

I groan and lean in to kiss her, but we're rudely interrupted when my alarm blares. I reach over to silence it and return to embrace her. "I'm sorry. I think that five minutes might have just turned into twenty," I admit.

"Hmm. Then it's a good thing it should only take another minute to wrap this up," she replies, clasping her hands behind my head.

I furrow my brow, unsure whether she's egging me on or shutting me down. Then a smile slowly spreads over my face as I figure out what she's after. "You want me to propose right now, don't you? But only so you don't have to stress about when and how I'll do it later."

She pulls me down until our lips touch and kisses me deeply for a few seconds, leaving me unable to think with my brain again. "Yes, I'm not a fan of surprises. And although I hate asking you to give up the opportunity to plan some elaborate proposal and wedding, because I know how much you would enjoy all of it, I also want to be married to you, like, yesterday."

I stare back at her, my eyes heavy-lidded. Is this really happening? Is she actually begging me to propose?

Well, you don't have to ask me twice, babe.

"Tenley Jean," I begin. "Even though we've only been dating for a short time, it hasn't taken me long to figure out you are all I've ever wanted. You're so smart and capable, you're kind and selfless, you're honest and loyal ... you care about all the right things and don't bother faking stuff that shouldn't matter. You've already started helping me grow in holiness. Not to mention, you're the most beautiful woman I've ever laid eyes on. You check all my boxes, and then some. I love you, and I would really like to spend the rest of my life annoying you, watching football with you, raising Ethan with you, kissing you, making babies with you ..." I punctuate that last point by placing my lips along her jaw. Then I glance up again. "And trying to get each other to heaven one day. But the thing is, I don't want to wait another minute to get started. Will you marry me, like, yesterday?"

She grins, and tears pool in her eyes again. "I love you, too. And yes, JD, of course I'll marry you. I thought you'd never ask."

I pull her in for more kisses, attempting to show her how happy she's made me with her *yes*, and we end up making out until the next time my alarm goes off. Then we resolve to get dressed, and I pretend not to look when she turns and asks me to refasten the hooks of that infamous black bra. Although, I suspect she only requested my help because she wanted me to at least get a peek.

"You know," she begins as she pulls my jacket down over her head. "You're never getting this hoodie back."

"It'll be community property soon enough," I assure her as I reach out and yank her down onto the bed again because she looks too hot wearing my clothes. "And I don't mind sharing."

"I suppose you're going to claim partial ownership of my bras next?" she teases.

"Yep. We'll just start putting 'Bourgeois' labels on everything. In fact, I'm looking forward to seeing that name on your fancy lab coat alongside all those capital letters." But I immediately regret saying it, since we've never actually discussed the idea until now. What if Tenley doesn't want to change her last name, at least not professionally?

She grins. "I suppose it's a good thing Dr. Simms hasn't added 'Tenley Robin' to the sign in front of the clinic just yet."

And after that, I can't help but pull her back in for five more minutes together.

CHAPTER 38
JD

My head is still pounding when I finally climb into my truck a little later that morning, but it's all been worth it. My phone chimes with a message from my brother, but even the dread of telling Blake about my plans with Tenley can't dampen my mood. I'll just have to play dumb for a while until I can figure out a reasonable explanation for what I'm about to do with the woman who refused to give me the time of day only a few months ago. Maybe we should just elope and come back married so that Blake will have no choice but to accept it.

BLAKE THE SNAKE

Good morning, sunshine. How's it hanging today?

JD

Fine.

BLAKE THE SNAKE

Cut the shit. I just passed by your house and saw Tenley's car in the driveway.

JD

Okay, FANFREAKINGTASTIC.

BLAKE THE SNAKE

gif of ref signaling touchdown

??

JD

We made up.

BLAKE THE SNAKE

?

JD

Talk later. I'm late for work.

BLAKE THE SNAKE

It better be because you had to kick her out of your bed and it took too long to help her find her clothes.

JD

IT WAS, OK.

I sigh as I toss my phone into the cupholder in my truck, and it begins ringing a second later. "Blake the Snake is calling," the audio system announces.

I hit the phone button on my steering wheel. "WHAT?"

"Tell me you finally closed the deal."

I groan. Might as well rip this Band-Aid off. "In a sense. We're moving in together."

"You're *what*?" he chokes out.

"Tenley came over last night to offer a very sincere apology, and we were able to overcome some pretty big hurdles in our relationship. Plus, once I realized how much I enjoyed waking up next to her this morning, I suggested we make it a permanent thing."

"Wait, let me get this straight. You finally got Tenley to spend the night, and all you did was *talk*?"

I know he's about to give me a hard time, so I might as well mess with him first. "I guess I'd call it some really productive pillow talk."

"So, you did score?"

"Your interest in what does and does not happen in my bed is starting to get a little creepy, man," I say, enjoying his frustration.

He clicks his tongue. "And you're obviously deflecting."

"Maybe." I'm holding back laughter at this point.

"Dude, you're pathetic."

"Just wait, there's more," I deadpan.

"What, does she not realize she'll have to put out if you're living together?"

"Don't worry. She understands my expectations regarding sex once she moves in."

"She does?"

"Well, yeah. We'll be married by then, so she'll be expecting me to put out, too."

"You'll be WHAT?" he yells so loudly that I have to turn down the volume.

I chuckle. "I suggested we get married before the custody hearing, and Tenley very enthusiastically agreed."

He's practically wheezing. "*Married?* But you weren't even on speaking terms twenty-four hours ago!"

"Like I said, she came through with one hell of an apology. It was also a lot easier to hear her out once I saw how good she looks wearing my t-shirt as a nightgown."

I'm still laughing while his tone is pleading. "You're totally serious, aren't you? JD, *please*, don't rush into this. I know you want to help her get Ethan back for good, but this is a disaster waiting to happen. I can't guarantee that a wedding will be enough to sway the judge. And how can you be so sure Tenley won't change her mind? Or that you won't get stuck in a custody battle of your own if you have kids together and things don't work out?"

"Look, Tenley's a very analytical woman. If she thinks this is a good idea, who am I to pass up the opportunity?" I drive up to the school, almost forgetting to park in the "Reserved for the Assistant Principal" spot in front.

"Okay, but what's the hurry?"

"We love each other. We want to get custody of Ethan and raise him together. And we want to cohabitate and have a lot of sex. Why shouldn't we get married?"

One of the students passing by on the sidewalk in front of me gives me the side-eye, so I switch the call to my phone. "Maybe it won't make a difference in the outcome of the hearing, but I'd still like to do things in what I believe is the right order, and I need to be a good role model for Ethan. I want the three of us to officially become a family as soon as possible. Is that so hard to understand?"

"This isn't just a quick fix, man. I believe that Tenley loves you, I do. And I know that Ethan idolizes you. I just don't want to see you get stuck in a situation that you'll regret within a few years," he pleads. "You can't jump into a marriage based on an infatuation and expect it to work out."

I groan in frustration. "Blake, you're not hearing me. Remember how you thought I was crazy for passing on free agency? As much as I enjoyed playing football, I never quite felt like that whole lifestyle was a good fit for me, so I didn't have any regrets about not going back after my injuries. Then I stepped into coaching, and I knew it was my calling, that I belonged here. That's the same feeling I get when I'm with Tenley and Ethan. It just feels *right*, because this is exactly where I'm supposed to be." I debate telling him this next part, but it's time I started owning it. "All this time, God's been leading me to them, to the family I've always wanted."

"So, let me get this straight—God's answering your prayers for a family by having you marry the woman who strung you along for months so you can act as a stand-in father for her teenage nephew? I don't think that's how this works," he retorts.

"Actually, that's exactly how it works," I confirm.

He grunts, and I continue. "Maybe you just need me to translate this into a language you'd understand. I have a girlfriend who loves football, is an awesome cook, has a doctorate, and holds the same values I do. She's selfless enough to foster her teenage nephew—who I'd also like to inherit—has an amazing sense of humor, *and* she makes enough money to support our family on her own. Oh, and did I mention that she's the hottest woman I've ever seen and that she needs three rows of hooks on the back of her bra to hold up her fantastic rack? Because she's got that going for her, too, and I'd really love to lock it all down while I can."

Just then, a loud knock scares the daylights out of me, and I tell Blake to hold on while I roll down my window.

"Hey, there, Coach."

"Oh, hey, Lo."

"You, uh, might want to lower your voice a smidge. I just accidentally overheard 'fantastic rack' as I passed by. While I'm assuming that means congratulations are in order and that you and Tenley have made up, you may not want all of Camellia High to be privy to your conversation."

Blake's laugh is obnoxiously loud over the phone, and I roll my eyes. "Thanks, and sorry about that. I'm just over here having a yelling match with my brother about my future."

"Okay, then. Have a great day, Assistant Principal Bourgeois," Loren says loudly, then mouths "text me" while miming typing on the phone. I nod in return, rolling the window up.

"Blake, I've got to get to work, all right? We'll talk later."

"But—"

"Oh, by the way, I'm going to need Mom's ring."

I'm only teasing him again. Tenley already nixed the idea of an engagement ring since it would just interfere with the medical gloves she wears all day, so I'm going to buy her a wedding band for now and get her something nicer later.

"WHAT? You've got to be f—"

I end the call and hurry into school since I'm already late, chuckling when Blake texts me a warning.

BLAKE THE SNAKE

JD, I swear, if you touch Mom's ring …

JD

gif of Gollum saying "my precious"

Don't worry, Mama's Boy. Your precious ring is safe for now. But if you don't find someone to give it to in the next few years, I'm confiscating it.

Maybe I'll have a daughter or two to pass it on to by then.

BLAKE THE SNAKE

You'd better figure out how babies are made first, kid.

CHAPTER 39
TENLEY

"Hi," I say quietly as I step into Blake's office, and he rises to greet me. "Don't stand on my account."

He clears his throat and sits, avoiding eye contact, presumably because he's still angry with me for breaking his little brother's heart after promising him I wouldn't. I imagine JD's also told Blake about our impending nuptials by now, which means he probably suspects I've been holding out on JD so I'd have a carrot to dangle when I swindled him into proposing to me.

Maybe I should tread lightly here.

"Look, Blake, I—"

He holds up a hand. "I'm your lawyer, not your friend or your brother-in-law. So let's just keep it professional," he says curtly.

I glare in return. "Fine. What are we doing about Ethan?"

He sniffs indignantly, then looks down at a file on his desk. "Your court date has been set for six weeks from now. As I said before, you still have temporary custody. If you want to exercise your rights, you can call the sheriff's department and demand Ethan be returned to you. However, I'd advise you to consider what he actually wants, since he's old enough for his opinion to matter at the hearing."

"Ethan wants to come home, but he wants a relationship with his father and his siblings, too."

"And he's told you that himself?"

"He has."

Blake nods solemnly and scribbles some notes. "Then I think your best option is to counter with a joint-custody offer. We can still request that you be named Ethan's domicile custodian but concede visitation privileges for Ryan. I'll warn you, though, he's probably going to fight it, because he wants to have the upper hand. And he's going in with an advantage."

"Because he's married and established," I mumble.

"Yes, but mostly because he's Ethan's biological father." He drops his pen and exhales, sounding frustrated. "Tenley, I have a confession to make."

"Okay."

He scratches his head, ruffling his perfectly coiffed hair. "In hindsight, I believe I made a mistake at the first hearing."

"What kind of mistake?" I ask hesitantly.

"Do you remember when the judge assumed you and JD were going to be living together? And I corrected him?" I nod silently, and he continues. "I don't think he meant to question your morality. He actually wanted to hear you and JD were shacking up so that Ethan would have a male authority figure in his life. That's why he ruled the way he did and encouraged Ethan to seek out his dad. If I'd let the judge believe you and JD were planning to raise Ethan together, as a family ..." He sighs. "Things might have turned out differently for all of you. I'm sorry."

I blink a few times, his transparency taking me by surprise. "Why are you apologizing now?"

"Because, as your attorney, I made a mistake, and I rarely make mistakes. I allowed my personal feelings about what I thought was best for JD to cloud my judgment, and I failed to pick up on something important, something that could have changed the trajectory of your case. I should've just let the judge make his assumptions, but I was worried about my brother getting more deeply involved in the situation."

"Oh."

"I'm also stepping down and handing your case over to Mr. Mark. I can't be completely impartial after everything that's happened, and I'd rather not risk another oversight due to a conflict of interest."

I recoil from his declaration. "So, you're just going to abandon us now?"

"I'll make sure all the prep work is done, and I'll brief Mark on everything before your court date."

"Hold on, Blake. I don't want anyone else to represent us. I want someone who cares about Ethan, who understands he's a great kid who made a naive choice, who's actually invested in what happens to him."

He stands and clears his throat, signaling my dismissal. "I'm sorry, Ms. Robin, but this is the most ethical course of action, given the circumstances."

I cringe, willing myself not to cry. "Is it really ethical to leave us hanging because you're butthurt over your brother ignoring your advice to be with me?" He looks away, shoving his hands in his pockets. "Is it also professional to sabotage my case so you can get what you want?"

"Excuse me?" He whips his head around to scowl at me.

"You just admitted you didn't want JD to get more involved in this situation, i.e., with *me*."

"That's not what I said."

"It's what you meant, though. I assume you've spoken to him today."

"I don't want to talk about this with you."

I ignore him and continue on. "Then you know about his offer to marry me, to help me get Ethan back. I tried to talk him out of it, because I don't want him to keep making all these sacrifices for me," I say, standing and raising my voice. "But he wouldn't take no for an answer, of course."

He purses his lips and looks down, shaking his head slowly. "Please stop, Tenley."

"We're guilty of the same thing, though, aren't we? Neither of us can refuse him." He glares at me. "I'm not using him, Blake. I love JD, and I actually want to marry him, regardless of whether it makes a difference in the outcome of the hearing."

"You should go. I'll have Mr. Mark reach out to you later."

I throw my purse over my shoulder, preparing to stomp out of his office. "Good, because I think I'd prefer to work with someone who has the balls to help me do whatever it takes to get my kid back."

"What did you just say?" he asks, leaning over with his hands on his desk.

"You heard me," I step closer again, hoping to show him I'm not intimidated.

"And you seriously think I'm the chicken here?"

I shrug. "I'm not the one running ... not anymore."

"Then why the hell did you torture him for so long? How am I supposed to believe you really want to marry him when you're always leaving him hanging or letting him wonder whether you even care?"

I frown. "I knew he was far too good for me from the beginning, so I pushed him away at first. I didn't think I deserved him, and I couldn't trust myself not to screw things up."

"None of us deserve him," he mumbles.

"You're right. But I've finally given up on trying to keep my distance. I'm not going anywhere, and I plan to spend the rest of my life trying to make him as happy as he makes me, with or without your blessing. So, think you can get over yourself and help me, at least for your brother's sake?" I stare him down with my hands on my hips.

To my surprise, he laughs. "For my brother's sake, huh?"

"Yes, because we both know JD and Ethan need one another, too."

He stares at me with an amused expression for a second longer, then he gives me a short nod and settles behind his desk. He picks up the phone and asks his receptionist to get Ryan from the Jameson Law Office on the phone, narrowing his eyes at me and gesturing for me to sit.

"Hey, Ryan? It's Blake Bourgeois. How's it going, man? Yeah,

yeah," he begins, leaning back in his fancy chair and crossing his legs. "Listen, I'm sure you already know why I'm calling, right?" he says with an obviously fake laugh. "Right. But look, you know Tenley still has custody for now, and Ethan wants to come home. Sure, he does. Well, have you asked him, buddy? Oh, yeah, teenagers, right?" He forces another laugh before his tone gets more serious.

"Anyway, she's willing to call off the sheriff's department and give you some weekend visitation for now if you send him back this afternoon. No, no, we know he's not in school over there yet. He was never withdrawn from Camellia High. *How* do I know? Come on, Ryan, I'm sure he's told you that JD and his aunt are pretty hot and heavy, which means E and I are tight, too."

I can't help it when Blake's claim on Ethan warms my heart.

"No, I understand. I do. But I've got friends at the DA's office, same as you, and this is personal for me. So, what do you say, man? Are you sending Ethan back today so you can have him next weekend, or do you want the whole neighborhood to witness the deputy knocking on your door within the hour?"

Blake's cocky expression looks promising. He winks at me, and I bite my lip as I grasp at the sliver of hope.

"Great, no, that's great. I'm just glad we're all on the same page. Oh, yeah. Appreciate it. See you next month in court. All right, later, man." He hangs up the phone and waggles his eyebrows. "Big E should be home for dinner."

"Oh, my gosh, Blake, that was amazing!" I lean over his desk and squeeze his forearm in a gesture of gratitude. But I pull my hand back quickly once I realize it's probably unwelcome.

He shrugs, ignoring the contact I initiated. "I did it for Ethan."

"You could have done it for Ethan a few days ago, you know," I grumble playfully.

"I wasn't sure it was in Ethan's best interest until today," he replies. "And I wasn't going to make empty threats unless I knew you'd be willing to back them up."

I smile. "Blake?"

"Yeah?"

"Thank you. And I meant what I said before. I'll do everything I can to make JD happy."

He nods. "I'll hold you to it, Tenley."

CHAPTER 40
JD

I step out of my new office and into the hallway to greet the students as they shuffle along to their homeroom classes. I notice Ethan glaring at me from across the way, and I flash him a cheesy grin as I think about the plans Tenley and I have been discussing over the past couple of days—the ones about getting married before we're awarded custody of Ethan and moving into my place together as a family.

There are also the plans we made for our wedding night, which have already become a permanent fixture in the back of my mind. But I've been trying my best to curb those thoughts, because catching a glimpse of the finish line hasn't made the last leg of this race any easier.

I spend the first half of my day monitoring the kids during transition and completing an endless stack of paperwork for the baseball team's eligibility with the state athletics association, then I take a break to scarf down some lunch. I text Tenley to check in, and I'm relieved when she replies that she still wants to marry me, though she admits she hasn't spoken to her family about it yet. Then I glance around my office, which still looks pretty sparse. I should start unpacking my things since I've gotten the majority of my work done for the day, but I bite the inside of my cheek as I debate my next move, my leg bouncing up and down restlessly.

"Aw, hell," I mumble to myself, already picking up my desk phone. I ask the secretary to make a quick announcement, and her voice resonates over the intercom a few seconds later.

"Ethan Robin, please report to Coach JD's office." She repeats it three times, making me smile.

Ethan knocks shortly before he walks in, and his expression says he isn't thrilled about the intercom summons. "Did you really have to get Ms. Sam to do an all-call to the whole school for me?" he asks angrily.

I snicker. "No, but it's more fun that way, right?" He rolls his eyes as he drops his backpack and sits in the chair across from my desk. "How's your first day back?"

He slouches and lifts his feet as if he's planning to prop them on the edge of my desk. That is, until he catches my expression. He clears his throat and straightens his posture instead. "People are still trying to figure out where I've been, but it hasn't been so bad."

"Have you talked to Caidence?"

A smile creeps across his face. "We were actually sitting together at lunch when you called me out."

"My bad, bruh." I laugh through the apology.

"So, can I go back?" He hitches his thumb over his shoulder.

"Hold on." I'm suddenly more nervous than I've ever been for a conversation with Ethan. "I'm sure you heard Tenley and I made up."

"She told me."

"Right."

He fidgets uncomfortably for a second before he speaks again. "Look, I know I texted you before, but while I'm here, I want to apologize in person for everything. I acted like a jerk, and I'm sorry for being so selfish and disrespectful."

I give him a half-smile. "Thanks. And I'm sorry about the way I handled things, too. I never meant for you to get stuck in the middle or for my relationship with Tenley to make you feel bad."

"I know, and I won't interfere with you guys again," he adds. "So, are we cool?"

"Yeah, man. We're cool."

"Good. Is that all?"

"Not exactly. I need to talk to you about something else ... important." I pause, still worried about his reaction. Maybe I'm supposed to let Tenley deliver this kind of news, but it feels like Ethan should hear it from me. "Your Pop and I, well, we kind of already discussed this, but I thought it was only right to defer to you now."

He blinks and swallows hard. "Oh."

"Yeah." I lean forward with my elbows on my desk so I can get a little closer to him. "Tenley and I are thinking about getting married very soon, and we want to make sure you're okay with that."

This time he takes a deep breath and blows it out before he speaks. "Damn. You like, *really* made up."

I chuckle. "I guess we did."

"I don't know, though. This seems pretty crazy." He shakes his head. "The other day, Aunt Ten freaked out when you brought up marriage, and now you're getting engaged? I mean, she did warn me that you were going public now, but what changed while I was gone?"

"We had a serious discussion about our future, and once we were completely honest about our feelings, we realized we both want the same things. We couldn't come up with any reasons for waiting to get married, and Tenley assured me she's ready to make that commitment," I explain carefully.

"And you're ready?" he asks. I smirk at him. "You've been ready." He says it as a statement this time.

"I'd like to know how you feel about it, though, since this means that you and I will be family, too."

"Well, yeah, I sort of assumed that's how this works," he says with a smile. "But I guess you're talking about living together."

"I am. I want you both to move in with me." My voice is a little shaky now.

"That all makes sense, except for the part about you and Tenley getting married so soon."

"You don't think it's a good idea, then?"

"I'm not doubting you guys belong together or that you'll take care of her and all that. It's just … this is all happening so fast for something so … permanent. I don't want either of you to rush into marriage because of me," he explains.

"Maybe we'd have been less likely to consider getting married right away if you weren't in the picture, but we have other reasons."

Ethan huffs. "Is she pregnant or something?"

I look away, unable to meet his eyes. "No, she's not. But Tenley and I agree we should be married if we're going to be living together."

"Because you want to get her pregnant?" he ventures with a smirk.

I clear my throat, resisting the urge to revert to the maturity level of the kid sitting across from me. "I don't know how soon we'll be ready to have more kids, but that's definitely something I'm looking forward to, as well as the sanctioned, regular practice."

He shakes his head in amusement, and I'm relieved. "I'm not sure how you went from being desperate for her to go out with you to getting married and having babies this quickly, but I guess I shouldn't be surprised."

"It's possible that God had a plan to bring us together and that we bonded over our mutual fondness for you. But, then again, it could have been the topless lawn service," I answer, leaning back in my chair and crossing my arms. "Or maybe the time you passed out at the homecoming dance and made me carry your little punk-ass home. Either way, she's a fan of all this." I flex my arms, and the teenage-boy half of my brain is satisfied when Ethan cringes.

"Are you going to do that kind of crap around the house? I don't know if I want to live with you guys if it means I'll be subjected to any more of you walking around half-naked and trying to impress her. I'd rather not be stuck in a documentary about the mating habits of thirty-year-olds for the next few years."

I tilt my head back and laugh this time. I'm still not sure where the kid gets his sense of humor or his ability to read people, but he's absolutely one of a kind.

"Best I can do is offer to keep most of that stuff contained to our bedroom. Not to mention, one of the only benefits of living alone all this time has been the clothing-optional dress code at home. I suppose we can make wearing shorts a house rule, though."

He groans. "Aren't you supposed to be convincing me to move in?"

"Hey, that's actually pretty generous. I'll be sacrificing a lot of my rights and privileges as a married man."

"Ugh, make it stop," he grumbles, covering his ears.

I glare at him until he drops his hands. "Remember that reproduction chapter we covered in bio last month? You do realize that process works the same for Tenley and me as it does for other humans, right?"

"Yeah, but I'd rather just pretend otherwise. Besides, Aunt Ten makes enough jokes about that as it is. I don't need to know that she's not actually kidding."

"Does she?" I ask with an eyebrow cocked.

He looks at me strangely. "I'm not ... just—no. Changing the subject, Coach Thirsty."

"Fine. But what do you say, wingman? Do we have your blessing?"

His expression softens, and he looks genuinely pleased when he nods his approval. "Of course. But, uh, how soon is *very soon*, anyway?"

"We'd like to get married before the custody hearing, so sometime within the next month?"

He narrows his eyes. "I thought you said you weren't doing this for me."

"I said we have our reasons, and you're one of them. You know how important you are to both of us. And I'm not saying we need your permission to get married, but we do want you on board with everything. Like I said, we're a family now. This is about all three of us."

He's quiet for a while. "What if it doesn't work? What happens if they send me back to Ryan's?"

"Is that what you want?" I ask, trying to keep my tone neutral. "Ethan, don't guilt yourself into making a choice between Ryan and us. While we'd miss seeing you every day, this is your decision to make, and I know I speak for Tenley when I say there won't be any hard feelings if you'd like to get to know your father better."

"I want to stay here with you guys," he replies quickly, to my relief.

"I'm glad. Just be sure you aren't saying that to make the rest of us happy."

He huffs. "You know, that's the funny thing. Ryan only tried to convince me I'd be making a mistake if I came back here, because he can give me 'so much more than Tenley ever could.' "

I clench my jaw, trying to keep my voice even. "He may be right. I don't have a mini mansion. We can't offer you a brand-new car, and we probably never would, on principle alone. We don't have a trust fund set up for you, and you're stuck in public school. Chances are you'll be babysitting and helping us change diapers before long. And as long as you live here, you'll have to pull your weight and adhere to our rules."

"I think I'm more than okay with all that, even diaper duty," he says, smiling until he adds, "Ryan's confident he's going to get custody, though."

"Well, I heard Ryan crawfished when Blake called him out the other day," I retort, and he grins even wider. "But we don't want you worrying about it. Tenley, Blake, and I will handle Ryan."

"Okay," he exhales. "As long as this is what you really want, too."

I smirk at him, warming myself up for another, more G-rated proclamation than the one I made for my brother. "It is. I love your Aunt Tenley, I want to spend the rest of my life with her, and I don't see the point in waiting to get started when my feelings aren't going to change."

He looks relieved. "It's too bad you won't get to do one of those grand-gesture proposals. I was looking forward to watching you embarrass yourself."

"I am a little disappointed, but we both know she'd hate that, anyway," I say with a short laugh before my expression turns more serious again. "Thanks for being my wingman, Big E."

"No worries, Coach."

"I mean it, kid. I appreciate everything you've done to help me. And I promise I'll make it up to you by trying my best to be a decent uncle."

"Yeah, bet." His voice cracks, so he looks away and clears his throat. Then the bell rings, providing a welcome interruption.

"How awkward is this going to be around school? Everyone's going to have questions once you randomly start wearing a wedding ring." He stands and throws his backpack over his shoulder.

"At least we don't have football for a while. And I'm not your teacher anymore," I point out, walking him to the door.

He rolls his eyes. "Just the assistant principal."

"I can yell at you in front of everyone if it'll make you feel better," I offer.

He laughs. "Yeah, I guess I've got no chance of flying under the radar now that you can make all-calls. Who wants to be the principal's kid, anyway?"

"Oh, I'm sure there'll be some perks," I return, trying not to let him see how happy he's made me by referring to himself as *my kid*. "I very seriously doubt anyone will dare to TP our house next homecoming, for example."

"Good point."

"All right. Now get your scrawny behind to class, Robin. Don't make me write you a tardy slip."

"Right. Because then you'd have to sign both sides, for the administrator and for the parent," he says mockingly before he leaves my office. And I take a deep breath and blink away the moisture in my own eyes before stepping out into the hallway again.

CHAPTER 41
TENLEY

It's been less than a week since our decision to move forward with a wedding, and JD has already scheduled an appointment with the priest. I have to admit, his impatience is endearing.

"Hi, Father. Thanks so much for letting us come in on short notice," he begins on the first morning of his Christmas break.

"It's no problem at all," Father Conrad says, shaking each of our hands and gesturing for us to sit. "I understand congratulations are in order?"

"Yes, sir, thank you," JD answers, reaching over to intertwine our fingers.

"Do you have a date in mind?"

JD clears his throat. "Well, that's the thing. How far out are we talking here?"

"Usually, six months would be the minimum."

He squeezes my hand gently. "Do you think we could possibly bend those rules for special circumstances?"

Father Conrad's eyebrows rise sharply. "I see. But I imagine you still have a few months before things become obvious, right?" he asks, peering at me.

"A few months?"

"You shouldn't worry about rushing to the altar before you're showing. It's more important that you take enough time to think this commitment through," he explains gently.

"Oh," I reply. "Actually, that's not—I'm not pregnant."

Father flashes an apologetic smile. "I'm sorry for assuming, then."

"Yeah, that's definitely not the reason we're here," JD says, a tinge of humor in his voice. I glare at him out of the corner of my eye.

"So, what's your hurry?" the priest asks.

"We're trying to get custody of Tenley's nephew. The court date is in just over a month, and we'd really like to keep him here with us instead of allowing his biological father—whom he's only just met— to force him to move away."

"Ethan, isn't it? Great kid. He's in our confirmation class this year," Father Conrad says warmly.

"Thank you, Father. You probably know my parents have been raising him since my sister passed away after Ethan was born. But, JD and I would like to take over as his permanent guardians. We really want to provide him with the closest thing to a traditional family unit that we can, and the judge will look more favorably on us if we can prove Ethan will have a father figure at home."

He nods and leans back in his chair, steepling his fingers. "While it's very charitable of you to want to do this for your nephew, I'm still concerned about your reasons for getting married. You haven't been dating for all that long, have you?"

JD swallows hard as the priest stares him down, and it's almost as if they're having a silent exchange. "A couple of months."

"Now, you know it would be irresponsible of me to let you rush into the sacrament of marriage without a true understanding of these vows. And there are still other logistical issues and requirements you must meet, such as completing Pre-Cana and natural family planning classes—"

"We know it seems fast," I interrupt him. "But we're both established in our careers and ready to take marriage seriously. In fact, I think my friend Sybil already mentioned to you that I'm a certified

NFP instructor, so that's another thing we can check off the list, right?" I volunteer.

I see the priest's eyes dart down to my hand as JD rubs the back of it softly. "When exactly were you hoping to have the wedding?"

"Literally as soon as possible," JD deadpans.

"We don't want anything big. The smaller, the better," I add.

"Within the month? It'll have to wait until after Christmas."

"Name the day and time, Father," says JD. "We'll be there."

"And you're both absolutely sure about this, that you fully understand the gravity and the permanence of this commitment?"

"We do. That's why we're here, because we want to do this right. It's also why we want a sacramental wedding in addition to a legal one." JD hesitates and clears his throat before continuing. "I've definitely been feeling it. You know, that pull from the Holy Spirit we talked about a few months ago? This is it."

He's referenced this "call" in front of me before, but I'm surprised to hear JD's also spoken to Father Conrad about it. The priest glances back and forth between us, a smile taking over his features. "Hmm. I think I get it," he says, smirking at JD. "You're very much in love, aren't you?"

"Oh, yeah," JD answers with a sigh.

"And by wanting to do this right, you mean that ..."

"I'm afraid it's either the altar or the confessional by next month, Father," JD admits, shaking his head.

I let out an embarrassed groan and tug my hand back to cover my cheeks, but Father only leans back in his chair and laughs heartily. "You could have just led with that, you know. You're only human."

JD turns to face me. "See, I told you he'd understand," he whispers with a wink.

"I'm sorry about him," I say, ignoring JD. "What he should have said is that we need to move in together for Ethan's sake, and we don't want to risk subjecting one another to that much temptation. Or, you know, we'd probably be back in a few months, asking you to move up the wedding for the first reason you mentioned."

Father laughs lightly again. "It's fine. Your honesty is refreshing and reassuring, and your willingness to sacrifice the big ceremony in an effort to protect one another's souls speaks volumes about your true intentions. You've already learned that real love is about humility, service, and compromise." He grabs a pair of reading glasses from his desk and puts them on before peering down at a calendar. "How is next Saturday morning, just after the New Year?"

"Really?" I gulp.

"That's what you wanted, right?"

I glance back at JD, my heart thumping loudly. "Yeah?"

A grin spreads across his face, and he brings my hand up to his mouth to kiss the inside of my wrist. "Yeah, let's do it."

I sigh, melting into my chair. The way he looks at me with so much adoration never gets old. "Okay. Next Saturday, it is," I agree, my voice sounding more breathy and desperate than I intend.

"Wonderful. And until then, I strongly recommend the two of you not spend any time unchaperoned," Father Conrad offers with an amused smile.

An hour or so later, we complete our first pre-marriage counseling session, and I walk out even more in love with my fiancé than I was when I first arrived. JD finally got the opportunity to share some of his deeper convictions, like his intense desire for a family and the promises he'd made to my dad, leaving me in awe of his faith and the way his mind works. I'm also unbelievably grateful that he never gave up on me.

I text my mom, Ethan, and Loren as soon as we're done to let each of them know we set a date for the wedding. Though I warned my mom about the possibility of Ethan and me moving in with JD in the near future, I'd left out my intention to get married first. To my surprise, she reacts as though she's been waiting on this news all day, like I'm just confirming the details of the ceremony she's already started planning.

Ethan receives the announcement as enthusiastically as his age and gender allow, as opposed to Loren, who's giddy about joining my mom and me for some impromptu dress shopping. JD and I part ways. (Okay, so we make out in the parking lot first, but he started it when he leaned in to declare some of the ways he plans to *show* me how much he loves me in under two weeks and counting.) Then I head out to meet my mom and Loren at a bridal shop in the next town over.

Although I'm dreading this part of the process, I've already taken the day off, and there isn't much time to find something off the rack. I'd honestly prefer to skip the fancy wedding dress altogether, but I want to do this for JD. I know he's been looking forward to having a big, traditional wedding, even if he won't admit it. And showing up to our small ceremony in a white dress and a veil seems like the least I could do.

The problem is that I've never been able to wear a formal dress without alterations before, and with the time crunch we're facing, I'm certain it'll be impossible to find anything decent to fit. For efficiency's sake, we start by pulling any and every dress that might possibly work with my current measurements, regardless of style, leaving me with a half-dozen options to start.

My mom and Loren each get one veto, which they agree on, and I eliminate two dresses, one that's too revealing and another that seems too complicated. I realize where my priorities lie when I catch myself worrying about JD having trouble with all the tiny buttons. Somehow, setting a date has made it even harder to concentrate on anything else, which reminds me—I'm going to have to keep a close eye on my chart in case my window of fertility opens early this next cycle. I can't imagine telling JD that we'll have to wait another week to consummate our marriage if we want to avoid getting pregnant, though he may be open to taking that risk if it happens. Either way, we should probably talk about our intentions beforehand.

But back to dresses—I need to pick out a dress before I can worry about what happens once it comes off.

The saleswoman, who'd introduced herself as Nicole earlier, holds up the first option. It's simple but surprisingly pretty. I step into the dress and pull the long sleeves up over my arms. Immediately, I'm impressed by the coverage the square neckline offers, despite the fact that I'm stuffing myself into a top that's at least a size too small.

Nicole zips up the back to reveal a trumpet silhouette. "Oh, wow," she says. "It's gorgeous … like it was made for you."

"Sounds like I need to check this out—oh, my word," Miley, the other stylist, gushes as she joins us in the dressing room. "Honey, you'd swear they sewed you into that dress!"

I bite my lip as I stare at my reflection. I'm not confident about my body very often, but I have to admit this dress is flattering. I turn to the side and survey another angle, and I'm mostly pleased with the way it fits over my hips and butt, which never happens. Something about the cut and the plain fabric allow everything to fall just right.

"Shall we go out and show Mama?" Miley proposes.

I nod. "Yes. I think so."

She leads me on while I fist the skirt in my right hand and stumble awkwardly over to the platform. My mom and Loren immediately fall silent behind me. I cast a nervous glance at them in the mirrored wall, but their expressions are blank.

Miley circles me as she smooths out the dress's train, and my heart starts racing when Nicole clips a veil over my head. My mom gasps at the same time my vision begins to blur. "Oh, Tenley," she murmurs as her hand flies to her chest. "You're absolutely beautiful." She sniffles a few times and reaches out for a box of tissues. I'm tempted to question her, but the truth is that for the first time in my life, I believe her. I *feel* beautiful.

I inhale sharply as reality slams into me. The veil is making it all too real.

I'm wearing a freaking wedding dress. Because I'm about to get married. To a man who's not only younger than me, but also a former NFL player. After dating him for under three months. None of this even makes sense, yet I've pretty much quit caring about what makes sense in the first place. It's like Sybil said, nothing else seems to matter as much anymore.

I swallow hard, attempting to keep my voice level. "I think I kind of love this one. It's nice, right?"

"Nice? *Nice?*" Loren yells as she dabs her eyes with a tissue. "Tenley, I've got half a mind to hate you after this. Who lands a husband like JD without even trying *and* looks this freaking good in the first wedding dress she puts on? Can't you save some luck for the rest of us?" I laugh as I dry my own eyes.

"Wait, you're marrying JD, as in *the* JD Bourgeois, the former LSU tight end with the big guns and the tight end?" Nicole asks, bouncing her eyebrows.

I snort. "That's the one."

She tilts her head and sighs. "Wow … I sorta hate you a little, too," she adds in a playful voice. "I went out with his brother once. He was fun, but I doubt we'll be seeing another Bourgeois bride in here any time soon, if you know what I mean." I roll my eyes at her somewhat accurate assessment of my future brother-in-law.

"Okay, I absolutely need to see a picture. And can someone please spill the tea? What's with the quickie wedding?" Miley asks as she readjusts my veil. "Will we need a bigger dress?" she adds quietly.

I reassure them that I'm not pregnant and explain the custody situation again while Nicole pulls up JD's Instagram account on her phone. I make a mental note to ask him to set his socials to private after this. But they only simper over a few of his photos and shower him with compliments, which I suspect is mostly to get me to laugh and help defuse a potential bridal breakdown.

I turn to face Mom and Loren after staring at my reflection a little longer. "Are you sure it's not too fitted? It feels pretty snug."

"She may be right, Mrs. T. Our boy is never going to survive the ceremony if we let her walk down the aisle like that," Loren says, nudging my mom and smirking mischievously. "This dress is basically obscene—like, spicy romance-novel material."

"I'm afraid so, Tenley-girl. Coach is going to lose it when he sees you in that dress. *Pauvre bête.*"

Loren giggles and snorts before she adds, "He's going to carry her right out of that church, all the way home to bed, I'm sure."

I cringe as Miley and Nicole join in. "You guys are the worst."

"If you'd have noticed the way he's been looking at you for the past few months, you'd think it was pretty funny, too," my mom returns.

Oh, I've noticed, but I can't think about JD's smoldering stare right now. I turn my attention back to the mirror, trying to change the subject before my cheeks flush any darker. "So, this is it. It looks like I'll be getting married in this dress," I remark, still in disbelief. "Because I'm a crazy person."

"Yeah, but the best kind of crazy, Ten," Loren replies with a smile.

CHAPTER 42
JD

I PULL MY ARMS THROUGH THE SLEEVES OF MY NAVY SUIT jacket, the one that Tenley likes so much, then I turn to face Ethan.

"My tie straight?"

"Yep. Nervous yet?"

I look down at my hands, willing them to stop shaking. "Nah, I'm good."

"Are you sure?" I figure he's referring to my decision to get married this time.

"Absolutely," I say on an exhale. It probably sounds less convincing than I mean it to, but it's the truth.

"You know, no one would blame you if you backed out," he adds quietly. "But it's now or never, right?"

I grin at him and let my hand fall onto his shoulder, feeling pretty damn lucky to be gaining him, too. "I'm not going anywhere, E. But thanks for the reminder." I reach in for a hug, which he willingly returns. Then I furrow my brow as I pull away. "Wait, you're not trying to tell me that Tenley's getting cold feet, are you?"

He shakes his head quickly. "I don't think that's going to happen. You know her. If she's come this far, she won't back out now."

I laugh because he's right. "Listen, Ethan," I begin. "I know it probably feels like everything is changing right now, but I still mean what I said before. You'll always be a priority for both Tenley and me, and I'm happy to play whatever part you want me to in your life. I could never replace your Pop, and I don't want to impose on your relationship with your father, but I'll be here for whatever you need."

He lets out a deep breath. "I know you will. I mean, I'm glad I met Ryan, but he's never going to be my dad. And he's nowhere near crazy enough to get married just to set a good example for me," he says with a sardonic laugh. "But seriously, I'm really grateful for you and Aunt Ten. Thank you for doing this."

I have to swallow the lump in my throat before I can answer him. "I'm pretty sure I'm the one coming out ahead here. Nothing would make me happier than having you around all the time."

He smiles. "Except maybe bunking with Tenley."

"Fair enough." I smirk. "But I haven't forgotten that you were my loyal sidekick before she showed up."

"That's true. Maybe that's why we've always gotten along. We were meant to become a family one day," he says softly, looking down at his feet.

My heart swells a few sizes, and I'm afraid it won't fit in my chest before long. "You're right, man. And, hey, I'm proud of you and the way you've handled everything. Don't take this the wrong way, but I kind of love you, kid."

I figure Ethan knows how I feel about him by now, but today seems like the right day to say it outright.

His cheeks darken and he looks away, obviously embarrassed. "Thanks. You, too, I guess, Uncle JD ... ew, no. Too weird."

"Yeah, Coach JD's fine," I tell him.

Father Conrad comes over to greet both of us with handshakes, and we make small talk until Blake saunters in from the back of the church.

"I still can't believe you're letting him do this, Father," he grumbles as we approach the altar, though I can see a smile lurking behind his grumpy mask. I'm starting to think my big brother has gone soft —not that I'm brave enough to call him out on it. Over the past couple of weeks since Tenley and I decided to get married, he's been way more supportive than any of us could've imagined, even helping us apply for a marriage license and deigning to play nice with Loren. And, although he voiced his disappointment when I turned down his offer to throw me a "real" bachelor party, he respected my wishes and agreed not to do anything too crude in front of Ethan or to decorate my truck with condoms today, especially since Tenley and I won't need them to practice NFP.

"Oh, I think he knows what he's doing," Father Conrad says with a chuckle. "At the end of the day, I believe JD will be awfully happy with his decision to enter into the sacrament of holy matrimony."

"I'm sure he'll be *very* pleased," Blake retorts, and my face flushes just a little.

"I'm counting on it," I murmur, my breath catching when the door opens to reveal Tenley in an actual wedding dress. It's simple, but it drapes over her curves just right, the neckline offering just a peek at her cleavage without being immodest. Mrs. T and Loren are still fussing over her and adjusting her veil as they walk this way, and I blink away my surprise. I'd assumed Tenley would wear something nice, but I honestly didn't expect to see her in anything so formal and traditional. She looks like a real bride.

My bride.

My heart pounds as I wait patiently for her to look up, and the smile that spreads across her face when our eyes finally meet doesn't disappoint. It sounds cliché, but I've never seen anyone look so beautiful.

"Are we all ready, then?" Father Conrad asks, bringing me back from my thoughts, and everyone shifts into place. Blake stands next to me, Loren walks across the way, and Ethan and Mrs. T flank Tenley's sides. They step forward, and I think Father asks them about giving her away, but I'm still so floored to see her standing in front of me in a veil and a white dress that I tune out most of what they're saying.

They take turns embracing Tenley before Ethan grabs her hand and places it in mine the way we practiced the day before. I automatically bring it up to my lips, kissing the inside of her wrist and causing her cheeks to redden. She glances up at me coyly, as if she wants me to know that she's wearing all of it just for me, and I find myself staring at her again and contemplating how lucky I am. Blake coughs out some mention of Holy water a few times until I get the hint and turn us to face the altar.

I struggle to focus on what Father Conrad says after that, my attention consumed by the feeling of Tenley's hand quivering within mine and the sound of her unsteady breathing beside me. After the liturgy readings, Father cracks a joke about "becoming one flesh" and being open to life that makes everyone chuckle, but by now I couldn't care less about everyone knowing my plans for the rest of the afternoon.

I try my best with the vows and the "I do" parts, though I'm forced to choke down the emotion in my throat a few times. Tenley tears up and her voice cracks when she repeats "in sickness and in health," and it takes all I have to keep my eyes dry. I know we're both wishing my parents and her dad could be here. I make sure not to glance over at Mrs. T, since I can hear her sniffling from where I stand. But when I turn to take the rings from Blake, the big softie nearly causes me to lose it. He clears his throat and avoids my eyes, and I elbow him in the ribs to signal that he isn't fooling me. He looks away, smiling shyly.

Tenley and I manage to slip wedding bands on one another despite our trembling hands, then Blake and Loren join us in signing the marriage license. Finally, Father Conrad has us bow our heads for a blessing before introducing us as "Mr. and Mrs. Joseph Drake Bourgeois, III" for the first time and inviting me to kiss my bride.

I wink at Tenley and shoot her a smug look, and her eyes widen before I yank her in and press my lips against hers greedily. I can hear some applause and laughter from our small audience, but I figure we're entitled to make out anywhere now, right? I force myself to pull away, and Tenley stands unmoving for a second, wearing that heavy-lidded, intoxicated look I love so much.

"All right, not in front of the kid," Blake calls out before he moves closer, draping his arm affectionately over my shoulder.

"Yeah, that's not exactly church tongue," Loren adds in a loud whisper before she offers her congratulations. My only reply is an unapologetic shrug before I pull her in for an embrace. My mother-in-law is next, and she squeezes me hard enough to make me check my ribs once she turns to fawn over Tenley again. Then Ethan humors me with another bear hug. Loren instructs us to pose for a few photos, but she gives up after having to reprimand me too many times for staring at my wife instead of looking at the camera.

"Why don't you two go on home and change into something more comfortable? We'll meet up later," Mrs. T says with a wink as we all walk out of the church together. Tenley rolls her eyes but doesn't protest when I clutch her hand and haul her toward the parking lot.

"Okay, then. Thanks for coming! See you all soon, but not too soon," I proclaim, dragging my bride along. I grab her sides to lift her and place her in my truck, making her giggle as I frantically stuff the rest of her dress in after her. Then I slam the door and jog over to the driver's side.

"Hey, don't hurt yourself, bro," Blake tells me, snickering at me as he ambles by. "Be safe. And remember, I'm expecting a full report later," he adds.

"I'm turning my phone off. And someone *better* be dying if you so much as attempt to contact either of us before tomorrow afternoon." I realize I'm growling at him, even though I don't mean to.

"Come on, Blake." Loren appears and tugs lightly on his arm. "I think Little Brother can take it from here."

He smirks at me before he obliges, slipping his hand over hers as they walk away together. I suppose they could've called a truce for the occasion, but Blake and Loren seem to be getting along unusually well.

Then I lose the ability to care about anything else once I climb into the driver's seat and glance over at my wife, and she smiles bashfully. "I can't believe we really just did that," she says.

"Well, Mrs. Bourgeois," I begin, cranking the truck and shifting gears before I reach over to clasp her hand. "I hope you're not having regrets already?"

"My only regret so far is wearing a dress this tight. It isn't exactly sitting-down friendly," she admits with a strained laugh.

"Ten, you're beautiful. I don't understand how you managed to find that dress so quickly, but I can't imagine you looking more perfect than you do right now." I keep my eyes on the road as I run my thumb across her hand to brush over the wedding band I just added to her left ring finger. "Or more sexy," I add, my voice deepening. Then I trail my fingertips lightly down her wrist and up her forearm.

She's biting her lip demurely and staring at me when I look back again. "You look really nice, too," she says after a second. "You wear a suit pretty well, husband."

I grin. "You know—"

"Yeah, yeah. I just set myself up for a birthday-suit joke, didn't I?" she cuts me off, already laughing. "Or are you trying to work in a 'my wife' in your best Borat voice?"

I snort. "Actually, I was going to say that as much as I like seeing you in that dress, I think it'll look even better on our bedroom floor in a few minutes."

She glares at me, but I notice how she's squirming in her seat. I slip my hand under her veil to rub the skin exposed by the low back of her dress. Then she sighs and reaches up to pull out some kind of comb before she loses the veil completely. While her intentions are likely innocent, she's unwittingly flipped a switch inside me, just by removing the first layer.

We pull into the driveway at my—*our* house a minute later. I notice she's staring down at her ring, probably waiting for the full weight of what we've just done to settle, so I take my time going around to help her out.

I guess she figures today is as good as any to humor me, because she allows me to scoop her up from her seat and carry her all the way inside. She wraps her arms around my neck while I kick the front door shut behind us, and I stare down at her as I slip my shoes off before walking us over to the bedroom, still in disbelief that I've actually managed to make Tenley my wife and that we're *finally* going to consummate this relationship.

I lean in for a kiss before placing her down gently on the bed. "You, uh, need any help with that dress?" I ask, my voice sounding strained. Her eyes widen when she realizes I'm not wasting any time. I'm certainly not giving her the chance to change her mind or waiting for someone to interrupt us again.

"Maybe the back," she says as she sits up and unbuckles her heels. "Don't you want to get that door?"

"No need. Ethan's gone to Ryan's. We both agreed he should stay elsewhere for the night."

"Oh. Won't he miss the dinner we planned for later?" She stands and turns so I can slide the zipper down.

"There is no dinner," I reply matter-of-factly, lingering to place a couple of kisses down her back.

"But I thought—"

"I told everyone to give us at least twenty-four hours to ourselves and not to bother us unless there's a major emergency," I explain as I continue undressing her, pushing the sleeves away from her shoulders and pausing for a few more kisses over her collarbone. Just being able to take her clothes off is already making me feel so good that my head is buzzing, and she hasn't even really touched me yet.

She bites her lip, stifling a laugh. "Did you really?"

"You're damned right I did. This is going to take a while ... and probably more than one attempt," I admit, smirking at her playfully and making her giggle.

"I don't mind if it takes a couple of tries."

"Don't worry. I've been reviewing my data. I'm confident I can get it right by round two, though I'm prepared to run this experiment as many times as you see fit," I tell her, kissing her on the lips while she laughs again.

CHAPTER 43
TENLEY

I WAKE UP THE MORNING AFTER MY WEDDING WEARING one of JD's T-shirts and a satisfied smile. I can hear him in the kitchen, so I stretch and shuffle over to the bathroom to freshen up before venturing out.

"Good morning, beautiful," he calls over his shoulder, a proud grin plastered across his face as he plates his scrambled eggs. "Would you like some breakfast?"

I smile back warmly. "I'm fine, thanks." He walks over with his plate and sets a cup of coffee down beside me. I know the mug is meant for me because JD doesn't even care for the smell of it.

"Did you buy a coffee maker?"

He leans over to place a quick kiss on my lips, his hand lingering on my bare thigh for a second before he sits. "I asked Loren for a recommendation last week."

"That was really thoughtful. Thank you," I reply, taking a sip. He's fixed it just the way I like it, but I shouldn't be surprised. Then I notice that the kitchen and living room look tidier than usual. "Have you been awake a while? Wait—did I accidentally marry a morning person?"

He raises one of his shoulders and drops it again. "I think I just had a lot of pent-up energy this morning." Then he takes a bite of his eggs and chews thoughtfully.

My cheeks warm as I attempt to hide behind my mug. I'm feeling quite the opposite after last night's marathon. It turns out that, professional knowledge and expertise aside, whatever I thought I knew about sex before was wrong. Despite our chemistry, I'd kept my wedding-night expectations low, especially considering our circumstances and my past experiences. But JD hadn't been kidding before about putting all his research to good use.

Whether it was due to a physical or an emotional connection, or even that he'd stumbled upon some kind of cheat code, he'd managed to get it right on the first try. Like, he'd gotten it *so right* that I literally cried, because I hadn't even understood how right it could feel before then. This went beyond mere gratification. And for the first time ever, I was comfortable in my own skin (and nothing else). Instead of being embarrassed, I felt safe, loved, cherished ... whole.

Then I fell apart and turned into a snotty, sobbing mess. JD was forced to comfort me while I apologized for letting my insecurities get in the way of our relationship for so long and explained how I never imagined I could love someone this much. Of course, his answer to my hormone-induced declaration that marrying him was "already the best decision I've ever made" was to say that if he'd known he was this good in bed, he would have just led with that a few months ago.

"You're going to be unbearably cocky after this, aren't you?"

He shrugs but his grin never falters. "Maybe. Should I be?" he asks, though his expression says he already knows the answer to that question.

"You just accomplished a twenty-four-hour job in a single attempt," I reply. "I may never let you put your clothes back on."

He chuckles and tilts his chin up. "Is that so? Well, just wait until you see what I can do with the rest of that time. I have been taking notes for a while, remember?"

I feel another flash of heat as he trails a line of kisses down my chest and up again. "I guess you really have become a Tenley expert, then."

"I'm working on my terminal degree," he murmurs. He reaches

over and picks up my hand, bringing my wrist to his mouth. I shiver, my body having already decided that I'm at his mercy.

"I love you," I whisper, my eyes watering again.

"I love you, too, wifey," he returns before he captures my mouth with his again ...

I clear my throat and take another sip, bringing myself back to the present. Am I supposed to be fantasizing about my own husband while he's sitting right beside me?

It must be the oxytocin talking ... or an estrogen rise.

Shit. I should probably warn him, then, just in case I end up ovulating early this month.

"So, um, what do you have planned today?" I ask, glancing sidelong at his arms and hoping my thoughts aren't as obvious as they seem.

"Eh, I've got a short to-do list. But it'll probably take all morning."

"Oh. Okay." I'm a little disappointed that he isn't even trying to bring me back to bed, in all honesty, but I suppose we can't stay in our honeymoon bubble forever.

"Wanna help?"

"Sure," I agree hesitantly, since I'm not exactly big on gardening and yard work. Unless it involves watching JD mow the lawn without a shirt.

"All right, then. Let's get started." He drops his fork onto the empty plate and turns to lift me from my chair.

"What the—JD!" I squeal as he throws me over his shoulder and carries me back into the bedroom.

"You're it, Mrs. Bourgeois," he says plainly, punctuating his sentence with a light smack on my butt.

"What?" I repeat from behind him. I have to admit, the view isn't all that bad from this angle.

"My to-do list." He flashes a cheesy smile after he leans over and carefully sets me down on the bed. Then he stops to peel his shirt off, and I sigh contentedly since he's all mine to stare at now. "I told you. I blocked out our whole morning. We're still under our honeymoon quarantine for the next few hours."

I throw my head back and laugh, until I remember I was supposed to initiate an important conversation before I let this happen again.

"You didn't really think I was done trying everything I learned after collecting all that data, did you?" he teases as he joins me in bed, kissing down the side of my neck and sliding his hands up my thighs and backside. Man, do I love his massive hands and the way they fit around me. As corny as it sounds, it feels like we were made for one another.

Stop getting distracted and spit it out, my brain scolds me.

"JD," I begin, my voice breathy. He leans back and tugs at the hem of my shirt until I raise my arms, allowing him to pull it up over my head and toss it to the side. Then he immediately returns his lips to my bare shoulder.

"Hmm?"

I hesitate to voice my concerns since I'm pretty sure we've passed the point at which he'll make any objections, but he deserves to know what he's getting himself into. "It's possible ... I think we could be nearing the second half of that experiment right about now."

He stops abruptly, and his eyes meet mine. "You mean, the procreation part? Already?"

"I really hoped we'd have more time before the safe-day cutoff, but I'm feeling like I should warn you first. The way my body's reacting right now tells me I might be closer to ovulation than I originally thought," I explain shyly.

He goes back to kissing his way over my collarbone. "Mm. You're gonna look so hot pregnant," he mumbles against my skin.

"I'm serious, JD."

"So am I," he growls, and I'm nearly embarrassed by the way I whimper and clutch at him desperately in response. I guess he notices, because he pulls away, looking concerned. "Should I stop, then?"

"I totally understand if you don't want to risk it," I spit out.

But we should totally risk it, my ovaries finish for me.

"Tenley, I have to confess—I've been dreaming about making you the mother of my children for months. And I have absolutely no reservations about getting pregnant, whether it's now or later, on whatever timeline works for you."

"Shouldn't we wait a little longer, though, especially with everything else happening so fast?" I try to articulate a real objection, but I already want him so badly I can barely form words at this point.

"Because you *think* we should wait, or because you *want* to wait?"

My stomach dips when I really consider his question. We'd be insane to go from strangers to married with a teenager in the house and a baby on the way, all within a span of five months, wouldn't we?

Absolutely crazy, right?

But then again, I'm already thirty years old, and I am a little more prepared for the ins and outs of pregnancy and childbirth than the average woman.

And BABIES.

My uterus is right. I do love me some babies.

There's also the fact that my hot-as-hell husband already knows me well enough to ask all the right questions and will undoubtedly be exceptionally good at fatherhood. He continues staring at me expectantly, waiting for my reply.

"I ... I don't know," I whine. "I'm sorry."

JD sits back on his heels, his expression softening. "No, babe, I'm the one who's sorry. It isn't fair of me to put this decision solely on you, is it?"

Dammit. His emotional maturity might be more dangerous than his kisses.

"At least not while it feels like I'd be disappointing you if I said no," I admit quietly.

"Yeah. And although I never want to pressure you or make you hesitate to stop me at any time, I'm not exactly reinforcing all that right now. I guess it's a good thing we waited this long, after all. I'm already screwing it up," he says remorsefully.

"No, you're not." I shake my head incredulously. "If anything, you're only making it that much harder to reason my way out of taking a risk, and I don't see it getting any easier with time. I mean, how am I supposed to stand a chance when you're able to figure stuff out and correct your behavior all on your own, and we haven't even been married a full day?"

He smirks. "If it makes you feel any better, the next thing I say is probably going to sound selfish."

"JD, you're incapable of being selfish, but I'd like to see you try," I say, grinning.

"I promise I'm not just trying to talk you into having kids before you're ready, but I'm really looking forward to sharing that experience with you." He brushes his fingertips lightly over my arm again, staring at me in a way that reminds me I've won the freaking husband lottery. "And I don't think I'll be able to get enough of you for quite a while, if ever, so it's only a matter of time before it happens, anyway."

I draw in a deep breath, and I'm pretty sure my uterus sighs wistfully along with me. I'll never grow tired of the way he makes me feel so loved and desired.

"And I think I would very much like to take our chances today and revisit our options tomorrow," I reply after a minute, and my ovaries celebrate with a secret handshake. "But in the future, I should probably initiate these conversations before I let you get me all JD-drunk and incapable of making responsible decisions."

"Noted," he says before he crushes his lips against mine. Then he whispers, "I love you, Tenley Jean," between kisses, and he makes good on his promise to *show* me how much he means it.

EPILOGUE

(THREE WEEKS LATER)

TENLEY

My nerves are worse than ever and my stomach churns as we walk toward the courtroom. JD's hand on the small of my back helps to ground me, but I still have to force a few slow, deep breaths, willing the acid back down.

"You okay?" he asks, leaning down to whisper into my ear.

"Yeah, I'm just so anxious. My stomach's in knots." I gulp and attempt to get my bearings again until I realize I'm about to be in a major bind. I turn in a panic, covering my mouth and bolting into the nearest restroom. I barely reach the first stall in time for the heaving to commence.

Once the nausea finally settles, I clean myself up and attempt to wipe the smudged mascara from under my eyes, hoping to look somewhat presentable again. But the woman in the mirror looks a bit worse for the wear, her skin pale and her hair sticking to the back of her sweaty neck. A fresh coat of lipstick isn't helpful either, and I'm just about to give up when JD cracks open the door and calls out to me.

I force a smile and attempt to reassure him that I'm fine. But he pushes his way in, anyway. "I'm sorry. I started feeling sick all of a sudden. I probably should have put something in my stomach to settle my nerves," I explain, figuring it's best to just let him make a proper fuss over me. By now I've learned when he's not going to take no for an answer.

Once he's finally convinced I'm not dying, he leads me out to the hallway with his arm around my waist. Ethan frowns when he sees me, his eyes running over my messy hair and smeared makeup before they land on the red splotch I left on JD's collar after trying to remove a lipstick stain earlier this morning.

"Ugh, you're not seriously faking sick to do *that*," he protests in mock disgust. JD backhands him playfully in the shoulder, and Ethan hisses and rubs his arm dramatically.

"Right, because we just couldn't wait until we got home," I add sarcastically, rolling my eyes. Then I glance at JD, and his smirk says he's thinking about how my lipstick got transferred from his neck to his collar in the first place.

"You forget I'm forced to wear noise-canceling headphones to bed in my own house," Ethan retorts, making JD's smile stretch wider.

"What can I say, man? *It's like that* now," he declares, his eyes still glued to me. Then he leans down and places a warm kiss below my ear, forcing me to take another deep breath.

"Gah, I can't take you two anywhere!" Ethan throws his hands up in real exasperation this time, and JD and I snicker as we make our way into the courtroom. My mom joins us a minute later, just before Blake saunters in with his trademark confidence.

We gather around as he reminds us of the game plan. We're going to offer visitation rights to Ryan but stand our ground on the domicile-custodian part. We're also hoping to appeal to the judge by foregoing any child support and proving Ethan will have a male authority figure in the household.

Ryan struts in shortly after with his expensive suit and fake smile. His trophy wife follows closely behind, looking flawlessly polished and faintly bored. I try not to make any ugly faces behind their backs, mostly for Ethan's sake, but it's hard not to roll my eyes, at least. They settle on the other side of the courtroom, and Ryan looks peeved when Ethan brushes him off.

The bailiff announces the judge's entrance a few minutes later. Luckily, we're first on the docket. Blake and Ryan trade a few formalities, and the judge invites Ethan to join him in his chambers, along with his custodians and their lawyers. I figure that means JD will stay behind, but Blake motions for him to come along. He happily clasps my hand as we walk in together.

"Well, hello again, Ms. Robin," the judge begins, eyeing JD instead of me.

"Actually, your honor," Blake interrupts him. "It's *Mrs. Bourgeois* now." I'm still getting used to that, but I certainly don't mind the title.

The judge's brow rises sharply. "Is it? Then I assume congratulations are in order to your brother," he replies with a short chuckle.

"Thank you, your honor," JD says, his thumb tracing a circle over the back of my hand.

The judge pauses and stares at both of us before continuing. "I could have sworn the two of you were only 'family friends' the last time we did this, which was only a few months ago, if my memory serves me. So either Mr. Bourgeois here works fast, or you all have staged something and are trying to pull the wool over my eyes."

I glance over and see a satisfied grin spread over Ryan's face. The judge isn't wrong. Even though it took a few months to convince me to give him a shot, JD *had* managed to get me to the altar in record time. But I stand by my statement that it was the best decision I've ever made.

My mind drifts through last few weeks: snuggling up to JD on the couch to watch a football game, laughing through dinner as he and Ethan tell stories about their day, arguing with both of them over what cereal to pick at the grocery store or which toppings to get on a pizza, and simply watching the two of them interact. I never would have believed I could make the transition from forced detachment to marital contentment so quickly and easily, but I already can't imagine my life any other way.

And surely the honeymoon effect is still an influencing factor, but I seriously can't get enough of my husband, in every sense. I don't understand how or when it happened—all I know is I want to be around him all the time, I find him completely irresistible, and I love him more deeply than I ever thought possible. He's become my favorite person, and I never have to doubt whether he feels the same about me. As predicted, JD really does make for a fine husband and an amazing partner—barring his inability to properly dispose of his dirty socks and clean around the sink after trimming his beard or to control his flatulence for extended periods of time. Apparently, the "privileges of being a married man" include the God-given right to fart in his sleep. Unpleasant, sure—but not intolerable. And he more than makes up for it with the other privileges he exercises in our bed—

I mean, he's just so good-natured that it's impossible to dwell on any minor imperfections, especially since none of his flaws seem to affect his ability to complete our little family and make both Ethan and me feel so unconditionally loved.

I'm grinning to myself when Blake clears his throat. "I apologize, your honor, because that was due to a misunderstanding on my part. I did say they weren't romantically involved at the last hearing, but it turns out JD and Tenley were just keeping their relationship private, for Ethan's sake."

Technically, he's not lying.

"Hmm. And how long since this wedding?"

"A few weeks now, your honor," JD replies.

"Then, you only got married *after* you found out Mr. Jameson was filing for custody?" The judge turns and glares at me, making my stomach roil again.

"If I may, your honor," Blake interrupts again. "While Mr. and Mrs. Bourgeois did pursue an earlier wedding date in light of their current situation, I can assure you their intentions were to establish a stable household for Ethan and to provide him with a respectable father figure, especially since the recent passing of his grandfather, Mr.

Jude Robin, the man who raised Ethan in Mr. Jameson's absence for the past sixteen years."

Nice job, Blake

I glance up at JD, who's smiling proudly. Then my stomach flutters yet again, and acid begins rising in my throat.

Oh, no. Not now.

"I suppose that's reasonable. But how can I be sure this wasn't forged simply to win a custody hearing?" the judge demands.

"We did convince Father Conrad to marry us, even on a tight timeline, and we also completed pre-marriage counseling through the Church," JD answers for both of us, since I can barely handle simultaneously breathing and standing at the moment.

But the judge seems to be too busy staring at me to hear it. "Mrs. Bourgeois, are you unwell? You look a little … green."

I lick my lips, trying to nod because I know I'll be in trouble if I open my mouth now. My eyes dart around the room, only to discover that everyone is watching me closely. Then my face flushes, my heartbeat throbs in my ears—and suddenly, everything goes black.

———

Tenley, babe, wake up.

I hear JD's voice off in the distance, but I can't seem to open my eyes. Then I taste bile in the back of my throat and turn to the side, attempting to spare my husband from having to wear my vomit on his fancy suit for the rest of the morning.

A trash can appears quickly, and I think I see Ethan in my peripheral vision. I heave over the bin a couple of times, and he hands me a paper napkin while JD holds my hair and rubs my back gently.

"I'm so sorry," I murmur, my hands trembling as I try to blot my face.

There's a welcome gust of fresh air as Blake stands over us, fanning me with a legal-size manila folder. "Well, wasn't that well-timed, Mrs. Bourgeois," he says with a cocky smirk.

"What?" I barely manage to get out. Then the realization hits me, and I almost hurl again. "Oh. Yeah. *Shit.*"

"What's wrong?" JD furrows his brow. I glance over to find Ethan looking just as concerned.

"Should I run with it or what?" Blake whispers, still smiling.

I exhale slowly, my head still feeling fuzzy. My boobs are also sore, and my stomach is still cutting flips. And my period is due any day now. But this isn't PMS, and Aunt Flo is not coming this time.

"I ... I, uh ..."

"Tenley?" JD speaks up. "What's he talking about?"

I visualize my chart and count backward in my mind. JD and I ended up spending the day after our wedding in bed, which appears to be a risky decision in hindsight, given the way my cycle panned out. I scold myself for not paying more attention since then, having confirmed the end of my window of fertility before my only concern became adding tiny hearts to my chart each day. Not that my husband seems to mind helping me keep that streak going.

Regardless, I'm certainly aware of which symptoms to look for, like a secondary rise in my basal body temperature, but I've been so busy with adjusting to married life and preparing for the hearing that I just ... forgot.

I look back at Blake and nod solemnly. "Yes," I answer weakly. "It's definitely possible ... actually, *probable* would be more accurate."

"This ought to make for a funny story one day," Blake mumbles, laughing to himself. Then he slaps JD on the back heartily.

"Anyone wanna tell me what the hell's going on?" JD demands, his tone changing.

"I'm just guessing here," Ethan begins, trying to keep a straight face. "But it sounds like you're still an overachiever, Coach."

"He always did go for the touchdown on every drive, you know," Blake adds, cracking himself up.

Ethan bites his lip. "I guess this is what happens when you make it too easy for him to score," he barely manages before breaking out into his own fits of laughter. I reach over and backhand the same shoulder from earlier.

JD shakes his head again, still confused. "Can you please explain why I should be okay with them making fun of you while you're sick?"

I sigh, cradling his cheek and sitting up to whisper next to his ear. "Because it means that experiment might have been a success, after all."

"Oh," says JD, blinking rapidly. "*Oh.* Ah, are you sure?"

"Not exactly, but I'm thinking it could be the reason I'm feeling like death warmed over right now," I reply, gesturing to the trash can beside me.

He stares down at me for a second longer, his expression softening and his lips curving into a silly but elated smile, just as the judge reenters the room with Ryan on his heels.

"How are we doing, Mrs. Bourgeois?" the judge asks, seemingly amused by my syncope.

"Much better, your honor," I answer as JD helps me return to a standing position, keeping his arm wrapped around me protectively. "And I'm sorry about all that. It's ... new."

"Are you sure you're okay to continue, Ms. Tenley?" Ryan asks, a hint of bitterness in his tone. "Of course, I don't mind if you need to postpone. We could always come to a better temporary arrangement today and meet later to finalize everything."

"That won't be necessary," Blake interrupts him. "Postponement won't solve anything since Mrs. Bourgeois's ailment isn't likely going away for, oh, the next nine months or so."

"She's pregnant?" Ryan scoffs.

"I guess that accounts for the short engagement," the judge surmises with a twinkle in his eye.

JD beams at me a second longer before he speaks. "Your honor, I know our situation seems unconventional. But I believe my wife and I were initially drawn to one another because of the individual bonds we'd each forged with Ethan. And by the time we fell in love, we didn't see the point in waiting to get married or have babies when the three of us had already formed a family. Now, all we need is to settle this arrangement, because we love Ethan, and we know he belongs here with us, *his family*." He states the last part firmly.

Ethan exhales audibly beside me, and even Blake looks a bit misty-eyed. I reach over to secretly pat my husband on the backside, because he deserves a token of appreciation after that amazing speech and heartfelt delivery. Plus, I find it unbelievably hot when JD gets assertive and authoritative, and I'm pro-PDA now. I grin when I hear a low growl from him in return.

The judge smiles down at us, and I wonder whether he's noticed our exchange. "I'd like to speak to Mr. Robin alone for a minute. We'll join the rest of you shortly."

I stop to squeeze Ethan's shoulder before he and JD casually trade fist bumps on our way out, though my eyes start to sting when I catch a glimpse of Ethan regarding JD with a look of sincere gratitude and affection.

We return to the courtroom, where my mom is waiting with a hopeful expression. "He's still talking with the judge," I explain, trying to regain control of my emotions as we settle in beside her.

Then my husband's hand curls in around mine before he brings it up to meet his lips. "I *really* want to kiss you," he says softly. "But since it's probably not the right time or place for that, and you just vomited in a trash can back there, your hand will have to do for now." And I blush a little, because I'm married to the most amazing man on the planet.

"Are you sure you're okay?" he adds in a whisper. I nod reassuringly, even though I still feel like I could use a few saltines and a place to lie down.

"I'm sure it's only the beginning," I remark with a short laugh.

"Aren't you going to tell her?" he asks, gesturing toward my mom. She turns quickly. "Tell me what?"

I glare at him. "I was going to wait until I knew for sure—"

"Yeah, well, apparently she's not above staging a shotgun wedding to get her way," Ryan complains loudly to his wife across the aisle.

I bite my lip and cringe, and Blake snorts. When I open my eyes again, my mother is staring back at me expectantly. "Tenley Jean?" she ventures, her voice higher than usual.

I lean over to explain quietly. "It's not true. We're just letting them believe what the judge wanted to hear."

"So, you're not ..." She trails off, her disappointment evident.

"Oh, no, I'm probably pregnant," I correct her. "I'm pretty sure I just had my first taste of morning sickness back there. But this would be a honeymoon baby, if you could call it that." She presses her lips together, and her eyes glisten. "I haven't confirmed anything yet, okay? So don't get your hopes up."

She shakes her head, because we both know that's impossible, and she pulls me in for a hug so tight that it takes me a second to catch my breath again.

"Okay, Mom. Just, could you stop crying? We probably don't want them thinking you're surprised by this news."

"Mm-hmm. Okay," she squeaks, trying to collect herself.

I turn back to JD, and his eyes are watery, too, now. "Don't you dare."

"I don't know what you're talking about," he replies, his voice thick. Then he scrunches his nose and looks up, exhaling through his lips. "I'm fine. It's just ... I've been looking forward to starting a family of my own for so long, and now I might be gaining two kids in one day."

I squeeze his hand tightly as my eyesight gets blurry. "Dammit," I curse, willing the sensation away. But my tear ducts hear "let's do this," and another pregnancy symptom makes a grand appearance.

"*Mais la*, people. Get a hold of yourselves," I hear Blake grumbling as he leans over and offers a box of tissues.

"At least I have an excuse," I retort, wiping my nose and making the others laugh.

Seconds later, Ethan reappears and scoots down to wedge himself between JD and me. He glances hopefully at each of us, a wide grin stretching across his face. The judge takes his place, and the proceedings begin much the same as the last time we were here.

Except this time, we walk out as a very happy family of four.

ACKNOWLEDGMENTS

Y'all. Is this really happening? *Mais,* gah-lee.

I don't even know how to begin to thank all my friends and family for their support, which is unfortunate because I'm supposed to be good with words and all. (Sorry, this will be long. It's my first book, and I don't usually do feelings, okay?)

This story was written with the intention of bringing glory to God and highlighting His greatest gifts—His infinite love and mercy —and to provide a reminder that, though we are human and we make mistakes (especially when hormones and emotions are involved), we can always strive to do better next time. Let's not forget that we need His grace to get it right. The Sacraments help, too.

To my loving and doting husband—thank you for being my muse, for acknowledging my dreams, for pushing me to do this, for putting up with me, and for not allowing me to quit. Thank you for being the romantic one, for always kissing my hand, for taking me to Saints games, and for indulging my silly whims. Also, shout out to you and the guns for posing for the JD art. I love you. I think I'll take you to Walk-On's to celebrate once this is all over.

To my amazing children, A, E, C, and R—thank you for fending for yourselves for the past year. I appreciate how often you tolerated chicken nuggets and take-home pizza for dinner while mom worked on her "project." To A—thank you for being my Ethan, my gift, for teaching me how to be a mom. To E—thank you for being patient with me, for stepping up and becoming a responsible big sis, and for encouraging me to write, though I'll never be the talented artist that you are. To C—thank you for being my sweetheart, for loving uncon- ditionally, and for always knowing when I need a hug. And to R—

thank you for making life interesting, for teaching me to laugh, for being unapologetically *canaille*, and for not burning the house down while I finished this. I love you all more than words can express.

To Kait—my BFFF, my main PIC, my enabler, my homegrown writing buddy, my Lo. Thank you for your encouragement, your ideas, the memes, the Bougie Bro inspo spam pics, the tough love, and most of all, for always being my safe space. I literally could not have done this without you. For your efforts, I gift you Blake. If I weren't such a jerk, I'd tell you that I love you, but alas, I love...cake.

To my friends and coworkers—especially my MGs (RG, ST, and KJ), Kate, Emily, Kim, Elizabeth, Jahn, Rebecca, and all the rest of you who suffered through months of my hyper-fixation, who read a million different drafts and smiled through my Watt-brothers "research" reports, who provided counseling and spiritual direction when I needed it most, thank you for your input and your support and for not letting me give up. I may never become a successful novelist, but I know have the absolute best inner circle and that I am loved.

To my alpha and beta readers—especially Claire, Dori, Kira, Savanna, Rose, Joanna, and the rest of the 'Fettes, my mom (L) and sister (A), Shaley, Crystal, Kelly, Carmen, Mel, Cindy, Nancy, Bibby, and anyone else I may have missed—I can't tell you how much I appreciate the time and energy you wasted on me and my silly story. I love you all.

To my revised edition betas, Moni, Amber, Logan, Krissi, Katelyn, Madeline, Laura, Cindy, and Kait—I can't thank y'all enough for your input and for helping me make some much-needed improvements to JD and Tenley's story. I appreciate all of your time and energy.

To my cover designer and favorite ARC reader, Cindy R—thank you for your support and for humoring me by accommodating my ridiculous imagination and using your talents to bring my Camellia Crewe to life. Most of all, thank you for your friendship. I can't wait to read your book.

To my editors, Emily P and Jen S—thanks for helping my crazy ideas make sense.

And to all my readers, especially my ARC readers—thank you *so very much* for taking a chance on me and for sacrificing your time to read this book. I am truly grateful for your support and reviews. I hope you each get something from this, at least a few laughs or a character crush and at most appreciation for the Catholic faith, the Sacraments, and NFP. I would love to keep entertaining y'all, if you're still interested in hearing about my made-up world.

Finally, to my parents—thank you for instilling your faith in me, for encouraging me, and for letting me believe I could become anything I wanted, even a writer. It's a bit more grownup than a *Little Golden Book*, but I finally did it. I love you.

ABOUT THE AUTHOR

A former high school literature teacher from South Louisiana, Marie Veillon is still learning to balance her ridiculous accent, Cajun-French—inspired vocabulary, and horrible speaking syntax with writing humorous stories and creating characters and situations relatable enough to make readers forget they aren't real. She enjoys reading books about her Catholic faith and rom coms with guaranteed HEAs, watching football, fangirling, and spending time with her amazing family.

Thank you for reading and reviewing!
marievwrites.com
@marievwrites

instagram.com/marievwrites

threads.com/@marievwrites

marievwrites.substack.com

facebook.com/marievwrites

tiktok.com/@marievwrites

bookbub.com/authors/marie-veillon

goodreads.com/marie_veillon

amazon.com/author/marieveillon

ALSO BY MARIE VEILLON

THE CAMELLIA ROM-COM SERIES

Third and Ten
Going for Two
Hail Mary Catch
Walking Green Flag

LAGNIAPPE
...A LITTLE SOMETHING EXTRA

Sign up for my newsletter and join the Camellia Crewe Facebook group to receive updates and announcements, including free content and the latest news regarding the next installments in the Camellia Rom-Com Series!

Continue the Camellia Rom-Com series with **Blake and Loren's story** and read the first chapter of ***Going for Two*** for FREE!

Need more JD + Tenley?
Get a Bonus Epilogue, a Cajun Glossary, NFP Resources, and more at
marievwrites.com